CW01391811

THE CAMBRIDGE SIREN

By Jim Kelly

a&b

THE CAMBRIDGE SIREN

JIM KELLY

Allison & Busby Limited
11 Wardour Mews
London W1F 8AN
allisonandbusby.com

First published in Great Britain by Allison Busby in 2025.

A CIP catalogue record for this book is available from
the British Library.

First Edition

ISBN 978-0-7490-3139-8

Typeset in 11.5/16.5 pt Adobe Garamond Pro by
Allison & Busby Ltd

By choosing this product, you help take care of the world's forests.
Learn more: www.fsc.org

FSC
www.fsc.org
MIX
Paper | Supporting
responsible forestry
FSC® C171272

Printed and bound in the UK using 100% Renewable Electricity at
CPI Group (UK) Ltd, Croydon, CR0 4YY

EU GPSR Authorised Representative
LOGOS EUROPE, 9 rue Nicolas Poussin, 17000, LA ROCHELLE, France
E-mail: Contact@logoseurope.eu

To all those men and women who failed their
Armed Forces' medical, but went on to serve their country.

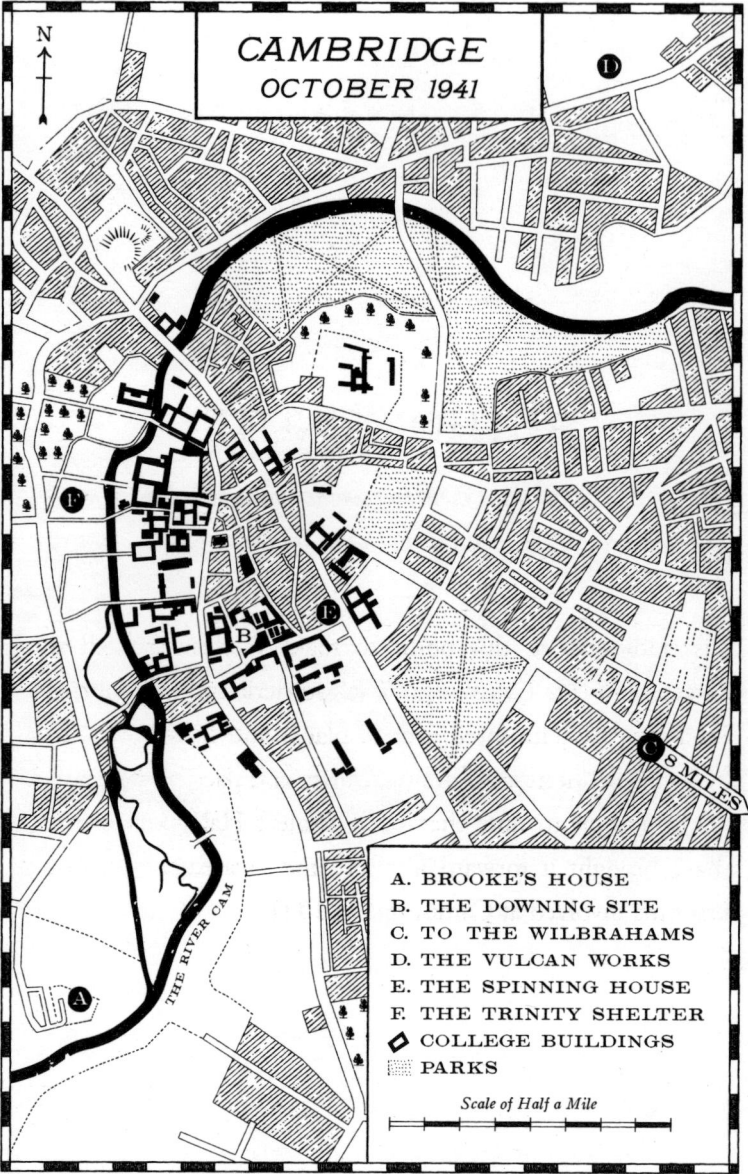

CAMBRIDGE
OCTOBER 1941

N

D

F

E

B

C 8 MILES

THE RIVER CAM

A

A. BROOKE'S HOUSE
B. THE DOWNING SITE
C. TO THE WILBRAHAMS
D. THE VULCAN WORKS
E. THE SPINNING HOUSE
F. THE TRINITY SHELTER
◇ COLLEGE BUILDINGS
▦ PARKS

Scale of Half a Mile

AUTHOR'S NOTE

It is traditional at this point to make it clear that all the characters in *The Cambridge Siren* are fictional; I should add that I have also invented events, places and institutions, but always in the interests of drama, clarity and pace. In particular, it is important to note that while Project Habakkuk existed, I have brought it forward in time, and created the scientific personnel involved at Cambridge in 1941.

CHAPTER ONE

Wednesday, 8th October 1941

Detective Inspector Eden Brooke sat on a wicker chair in his front garden watching the river flow by, dragonfly green in the evening light, pitted with miniature whirlpools, sliding towards Cambridge along its chalky bed. Beside him, on a kitchen stool, was his wife Claire, while their daughter Joy knelt with her baby on a rug. Iris was a year old and determined to crawl to the grass, only to be returned methodically at each attempt by her mother. Her first steps were eagerly awaited.

A punt went by; a rare sight now, in the third year of the war. An old man was at the pole, expertly running it through his hands, using it as a rudder to steer away from the bank as the river took the long slow turn around Newnham Croft. A fisherman certainly, the boat laden with rods and tackle, even a picnic basket. One of the war's irritating burdens was the idea that enjoying yourself was somehow unpatriotic.

Morale, Brooke knew, was vital if you wanted to win the war on the Home Front.

'Any luck?' he called.

The man leant on the pole, bending down to retrieve a shining silver fish in a canvas bag, which he held out like a trophy.

Brooke tipped his hat by way of approval, and the fisherman went back to steering his punt, drifting downstream.

'That reminds me,' said Claire, who was sitting in the last of the sunlight, her head back, letting the warm rays fall on her upturned face. 'Supper is Asquith Pie.'

This was a family joke, the derivation long lost, but possibly a dimly remembered echo of the great prime minister's call to 'make do' with anything available during the long winters of the Great War. Asquith Pie contained leftovers, and anything else inedible if not concealed within pastry.

There was a long silence. The summer had been wet and grey, with only a few spells of blue sky. The winter before it brutal, cloaked in snow. It had all been a heart-breaking contrast to the brilliant blue Blitz summer which had marked the first year of the war.

Gradually, the shadow of the house fell entirely over the garden. Joy wrapped a shawl around the baby and held her fast. Claire took up a book on the treatment of malnutrition in children: she was a nurse, sister on the children's ward at Addenbrooke's Hospital. She could read the effects of war, and rationing, in the faces of her poorer patients.

The Brooke family home was one of a pair of modest riverside villas built in a playful style, a cross between a country railway halt and the gate lodge of a Scottish stately home. The garden ran down to the towpath; the gate – latch broken – always stood half open.

Brooke knew this idyllic scene was threatened on many sides by war, but recalled his favourite aphorism, from the *Rubaiyat of Omar Kayam*:

Be happy in this moment, this moment is your life.

'You go first,' said Claire, setting her book aside.

It was one of several enduring family games. They had to imagine what all the missing Brookes were doing at this very moment. Given the worldwide scale of the war, the first task was imagining where they were.

'Luke?' asked Brooke, lighting one of his precious Black Russian cigarettes, and adjusting his green tinted glasses. For a moment he watched the tip glow, burning the black paper, edging down towards the gold filter.

Their son had ignored his father's one piece of advice in life: never volunteer. This had not carried much weight, as Luke knew his father had himself volunteered in the Great War. The result of that mistake had been his capture, and torture, in the Middle East campaign. They'd staked him out in the sun for three days, without water, and his eyes were damaged beyond repair. Hence the fondness for shadows, and a series of tinted glasses: ochre, green, blue and black, depending on the intensity of the light.

Brooke looked at his watch. 'Given his last letter I suspect he's back running between telegraph poles on a stretch of Scottish moorland. He'll be sick of it by now. Then they'll have to run back to the castle.'

Achnacarry Castle was the HQ for commando training, six miles from Fort William. Luke had already done basic training, and taken part in a brief raid on the Normandy coast. Now he was back in Scotland, no doubt preparing for some other adventure. But the daily grind of keeping fit would be unchanged. Mr Churchill was desperate for the commandos to deliver a morale-raising raid behind enemy lines. Or – as the prime minister put it – 'set Europe alight'. Only that morning the Home Service had reported a raid on the Norwegian coast. But Brooke decided to keep this news to himself. As far as Claire was concerned, her only son was back in training, and would be for several months, if not years.

'When they do get back to the castle, there'll be tea – so that's what he's thinking about right now. Food,' decided Brooke.

'Ben?' asked Claire, knowing her daughter had a vision of her absent husband in mind at all times.

Joy picked up Iris with brisk efficiency. Like her mother, she was a nurse, and was competent at all things. 'I think they're on the surface – in the sunshine. I hope so. They've decided he's the scientist on board – on the flimsy basis he's a medical student. He might be recording the weather for the log. He'll be thinking about Iris.'

Brooke's son-in-law was a submariner on HMS *Unbowed*, currently stationed at Rosyth, on the Firth of Forth. But he'd be at sea and, Brooke thought, quite possibly in the sightless depths. He'd met his son-in-law half a dozen times and felt, fittingly, that he could be a bit of a cold fish. He'd once asked him what he did when the sub was lying low with an enemy ship above. His answer – that he read a book – revealed a level of cool detachment Brooke found inhuman. But everyone on a sub was a volunteer, so he couldn't fault his courage. Ben's first boat – *Silverfish* – had caught fire in the North Sea due to engine trouble, and he'd been captured, and taken to a POW camp, from which he'd escaped. Not only escaped, but led an escape. So – courage certainly, and leadership. Joy was smitten, and each time Ben came to Newnham Croft, Brooke felt he detected a little more of a hidden vulnerability – again, fittingly, just beneath the surface.

They heard a car breaking on gravel with a theatrical skid.

The house faced the towpath; the road was at the back. From where they sat there was not a single clue that they lived their lives in the twentieth century. Brooke always said that time spent by the river was so peaceful because he had nothing in front of him and the world behind him.

But the world often came calling.

Steps, slow and steady, announced the arrival of Sergeant Ralph Edison, long before his substantial form appeared, pushing open the side gate. Edison had retired in 1938 after thirty years in uniform. Now he was Brooke's right-hand man, and in plain clothes, although he still managed to radiate the authority of the missing uniform. The unseen slalom with the motor car on gravel was a rare glimpse of an unruly side to his character.

'Sorry, sir. Ladies,' he added, lifting his hat.

'Hello Edison,' said Joy. 'Tea?'

Edison looked helplessly at Brooke.

'I can see by the way Sergeant Edison is holding onto the gatepost that he expects me to follow him to the car,' said Brooke. 'I shall. I'll just get my jacket.'

Claire stood. 'Food in the oven, Eden. We're both on nights this week. Iris will be with Mrs Mullins.'

A minute later Edison's gleaming Wolseley Wasp was on the road into the city past the millpond at Newnham. A significant factor in Edison's return to the force was the petrol coupons he could draw to run his own – treasured – car. Its crimson paintwork was a mirror to the passing world.

'What do we know?' asked Brooke.

'Fatality, sir. The Trinity Shelter.'

'Something suspicious?' said Brooke, swapping the green tinted glasses for the ochre, the sun finally setting.

'Possibly, sir. Constable who phoned it in said it had the hallmarks of suicide, but that there was a lot of blood. I thought it best to play it by the book.'

Brooke nodded. It wasn't good news. The shelters were supposed to represent a haven of safety in a violent world. They often offered sanctuary to the desperate. Suicide was not unknown. Pills had flooded the market at the outbreak of war as many families decided that if the invasion came, they couldn't face the invaders. The fate of the Jews, especially, was growing darker by the month as news emerged, piecemeal, from Poland.

Newspaper coverage of shelter deaths – often a single paragraph in the *Cambridge News* – had not helped to burnish the reputation of the city's communal public shelters. Brick-built, with a concrete 'cap', they were widely seen as death-traps. In London – it was said – several had failed in the Blitz, the walls crumbling, the concrete ceiling falling on the helpless within. More and more families opted for shelters at home: Andersons in the garden, Morrisons in the house. But not everyone had a garden, or the space indoors, so the poor were often left with no alternative to the public shelters, unless they wanted to trust in fate and stay in bed – which many did, especially as the Guildhall siren went off every other day, although bombing raids were rare.

Edison drove along the Backs, the ancient colleges appearing through the trees on the far bank of the river. A slight wind, so often a herald of the dusk, prompted a shower of falling leaves, through which they glimpsed King's College Chapel, its stained glass now stored in a nearby basement, its windows boarded.

On this side of the river, on the rough pasture where cows had been kept in peacetime, a set of three shelters had been built. Keen to do their bit, three colleges – King's, Trinity and St John's – had each put up the money for shelters for the use of the residents of Castle Hill – a nearby warren of cramped housing, a refuge for the city's Irish labourers and the poor.

The Trinity Shelter boasted a stone version of the college crest over the door: Tudor roses, a lion and – a bad omen for a detective surely – two closed books.

The shelter warden, provided by the college, was a woman called Mrs Flaherty. Given the Irish brogue, and the spotless hands and nails, Brooke guessed she might be kitchen staff.

'I should have seen him this morning,' she said, distressed, covering her mouth with the back of her hand. She'd met them on the threshold of the shelter, as if it were her own front door.

'Why don't you show us, and start at the beginning,' said Brooke, taking off his glasses, ready for the gloom within. Ready, also, for the sight of death. Since his ordeals in Palestine, and especially on the long march to Gaza, he'd found it almost impossible to view a corpse without prompting a psychological return to the battlefield. But this was his job, his duty, and so he steeled himself.

The door led into a small porch, set at an angle to the main shelter, presumably to stop draughts. Inside, the main room held fifty according to a sign, with two long benches on either side. At the far end there was another right-angled turn into the toilets. There was a short bench here too, and under it the body of a man, turned away, with his back to them.

A uniformed constable, PC Alby Durrell, stood guard. The Borough was the country's smallest police force. Brooke knew its dozen uniformed PCs by name – first, and last.

'When did you find him?' Brooke asked Mrs Flaherty.

'When I got here this evening at five. There was a raid last night – well, a siren – so I thought I'd better give it a clean and make sure I hadn't got any roadsters.'

The number of homeless tramps had grown with the coming of spring. Most of the shelters sent them on to Market Hill where there was a special shelter. Otherwise, there were complaints about the smell, and the drink. But the shelters were open at all hours, and so presented an irresistible temptation to the needy.

'The shelter was full last night?' asked Edison.

'Half full. The siren went at two, the all-clear at six.'

'You think this poor man may have been here last night?' asked Brooke.

She shrugged. 'Maybe. The toilet isn't popular. The light wakes people up so most of the men go outside and use the bushes. I can't stop them. The women use it – but they just trail a hand along the wall.'

There was a blurred mark on both sides of the passage.

'People sleep under the benches all the time,' she offered.

'You can't perch on a wooden bench for ten hours. Everyone lies down in the end. It looks like bedtime at a kennel. If you bring enough bedding, it's fine. Does for me.'

'And you sleep where, Mrs Flaherty?' asked Edison.

'By the entrance, in the little hall. I've got a gas burner, so I do tea.'

The electric light, even when it was on, was dismal, so Mrs Flaherty fetched a lantern and lit it, setting it by the body, but not looking *at* the body.

'Oh God,' she said, catching sight of the blood.

A trickle – about two inches wide at most – led away from the corpse and the slight ledge beneath the seat, and then formed a pool about three feet away.

The blood was black, coagulated.

Brooke turned to PC Durrell. 'The blood – has it spread since you first saw him?'

'No, sir. Not an inch.'

Mrs Flaherty was distressed. 'I didn't check back here when I left this morning. I never do. It's the stink of it.'

'Is there another way in or out?'

Mrs Flaherty led the way, beyond the last Elsan toilet and around yet another corner. Brooke thought she was right about the smell. The place reeked of it – the whiff of a chemical toilet would be one of the engrained memories of war.

Brooke stepped out through the small back door and found himself in the trees beside a water-filled ditch. A neatly mown grass path led to Trinity Bridge, then over the Cam, to Wren's Library. He thought security was lax, but then there was little to worry about when the real danger was a thousand-pound bomb.

Back inside he found the Borough's pathologist, Dr Henry Comfort, briskly attempting to roll the victim out of his niche. The doctor was a large man, with a boulder-like head, and a butcher's meaty hands.

'There you are, Brooke. Help me lift him clear of the blood,' he said.

Brooke took his knees, Comfort the armpits.

'Poor man,' said Mrs Flaherty.

Once they had him in the light they could see that his clothes were clean, if worn, but of good quality. Both of his wrists were slit, and a bloodied cut-throat razor had fallen from a fold in his jacket.

Brooke recalled that less than half an hour ago he'd been sitting outside his riverside house thinking about happiness.

The features of the face already had the plump plasticity of the dead. In life he might have been handsome, with a wide face, a good jaw and fine skin – and here Brooke detected an olive tone, so perhaps Italian, Mediterranean certainly. There were several POW camps in the Fens full of Italian internees, a large number of them chefs and waiters from London's West End – an unintended consequence of government policy which had, it was said, upset several members of the Cabinet.

Edison, notebook open, told Dr Comfort what they knew. It was an expert summary, for his sergeant had a logical mind. As they listened Mrs Flaherty's lips were moving and Brooke guessed she must be saying a prayer.

'Time of death?' asked Brooke, braced for the usual rebuttal.

'As you well know, Inspector, that is a question for the laboratory later.'

Comfort opened his black bag and slipped on a rubber

glove, using his finger to test the consistency of the blood.

'But if you have an urgent need to know, I'd say between twelve and twenty-four hours . . .' He looked at his watch. 'Between six last night and six this morning. The blood's nearly dried. But it's been a warm autumnal day – so don't hold me to it.'

Comfort picked up the man's arm and tried to articulate it at the elbow, wrist and shoulder.

'Rigor's gone. The blood's almost black. I'll stick with my estimates of the time of death – but the autopsy may throw up the odd surprise. Although I doubt it.'

'I'd like to check the pockets,' said Brooke.

'Please yourself,' replied Comfort, taking a cigar tube from his pocket, extracting the cigar within, and lighting up.

'Nothing like a decent Cuban to give a chemical toilet a run for its money,' he said.

Mrs Flaherty looked appalled.

Edison and Brooke emptied the dead man's pockets. There was no wallet, no ID card, no name tags, no letters, no watch, no rings – although there was a pale band where the watch strap should have been. There was the usual litter: sweet wrappers, small change, a golf tee, a handkerchief – ironed, and fairly new. Brooke picked up the cut-throat with his handkerchief.

'No means of identification,' he said.

'A bit odd if you want to end it all.'

'Shame?' suggested Edison. 'Perhaps he wanted to spare others.'

Nodding, Brooke agreed: 'Yes. Perhaps he just wanted to slip away.'

He was staring at Edison as he said this, eye to eye, but

at this moment his sergeant looked down at the corpse. There was something furtive in the sudden gesture. A hint of guilt perhaps. But for what?

Brooke had no time to give it further thought, as the pathologist had returned to his examination of the body.

'Early twenties. Good condition, excellent even. Fair hair.' He knelt down and slid an eyelid open. 'Green eyes – glazing has set in. So again – my money stays on twelve hours or more.'

'Something wrong?' asked Brooke, because Comfort was simply contemplating the victim's face.

'Just a note of caution. It takes some determination – a steady hand – to slit *both* your wrists. It's actually very rare – the second wound is often botched. Not here. Both wounds are straight, and deep enough to sever the arteries.'

'What's that?' asked Brooke, pointing at the palm of the left hand. There were inky letters, obscured by blood.

Comfort gave him a piece of clean bandage, and a bottle of white spirits, from his black bag. Carefully swabbing the skin, he revealed what turned out to be a line of numbers: *78891*.

Brooke stood, staring at the hand.

'What is it, Brooke?' asked Comfort.

'It's my telephone number,' he said.

CHAPTER TWO

Brooke bought two pints of Ridley's Best Bitter at the bar and found their usual table to one side of the fireplace. The Cricketers was only half full: a Wednesday night, like any other since the war had begun, and the price of beer now sky-high at five pence a pint. Their table was beside the frosted window, one pane of which was etched with figures playing cricket in happier times. The rest of the windows were new, blown out by the bomb which had fallen on Elm Street the previous year, and which had come within fifty yards of ending Brooke's life – which, Claire had pointed out, would have been an ignominious end for a man who'd got a medal from the king for refusing to divulge military secrets despite the tortures of thirst. She said that if the Elm Street bomb had killed him, he'd have been a hero all over again, but only in his obituary in the *Cambridge News*.

Grandcourt arrived, precisely on time, already filling his pipe, and as cheerful as ever. He sat down and took an inch off the top of his pint, wiping suds from his moustache.

They touched glasses: 'Sir,' said Grandcourt.

Edmund Grandcourt had been Brooke's batman in Palestine, and was virtually part of the family, but the 'sir' never faltered, even if its deferential tone had faded away.

Momentarily, he disappeared in a cloud of pipe smoke and sizzling sparks.

Grandcourt was perfectly at home in a well-run public house, despite modest habits when it came to beer. The atmosphere of carefree sociability suited him, largely because he felt able to stand aside and observe. He was that rare example of someone who delighted in the joy of others. Brooke had never seen him the worse for wear, not even in Alexandria when they'd headed back for the boat home.

England had looked green and pleasant in 1919 as they steamed past the Isle of Wight and into Portsmouth, but jobs were scarce, and so Brooke had secured him a position as a storeman in the university's engineering department. It was meant to be a temporary appointment, but jobs were even more difficult to find in the lean years of the thirties, so Grandcourt – despite ambitions – had stayed put.

Since a new war had broken out he'd volunteered as a shelter warden, and so was one of Brooke's many nighthawks – a network across the city, the product of twenty years of intermittent insomnia, another consequence of his ordeal in Palestine. The nighthawks were always there for Brooke, and often on hand to help with his most testing cases.

'Any news of young Mr Brooke, sir?' asked Grandcourt, stretching out a stiff leg.

'Nothing you could call news,' said Brooke, lighting one of his Black Russians – an affectation he'd picked up in the officer's mess in Cairo.

He tried to concentrate on his friend's question.

'Luke should be in Scotland training. But you never know. There's been another raid on some islands off Norway – the radio this morning said commandos took part.'

He produced his notebook. 'Some place called the Lofoten Islands. Said they took more than a hundred prisoners. No casualties on our side. They brought a bunch of Norwegians back with them – volunteers, local partisans I suppose.'

'Official?' asked Grandcourt, who, while a conduit for gossip and 'intel', was a sceptic in all things.

'The Home Service said a statement was issued by the Admiralty. Not much detail. And, of course, no date. They never give dates. But it must have gone well, otherwise they'd have brushed it under the carpet.'

Grandcourt's pipe produced a billow, which actually shut out the beams of sunlight for a moment. He was a small man – bantamweight – and his choice of pipes made him look even smaller.

'They'll be newsreel in the cinemas if they want to make a splash of it,' he said. 'Bogart's on at the Regal – *The Maltese Falcon*.'

'Claire's already marked my card,' said Brooke. 'We're going Sunday night with Joy.'

They synchronised the sipping of ale.

Brooke asked after Grandcourt's grown-up children and his wife. If he was honest with himself he wouldn't have shown an interest normally, but Claire would ask if he'd asked, and expect the latest family news. But neither he nor his one-time batman were especially relaxed talking about personal matters. The conversation tended to centre on pies, bacon, cricket and town gossip – unless Brooke had a case to crack, which might benefit from Grandcourt's common sense about the everyday world. He was a walking encyclopaedia of the practical; one of those people who seemed able to turn their hands to any task. In the desert he'd proved a gifted organiser, with enough astute intelligence for the whole troop.

And Brooke often needed the help. The Borough, being a miniature police force, with scarce resources, left him in effective command of the plain-clothed division – in that the other inspector dealt with road traffic, and the courts. In terms of criminal detection, Brooke was the only senior officer in a city swollen by evacuees and civil servants shipped out of London. He'd take any help he could get.

'I've got a nut to crack,' said Brooke. 'A body was found in one of the shelters on the Backs. Looks like suicide. Thing is, he had my office telephone number on the back of his hand.'

'Good God,' said Grandcourt. 'Wasn't there one up at Chesterton in the summer – a suicide? I get plenty of tears in my shelter – and it's not just the women and kids.'

'We all lead lives of quiet desperation,' said Brooke.

Grandcourt had developed a sixth sense with respect to Brooke's philosophical musings, so he knew when his spoken thoughts needed no response.

'Autopsy tomorrow,' said Brooke. 'Which makes the beer all the more refreshing tonight.'

Grandcourt, who had seen his commanding officer pass out at the sight of blood several times in the desert, took the hint and provided refills.

Brooke took a gulp and outlined the facts of the case. 'Dr Comfort has his doubts too. And given the victim was going to call us, I think we should leave no stone unturned. And there's something else,' he added. 'There was nothing in his pockets that could lead us to his name.'

Grandcourt's pipe produced a miniature impression of the *Flying Scotsman* – a sure sign he was thinking. 'Maybe someone found him in the shelter – you said he was at the back, by the loo? Maybe they did find him at night, rifled his pockets, then made off through the back door.'

Brooke hadn't thought of that. Maybe it was suicide after all. Closely followed by robbery.

'I suppose the other question is why *wasn't* he in uniform,' said Grandcourt. 'Young fella like that.'

Another good point. Brooke had assumed he was RO – reserved occupation. But now he thought it through, it was rare for someone so young to avoid conscription unless they were a farmer, factory worker, fireman or policeman. And he'd put money on the victim being an office worker. Smooth hands, smart clean suit (if worn), clean skin.

'You're right,' admitted Brooke. 'I think he was an office worker, white-collar.'

'A nobby clerk, then,' said Grandcourt. 'Even if he was RO, he'd have got a lot of stick. White feathers and all that. People can be nasty. Mean. Maybe it was all too much. There's plenty that want to fight, but the government won't let them go. What will they say when their kids ask them what they did in the war?'

They finished their drinks and strolled back though the Kite, a working-class district set between a parallelogram of thoroughfares. There was a shop on most corners, although many had closed for want of shopkeepers, and some of the corner pubs had fared no better. Brooke felt the streets hid a lot of private despair. Everyone was getting by on hoping that better times were just round the corner.

Grandcourt stopped outside a boarded-up pub, called The Rose, with an ornate iron flower, painted gold, rather than a sign.

'Good old pub this,' he said. 'Shame to see it shut up. I used to come here with the wife after the war. Dominoes team as well. Darts. We used to travel for away games, far as Ely. Trip to Gorleston in the summer in a charabanc. A lot more like it won't survive the Duration.'

Grandcourt shook his head. There was a strange wistful look on his face which Brooke had rarely seen, except in the desert when he'd admit to missing his wife and boys.

They emerged on the edge of Parker's Piece. As well as the line of concrete shelters, one of which was Grandcourt's new domain, the army had bivouacked on the grass in neat lines of bell tents. Brooke was unsure why Cambridge needed such a military presence. Last summer had seen speculation a German invasion would come on the east coast, but now Hitler seemed to be biding his time. The absence of news – the papers and radio were strictly censored – added to the feeling of isolation. The whole city felt like a backwater.

From his knapsack Grandcourt produced a helmet with the words HEAD SHELTER WARDEN painted neatly in white on the front.

'Promotion,' said Brooke. 'That was fast.'

'Nobody else wanted the job,' said Grandcourt.

He set the smart helmet straight and gave Brooke his customary salute, then marched away.

CHAPTER THREE

Lieutenant Ben Ridding raised his binoculars to his eyes to scan the horizon. The sun had set in the west, the first stars multiplying, the sea dark, the white horses luminous. He was on third watch, alone in the conning tower of HMS *Unbowed*, a U-class Royal Navy submarine. The boat (never a ship) was 300 nautical miles west of Norway, and 250 nautical miles north-east of Orkney; its task was to protect Convoy PQ-7 en route to the Soviet White Sea port of Archangel. The sea state was rated 1 on the Douglas Scale – calm (rippled). There was a salty whisper as each wave broke over the bow.

The day he'd left Cambridge to join the boat, he'd told his father-in-law – Detective Inspector Eden Brooke – that if he was lucky, he might get to see the Northern Lights. Brooke, a natural scientist of the old school, had put a hand on Ben's shoulder.

'Come back and tell us all what it was like – not the picture-book stuff, what it was *really* like. You can tell Iris.'

At the thought of his daughter, Ben's insides clenched, the fear of not seeing her again now as dull and everyday as the bedbugs and the nits, and the damp stink of the mess.

So, what would he, God willing, one day tell his daughter?

Above him now the sky was alight.

As soon as the sun had gone the colours had appeared. A curtain, certainly, strung south-west to north-east across their bearing. An emerald-green screen which buckled and pulsed with that extraordinary light. Within this a gold band, a swathe of lemon-yellow, billowed. An orange motif was less fluid, more structural, as if the whole fantastic canvas been hung up in the Arctic sky on hooks.

What words to use? Brooke had given him some helpful technical terms, only marginally undermined by the fact they were nearly 2,000 years old. He should look out for *pithaei* – barrel-like shapes; *chasmata* – chasms; *pogoniae* – bearded lights; and finally *cyparissae* – the green layers of the cypress tree. There was a vast shimmering barrel certainly, and even some clear bearded shapes just above the horizon, as if the curtain was weeping, but the overall impression was the chasm: a vast series of caves within which lights played.

But to answer his father-in-law's real question, he had to abandon colour and describe the scale. Ben was a sailor and he didn't often find the sea romantic, but this was not the sky at dusk, this was the heavens. And it drew him in, towards magnetic north and beyond. There was only one small disappointment.

He was a submariner: living – surviving – below the sea was above all an auditory experience. And Brooke had been told that the aurora had its own sound, which varied from claps and rattles to something close to birdsong; but it was rare, and as hard as Ben listened, all he could hear was the sea.

To balance out that disappointment there was an additional wonder. For the sea was alight too. The bow of *Unbowed* – running forward at ten knots – pushed aside the waves which rolled smoothly over the for'ard section. Each of these bow-waves flowed silkily around the conning tower, each studded with pinpoints of luminescent green, plankton mirroring on a microscopic scale the overarching vision above.

That was the beauty of it all.

His job was to keep watch for the beast.

It would strike at night. Possibly, tonight.

Its prey was Convoy PQ-7, currently eighteen miles away, just over the horizon, at a bearing of 120 degrees.

He could see one of the ships, the 5,000-tonne tanker MV *Airdrie*, carrying an entire wing of RAF fighters for the protection of Soviet Arctic ports. Since the German invasion of Russia in June, the convoys had developed quickly into a vital lifeline for an effectively landlocked ally. Ben simply noted the irony that a year earlier Stalin and Hitler had connived in the destruction of Poland. But his job was to keep an eye out for MV *Airdrie*, not muse on global geopolitics.

And keeping an eye on the ship was harder than it sounded. Night was falling and all he could see was the smoke from its furnaces, for its lumbering grey bulk was obscured by the curvature of the Earth. The smoke started at the horizon as a narrow funnel which then widened out, in the shape of a tuba held in the orchestra, until it blended into the aurora. Just behind it was another tuba, slightly smaller, but identical, on the same bearing.

According to the skipper's briefing on the chart chest at the start of the watch, there were sixteen merchant vessels in all, including one troop ship, all heading for Murmansk.

Their orders were to shadow the convoy and attack any German warship that approached. They had no name for the beast – any battleship in the Kriegsmarine would qualify, but they all knew the *Tirpitz* was in the sector, and her job was to stop the Soviet fleet breaking out of the Baltic. But she might take time off duty to destroy a convoy.

The moon had risen to starboard, which would reveal them in silhouette, the conning tower cutting through the silver sea like a shark's fin. But they were invisible at more than five miles, and Ben was satisfied this stretch of ocean was theirs alone.

One of the engine room ratings clattered up the spiral steps with a mug of tea.

'Jenkins says you've fixed the periscope, sir – that we won't miss next time.'

'Tell Jenkins to concentrate on the port-side diesel engine. It sounds like a clapped-out motorbike.'

'Sir. Did you fix it though?'

It was Able Seaman Tonks, one of the junior ratings.

Ben ignored the question. The boat had a crew of twenty-three. Traditional deference to ranks was difficult to maintain outside of battle stations.

The boy lingered. Ben was a favourite with the crew. This wasn't his first boat. He'd helped scupper the *Silverfish* off the German coast the previous year because of an engine fire, and he'd then spent six months in a POW camp as a result. He'd escaped, a feat which seemed to impress the deckhands more than any amount of nautical knowledge.

Which made him feel a fraud, because when the *Silverfish* had caught fire the sub had filled with smoke, and the lights had gone out, and he'd spent vital minutes holding onto the metal frame of his bunk, praying he'd see Joy and Iris again. If he hadn't been so terrified, he'd have screamed. His bunkmate Johnnie Phipps had saved his life, coming back down to drag him up the corkscrew stairs of the conning tower and bundle him into a raft. If they hadn't escaped from Luft III he'd have cracked up in there too. He'd told no one when he got back to Cambridge, but the nightmares betrayed him to Joy at Newnham Croft, although he could never quite bring himself to tell her the whole truth.

He didn't really deserve to be treated as a hero. He was only waiting to crack up again. His nerves were shot. The real problem was that, as always, he could hide it so well with a kind of blithe stillness. He'd never broken a sweat in his life.

Tonks was still waiting for an answer to his question.

Had he fixed the periscope?

Every man on a sub was a volunteer, Ben often reminded himself of that, so he hardly felt he could treat them like swabs. Tonks deserved an answer because his life might depend on it.

'I did what I could, Tonks. Optics isn't my strong point. I'm a medical student. But we'll find out soon enough.'

Tonks still lingered. He was like a dog.

'Now, go and tell the man at the day book the moon's up and there's nothing to report. Inform the skipper that we are now visible at five miles.'

Tonks dropped from sight, and Ben heard him turning the locks on the hatch.

Six days earlier they'd had a German corvette in their sights: 1,000 yards on a flat sea, almost beam-on. The skipper fired two torpedoes from periscope depth – forty-five feet. They'd crowded into the command room by the blue light of the sonar screen and waited for the tell-tale explosion, the inevitable pulse of the shock wave, the crump of bulkheads folding under pressure as she went down.

Both fish missed.

Ben had been summoned to the mess once they'd withdrawn from contact. The periscope eyepiece was on the tabletop. Was it the culprit, or had poor seamanship allowed the enemy to escape?

'The eye of Polyphemus,' said the skipper, whose name was Lynch-Forbes, but everyone called him Skipper. He was old-school, a veteran of the Great War. They were treated to the story out of the *Iliad*, but Ben knew it, because Brooke was always quoting chunks of the text over dinner at Newnham Croft, as he'd been given a copy by his father at Cambridge railway station the day he'd set out for Egypt in 1915.

Polyphemus was a Cyclops. Ulysses' men got into his cave and stole his food and when he was drunk they blinded him, and then hid outside amongst the sheep, so he couldn't feel where they lay. Which made Ben think of *Unbowed* blundering around looking for the enemy by sonar alone.

'Our Polyphemus isn't blind – but he bloody well might as well be,' said the skipper. The chief was there too, but everyone seemed to think this was Lieutenant Ben Ridding's problem. This seemed unfair. As a medic he'd specialised in optics and diseases of the eye. In scientific terms this expertise was useless when dealing with a periscope. But given the size of the crew it had been sufficient to land Ben the job.

'Can you check it out?' asked Lynch-Forbes. 'If we can't rely on her we might as well get back to port. I've asked the Admiralty to contact the factory – place called the Vulcan Works, Cambridge. Isn't that your neck of the woods, Ben?'

Ben nodded. It was home now. He'd gone straight to Rosyth after the wedding, and the deckhands had thrown him in the dock.

'We're not the first to spot a problem,' said the skipper. 'It's probably shoddy workmanship. Unfortunately, they can't spare an expert so they're sending in the local coppers. God help us.'

The skipper looked at his watch. 'Hargreaves can cover your next watch. This is a priority. If we can't shoot straight, we'll skedaddle.'

After that, it had taken Ben three hours to set up a makeshift lab table in the torpedo hall.

There were three lenses – the object, the field and the ocular, and he used a torch beam through a hole cut in a card to check the angles, and the degree of refraction through the two prisms. (He'd learnt that much at Dartmouth: prisms, never mirrors, because they'd shatter anywhere near a depth charge – or mist up once the damp got inside the periscope tube. A decent prism was as durable as a rock.)

There was nothing wrong with the kit, but the periscope's optics were off-line by three degrees. The third lens, the ocular, was the culprit. It was a millimetre closer to the field lens and set very slightly off a right angle. Ben used an eyepiece to examine the assembly and found a very fine washer had been inserted – one side bevelled to produce the angle. There was nothing 'shoddy' about the workmanship here: it was a fine piece of engineering.

He checked everything again. Then a third time. After speaking to the skipper and assuring him the periscope was now usable, he went to the radio room to send an agreed message to the Admiralty, with a copy to the War Office.

In it Ben set out his precise measurements.

The message ended with:

NO DOUBT: CAMBRIDGE FACTORY. SABOTAGE.

CHAPTER FOUR

The Spinning House – heart and soul of the Borough – stood on St Andrew's Street, one of the arrow-straight sections of the original Roman road which cut through the city like a cheese-wire. In its former life the medieval building had been a prison for 'fallen women' run by the university, which had taken upon itself the role of policing the streets and safeguarding the morals of its students. (Or more likely, wished to remove a temptation which proved too much for so many.) It looked like a gaol, with small windows and blank walls, and it radiated a certain grim determination to punish. In the final years of the last century it had operated as a workhouse – the women set to labour in its lofts at spinning wheels and looms.

Brooke met Edison on the threshold, the sergeant's arms full of excess produce from his allotment, destined for the uniformed branch's mess room. For thirty years he had been one of them, not a detective, and the mess was in some ways a home from home. While Edison's generosity with carrots, cabbages and Russian kale was legendary, Brooke felt that this time he had gone too far. His sergeant was practically obscured by largesse, a walking grocery stall.

'Everything's got to go,' said Edison. 'We've got a garden, sir. The wife can grow what we need. I think the allotment's had its day.'

It was a small clue, and now he recalled others, that in some way Edison's life was shifting from its well-worn path. During the three years they'd worked together Edison had made it clear that while the Wasp was his pride and joy, the allotment came a close second, its hut a welcome refuge from the world. Now he planned to simply give it up.

Edison hurried off. 'I'll dump this. Will you want me for the autopsy, sir?'

'In an hour.'

Brooke went to his office and carefully adjusted the blinds to decrease the light, taking off his glasses to read the post. The autopsy on the man found in the Trinity Shelter was scheduled for ten. A sense of hopelessness kindled in Brooke. He knew that he'd soon see that face again, in the unforgiving light of Dr Comfort's laboratory. Cold, pale and once handsome. He had to hope that within hours someone would step forward: a girlfriend, a wife, a mother, a brother. Otherwise, they might never know his story, and why he'd wanted to share it with the Borough.

DC Vanessa Turner appeared at his door, reporting for duty. She was a new recruit to the Borough, after the war put a stop to her studies at the art college beyond Parker's Piece. Attracted by the concept of detection, and its emphasis on detail – which was central to her artwork – she'd signed up as a special constable, her diploma studies suspended. She'd gone into the uniformed branch, but Brooke had spotted a sharp brain and an even sharper eye and whisked her up into the plain-clothed division.

For a moment she stood, patting down her dark jacket and skirt. Brooke had noted she had the arresting habit of appearing still, while her eyes ran sinuously over everything around her. Brooke suspected any nerves exhibited were limited to her hands, which she often held behind her back. Her file had listed a passion for exercise, specifically lacrosse. As a child he'd often seen matches on Parker's Piece – the girls charging around with lethal sticks, throwing up turf like galloping horses. Turner exhibited all the signs of suppressed energy. Her movements were slightly awkward, a common trait in the tall. But he suspected that at speed, and under pressure, she would achieve an effortless grace.

She had accepted, at least for now, that her duties were to be mundane.

She offered to fetch tea from the canteen.

But Brooke had a sudden notion, which he recognised called for immediate action.

'Art – at the college? Wasn't that it?'

'Sir. Third year of a diploma.'

'They teach anatomy?'

'Sir. Medical school at Queens'. Twice a week.'

'Good. If you feel queasy don't eat now. It never works. We've an appointment at the Galen for an autopsy at ten. Bring a pencil and sketchpad. I'll meet you at the duty desk at five to the hour.'

She nodded, and he thought she really did look keen.

Then he settled down to deskwork, an aspect of detection he found loathsome. He asked the switchboard for a line and began a series of calls designed to confirm that no missing persons had been registered at County, or the neighbouring counties, in the last forty-eight hours. A young adjutant at Madingley Hall, the country house on the edge of the city requisitioned by the military as a regional HQ, assured him the last soldier registered as AWOL had been found at his home address in Shoreditch two weeks earlier, and no one else was missing. The university was a trickier matter. All students and most of the able-bodied academics were now in the forces. Those that were left were essentially AWOL for the Duration. With no one to teach, the staff were either lost in the maze of college libraries or dragooned into work related directly to the war effort, at various ministries or laboratories. Keeping track of them was impossible, certainly at short notice.

Taking a break, he stood at the blinds, feathering them to look out over the rooftops. As he watched, a barrage balloon rose slowly from the riverbank, the university library its backdrop. In the sky above a bomber limped home to one of the Fen aerodromes. The war was the backdrop to everything, but nonetheless oddly distant.

Perhaps it was the thought of the autopsy to come, for he was never at ease in the company of the dead, but he felt a sudden, crippling fatigue. Ever since his ordeal in the desert he'd been a victim of insomnia. This had suited his aversion to light. He'd attempted to follow a new regime for sleep: an evening meal, a hot bath and a darkened room at the appropriate time. But almost every night he was awake by two and had simply to wait for dawn. More often he'd simply get up and set off across the city in pursuit of the company of nighthawks.

The effect of his sleepless nights were these sudden collapses, a brief plummet into sleep and dreams. Or nightmares.

He lay down on the day bed he'd bought in Cairo. It was in a light flexible wood, painted with a scene comprising reeds, and birds, and the Nile. Sleep came, and nightmares flitted, interwoven with a single image of the dimly lit bomb shelter, which for some reason incorporated a makeshift gallows, a man standing on the bench, the rope around his neck attached to an iron ring in the concrete roof, set to hang a lantern. In the desert he'd had to order the execution of a looter south of Jerusalem. He heard now, in his sleep, his own voice giving the final order. He looked down at the shadow on the colourless sand, the tied legs swinging. He wanted to cut him down, but his own limbs wouldn't move. It was typical of his time as a soldier, in that he felt he'd been made to do something to meet the expectations of others. The man's name was Omar – which he knew was derived from the Arabic for 'flourishing'.

Which is how it always ended, with him trying to say 'Omar', but the sound getting stuck in his throat.

A hand on his shoulder woke him. It was PC Turner. He wondered if she'd heard his struggle to speak.

'Time, sir,' she said, unsmiling.

They set out quickly for the Galen Anatomy Building, just three minutes' walk through the grounds of Downing College.

Completed in the last months of peace, it was a pale vision of tiled brickwork, rising five floors, a shining addition to the medical faculty and the other anonymous post-war science buildings making up what they now were asked to call the Downing Site – although as a child he'd known it as Pembroke Leys, a marsh, where he'd hunted for frogspawn, a secret world of puddles, streams and ponds.

They climbed the steps to the Galen's imposing doors, past the two male statues on guard to either side: classical carved figures set in stone; warriors, armed with spears. Brooke could never ditch the illusion that as he passed they turned to watch him, amplifying the feeling that he was going into battle again, and that he'd soon have the company of the dead.

Recognising Brooke, the porter touched his cap. 'The doctor's upstairs, sir. You're expected. He's got a lunch at Catz, so he'll whistle through it.' The pathologist was a fellow at St Catherine's College, and a stalwart of the High Table.

Noting Turner, and the uniform, the porter seemed confused, and simply mumbled 'Ma'am,' before returning to his ledger.

Dr Comfort's laboratory was on the top floor. His modest duties as the Borough's pathologist were combined with a university position in medicine; a double appointment which stretched back to the period of Victorian efficiency. The city was tiny, and since the days of open warfare between 'Town' and 'Gown', instances of unnatural, unexpected or violent death were very rare. The County force, up at the Castle, had its own arrangements.

Brooke took the concrete steps two at a time, rising up through the silent building. He noted that PC Turner matched him step for step without any obvious need to take extra breaths, or even any breaths. He got the impression she was disappointed to reach the top, where she straightened her tunic.

The pathologist was waiting at the doors of his laboratory, struggling with a bowtie. Brooke introduced PC Turner, adding that she was present to observe. Dr Comfort's entire attention switched to the one occupied dissection table – one of three set in the centre of the laboratory. Three walls of the room – which served a double role as the city's mortuary – held windows, and so the light was penetrating. Brooke switched from the ochre to the blue tinted lenses. He always preferred to see a corpse by dim light. Here, in Dr Comfort's kingdom, the dead were revealed in dazzling detail, which reminded him, yet again, of the desert.

The deceased was naked, the re-stitched flesh jagged with wounds. Dr Comfort had known Brooke a decade and was well aware of his violent aversion to blood and gore. He always strove to complete the butchery well ahead of time, leaving Brooke to deal with the findings, and, briefly, to examine the corpse.

So, the brain had been removed, although Brooke just had time to see it floating in a glass jar before he looked away. In Egypt and Sinai, he'd learnt, eventually, that he couldn't emotionally connect with every casualty, and that he should reserve his concern for his men. The problem was that in a real sense this man *was* one of his men. The dead – the murdered – were now his soldiers.

One thing struck Brooke immediately. Naked, it was obvious the olive tone of the skin was not hereditary at all. The victim had a suntan, which covered his body except for the area delineated by a pair of swimming shorts. There was no doubt he had been in strong sunlight quite recently. Given the appalling summer so far, that raised its own questions.

Comfort, smiling, watched carefully, and then took Brooke's eye to the left wrist.

'The Tropics?'

'Well. Certainly not the English summer which has just passed. Certainly not a bank holiday in Margate – if we had bank holidays any more.'

'Natural?' asked Brooke.

'Oh yes. I've run a few basic tests – the dye is easy to detect. No – he's been in the sun alright. And recently. Over time tans go – don't we know it. But exposed areas whiten first. Unexposed areas reveal the depth of the original tan – here at the chest, or the legs. He's been sunbathing.'

'How recently?'

Comfort rocked his head side to side. 'I'd hazard within the last fortnight.'

Brooke stared at the corpse. Who could afford a sunshine holiday abroad in the midst of a world war? Or was he a foreigner? American perhaps – newly arrived? The newspapers were full of stories of brave young Americans volunteering, even though Washington was adamant about remaining officially neutral. Was he part of the advance guard?

Turner was examining the naked corpse with frank professional interest. Again, her body still, the eyes in constant motion.

'Bit of a conundrum,' said the pathologist. 'Never seen anything like it,' he added, staring at the stone-like face, as if the rest of what he had to say was going to be an entirely interior dialogue.

'In what sense?' prompted Brooke. 'The tan?'

'No, no. That's entirely for you to consider, Inspector. The sun didn't kill him – did it? And he's in excellent condition. Wouldn't look out of place on the Elgin Marbles. But for some intervention he'd have lived a long life. No. The blood loss didn't kill him, you see. That's post-mortem.'

'What did kill him?'

'A massive heart attack, but there's no evidence of cardiac disease at all. Which would lead us to some kind of violent shock – I'd guess toxic.'

'Poison?'

'Yes. The broken blood vessels behind the eye are particularly telling. Can't say anything definite until we have the toxicology. Which would mean in turn sending off samples to the Yard, which would demand delaying burial. But then I presume we still don't know who he is – so that's hardly a problem. Correct?'

'Correct,' said Brooke. 'So someone killed him and then slit his wrists to make it look like suicide?'

'That's it. Death occurred in the time frame I gave you – twelve to twenty-four hours. Otherwise, the blood wouldn't have flowed at all. But it could have occurred anywhere – not necessarily in the shelter. The body could have been dumped. In fact, I think that's likely because his blood has pooled evenly on his right side and left side – but he was found on his left side.'

All of which, thought Brooke, *makes the telephone number more interesting. Did the victim suspect that his life was in danger?* Brooke's telephone number was in the directory for the Borough. Or more precisely, listed for CID. It would have taken less than a minute to find it in any telephone box, or post office, or library.

Comfort swept the shroud back over the corpse.

'None of which is good news, because the chances of catching a poisoner are thin. But then that's your job, thank God. I'll do the paperwork now. We'll get samples down to the Yard by courier today. And chummy here will have to stay on ice.'

Comfort was putting on a jacket, patting pockets for his cigar and lighter, no doubt contemplating his lunch at Catz.

But Brooke wasn't finished. 'I'd like to suggest a somewhat unusual course of action, Doctor. Can the servants leave the victim here for a period of time.'

'Why?' asked Comfort, frozen in the act of straightening his tie.

The 'servants' were the doctor's assistants. Well trained, they provided muscle when needed to operate saws and other specialist instruments, and ferry the dead to and from the outside world in the capacious lift.

'So far we have no reports of a missing person, or persons . . .' said Brooke. 'The deceased had no visible means of identification – quite the opposite. If he's from out of town – and given the tan, it could be well out of town – we may never know who he is. I accept that there's a war on. Thousands will die and lie in unmarked graves. I can't do anything about that.

'But this could be cold-blooded murder. Executed with some skill and planning. I know we can't prove that yet – but that has to be a working hypothesis. I think we should try and find his killer.

'The town's full of outsiders. Evacuees, their parents, soldiers, airmen, civil servants up from Whitehall. Thousands. Visiting academics. But someone might remember his face.

45

'PC Turner is part way through a diploma in fine art. She has experience of attending the anatomical theatre. I want her to sketch the face as if in life. Then we could get County's help in running out a poster.'

Comfort was standing on one leg, polishing his right shoe by running it up and down the back of his left leg.

'And what does PC Turner think? Asked her, have we?'

PC Turner produced a pencil from behind her left ear, and a sketchbook from a satchel over one shoulder.

Comfort sank his chin into his chest, a sure sign of deep thought.

'We don't need to say the man was murdered,' said Brooke. 'We want to ask if anyone has seen him or recognises him. In fact, we should say that suicide is suspected – that way the killer may relax. Yes. That's best I think.'

Comfort looked at the corpse. 'Alright. But you must wait another twenty-four hours before publication. I know there's a war on and death is all around us. But there's no indication this is about the war. Let's hold onto what shreds of civilisation we still have. How long do you want?' he asked Turner.

'Half an hour, sir,' she said. 'And a high stool?'

They fetched one from a store cupboard.

'And you can achieve a living likeness?' asked Comfort.

She nodded.

He puffed at a freshly lit cigar, still troubled. 'If he had a name, he'd have a next of kin and I'd have to ask for permission. It's ghoulish. Kind of thing the Yanks do all the time – crime scene pictures plastered across front pages. Blood and guts . . .

'But if you must . . . One precaution. I'll inform the coroner, Brooke, and if he thinks we've gone too far then I'm afraid you can't use the image. Agreed?'

Brooke nodded.

Comfort pressed the electric button to summon the 'servants' and almost immediately they heard the lift motor whirr. There were two, in white surgical jackets, eyes down, workmanlike and brisk. It took them five minutes to turn the corpse, elevate the head and remove the shroud.

Turner perched on her stool with the sketchpad on her knee and got close to the cadaver. She pushed back the Anglepoise lamp, turned off the neon tubes above and set a desk lamp to one side on a trolley.

The victim's face was reinvigorated by shadow.

As she moved the lamp, the flesh seemed to come alive, and Brooke had to look away.

Comfort went to lunch, and the servants back down in the lift, asking only for someone to press the bell when they left.

Brooke smoked at an open window.

After twenty minutes Turner handed him the sketchbook.

A pencil image, strikingly vivid, with the pale green eyes – suggested by their light tone – bringing it all to life. In the shelter, in his suit, he'd looked anonymous. But the artist had found something else in the face, drawing the lips together to hide the teeth, and capturing a facet of character: weakness certainly, but self-knowledge too.

CHAPTER FIVE

The Arbury was a stretch of heathland to the north of the city, a bleak precursor to the Black Fens which began beyond the twin lost ports of Waterbeach and Landbeach. Brooke's father may have won the Nobel Prize for medicine, but Sir John was nothing if not a polymath. On blustery summer days he'd take his son out on the Arbury to see the dimly discerned earthworks of an Iron Age fort built on the last solid ground before the great watery wastes engulfed the land. Brooke had enjoyed careering up and down the slopes and running along the ditches. But they'd once come at Christmas – his mother in tow – and it had been misty, and he'd been spooked by the conviction that he could see the shadowy figures of Iron Age warriors, as if glimpsed through tracing paper.

The landscape's ragged splendour had been undermined by the arrival of the suburbs. There was a cluster of shops now where the Arbury Road left town, and a pub half a mile along the lane. The Vulcan Works comprised a low-slung line of buildings in red brick, with corrugated roofs and a flagpole with no flag. There was a ten-foot wire fence and a manned gate. They were all asked for their warrant cards, and their ID cards. Police officers were issued with photographic ID, unlike the general population, so there was always a short performance as their faces were scrutinised.

'Mr Chubb's expecting you,' said the guard. 'Can you park to the left where indicated?'

There was even a smart salute, although the man's uniform simply carried a badge marked VULCAN. Brooke thought everyone was saluting these days. And uniforms had proliferated, perhaps in part to make life easier for those who'd been denied the opportunity to serve in the armed forces. It reinforced the idea that everyone was part of the war effort, even on the Home Front. It also empowered a growing band of officious officials – widely dubbed 'little Hitlers'.

The 'car park' consisted of five bays, one marked VISITORS. A bike rack ran for a hundred yards and was packed solid. Strains of the BBC Home Service echoed from the open doors of the factory vehicle bay. The whole factory had the dusty commonplace feel of the working man – and, increasingly, the working woman. With conscription at full tilt, factories across the land had been forced to turn to women to keep the war economy in action. Not just factories, but bus companies, rail companies, anything, in fact, requiring 'manpower'.

A message for Detective Chief Inspector Carnegie-Brown, delivered that morning by motorcycle messenger from the Admiralty, had set the visit in urgent motion. The Admiralty orders had been waiting on Brooke's desk when he got back from the Galen. Sabotage was suspected at the Vulcan Works. The Borough was to investigate and report back within twenty-four hours. If possible, the workforce was not to be alerted to the investigation. A scrawled note from Carnegie-Brown had stipulated that the inquiry was now the Borough's 'top priority' – a snippet of managerial hogwash which always annoyed Brooke: what other kind of priority was there?

Given the sensitivity of their visit, Brooke had decided to bring an extra pair of eyes in the shape of PC Turner. Her job was to observe. Nothing more, nothing less. Sergeant Edison would do what he did best – watch Brooke's back. He had an unerring ability to ask the one question which could open up an inquiry.

'Mr Brooke!' called a voice, as a man emerged in brown overalls from the inky interior of the main shed. He wore a shirt and tie and was shadowed by a woman with spectacles on a chain round her neck.

'Mr Chubb?' asked Brooke, taking off his hat and the blue tinted glasses. 'Sorry to interrupt the working day.'

'Unavoidable, Inspector. We're on three shifts now – round the clock production. But it's not a problem. This is the office manager, Mrs Bavidge.'

Brooke nodded.

'Always a pleasure to see the Borough,' said Chubb, loudly, as a group of workers filed past. 'We take security very seriously here on the Arbury. We're happy to show you anything, anywhere. Routine checks are part of the working day.'

Chubb had a nervous habit of nodding rapidly as he spoke, as if his vocal cords were attached to his spinal cord. He was about forty, with thinning red hair. Brooke felt he'd slightly overdone the cover story. The word sabotage would not be uttered in public. Their visit was simply part of a Whitehall-inspired programme of security checks on factories manufacturing military material. The Admiralty had suggested a bulletin to this effect should be posted on the canteen noticeboard, and a brief item inserted in the *Cambridge News*.

They wanted to catch their saboteur, not set them running.

Outside the Borough, only Chubb knew the truth.

Head bobbing in a short bow, he led the way.

'The office is probably best, but I can do the quick tour . . .'

'Good. We won't take up hours,' said Brooke. 'We're off to Unicam next, and then the rail works.' This was all part of the cover story too, as he had no intention of visiting either. He produced a packet of cigarettes.

'No smoking, I'm afraid,' said Chubb. 'Not in the factory – but my office is fine.' Despite the nervous disposition he was clearly still master of this small world, and no doubt set its many rules.

The atmosphere inside the factory was brisk but dull, enlivened by the radio and a circling tea trolley.

There were production lines but no conveyor belts. Items were worked on at a preset station and then set aside to be taken by a hand-pulled forklift to the next station. Some of the workers, mostly women, stood and repeated simple tasks. More skilled operators, mostly middle-aged men, sat at their stations. Drills and small circular saws hummed at intervals. There was a strong smell of oil, and soap, and inevitably, long-brewed tea.

The first three sheds – about the size of badminton courts – were making galvanometers for measuring and detecting small electrical currents, while the next two were turning out optical equipment for laboratories: Chubb showed them a set of boxes marked up for shipment to the government labs at Porton Down. A separate, larger shed was producing a variety of instruments for the new Mosquito, which Chubb called 'the Wooden Wonder'.

'The de Havilland engineer – he comes over from the plant – he says it'll win us the war if we can get enough in the air.'

Brooke thought the engineer from de Havilland might like to keep his mouth shut.

'We'll see,' was what he said.

The periscope plant was new, this time made of corrugated iron, and they had to sign a book to get past a woman on the door. The air inside was stifling because the light flooded in through skylights – as in the other sheds – but these were plexiglass and had no vents. The building comprised two sheds: in the first, men wearing the kind of single-eye magnifying glasses used by jewellers worked at grinding machines producing lenses and prisms.

In the second, women were assembling the periscopes. Edison stood at one woman's shoulder, patiently watching her skilled hands manipulate a series of lenses into position. Someone had brought in a gramophone player and Brooke couldn't help but smile at the choice: Beethoven, a piano sonata. Just after the Great War was finally over he'd taken Claire on a cycling holiday – another recommended exercise designed to heal his injured leg. They'd caught the ferry to Hamburg, and idled down to Bonn, taking time to find the great composer's birthplace. Brooke wondered what the city looked like now. Every night the bombers flew south. He could only imagine the devastation.

The sonata played on, and the work – mostly silent – was steady. The metal components and unground prisms and lenses arrived by lorry, said Chubb, the brass and steel already broadly finished. The skilled work was in grinding and polishing the 'optics'. The factory then provided precise, skilled assembly – a job they'd found suited the women. The finished items were checked before shipment in the testing room, which comprised the ground floor of a small, new two-storey admin block. Chubb took them through and up a metal staircase to a set of modest offices.

Tea had been ordered and was set out on his desk. There was an awkward moment as everyone waited for Mrs Bavidge 'to do the honours'. PC Turner pointedly stood by the door, her notebook ready.

Chubb picked up his chair from behind his desk and brought it round so they could all sit together, which Brooke thought was smart, and revealed a surprising degree of subtle management.

'What did the ministry say?' asked Brooke.

Chubb glanced at Turner and Edison.

Brooke replaced his teacup in its saucer. 'The chances that PC Turner and – or – Sergeant Edison are Abwehr spies is slim, Mr Chubb. If the problem is anywhere, it's here in the factory.'

Chubb looked shocked but nodded a few times as if pulling himself together. 'The message I got was brief but unsettling, to say the least, Inspector. They've ordered visual checks on the new attack periscopes across the U-class fleet,' he said. 'A number – unspecified – have been found to be faulty. All those failing tests

53

were made here. They said you'd have more information.'

The sudden sound of aircraft engines made them all look out the window over the brown heathland. A bomber appeared to the east, coming in at the airfield at Waterbeach. It was trailing smoke and the engine kept cutting out, or at least misfiring. It was very low and seemed to heave itself up with an effort to clear a line of poplars before disappearing from sight. They all knew enough of the reality of bombing raids over Europe – as far as Berlin itself – to know it might have been shot up so badly the landing gear was out of operation, so they waited, teacups poised, in case there was a slow crump and a burst of flame. But the moment passed.

Chubb looked at his tea. 'But that's not why you're here, is it Inspector? I don't think our problem is seen as shoddy work – is it?'

'No, sir,' said Brooke. 'So far eight periscopes have been found to be faulty. In each case it is sabotage. When disassembled, the faulty periscopes are found to have a misaligned lens – the "ocular" lens.'

'How . . . ?'

Brooke held up a hand, and with the other produced a small washer from his pocket. 'In each case, as I say, one of these has been slipped between the lens and its slot.'

Ben had been the first to find the washer. A quick inventory of boats at Barrow, ordered by the Admiralty, had identified two more to add to the six at sea. This one had been driven south by a motorcycle messenger to the Spinning House.

'These are the delivery dates for the faulty periscopes,' said Brooke, handing over a typed sheet.

Chubb studied the washer. 'This has been manufactured

for the periscope. It's of high quality. This is most disturbing, Inspector.'

Chubb got up and began to sift through a filing cabinet.

PC Turner took the opportunity to slip out of the office, announcing she would check perimeter security. This had been prearranged by Brooke. He wanted her to tour the entire factory – inside and out.

Chubb sat down with the files. 'Two each from four batches. There's a dozen in each batch. We've had ten batches since production began. That's 120 periscopes in total – with eight faulty, as you say. The last lot went out three weeks ago. They were all tested and passed. The dates on which faulty periscopes were delivered seem random.'

Brooke leant back in his seat, and Edison cleared his throat. This kind of choreography was now innate. The sergeant would take up the questions, giving Brooke time to think.

'Why do our submarines need new periscopes?' asked Edison.

'Every sub has two, Sergeant. Attack and search. The attack is smaller – less visible – and can provide data on range and bearing. We produce attack periscopes. A firm in Glasgow – Barr and Stroud – developed the kit, a new design for the navy. They've found a way of keeping moisture out of the optics – that improves everything. They needed to find someone to do the routine manufacturing work. We got the contract – well, the lion's share of the contract. The rest went to an outfit on the Tyne. That's standard practice, so that if we were bombed they could simply switch north and expand production.'

Edison closed his notebook, then asked another question. 'How is the testing done? And where is it done?'

And there it is, thought Brooke. *The central question.*

'Each periscope is bolted into the test bench – downstairs – and a light shone through. The resulting pattern is matched against a pre-printed card. An exact match shows us that the optics are in perfect alignment. It's very simple, a child could do it.'

'Who did do it?' asked Brooke.

Chubb fetched a large ledger from the top of a bookcase. Opening it, he rested a finger on the left-hand column.

'Each periscope has a serial number – 043, etcetera – and this is punched on the periscope tube here in the factory before assembly. The serial numbers run in an unbroken series from 001. We've now reached 120, as I said. When tested, the signature of the test engineer is set beside the serial number in the log if all is well.'

Brooke took off his glasses: 'P. F. C.?'

'P. F. C. – Peter Faraday Chubb. Sorry – my father always wanted his son to be a scientist.'

'And the other faulty batches – who tested them?'

Chubb flicked back. 'I did the first, and Dr Simons did the next two, then I did the last. He's a fellow at the university, St Radegund's. He was one of the founders of this factory back in '33. Member of the Royal Society. Expert in instrument calibration. Most of his time these days he's in London for the War Office.'

Unless they had two spies in the Vulcan Works testing team, it looked like the periscopes had left Cambridge in mint condition, thought Brooke.

'Does the tester load the instruments for delivery?' asked Edison.

'Yes. Each one is tested, placed in a wooden box, and sealed at six o'clock on the evening before the consignment goes north.'

'How sealed?'

Chubb held up a lump of red wax which sat on his blotter beside a candle, and a small seal stamp etched with the letters VW and a motif of a hammer and fire.

'What happens once they leave here?' asked Brooke.

There was a map on the wall – in fact covering one wall – showing the British Isles and the major roads and rail routes.

'Pretty simple. North on the Lynn Road then over to the Great North Road and up to Scotch Corner, then over the Pennines and into Lancashire and out to Barrow. It's a long old haul with a delicate cargo – two days. Stop over at Scotch Corner.'

'Driver?'

'We provide the driver. The navy provided the reinforced van. We don't add a security man because it only advertises the fact we've got something sensitive on board. And the van – from the outside – is a standard Morris Eight. As far as anyone else is concerned, it's a consignment of "laboratory equipment" for the navy labs at Barrow. The various police forces relay us all the way up, and all the way down. But it's only a watching brief, they just make sure we get to where we're going. There's no outriders or anything. It's all very low key.'

'But County see you over the border here?' asked Edison.

The County force, based up on Castle Hill, had jurisdiction over all of Cambridgeshire except the City of Cambridge – leaving the Borough, based at the Spinning House, as the country's smallest police force. Enmity between the two forces was long established, so long that nobody could recall how it had begun, but Edison considered all those 'up at the Castle' to be overly officious, and he was prepared to list their other shortcomings at length if asked, and occasionally if not. His question was designed to show that if there was a problem on the road, it was not down to poor police work on the part of the Borough.

Chubb nodded. 'But as I say, the surveillance is cursory.'

'How many drivers?'

'One – same one each time. You don't want anyone getting lost and this way there's a drill and it never, ever varies.'

'What's his name?' asked Brooke.

'It's not a man,' said Chubb. 'It's our Eva, Eva Mappin. She's a very popular girl. Best driver we've got – everyone says so. I say girl, she's in her forties. I trust her completely.'

'Local?'

'No. Leeds, I think, or Sheffield. Moved down for the Duration.'

Brooke remembered when the 'Duration' was a code for a short war. Now it had a certain grim humour. It might mean for ever.

'Her aunt's bedridden. Here, in the Arbury. One of the sons was looking after her but he's a pilot out at Marshalls. She came down and left her husband to fend for himself. He's RO – factory worker. So he can't move of course, unless he can find a replacement. The rules are stringent.'

'Right. We'll still need to see her file,' said Brooke. 'In fact, we better check it out. Can we take it with us?'

'We don't keep files here, Inspector. All workers are selected by the Ministry of Labour and undergo a security check. So they'll have the file. They've an office here in Cambridge on Brooklands Avenue. But given Eva got the job, I can tell you she was rated A1 for security.'

'We'll double check,' said Brooke.

They went back downstairs, then out into the car park. PC Turner could be seen in the distance, pacing the outer security wire.

'When's the next consignment, sir?' asked Brooke.

'Tomorrow, Inspector. Production is scheduled to accelerate. The new kit – if not tampered with – has performed brilliantly in trials. The green light has been lit. The shipments will be weekly at least from now on.' said Chubb.

'Tomorrow?'

'She leaves at six when the shifts change.'

Brooke said they'd shadow the lorry all the way to the docks. The odds were nothing would happen – after all, six of the ten batches so far had been untouched. But there was little doubt the sabotage took place en route, or at Barrow once delivered. They needed to observe, even if the trip went without incident.

'The periscopes aren't checked again. They go straight into action, so to speak?' asked Edison.

'Yes. Why check them?' said Chubb. 'They leave here in perfect condition.'

'That may have to change,' said Brooke. 'Absolutely no part of this conversation is to be repeated,' he added.

PC Turner appeared, notebook in hand, so Brooke put his hat on and said they'd pick up Eva Mappin's van as it left the Arbury the following morning after six. They'd be in position one hundred yards west by five-thirty.

'The van – a Morris Eight. Colour?'

'Locomotive green,' said Chubb. 'Very smart. Eva puts a shine on the paintwork that's difficult to miss.'

'Right. No word of this to her.'

Chubb shook his hand. 'We all hope you find them, Inspector. And quickly. Anything I can do, anything. Just ring. I've given my home number to your sergeant here.'

As they drove back into the city, PC Turner summarised security at the Vulcan Works.

'The front gate's efficient. All those on foot have to sign in. Cars and occupants are logged in with their reg numbers. But they don't bother to log anyone out. The security fence is in good condition. But round the back there's a gate in the fence onto open country. It was locked. But it can't always be locked because outside on the grass was a football, a bench – cigarette butts underneath – and under a turf mound what looks like the factory bomb shelter. There's a netball post as well. I asked one of the girls and she said lunch hour, tea breaks, they open the gate.

'There's three security men – at the front gate – and a night watchman who takes over from six to six. Ex-Red Cap. There's a sign saying BEWARE THE DOG but no dog, apparently, since the last one bit a postman at the gate and had to be retired. The night watchman has an office, which I noted included a day bed.

'So, overall, slightly slipshod, sir.'

'But twenty-four-hour production. So there's always someone about,' said Edison.

'Yes, Sergeant. But the workforce is growing fast – currently one hundred and eighty. It was sixty-six three months ago. Would anyone spot an outsider in overalls? I doubt it.'

CHAPTER SIX

By the time Brooke stood on the doorstep of the Spinning House, lighting a cigarette, his desk clear at last of bumf and memos, it was nearly eight o'clock. The evening ahead was bleak. Claire was in the middle of her five-nights shift on Sunshine Ward. Joy was on an early rota in the geriatric ward, 'acting up' as sister, due to lack of staff. They'd both have eaten early, together, and taken Iris around to Mrs Mullins'. This routine caused Joy some grief, as she was loath to part with her daughter at such a young age. (And she was haunted by the thought she might miss those first steps.) There was nothing wrong with the care offered by Mrs Mullins, who was in her fifties, with three grown-up children. She loved babies, and needed the cash, and lived in Newnham village beside the Red Bull. But Joy felt these early months of life were unrepeatable, and therefore begrudged the loss.

Brooke was hungry but didn't relish a silent house and a cold grate, or an even colder dinner, ready to be reheated in a stone-cold oven. He felt the need of company and idle chat, so he turned down St Andrew's Street into the heart of the city, in search of fellow nighthawks. Halfway along Hobson Street – a dank thoroughfare on a sunny day, let alone after sunset – he heard footsteps and a woman appeared out of the shadows, hurrying home, so Brooke stepped back and tipped his hat.

With a nervous 'Evenin' . . .' she was gone.

The blackout brought its own fears and anxieties.

At the corner of King's Street – notorious for its many rowdy public houses – he stopped to smoke a second cigarette. The city centre was always quiet at this time; it was as if all the old stone, the ancient pillars and arches, towers and spires, was taking a collective deep breath to mark the end of the day. The result was the kind of silence in which you notice the oddest of intrusive sounds: the fluttering of a barrage balloon over the railyards, the sudden *thwack* of a flock of pigeons taking flight from the Senate House, or an oak door closing with the clank of a lock turning, a latch falling into place.

And then something out of place; voices, rebounding in a great open space. And then just once, a police whistle.

He set off in pursuit.

Echoes in an old city are misleading, and he'd drawn several blanks before falling out onto Market Hill – the city's central square. The stalls were all closed down, and the old fountain – fed by Hobson's Conduit – trickled. A small crowd of perhaps twenty people stood on the east side in front of the new Guildhall – a neo-Georgian monstrosity which had swept away the old shire house, and the tollbooth, and even Butter Lane, where his mother had taken him every Saturday as a child to fetch cheese and eggs, and frothing cream.

The only remnant of the old building was the clock, a circle of glass ten foot in diameter, lit from within, the Roman numerals in solid iron. In peacetime it shone out like a second moon. In wartime it was forced to enjoy a brief illuminated life between dusk and the blackout, which was ordained for nine o'clock until the beginning of November.

It was 8.16 p.m. precisely. (He'd heard the quarter chime as he'd entered the square.) Everybody was looking up at the clock – a hundred foot high, at the apex of the four-storey stone facade. A figure stood before it in silhouette, unnaturally still, arms held to his sides, head up, never looking down. Brooke was reminded of a sequence from *Metropolis*, which he'd seen at the Regal with Claire after the last war. A vision of a joyless future, dominated by factory work, regulated by a human clock – a man held fast in irons at the centre of the dial, forced to move the hands, forever part of the machine.

Brooke joined the crowd and saw now, with a sickening shock, that the man stood on a narrow ledge. It was quite clear to Brooke that he intended to jump.

The woman beside him held both hands to her mouth.

A hand gripped his elbow.

It was Inspector Jack Norton, his opposite number – his 'oppo' – in the uniformed branch at the Borough.

'Brooke. Not much we can do. I've got a man up there trying to talk him down . . . do you see?'

At the far northern end of the roof, a police constable was kneeling down beside the barrel-like frame of the city's principal air raid siren. By the stilted semaphore of his hands and arms they could see he was pleading, cajoling, beckoning the young man who steadfastly looked only ahead, across Market Hill, over the rooftops of Trinity Street.

'It's Dick Fenner,' said Norton. 'He's got the gift of the gab. I can't let him any closer. If we rush the kid he'll jump.'

'Not a night-climber?' asked Brooke.

For more than a century the city's students had enjoyed an illicit sport, after dark, scaling towers, spires, domes and roofs, despite the half-hearted efforts of the authorities to spoil their fun. The war had brought stricter rules; the idea somehow obscene, that a man would risk his life for fun while other men – and women – were risking theirs in a fight for national survival.

Norton was shaking his head. 'Well he won't speak, Brooke. But no – everything else apart, I don't think he's old enough to be a student. And he's got a working man's boots.'

A police constable began to push back the crowd, which was growing. The situation was obscene, but inescapable. A last-minute reprieve looked hopeless. He'd seen a man jump from a bridge over a wadi in the Sinai, mad with cheap liquor and the heat. His girlfriend had given him the push by letter. He'd been nervous, skittery, and eventually fell almost by accident. There was no evidence of torment here, just resolution. It was as if the young man was made of stone, a human caryatid, supporting a terrible, unseen weight.

A silence had taken hold of the crowd, set against the metallic clank of the minute hand of the great clock juddering forward.

'Let me try,' said Brooke. 'We can't just wait for him to step out into thin air.'

Inspector Norton lead the way. The inside of the building was cool and echoed as they ran up the great stone staircase, five flights to the top, where they found a young man sitting on a step, his head down, hands over his ears.

'This is the night watchman,' said Norton.

'Do you know this lad out on the roof?' asked Brooke.

Reluctantly he lifted his head, then shook it. 'I think he got in during the day and hid. I didn't let him in – the doors were locked. It's not my fault.'

There was a slight stammer on the 'l' of locked, and the shadow of a facial twitch on the left side. He was soaked in sweat. Brooke thought he looked terrified.

'Just show us the way,' said Norton. 'No one's blaming you.'

There was a narrow final flight of steps, a glass canopy, and they were out on the roof. To one side stood the air raid siren – the city's principal warning of raids. It comprised two drums – a bit like waterwheels, between a central box. It was metallic, and polished to a sheen. In its shadow knelt Dick Fenner, one of the Borough's most reliable constables. Norton was right, he could talk to anyone.

The young night watchman slipped back inside the building.

Brooke stepped out carefully, but his shoes crunched on the gravel, and the man on the ledge turned round at the footfall.

Brooke held up his hands, palms forward. 'I won't come any closer,' he said. Inspector Norton knelt down.

They were about twenty yards from the young man.

PC Fenner was still kneeling. 'I've tried everything,' he said in a whisper. 'Everything I can think of. He hasn't said a word.'

'How long?'

'Twenty minutes.'

A young man certainly, fresh-faced, in overalls, boots, hair short. It was extraordinary how still he was, thought Brooke. Even his hands, at his sides, were settled, almost relaxed, as if he were a high diver at the lido, waiting for his moment to leap.

'My name's Eden,' he said. 'No one's going to stop you. But I'm here if you want to talk. Leave a message. There must be people at home. Or have you left a note?'

There was no answer.

'Good,' he said. 'That's the kind thing to do if they love you. Or tell them. Go back, this time. Speak to them. It might be alright.'

There was a slight movement, a deeper breath, but nothing more.

Brooke thought the man must be physically fit – because immobility was tiring, but he hadn't shuffled his feet, or even flexed his fingers.

All he wanted to do was make him think, to break the spell.

'Why don't you sit. Rest. I've got a hip flask. You don't have to talk at all. Not a word. Time. Take some time. I'm not going to stop you. You're in charge here.'

He never knew if he imagined it, but there might have been a flexing of the knees, a slight rearrangement of the boots.

The clock whirred, the minute hand jumped to the half-hour, the clock struck, and he simply, and calmly, stepped off the ledge.

There was no time to blot out the noise, or the single scream which followed from the crowd below.

'Oh God,' said PC Fenner, standing, so unsteady he put a

hand out and leant on the siren.

Brooke knew it was selfish, but he understood immediately, and dispassionately, that he'd be haunted by the sight of him just disappearing, descending, as if into hell. He almost expected a sudden updraught of smoke, ashes and flames. Even as they took the stairs down from the roof he'd moved on to the second tragedy: the family, the friends, the lovers, who would soon hear the news but might never know why he'd jumped. And the third – smaller, corrosive – tragedy, that every time Brooke saw the moon-like clock he'd see that calm silhouette.

CHAPTER SEVEN

He'd loitered in front of the Guildhall, until the ambulance had removed the shattered body. The crowd, silent, had simply melted away. He'd manufactured kind words for PC Fenner, who was badly shaken, and had to be taken back to the Spinning House by a volunteer from St John Ambulance. Brooke thought they would all want to forget what they'd seen, but that none of them would. He walked on in a daze, the indelible images already part of his memory for life.

The city streets were a comfort. His mother had died when he was six: she'd disappeared too – just like the man on the Guildhall roof, one minute standing in front of him, explaining that she had to go into hospital for a minor operation, then never coming back. Left to his own devices between the end of school – a private 'prep' in Trumpington – and a late tea at Newnham Croft, he'd become a wanderer. His father often stayed in his laboratory in the cellar, the food ferried down by the kitchen help before she went home. There was no particular urgency in going back to Newnham Croft at all. He knew the city, stone by stone.

Opposite the gates of Trinity College he cut left into an alleyway which led into the old Jewish ghetto, a miniature maze of courtyards and hidden doorways. Here he knew his way by touch, reading the cobbled lanes as if they were Braille. He took two left turns and a right and fetched up where he wanted to be, outside the great doors of his old college, Michaelhouse.

He tapped out his usual code using his signet ring on the metal key plate.

Brisk steps were followed by the rattle of the great keys and then the small 'Alice' door set in the oak swung in, revealing a pool of light from a lantern, and a pair of stout polished shoes.

Brooke ducked through and closed the door, following the porter into his lodge.

'I'm guessing food, Mr Brooke?' said Doric, the night porter. 'Good heavens, sir. You're as white as a sheet. Take a seat, by the grate.'

Brooke went through into the back parlour, which was panelled and polished like a captain's cabin, the wood catching the glimmer of coke from a small fire. A badly singed Union flag hung on one wall, beside a picture of the porter in uniform, standing to attention in a pool of what looked like Indian light – or possibly African. A colonial house was in the bleached-out background, with the statutory flagpole, although this one managed to boast a Union flag too.

Doric was a veteran of a long list of now forgotten wars.

Brooke looked at the glowing coals and tried not to think.

Doric appeared with a plate of food, a wine glass and a half-full bottle of claret.

'You look like you've seen a ghost,' he said.

'Sorry, Doric. I'll be fine. Young chap just took his own life – stepped off the roof of the Guildhall. I was trying to talk to him. No – I *was* talking to him. He was beyond listening.'

Doric took a breath to speak. 'I know,' said Brooke, holding up a hand. 'Not my fault. I didn't even know his name.'

Brooke searched his jacket pockets and found a letter, torn open.

'This was in his pocket,' he said. 'I know his name now. Peter George Hood. Aged eighteen – birthday two weeks ago. These are his call-up papers, Doric. Army medical tomorrow morning at ten o'clock.

'Which is a clue, isn't it? Because they use the Guildhall for the medicals. We'll never know, but I think he got in to see where it was going to happen. Face down his fears, whatever they were. It does work – can work. But sometimes it makes things worse. Maybe he thought he was a coward.'

'Maybe he thought he might fail the medical,' said Doric, kindly.

Brooke drank the wine.

'Sorry,' he said, suddenly realising how hungry he was, and tearing into a duck leg, some roast potatoes, a wedge of Wensleydale and a pear.

The war, and rationing, had not made a significant impression on Michaelhouse's reputation for good food. Most of the undergraduates had gone, which left the fellows, all of whom were men, all of whom were overweight, all of whom came to Formal Hall.

'Bravo, Mr Brooke,' said Doric, taking the empty plate. 'I've started leaving some of the food they waste out for the roadsters, there's more every week.'

Tramps had begun to appear again once Whitehall's grip on life on the Home Front had begun to slacken. Most were frail and elderly because anyone else was liable to be swept up for the services, or Civil Defence.

'Don't they have their own shelter now – off Peas Hill?'

Which was just off Market Hill, which brought back the image he was trying to slough off.

Doric nodded, 'Trouble is they don't like all the rules – that's why a lot of them go on the road in the first place. More and more people know how they feel these days. Not a moment goes by without another sheet of paper from the government, or the regional controller – whoever he is – or the university, or the council.'

Doric stood in front of the fire and bounced slightly on his feet. He was incapable of being still for an instant, maintaining constant motion, without a sense of panic.

Settling on his heels, he began to whistle tunelessly.

Brooke made a conscious effort to concentrate on the case in hand: sabotage at the Vulcan Works.

'Is Fergusan still here?' he asked. Dr Fergusan had been one of his tutors in natural sciences. He'd heard he'd had a hand in setting up a factory in Cambridge to make radio instrumentation for tanks.

'No – well, he's an *honorary* fellow, so you see him about

the place. But he's moved out. He's set up a works in Cherry Hinton they say. Took some of the laboratory technicians with him from the department, which didn't go down too well. But it's all government contracts, so it gets priority.'

Doric helped himself to half a glass of claret.

'They're all sniffy of course,' he said, jerking his head towards the Great Hall. 'They think its *infra dig*. Commercial enterprises – making money, it's all a bit beneath them, but then most of them were born in clover.'

Brooke nodded, happy to be part of any conversation on any subject that would take them a further step away from events on Market Hill.

'Bit of a gravy train according to Simkins at Catz,' said Doric. 'All guaranteed, and only the best materials. Thing is – apparently – the city's got the skills, what with all the labs and that. And it's all light engineering, it's not like they're turning out tanks or nine-inch shells for the Somme. There's got to be twenty new outfits – leaving out the big boys like Pye and all that in Barnwell.'

Brooke had a second glass of the claret.

'Right. Heard of the Vulcan Works, Doric? Apparently, it was set up by a don at St Radegund's – name of Simons?'

Doric thought it through.

'Yes. A link with the university certainly. Give me a second.'

Doric sat at the centre of a web of night porters across the city. He undertook now what he called a 'discreet' call, not a difficult manoeuvre as he was – during the night shift – the switchboard operator.

He turned his back on Brooke, and after three calls, a murmured conversation began.

Brooke stared into the fire.

He'd spent many evenings here as an undergraduate, escaping Formal Hall and his fellow students, and chatting instead with the dependable Doric. Putting aside the two weeks spent each year with a married sister in Cleethorpes, Doric's presence could be taken for granted. His long-term ambition was to become as fundamental a part of the college as its pillars and arches. He was indispensable on several levels. This furthered his master plan to overshadow his arch-enemy, the head porter, who ruled in daylight.

Brooke's degree had been interrupted by the war. The war had been interrupted by his capture, and ill treatment in the desert. (He avoided the word torture. The men who'd deprived him of sleep, and ruined his eyes with light, were trying to save the lives of their comrades. He'd have probably done the same). On his return to Cambridge his eyesight was shot. A degree in natural sciences was beyond him. Although, as time went by, he wondered if it had simply been a convenient excuse to avoid an academic life. His father's retreat into the shadowy cellar of his laboratory had seemed like a self-imposed exile from the world, a course Brooke wished to avoid.

He'd joined the Borough. It offered an intellectual challenge, a continuation of forensic observation, and appealed to his own overdeveloped concepts of good and evil. He never pretended that he was an unselfish person, but he did think he had the capacity to be selfless – to gain satisfaction through the advance of others. He'd often found unselfish people to be irritatingly pious. Brooke did what he could for others because it made him feel good about himself.

The only barrier to his new career had been the police

medical. But he'd found a patron – the detective inspector then running the Borough, who'd smoothed the way. Brooke had made it clear, from the first day, that he didn't mind starting at the bottom. Again, kind superiors – recognising his obvious abilities in logical, scientific detection – allocated him a night beat across the city to protect his eyes. Doric, revisited, soon became part of his expanding network of nighthawks – all denizens of the dark, either by choice or occupation or wartime duty. The porter had always given the impression that he enjoyed company. And they were both outsiders now, outside the academic coterie of High Table, which acted as a further bond.

Replacing the receiver, Doric took a moment to refill their glasses.

'You didn't hear this,' he said, standing over the table, claret in hand. 'Apparently not all is well with the Vulcan – my man says this Simons chappie, one of the Radegund fellows, is a technical adviser and an investor. Anyway, he's been moping around saying he might lose it all. Says the workforce is struggling to meet standards. This is periscopes apparently – but that's top secret.'

Doric went and closed the outer doors, as if this would radically increase security.

'My man says there's a shadow works. Whitehall wheeze this – so every factory has a twin which can take up full production at the drop of a hat. If a stray bomb falls, the navy's still got a supply line. They build them near an existing works – say a car factory. That way they can call in skilled men. The Vulcan's shadow is up north.'

'Indeed – just outside Newcastle.'

'Right. You can see the danger. One more foot wrong – says this Dr Simons to anyone who'll listen – and they could cancel the Vulcan contract. Switch production up the Great North Road. It could cripple the business – even shut it down. Simple as that.

'My man says they may do it anyway 'cos what with the bombing in Liverpool and Barrow, they're trying to get subs built on the Tyne too. Newcastle's got the skills. The periscope works would be up the road from the shipyard – sorry, *boat*yard.

'Best option if the shoddy work continues is they leave the Cambridge works mothballed in case Newcastle gets bombed.

'It comes with the usual disclaimer, sir. You heard it as I heard it. Doesn't mean it's true.'

Somewhere nearby, probably in the college chapel, they could hear the celestial voices of a choir in practice.

Doric bounced on his toes, enjoying the music.

'Remarkable,' said Brooke. By conventional means – a call to Whitehall – it would have taken him a week to get half as much information about the Vulcan Works. But the real nugget was unsaid: Doric's contact had made no mention of sabotage. Which was, for now, good news. They mustn't spook their quarry.

The mood of serenity, created by the choir, was shattered by the first low groan of the air raid siren on the Guildhall.

'Stay by the fire if you like, sir,' said Doric, shrugging himself into his greatcoat. 'I must warn Cooke, Weighton and Robyns. They're all in their eighties and hard of hearing. Typically, they're at the corners of the college.'

Doric stood before Brooke. 'I must open their doors, which are never locked, and perform the recognised signal for the

75

siren – in case at other future times I need to tell them there is a fire, or that they must evacuate the buildings, or that German parachutists are in the Great Court.'

With a straight face Doric indicated the sign: this involved sinuously flapping both arms in time with the waxing and waning of the siren's call. It was an oddly beautiful performance. Brooke imagined the three elderly academics patiently waiting in their beds, watching the night porter, waiting for his mime to reach its conclusion, before bolting – as best they could – for the shelter provided by the Great Hall's cellar.

Brooke would see out the evening by the fire.

CHAPTER EIGHT

HMS *Unbowed* had been on patrol since Lieutenant Ben Ridding had reassembled the attack periscope, still wary of the beast, still escorting Convoy PQ-7 north across the Arctic Circle. Ben was confident he had solved the problem, and so young Able Seaman Tonks was confident too. The young rating had taken the lieutenant a mug of tea at midnight but seemed reluctant to go below, and he was not alone. Half the crew were out on the narrow deck, breathing in the sea air, smoking, looking at the stars. There was ten degrees of frost but the sea was glassy calm, as if caught in the act of freezing. The aurora was absent, the sky full instead of cold silver stars.

They spent most nights on the surface, and if time and the

sea state allowed, the crew was given leave to walk the deck. Only moonlight kept them below, or the distant funnel smoke of an enemy ship. On the surface they could recharge the electric batteries, let fresh air blow through the mess rooms, drive out the stench and let in the metallic Arctic air. The men were never out of the clothes they stood in – for there was no time to get dressed if the claxon sounded, and there were no storage rooms, cupboards or cabins. When the hatch was open, and the order given, a brisk *volta* on the deck was the ideal way to try and lift from their clothes the miasma of old sweat, fear and fried food.

'Know what I heard, sir?' Tonks was persistent.

This was the standard gambit if anyone wanted to pass on gossip dressed up as 'intel'.

'Go on, Tonks,' said Ben, running the binoculars along a charcoal-grey horizon which separated the heavens from the depths.

The watch was vital at night. A single light. A gun flash. Anything could give the enemy away. Despite the presence of the able seaman Ben kept to his routine: a complete *tour d'horizon* with the field glasses, then by eye twice, then back to the binoculars. It was essential to maintain a strict routine and avoid distraction. It was surprisingly easy to ignore Able Seaman Tonks.

'Engine room crew reckon they're onto a fortune, sir. There's a scam on the dogs. Sunderland, Rosyth, Peterborough, Harringay, Moss Park, Cambridge. They've got this dog – trained in Ireland – fast as light. But the thing is it's got no form. They've trained it on some farm in Antrim or Kerry or whatever. It's a winner. But it's never run on the book. It's coming over and they'll run it at each course – seven races, seven tracks. Rank outsider. A hundred to one. That's it.'

On the deck, some of the chief's men were throwing a rope ring around in a game as old as the navy.

Ben completed another sweep with the glasses.

Tonks waited.

'But if it wins at the first track it will have form,' said Ben. 'The odds'll shorten. Where's the scam?'

'Different name at each track,' said Tonks. 'When they need to they paint the dog, so nobody spots it. Sounds daft but it's an old trick, apparently. So it's a first-time winner every time. It'll struggle to make a hundred to one – could be hundred and fifty to one.'

'And how will the engine crew know which one to back?' asked Ben.

Tonks looked over his shoulder, as if they might be overheard by the constabulary, on the conning tower of a submarine in the Arctic Ocean.

'There's a list of names.'

'Are they sharing?'

'Ten bob they want.'

'I'd give it a miss, Tonks.'

The lad looked disappointed, but determined, so Ben thought the decent thing to do was to scare him off.

'But I'll let my father-in-law know. He lives in Cambridge.'

'Does he like the dogs?'

'No, Tonks. He's a detective inspector.'

Tonks fled.

When Ben put the glasses to his eyes he saw it immediately: a funnel of smoke against the first blush of dawn, a warship at six miles. He was on his way down the steps in under fifteen seconds, battle stations already sounding. The sea closed over *Unbowed* – but not before they'd got a radio signal out to the convoy, which was fifteen miles ahead of them.

It was raining inside the boat, the cold air condensing on the pressure hull. It was a constant irritation each night and had already prompted the spread of moss and mould, and turned the sausages hung from the pipes in the engine room a strange cobwebbed white. Despite the hatch being up for an hour the stench was still incredible: the diesel engines were shut down as they were submerged, but the fuel still made Ben gag, as did the 'blown fuse' reek of the two electric engines.

After the sub-zero frost up top, it felt like a descent into a baker's oven.

The command room was crowded, all posts filled, the skipper at the map table.

A brief survey with the search periscope had confirmed the enemy ship was on a bearing to bring it within a mile of *Unbowed*. Ben was sure the obvious plan would unfurl: there was no reason to believe the enemy had spotted them, so they'd stay submerged, drop down to a hundred feet, slip a hundred yards to port or starboard, time the moment when they could rise up, then attack from periscope depth, side-on to the target.

Ben stood by a bulkhead. Anxiety had locked his limbs in place – one arm round the stanchion, feet apart, shoulder to the hull. Water dripped onto his face, and he brushed it aside with the back of his hand, alarmed to see that his fingers were shaking. His fears were simple: darkness, failure, panic, death.

Then his ears popped, as *Unbowed* leant into a steep descent. Images of the fire on *Silverfish* were difficult to suppress. He'd be fine, he told himself, as long as the lights didn't go. The command structure was above him: skipper, number one, chief. The operational posts were manned: navigation, sonar, torpedoes. He was a spectator, which oddly made things worse. If only he had something to do.

He had the overwhelming feeling he was about to faint. The ward room was next door – through that the galley, and the mess room. He thought that if he moved it would help, so he let go of the stanchion and strolled away, through the open hatch doors. He sat on his bunk and could look back all the way to the command room.

Then he lay on his front and took out his paperback copy of *A Tale of Two Cities*.

The book was a sham of course, he'd never got past the opening paragraph – with its prophetic coda. *It was the season of Light. It was the season of Darkness.*

There was a distant crump of a depth-charge. Somewhere, someone swore. They had, after all, been seen. The lights flickered. The shock wave reached them, and the pressure hull 'pinked'.

The lights went out.

Ben counted slowly in his head. At 'five', the emergency generator kicked in and the shadows fled. He'd been expecting the reprieve, but even so, the relief was overwhelming.

Then another depth-charge crump, this time closer, and then a third.

Given *Unbowed* was moving, and the depth-charge blasts were getting close, it seemed certain the enemy had picked them up by hydrophone. It was odd to think they were being listened to, stalked, hunted.

He headed back to the command room, each twist and turn in the half-light by memory, past the batteries, the galley, the ward room, the lights of the radio room ahead.

'Take her up,' said the skipper. An old hand, he always managed to radiate the bored mundane tone applicable to a training exercise. Taking her up meant he was going to attack. The hunter was about to become the hunted. It was the only feasible tactic – other than lying doggo. And no one wanted that. The enemy was coming straight for them, which meant the target was narrow. If they missed, they'd give away their position and end up sitting ducks.

The navigator counted down the boat's depth as she rose from a hundred feet.

At thirty feet the skipper closed the tanks and the momentum took them the last five feet. And then up came the periscope, up through the control room and out via the conning tower. The skipper waited, then dropped the handles on the attack periscope and hung there, swinging right, then left, by the hips. It was almost balletic and known on every boat in the service as 'dancing with the grey lady'.

The sonar operator in the radio room provided the only commentary: 'Distance four hundred yards. Speed thirty knots.'

They could hear the screws, churning. Then another double blast of depth-charges.

The crew not needed in the engine or torpedo room stood back in the shadows. The pitter-patter of the sweat from the hull was incessant. Several men were on their knees. Ben held on grimly to a ladder rung.

The skipper was suddenly still, then turned a half-circle, then back.

'Now Mr Ridding, time to test your handiwork. Three degrees starboard,' said the skipper, and they felt the boat turn slightly, widening the angle on the target, before coming back into firing position.

'Fire at two hundred yards.'

The navigator read out the narrowing sea distance: three hundred yards, two hundred and fifty yards. Two hundred yards.

The torpedo man fired. Ben felt the jolt and saw in his mind's eye the two light-green wakes flying forward.

The silence ticked away. At this distance impact was fifteen seconds. Ben counted. He got to fifteen. It was the first time he thought his life might be a failure. He clung to an image of Newnham Croft. The old gate off its hinge, the garden path leading to an open door.

And then the miracle: the impact of the first torpedo, then the second.

'Fool turned away,' said the chief, a note of genuine regret in his voice.

The effect on the crew was remarkable: the dimly lit silhouettes seemed to straighten, locked limbs falling loose. *Unbowed* tipped into the deep. Ben thought of the water beyond the hull, the colours changing from white, to green, to blue, to black.

They could only hear what was happening, but they could all see it too, because each one of them had imagined such a nightmare. The man in the radio room turned up the volume on the hydrophones, which broadcast a trembling rumble, and then the rush of water filling a sudden vacuum.

'Sir.'

It was the radio man, with a printout. 'Admiralty advises spotter aircraft ID on target, Zerstorer class, probably the *Richard Beltzen*. Five five-inch guns. Sixty mines. One hundred and thirty depth-chargers.'

The next sound brought complete silence. It was a crump, a collapse, and they all felt the pressure change in their inner ears. It was a bulkhead buckling, the ship sliding down, being squashed by the pressure. Ben could see the involuntary shudder of arms and legs, feet shuffling, as they all felt it: the hatches bursting, sea water flooding through in darkness, the annihilation of up and down, the fingers around anything solid, anything anchored.

'Complement?' asked the skipper.

They all looked at their feet.

'Three hundred and twenty-five, sir.'

'Well God help them,' said the skipper.

Ben thought that if the saboteur at the Vulcan Works had gone undetected, then all those men would be alive. In this moment they'd be reading, sleeping, keeping watch. It was an odd thought, and strangely unpatriotic. Then he looked at his own hand, in the flickering light, and thought *but I'm alive*. Then he realised his face was awash with sweat.

'Well done, Ben,' someone said.

Then he passed out.

CHAPTER NINE

Brooke got up just before five, the bedclothes swirled in a pleasing spiral with Claire at the centre, lost in a deep sleep, having got home in the early hours. For once he'd followed advice and gone to bed at a civilised time, hurrying home from Michaelhouse. He'd expected a descent into nightmares but, wonder of wonders, had slept soundly, the first such night in several years. Perhaps the ordeal on the Guildhall roof had been cathartic. A confrontation with death, rather than the fear of it.

Claire had not moved an inch since falling asleep. Her night-time ritual was a family legend, and she'd happily explain that the last thing she remembered each night – at any hour – was reaching out for the light switch by the bed. She wasn't insensitive to Brooke's condition, but had never exhibited any pity, reminding him when necessary that he was otherwise healthy, and had two inspiring children, a job he loved and a house by his own river.

In the bathroom he put on his shorts and slipped down to the grassy bank beyond the front gate. Floating, gliding, he thought about the day to come. The van bound for Barrow with periscopes had been loaded the night before after the consignment had been checked by Chubb in the testing room, the boxes sealed. Overnight the Morris Eight had remained locked in the vehicle bay. All doors were double-checked by the night watchman. Eva Mappin would leave when the day shift began at six.

The route was a set one, and laid out by the factory manager, following regulations laid down by Whitehall. It followed major roads, used established garages and cafés, mainly 'greasy spoons', all providing a public telephone. There were three set rendezvous points with police radio cars – one at Doncaster, near the racecourse, one at Scotch Corner, where the driver was reserved a room in a roadhouse and the van was checked regularly by North Riding police overnight. The last leg over the Pennines included a stop to check in with police beyond Bainbridge, in the Yorkshire Dales. Military police would take over once the consignment was through the gates at Barrow.

Hauling himself out of the river, he stood for a moment to drip-dry. Looking up at the house, he caught sight of Claire's face at the bedroom window. She shook her head once, and then dropped out of view. The general opinion in the Brooke family was that early morning swimming had the whiff of the hair shirt about it, and Claire pointed out that his swims were religiously observed. It was a point on which they differed, but only in that Brooke thought obsessions healthy.

Changed, he was on the towpath in ten minutes, cutting across the city to Barnwell; here the river had reached a stately grandeur, with just fifty miles left to the sea. He crossed by a footbridge to the Green Man at Chesterton, noting that one of the locals had clearly had a good night as he was curled up on a bench opposite, still clutching a bottle of brown ale to his chest.

Edison was waiting for him in the Wasp in a lay-by overshadowed by trees. The Ely Road was in sight, now reclassified by Whitehall edict as the A10.

They sat and smoked.

'It's green, sir, with padlocked back doors,' said Edison, his eyes on the rear-view mirror.

Brooke could sense, with relief, his sergeant's eager anticipation for the day ahead.

Edison checked his watch. 'Six o'clock, sir.'

The night before, Brooke had left a note for PC Turner on the shelter death inquiry. So far nobody had come forward to report a missing person. Comfort's reservations about the artist's sketch could now be set aside. The coroner had raised no objections. There was already general permission for the poster to be made public, but now the formalities must be observed. First, she was to ask Chief Inspector Carnegie-Brown to pull strings 'up at the Castle' and get the sketch of the victim copied and set as a poster: 200 should be enough, at key points in the city, the hospital, the railway and bus stations, and all public air raid shelters. A copy should be delivered to the editor of the *Cambridge News* – with a short statement asking members of the public who either knew the man or had seen him recently to come forward. It should add that he was found dead in an air raid shelter, cause of death as yet unknown, and that the police were not looking for anyone else in connection with the fatality – shorthand, in essence, for suicide.

Anyone with information should ring the Spinning House.

Turner was also to ring the Yard – Detective Inspector Woods was the contact, to check on progress with Home Office toxicology. Brooke would ring from Scotch Corner that evening at six – direct to his desk phone.

Impatient, he checked the near-side mirror.

He sensed that Edison wanted to tell him something.

'Mrs Edison?' he asked.

Edison looked startled. 'Fine, sir.'

A pause.

'Misses Ireland, has to be said. Her sister's with us for a week and so they've been reminiscing, which always brings on homesickness.'

There was an awkward pause, and then a note of relief as Edison spotted their quarry in the rear-view mirror.

'Ah . . . Here we go, sir.'

The van drove past, the gears running smoothly through the box, so that Edison had to accelerate to keep it in sight. Chubb was right about Eva Mappin's polishing skills – the Morris Eight was mirror-like. No one had told Mappin she would have company that day. She was still a suspect. Keeping her in sight, but not too close, would demand constant attention.

There was some traffic, and they knew the designated route, so they stayed back one or two vehicles. The rear of the van was like a thousand others – only cleaner, but the shining railway green helped, although they saw three other vans with exactly the same paintwork in the first hour.

The Fens swept past, like some vision of the Russian steppes. Horse-drawn carts were everywhere, and the fields dotted with farmworkers. Clouds of seagulls followed tractors across fields the size of an English county. At Downham Market they struck across country to the Great North Road, now proudly signposted as the A1. Then the long haul began – the flat landscape enlivened by fair-weather clouds. Free of the sheltered streets of Cambridge, Brooke started to enjoy the wide-open skies.

The first scheduled stop, a roadhouse called Crossways near Doncaster Racecourse, was a welcome reprieve from the unrelenting progress of the Great North Road. They let Mappin fill the Morris at the fuel pump while they grabbed tea and a sandwich in the greasy spoon. They then swapped roles: filling the Wasp while she had tea and smoked. They left first, letting her overtake them as they waited in a lay-by a mile to the north.

Given they were in a stream of traffic, they let her get several hundred yards ahead. She was in sight every few minutes. Chubb had calculated that it would take up to half an hour to sabotage two periscopes, which gave them a wide degree of discretion. Brooke, hat down over his eyes, managed a nap.

At Boston Spa she stopped again at a garage while they parked up short of a roadside inn – the Red Fox. It was their first good sight of Mappin. The Wasp's fuel capacity meant they had time on their side. She wore overalls, and a headscarf, and heavy-duty shoes with steel caps. They watched her march off confidently for the café, and through the window saw her take a table with two other women, also drivers, although the rest of the café was packed with men, mostly too old for service.

She was a diligent mechanic, and they saw her check the tyres and water, run a damp cloth over the side windows, and double-check the locks on the back of the lorry. Then she refuelled and was back on the road. The North arrived, and slipped past, Sheffield first – hidden in a cloud of smoke and grime. They were separated from her once – near Catterick Camp, where a roadblock had been set up due to a soldier going AWOL. Brooke showed his warrant card to get through and at first they thought they'd lost her. After ten minutes at thirty miles an hour there was no sign, so they slipped into a lay-by, and sure enough she went past a few minutes later. At the most she'd been out of sight for fifteen minutes. And there was no way she, or anyone else, could have predicted the roadblock. They'd only lost her because of the heavy traffic – most of it military. Convoys of covered lorries made it impossible to see clearly ahead.

The sun was down long before they got to Scotch Corner, where the road forked between the route to Glasgow and the west, or straight on to Edinburgh in the east. There were heavy clouds over the Pennines, and the lorry created a wake of spray as the rain began to fall. The light was fading as they watched Mappin park outside the roadhouse hotel.

'Blimey, sir, this is a bit upmarket,' said Edison.

The hotel looked new; a sign advertised AMERICAN BAR and SCOTCH BAKERY, while a hand-painted placard boasted of hot and cold water in every room, of which there were seventy. Brooke thought it showed how much the War Office valued submarine supplies. The lorry park also guaranteed SECURITY OVERNIGHT and DOG PATROL.

Edison parked carefully, so that they had a clear view of the van now that it was – as he put it – tucked up for the night. Eva again checked the locked doors, then headed for reception. For the first time Brooke could see her face clearly, because she'd pulled off her scarf: she had dark hair, cut roughly short, and a broad cheerful face.

They sat tight, leaving Eva to register and settle in. Time passed, and Brooke was reminded of dreary hours of surveillance on past cases, and the constant struggle to stay awake, let alone alert. The fading light finally gave way to the night.

'Hold the fort,' he said eventually, slipping out.

There was a yellow-and-black AA box on one side of the forecourt, which he could have used, but he was keen to see the interior of the new hotel, and felt sure that Eva would be resting in her room, or soaking in a bathtub.

The American bar was packed, although the elaborate transatlantic decor was undermined by the fact that a group of long-distance lorry drivers were drinking pints of bitter and playing darts.

Brooke declined the opportunity to order a Manhattan, one of ten cocktails on offer, and asked instead for a pint of beer, which he left on the bar with his hat while he slipped into one of three telephone booths, with flip-down seats.

It was precisely six o'clock and PC Turner was at Brooke's desk.

'Sir.'

'Constable. All well here. I suspect this consignment will be fine. Absolutely no chance the cargo could be tampered with en route so far. I've organised a double-check in the shipyard tomorrow, so we'll know for sure. Can you pass that on to the chief inspector?'

'Sir.'

'Anything to report?'

'Posters of our man from the Trinity Shelter are ready to go up and the *Cambridge News* is running it in the morning. I talked to Kett, the editor. He's happy to stick to our line: we need to find a name so we can contact relatives, etcetera. The story will imply suicide. The editor read me the copy.'

'Well done. Switchboard?'

'Three girls in from seven tomorrow. I've told them to just note names and numbers and we'll take it from there.'

'Fine. Fingers crossed. We need our man's name, otherwise we'll never know who killed him.'

Back with his beer Brooke picked up a local paper, which was full of news from North Africa, most of which was bad. Rommel was now leading the Axis desert forces, bolstering the battered Italian army. Greece had fallen. Yugoslavia could be next. British units were bogged down in faraway places of which the public, until recently, had known nothing. The war, for Brits, was in the Atlantic.

Brooke set the paper aside and considered getting two rooms on the Borough but decided they'd better stick to the plan, although the possibility that a saboteur could get into the van, access the periscopes, conduct a precise operation to render them faulty, and then replace them undetected was remote to impossible. Brooke thought it likely their saboteur was on the docks, and that they struck after the consignment was signed off at the gates. It was the logical solution.

That would fall to the Red Caps, the military police, and Scotland Yard.

He went back to the car and found a police constable sat in the rear seat.

'This is PC Garside, sir. Darlington. He's our contact,' said Edison, looking in the rear-view mirror.

Garside briefed them, although his accent was so impenetrable that Brooke's attention wandered. Security amounted to a night watchman and his Border Terrier. Lancashire would take over in the morning as soon as they crossed the Pennines.

'The bar's twenty-four-hour, sir – not for alcohol, but they do tea and sarnies.'

'Before you go, Constable,' said Brooke.

One of his minor obsessions was regional accents.

'Your accent. Not Tyneside, or Tees. Borders maybe – Berwick?'

'Spot on,' said Garside. 'It's a mangle of Durham and Scots.'

'Indeed. Do you know if security here is aware of our presence?'

'They're none the wiser, sir. We didn't tell them, obviously. And when I had a word – just routine – they never mentioned a thing.'

Brooke watched the constable get back on his motorbike.

'Not sure we can believe that, do you Edison? We've been sat here for hours. If it's true, security is pretty slipshod.'

Brooke considered Mappin's choice of parking spot. It couldn't be faulted: rear doors facing out, bonnet to a brick wall, under a security light – although once they passed nine o'clock the blackout would be observed.

They settled down on a shift pattern of two hours on, two hours off, after they'd both had steak and chips, separately, in the bar. They considered seriously the possibility that the steak was horsemeat. They saw the night watchman and his dog twice. And a young woman in a raincoat, who hung around the lorry park accosting drivers – one of whom eventually took her inside. Dawn illuminated the dismal scene. Edison fetched them what he'd been assured were sausage sandwiches.

Eva emerged with a brisk step at eight-thirty, and they were back on the road in a sudden burst of blinding sunshine. But it didn't last, as the clouds came down, so that as they climbed into the hills visibility shrank to a hundred yards of milky-white mist. Richmond passed: a high street of dripping stone, and then more fog until Leyburn, when they turned west and rolled down through pine forests.

Brooke drove to give Edison a rest, but he could see it was making him jumpy, and he was dog-tired himself, so he let his sergeant negotiate the final few hours. The last fuel stop was Bainbridge. The sun had come out and the road was steaming gently. There was an arrow on the wall of the garage indicating an air pump and hose at the rear, and Mappin took the Morris briefly out of sight before it reappeared a minute later, gleaming, the wet leaves and mud spray washed away.

Just beyond the town a police car shadowed the van for two miles, as per the plan, then turned away with a brisk salute. It was the afternoon by the time they reached the outskirts of Barrow, and the rain stopped, and there was a stunning view of Furness Island, and the ocean beyond.

They'd almost forgotten the reality of war on the journey, but you couldn't miss it in Barrow. The harbour contained two warships – destroyers – and the hills bristled with ack-ack emplacements and even some heavy guns. Almost everyone was in uniform, and there were two checkpoints to pass through, at which they held well back, so that Brooke could show his warrant card.

Vickerstown, around the docks, was a forest of cranes. Brooke, glancing down a street of two-up two-downs, saw a slice of open water as a submarine conning tower broke the surface. Which made him think of Ben and the crew of *Unbowed*, who were God knows where.

Eva Mappin wove her way through the chaos of the quaysides to yet another checkpoint signposted NAVAL SUPPLIES. She leant out of the cab to hand over papers and, as she edged the van forward, they lost sight of her at last.

An hour later Brooke was still in the Red Caps' office at the gates. He'd been given a brief tour of the dockside after Mappin had signed off the van. At no point was the shipment left unattended, until it was parked in a bonded warehouse on the quayside. This was guarded around the clock. Overnight a senior RN engineer would enter, unload the wooden boxes, and take them to the submarine stores. This comprised a separate warehouse, which was manned on a twenty-four-hour rota. As far as Brooke could see, security on the dockside was excellent.

On this occasion, following Brooke's request, the periscopes would be tested inside the bonded warehouse. This would take two hours, during which time he drank several cups of tea and started chain-smoking two packets of Piccadilly they fetched him from the NAAFI. Edison was released to the delights of Vickerstown. There'd been a further delay, it was explained, because a qualified submarine technician had to be brought ashore from one of the boats in the harbour. Eva Mappin, meanwhile, had left on foot for the town to her usual boarding house. She'd pick the van up at six.

Finally, a navy man in overalls arrived. He had a pencil behind each of his ears, narrow shoulders and a cheerful manner. Claire would have said he was 'chipper'.

'Inspector Brooke?' he asked, shaking his hand. 'Looks like you've got a problem, sir. Two out of the dozen from Vulcan are faulty. Off by three degrees – which at a thousand yards would mean a shot for midships would miss the *Bismarck*.'

This news was accompanied by a broad smile.

Brooke heard himself say 'That's not possible,' before realising just how stupid that must sound.

CHAPTER TEN

They split the return journey into quarters and drove through the night. The roads were deserted, England was under blackout, and hardly a light showed for eight hours. They were stopped at regular intervals at military checkpoints and their papers checked for permission to travel after dark. Brooke took the first and third watches, driving with as much concentration as he could muster given his constant determination to work out how the periscopes in Mappin's van had been tampered with in plain sight, inside a moving and locked van.

Possible solutions ranged from the bizarre to the surreal. Had Mappin thrown them off the scent long enough for the damage to be done? They'd lost sight of her twice, once near Catterick, once at Bainbridge: the first time for fifteen minutes, the second for two minutes. Impossible. That left two gaps: the first in Cambridge between the periscopes being tested and loaded, and the van leaving the works; the second between the van going through the final checkpoint in Vickerstown and the test being undertaken on the dockside. Brooke was now certain the dockyard was not the issue. Which left the Vulcan Works overnight.

They reached Cambridge at dawn. There had clearly been a raid overnight. A pall of smoke drifted from the railyards, and a dispiriting line of civilians snaked along Regent Street, hauling bedding and suitcases, quitting the shelters on Market Hill and Parker's Piece. (Brooke had always found the contents of such cases heart-breaking: cash, valuables, deeds, Last Will and Testaments, a favourite book for the children.) The *Daily Telegraph* – which Brooke had purchased en route – said the Cabinet was meeting that morning to discuss civilian morale. He thought it was a good job they couldn't see the scene: the citizens of Cambridge, like refugees, trudging home.

Brooke nodded at the duty officer at the desk, who simply pointed at the dispositions board – a primitive device of childish design, with sliding panels, which illustrated the location of the Borough's meagre resources of four radio cars, three motorcycles, a dog van and a single paddy wagon.

According to the board, three of the four radio cars were out on the road. A chalk addition indicated their location: Parker's Piece.

'Incident at a shelter, sir. Mr Grandcourt left you this . . .'

It was a note in his former batman's workmanlike hand.

Body found in Shelter 6 at four this morning. Some
witnesses have gone home. I have names and addresses.
Male, twenties, in civvies. No visible injuries.
G.

'Sir?' It was PC Turner, with a sheaf of forms. From the switchboard room Brooke had already detected the hum of incoming calls. The *Cambridge News* would be on breakfast tables in thousands of homes, or being read on buses, trams and trains.

'We've had over a hundred, sir. Nothing solid yet.'

'Keep going,' said Brooke, heading for the door.

It took him three minutes to walk to Parker's Piece.

Grandcourt, the senior warden in the park, met them at the entrance, pipe unlit and clamped between dentures. Nothing, even death, could dim his wide smile of welcome.

'Thanks for raising the alarm,' said Brooke.

Grandcourt shrugged. 'I've passed names and addresses to the constable.' He dropped his voice and stepped closer. 'If you need the warden – that's Jack Hurley – he's in the Cricketers.'

Brooke checked his watch. 'At a quarter past eight in the morning?'

'Brother's the landlord. To be honest he does a good trade after a raid, Mr Brooke. Thirsty work being a warden.'

Brooke filed that under *turn-a-blind-eye*, and moved on to the constable on guard at the door to Shelter 6.

It was PC James Crane, a stalwart of the Borough who'd spent twenty years in the traffic division.

'Jimmy,' said Brooke. 'Where are we?'

'Pathologist is inside, sir. Body by the Elsan. We've got a statement from the shelter warden. Nobody saw a thing.

We're still checking along the line.'

The other five shelters led towards Fenner's cricket ground.

Brooke paused and lit a cigarette.

'There's a back door?'

'Sir,' said the constable, checking his notebook. 'Opens onto the edge of the park and Lensfield Road. Nobody I spoke to saw or heard a thing. Woman found him when taking her kiddie to the loo at seven. Another woman had gone to the loo earlier – in the night – and says she's sure he wasn't there then. I've got a name and address. Woman with the child sat down while the little girl used the bucket. He was sat next to her, asleep – she thought. She said his hands "looked dead" – her words. Then she looked at his face. No question. She'd been a midwife before the war so she didn't spook easy. Called the warden in. He alerted the senior warden. That's a Mr Edmund Grandcourt.'

Brooke took off his glasses and entered the shelter.

It was much larger than the Trinity Shelter. Dr Comfort was setting up a lamp, illuminating the main chamber but leaving the side rooms in shadow.

'This way, Brooke,' he said, taking them around a tight corner, revealing an alcove on one side, the toilet closet on the other. The body was still sat on the bench, slumped against the wall, hands in the lap, head back, mouth open. The clothes were once smart, expensive, now worn but clean.

Brooke judged him to be mid-twenties.

'It's pretty clear,' said Comfort. 'I think he's been propped up, Brooke. If he'd died in this position he'd have likely slumped to the floor. There's no rigor, and no sign of rigor developing – so I think dead before he got here is my guess. So again – twelve to twenty-four hours since death.'

Brooke studied the scene. 'No blood?'

'No.' Comfort put on gloves and gave Brooke a pair. 'Shall we?'

They rolled him off the bench and carried him through to the light, setting him down on a tarpaulin Comfort had laid on the brick floor. The body was supple, flexing easily at the joints and waist. In holding the corpse slightly upright the shirt had been pulled down to reveal the lower neck, and part of the left shoulder.

'What have we here?' said Comfort, fetching scissors from the black bag, and neatly cutting away the shirt.

Brooke couldn't stop himself taking a step back. The skin was covered in vivid red sores.

They removed the jacket and shirt. The deceased body was perhaps thirty per cent covered in the marks. One of the staples of pub gossip in Cambridge was speculation on the secret weapons being developed in the university's laboratories. Biological warfare was the latest newcomer in this lethal field.

Brooke's discomfort was clearly visible.

'Buck up, Brooke. You won't catch this. It's psoriasis vulgaris,' said Comfort. 'Not contagious – but hardly inviting either.'

'Face and hands clear,' said Brooke. *And*, he thought, *clear signs of a tan on both.*

'Yes. Usual presentation for psoriasis. Everyone varies but yes – standard. Sunlight works wonders. Although that's odd . . .'

He used a spatula to lift the trouser belt away from the skin. There was a definite area of pustules, full of a white liquid.

'Von Zumbusch's psoriasis. Nasty. Fevers, shivers, joint pain, dizziness, erratic pulse. Comes and goes but living with it must be grim. Fatigue too – extreme lethargy.'

Brooke knelt, studying the face, before leaning forward and

checking the deceased's pockets: jacket, trousers, hatband – nothing except litter, loose change, a key, a box of matches. No rings, no watch – but yet again, the tell-tale pale strip of the missing strap.

One surprise. A pill bottle, glass, with a mark where the label had been scratched off. And, possibly, a grubby fingerprint.

Brooke, still in gloves, held it up to the light and then dropped it in a small bag proffered by the pathologist.

'We'll need the Yard for toxicology again,' said Comfort. 'But the Castle could lift the print – if you're willing to set aside the usual antagonisms. There might even be a residue of the pills in the bottle – but that would have to go to the Yard too.

'Is it médicine, or is it poison? That is the question. Or was it an overdose *of* the medicine? I think we're being led a merry dance here, Brooke.'

Comfort knelt by the corpse and lifted an eyelid. 'Same as our first victim. Broken blood vessels – a severe toxic shock.'

Opening the back door, Brooke stepped out onto Parker's Piece. Traffic passed on Lensfield Road. The shelter was twenty yards from the kerb. The back door of the Trinity Shelter had opened into trees, a path leading to Queen's Road. Again, less than twenty yards. The picture was clear; a hurried, furtive disposal of a corpse, probably unloaded from a vehicle.

Going back inside, he watched the pathologist at work, revealing a tan line between the lower leg and the top of the foot.

'Given it's now October, and we haven't had a decent summer's day since June, I think we can say he's been abroad. Recently. Just like our first victim.'

Brooke lit a cigarette. It was difficult to dismiss the

conclusion that they were dealing with a double killer. The removal of all forms of identification was particularly striking, as was the attempt to suggest suicide.

Comfort stood back. For once the bleak finality of his job seemed to weigh him down.

'No mystery as to the absence of a tan on the rest of his body. I suspect his skin was a burden unshared. Imagine going through life with such a secret.'

CHAPTER ELEVEN

On his return to the Spinning House, Brooke was informed by the duty sergeant that he had been summoned 'upstairs'. This was never accepted with a smile. The attic – once a dormitory for the women designated 'fallen' by the bachelors of the university – was reserved for Chief Inspector Carnegie-Brown, effectively the force's senior police officer, given the chief constable's role was ceremonial. An atmosphere of austere regulation had survived the centuries; a sense of spartan, joyless work.

Brooke stood at the duty desk wondering if he could duck the invitation, as he was now close to sure he had two murder victims on his 'manor', and no idea who the killer might be – or for that matter, who the victims were. The case seemed impenetrable, while his priority was supposed to be catching the saboteur at the Vulcan Works, an investigation in an even more parlous state.

'She said to make sure you'd got the message, sir,' said the sergeant. 'It appeared to be urgent,' he added, unnecessarily.

Brooke headed for the stone stairs which led to the upper floors. The same flight also led down to the cells – again, an original feature of the medieval building. Cold, shadowy, cramped, they'd been cut out of the living limestone five centuries earlier. Brooke would rather have descended than ascended. He occasionally slept in Cell 4 – the only one with a narrow glass grate to the street. The atmosphere of a catacomb suited him.

Brooke found the chief inspector's door open. Carnegie-Brown was standing at the window looking at the breeze flex the trees in the grounds of Emmanuel College. St Andrew's Street, below her window, was narrow at this point and the trees – horse chestnuts, a century old – seemed close enough to touch. Brooke felt he'd interrupted a moment of reflection.

The chief inspector was smoking, and she simply pointed at the open silver box for Brooke to help himself. For two years she had tried to keep this vice a secret, slipping away to smoke on a bench in the grounds of Downing College. Now, suddenly, she seemed not to care. It offered a rare glimpse of humanity.

For a moment they were both silent.

'Home Office wants to see me at Marsham Street next Monday,' she said, finally. 'An appointments panel – but I'm told it's just going-through-the-motions.'

'Congratulations,' said Brooke.

Rumours that Carnegie-Brown might join Scotland Yard

had been rife for months. She'd come down from Glasgow to Cambridge to secure the rank. Her brand of efficient, bureaucratic policing had caught the attention of Herbert Morrison, the Home Secretary. The wartime government ran on paper. At the current rate there would not be a tree left in the kingdom.

'I've recommended you to replace me,' she said, sitting down. 'The chief constable's supportive. It'll be yours if you want it. You are an outstanding officer. Don't let the chance slip.'

'Thank you, Ma'am.'

Brooke looked at the mahogany desk and the pile of paper obscuring the in-tray and wished, fervently, that she'd change her mind and stay. He tried to think of reasons why she should. A keen fisherwoman, she was often seen on the banks of the Cam, or up at Ely on the Ouse, decked out in the best Highland tweeds. The Thames was clogged with merchant shipping, a live fish had not been seen since Trafalgar, and the Yard would expect seven days a week. There'd be no fishing in London. But ambition knew no bounds. It wasn't enough.

'I see Sergeant Edison has spent three pounds ten shillings of the Borough's petrol ration. Was it money well spent, Brooke?'

Brooke took a chair unbidden.

'We shadowed the Vulcan Works consignment to Barrow, ma'am. The lorry was pretty much in our sights the whole way – including parked up at Scotch Corner overnight. Barrow checked the periscopes – two faulty. All perfect when checked at the works the night before the van left.'

She pushed a manila file on her blotter a further few inches away.

'The War Office wants an update,' she said. 'Given we know there is a saboteur, and we can track the goods, we'll end up a laughing stock if we can't actually find our man.'

'Or woman,' said Brooke.

'The driver?' asked Carnegie-Brown.

'Eva Mappin's her name. She was cleared by the Ministry of Labour. I've asked for the file. We lost sight twice, but not long enough for the saboteur to get to work. Or for her to get to work. It's much more likely that the culprit is in the factory and can get to the lorry between the last check and Mappin's arrival to drive the gear away.'

Carnegie-Brown looked unimpressed. 'In effect we know less now than we did twenty-four hours ago?'

Brooke took one of the cigarettes, deciding this was a question to which he'd be wise not to provide an answer.

'And nobody at the factory is aware the sabotage has been spotted?'

'Just the manager – name of Chubb. As far as I know, the workers think we're checking security at factories conducting government work. I've asked County to do a couple of visits out at the university farm research lab and the RAF workshops at Witchford and Mepal. So we fit a pattern. But who knows? The saboteur must have realised the faulty periscopes would be spotted eventually. It was only a matter of time.'

Carnegie-Brown placed a hand on her blotter for emphasis.

'We must catch the saboteur, Brooke. Not scare them into going to ground. Or worse, finding a new job where they can do more damage. We know they're there – we have to catch them while we can.'

Brooke nodded.

'I'll put someone in the factory overnight. They're recruiting, so we just need a willing officer.'

'Not one of ours,' said Carnegie-Brown. 'They must be no chance of recognition. County could help. They owe us a favour after the intelligence we gave them on the petrol coupon fraud at Newmarket. They could give us someone from Royston, or one of the southern villages.'

Carnegie-Brown reached for a fresh cigarette, but instead slapped the lid closed.

'We do need to bring this inquiry to a head, Brooke. The Cabinet is aware of the issue. The prime minister feels a certain duty of care to submariners.'

Brooke could only guess at the subtle pressures for results brought to bear on Carnegie-Brown: pressures which might one day soon be his. In the desert, when he'd been captured, he'd shown that he had the courage to overcome pain. Against boredom, however, he had almost no defences.

'We don't need diversions,' she said, taking a copy of the *Cambridge News* from her drawer and turning it round so that Brooke could see Turner's sketch.

'Is this necessary? It's hardly in good taste. I've had calls, Brooke. The United Churches Board. The chief constable up at the Castle – let alone our own chief constable. The town's MP. The university MP. As I say – was it necessary? Just to find the identity of some poor wretch who felt he had to take his own life?'

'There's been a second body, I'm just back from the scene,' he said, a trump card, unfairly withheld. 'Foul play is suspected in both cases. No ID – no watches, no rings. Public shelter on Parker's Piece.'

Carnegie-Brown gave him a penetrating look worthy of Scotland Yard.

'MO?'

'Similar. Body may have been dumped. No visible cause of death, but an empty pill bottle was found in his pocket. Perhaps someone wants us to think it is suicide. One oddity; both victims appear to have been abroad – they have deep suntans. The first young man was in A1 physical condition. This one not so – although out and about he'd have appeared healthy, there was evidence of psoriasis. In part a serious condition – according to Dr Comfort.'

Carnegie-Brown's nose crinkled slightly. Brooke had often observed her distaste for the pathologist's bluster, or was it the thought of the disfigured skin?

She stood. 'No obvious cause of death, you say?'

'No. Toxicology is our best bet. The Yard's always willing to run the tests but we'll have to wait in line. Comfort thinks they'll find poison. His instincts are usually sound.'

Carnegie-Brown straightened her necktie in a mirror set by her hatstand.

'A meeting, Brooke. The Castle. Joint policing committee.'

The thought of any committee made Brooke want to scream.

'I'll leave you to get on,' she said. 'But remember there's a war on. Sabotage is a threat to the realm. We can't waste resources on waifs and strays who may – or may not – have fallen foul of some sordid killer. The sabotage is our principal concern. Focus on it. I want answers. Mr Morrison wants answers.'

Brooke thought Mr Morrison should sling his hook and leave policing in Cambridge to the Borough.

'I'd like an answer too, ma'am,' he said. 'I'd like to know

why the first victim had my telephone number – here at the Spinning House – written in ink on the back of his hand. I like to think that any member of the public who turns to us for help has the right to remain alive long enough to make the call.'

Carnegie-Brown's eyes narrowed. Then a light flashed on her desk phone.

'My car's here,' she said. 'Next Monday, Brooke. While I'm at the Yard I'd like to brief the commissioner on our progress at the Vulcan Works. Don't let me down.'

CHAPTER TWELVE

Claire tightened her grip on Brooke's hand when the commentary on the newsreel hit a heroic note, as a battleship plunged through an angry sea, a lone signal light the only illumination in a world of grey on the edge of night.

A voice boomed. 'Their bows digging into the tumultuous seas, the British warships forge ever ahead!'

Smoke drifted across the screen of the Regal, picking out the light beams from the projector. They were in the second row from the back, and every seat was taken, but only because Humphrey Bogart was what the Americans liked to call 'box office' and he was on next.

Brooke could feel Claire stiffening in her seat, desperate to catch a glimpse of Luke, and terrified that if he was there the image would be gone in a second. Joy had passed up on the trip, deciding she could live without the stress.

As the 'daredevils approached the Nazi dominated coast' of Norway, Brooke lit a cigarette. 'Just shows you,' he whispered to Claire. 'The Germans aren't the only ones who can turn out propaganda.'

Reports in the paper had described the raid as a wholly successful attempt to destroy vital supplies of fish oil on the Lofoten Islands – the glycerin crucial to grease Germany's machinery and guns.

Brooke was sceptical. The whole enterprise had been caught on camera as it happened: a preparatory night raid, a dawn landing, raging gun battles, prisoners taken and 'Quislings' led blindfolded away – presumably destined for interrogation back in good old Blighty.

As the caption said: VICTORY WITH A CAPITAL V.

But there was no sign of Luke.

There was a dull bit with a piper playing a tune and various soldiers dancing a jig, during which everyone around them in the cinema began to talk, impatient for the main feature. Brooke felt it showed the British public had a genius for spotting puffed-up jingoism.

The woman behind him was talking to her girlfriend. 'I heard they'd had their throats slit – silent like, right there in the shelter. It's a thief, they reckon, 'cos their wallets are gone and rings and watches.'

'Milly – what's on the buses now – she said there were other cases at the shelters up at Chesterton, and Castle Hill, and Romney Town, and that it's all hushed up and the papers can't do nothing because of the censors. It's a scandal.'

Brooke thought that the truth would be better than this nightmare round robin of gossip. How had details got out so fast? The *News* had revealed only the first victim, and only then portrayed as a case of suicide.

'Eden,' said Claire, quite loudly.

He looked up at the screen. It was a shot showing the little street at the island port – Svolvær. Half a dozen soldiers were strolling back to the landing craft, smoking. For three seconds he was there. Claire always said she could recognise Brooke from a hundred yards by the way he walked: as if treading a thin white line, bringing the feet to the centre, so that with his hat on and overcoat he narrowed to a point, like a nail driven into the ground. Luke's walk was identical.

There was a flash of his old smile, the cigarette held jauntily between his lips, and then the audience was transported to troops on their way home below decks; exhausted in their bunks, or playing cards, or drinking tea.

Claire's face, lit by the flickering screen, was rapt. Then she smacked Brooke's hand away.

'He's taken up smoking. That's your fault.'

'He's well. Even thriving,' said Brooke. 'That's good enough.'

The news gave way to the usual announcements about what to do in case of an air raid, and so Brooke took his chance, kissed Claire, and slipped away as they'd agreed.

It was 7.30 p.m., and once the cinema doors had slammed behind him the city was silent, like a scene captured in a paperweight. He walked briskly to the Galen, nodded to the porter, and ran up the concrete steps to Dr Comfort's morgue.

The pathologist wore a blue velveteen jacket and smart grey

slacks, with the usual white shirt and a tie, this one emblazoned with the emblem of the Rotary Club.

'Game of bridge at the club,' he said. 'Frankly, I'd rather spend the evening here, but Mrs Comfort lives for the thrill of it all,' he said, lighting a cigar, which gave off a greenish, twisted trail of smoke, like a length of gut.

'Not much to say on chappie here,' he added, turning to the first mortuary table.

He flipped back the white sheet and took up a metal pointer. 'The psoriasis covers a third of the skin area. We saw that on the back. The Von Zumbusch outbreak – here . . .'

He used the pointer to indicate the area around the 'belt'.

'This is a recent inflammation. There have been others – you can see the scarring.' The pointer moved to the groin, and one armpit.

'Extremely painful – irritation would have been difficult to live with. I'd be amazed if he hadn't sought expert medical advice. Yes – constant pain.'

There was a distinct note of sympathy in the voice.

'No other health issues other than his skin?'

'No. Quite the opposite. He's A1 or A2 in medical board terms. But the skin would have ruled him out. Don't want to share a trench with a man covered in sores, do you? Or a tank, or a lorry, or a barrack hut. Showers wouldn't have been fun for him either. Soldiers can be unkind, Brooke. As you know. But his weight's perfect for height, excellent muscle development. Internal organs all clean – no sign of any disease.'

'Which leaves us . . . ?'

'Becalmed, Brooke, until we get toxicology. I've sent blood and organ samples to the Yard. There'll be something in the blood. Mark my words. Having two sets of tests will actually make it easier. A week maybe, ten days.

'And there's the fingerprint on the pillbox,' he added, picking up a thin file. 'The Castle has lifted a thumb print – and they can confirm it is not the deceased. They'll get us copies.'

'Good news – if we had a suspect,' said Brooke.

Comfort's eye drifted to the next mortuary table.

'I don't want to see,' said Brooke.

'Then don't look,' said Comfort, setting aside the shroud.

Brooke stared at his feet. But he'd seen the outline of the body under the sheet and knew, by its unnatural form, that it was young Hood, who'd jumped to his death the night before.

'Understand you were there, Brooke. You have my sympathies. Traumatic injuries, obviously. We advised the family not to view the body, but the mother insisted. We did what we could.'

He held up a St Christopher medal on a simple silver chain.

'This was round his neck. Present from his mother. She said he hadn't been himself since the call-up papers arrived. Two older brothers, both in the services. One got the Military Cross in Belgium. I suspect he felt he wouldn't match up.'

'Verdict?' said Brooke.

'That's for the coroner. No last letter or note. What was in his head will never be known. But he had his army medical papers in his pocket, I understand – so that's suggestive. Whatever troubled him he did not wish to share it in life, and certainly can't now.'

Comfort took a deep breath. 'What really was affecting was the dog.'

'What dog?'

'Irish terrier, beautiful animal, wonderfully affectionate

apparently. The mother had it on a lead. It sat on the threshold over there and wouldn't come another inch. It was the boy's of course. He'd have had to leave it behind.'

Comfort checked his watch, then draped the sheet back over the body. The outbreak of empathy had been suppressed. He might have been rearranging dust covers over furniture in a country house.

CHAPTER THIRTEEN

Brooke didn't sleep, but it didn't matter. He'd seen Luke alive and well – if smoking – and then dinner at Newnham Croft had been interrupted by a call from Ben. *Unbowed* was in Rosyth and he'd be home within days – especially if he could beg a lift from the navigation officer as far as York. That had left the girls in tears, locked in an embrace, until Brooke announced the need to celebrate with a bottle of his father's claret, and fled to the cellar.

Joy, on her second glass, had fallen around laughing when told of Luke's indiscretion with a cigarette. She cheerfully told them that he'd been smoking since he was fifteen, stashing the cigarettes and lighter in the 'hanging tree' stump out on the riverbank. Brooke said he now understood why the boy had always been so keen to go on cross-country runs in his spare time.

Now the house was quiet. Iris was asleep, so Joy would be lying beside her daughter. Claire had fallen into a blissful slumber. She always said that she had an unsigned contract with God that if she looked after her patients, currently the children of Sunshine Ward, He would look after her family. This deal had been sorely tested but never broken, although she recognised hostilities could last for years. The latest news showed that in some ways the house was still blessed, and so the bargain held.

Brooke didn't believe in a God any more, at least not in the sense of any actual intervention in the reality of life. He was perfectly happy lying awake considering his plain good fortune.

It was just past midnight when the phone rang.

It was PC Turner at the Spinning House.

'Sir. Sorry. We have an ID on the poster boy.'

It took twenty minutes, from standing in the chilly hall at the house, to thudding through the front door of the station.

PC Turner was drinking a mug of tea by the duty desk, the sergeant reading the previous day's edition of the *Cambridge News*; the 'artist's impression' of the Trinity Shelter victim still dominating the front page.

Turner didn't waste any time. 'Sir. Woman by the name of Peggy Lewis. She's in your office. She'd been out with friends, got back late, and picked the paper up off the mat.'

'And we're sure?' asked Brooke. So far they'd dealt with nearly 200 calls, most claiming vague 'sightings' of the dead man, all at least twelve months old, but none offering a name.

'She's got a photograph,' said Turner. 'It's him. Name of Philip Basford. One "l", one "s". They were engaged – well, she says they were, and she does have a ring to show for it.'

'Last seen?'

'That's the thing, sir. He disappeared last August. She hasn't seen him since. She's not in good shape, sir. I've got one of the radio cars to pick up her mother from out at Cottenham. She can take her home afterwards. Hope that's alright with you, sir.'

Brooke nodded. Turner was turning out to be a special constable in several ways.

They climbed the stairs, but Brooke paused on the landing.

'Ask questions, Constable. Let's make this a conversation, not an interrogation. If we ask the right questions we might make some progress.'

'Sir.'

Peggy Lewis was sitting on the edge of Brooke's Nile bed, a mug of tea untouched by her shoe. She was still holding a photograph that showed a couple, an embrace on a beach, a sunny day, in love, somewhere – Brooke guessed – on the north Norfolk coast.

He sat on the corner of his desk, while PC Turner stood with her back to the door. He offered the girl a cigarette and she took it, accepting the light, drawing in the smoke with a sharp catch of breath.

'It's him, it's Philip?' she asked Brooke, and he felt sick at heart when he saw the hope in her eyes. She'd thought, perhaps, that he could somehow put her life back together, set it running forward once again.

He nodded.

'Only I wasn't sure. I knew, but I wasn't sure.'

Brooke took the picture. 'Yes. There's very little doubt. There will have to be a formal ID. Not now – after a night's rest. But both I and PC Turner have seen him, and it's a match.'

'We were getting married,' she said. 'Holy Trinity – springtime.'

Advancing years made the young look very young, but Brooke thought she'd have looked like a child bride. Clear skin, bright eyes, slightly birdlike and fragile. She didn't look old enough to smoke.

'I'm sorry,' he said.

'There was no hurry,' she said. 'We're grown-ups. Just live for the day, that's what Philip said. I wish I'd got pregnant now, but nothing happened. Shame – least I wouldn't have been left alone.'

It was the first note of bitterness, even anger.

'He just went missing, Peggy?' prompted Turner.

'Yes. Checked out and just left.' She still couldn't believe it, Brooke could tell, sensing the corrosive impact of an inexplicable heartbreak.

'Checked out?' asked Brooke.

'The Laurels – it's a residential hotel out in the sticks. His family's from Chester, they're not close, so he didn't want to go home. He taught at a crammer near St John's when he had to stop studying. First year – history. It isn't that posh. Just a boarding house really. He had a room in the attic. His family are just run-of-the-mill like me. He's a scholarship boy, he was proud of that.

'He liked being out of the way. People can be so cruel, can't they. They'd come up and ask why he wasn't in uniform. But the Laurels is private – peaceful. Most of the rooms were long-term lets – old duffers, trying to see out the war. But people like him got a box room upstairs. And it's safe too – Cambridge gets the odd raid but there's nothing much out there.'

Brooke lit a cigarette. 'Out where?'

'The Wilbrahams they call it. Great and Small. They're pretty.'

'Why wasn't he in the armed forces, Miss Lewis?' asked Turner.

She looked bemused. 'Philip?' She looked at the picture again. 'Sorry – he always took them off for pictures. His eyesight was awful – short-sighted. The lenses are so thick – so he tried to bluff his way. Silly really – I didn't mind. He'd wear them with me – and out and about, to see a church tower, or the sea, but he'd slip them off to talk to strangers. Or in the street.'

'There were no glasses, Miss Lewis – when we found him,' said Brooke.

'Close up he was fine,' she said. 'Always in a book. I was a bedder on his staircase. G. It's my favourite letter. He always made me tea. Said why didn't I sit down for a minute.'

She looked at the now cold mug at her feet.

'Where did he study?' asked Turner.

'At St Catherine's – sorry, Catz. He said never to call it anything else 'cos it's bad luck. He "read" history – that's what you say, isn't it? He loved all that – living in the past. He was shy, until you got to know him. The plan was he'd hang around – do war-work, save up some of the cash from teaching, and then finish his degree when – you know, it's all over.

'It must have been going well – the teaching. The last time I saw him he said he'd got enough for a deposit on a small house. He'd seen one out at Newnham. We took a stroll – it was lovely.'

She looked down, reliving the memory.

Brooke wondered how on earth young Basford could afford such a house. His father had bought Newnham Croft after fifteen years as a professor. And his mother had a private income. Where had young Basford struck gold?

The Spinning House was silent. Outside they could hear a drunk singing on St Andrew's. Brooke thought that without help Peggy might fall into that silence.

'No letter, no note?' asked Brooke.

She shook her head.

'No. But I knew something was up because he was so scared.'

'Scared of what?'

'Too scared to say. He burst into tears once. Said it couldn't go on. That was about a week before he went.'

One of the joys of detection was watching the past make sense. Each piece of the jigsaw gave subtle indications of the pieces around it. A dim picture emerged.

'You said he had family?' asked Turner.

'I wrote. Nothing. They hadn't seen him for months. His dad's dead. The Laurels has a phone, so he'd talk to his mum – once a month. First Monday. Six o'clock. I don't think he'd been happy at home. She lived on a widow's pension.'

'I'll liven up that cuppa,' said Turner, taking the mug and disappearing.

Her absence created a sudden intimacy.

'What did *you* think had happened?' said Brooke.

'Silly things. He'd found someone else. He was in trouble. Maybe his nerve went – I don't think he ever expected marriage, or even a girlfriend. He couldn't see other people properly, I think he thought they couldn't see him.

'Then when he said he was scared, I thought he'd got caught up in something. The other lads were a rum lot – not his mates, but the rest. Liked a flutter, and a drink. He said it was like the "Sirens' call" – which was history, so I never asked what it meant.'

Brooke lit a cigarette. 'They lured sailors onto rocks with their enticing voices.'

Peggy took one of Brooke's cigarettes. 'Money didn't seem to be a problem for them, so I thought they might be up to something. You know – black market, theft. There's all sorts going on now you never see a copper.'

Brooke left a silence. 'Who were these other lads?'

'There was a bunch of them at the Laurels – a conscientious objector too, rejects like him. Like I say, a rum lot.'

Turner came back and this time Peggy took the mug, cradling it for warmth.

'But mostly I thought he'd found someone else,' she said, finally answering Brooke's question. 'Perhaps he was scared to tell me.'

Brooke gave Turner a glance, and she took up the reins.

'You said he did war-work, Peggy – what was that?' she asked.

'He was fit,' she said, and blushed. 'Good-looking if he only knew it. He'd rowed at Catz. And ran. He loved it. He was on the council labour gang two days a week. And ARP for the village. That was when there were raids. Some nights he'd stay at mine. I've got a room – off King Street, near the Champion. It's cosy,' she added, and took a sip of tea.

'What do you think happened?' she asked, looking at Brooke, then Turner.

'We don't know,' said Brooke. 'But we'll find out. We've got a name – that's a start.'

'I want to know the truth,' she said.

'Did he ever talk about going abroad?' asked Brooke.

She shook her head, incredulous at the idea.

'Philip? Getting up to the coast was an adventure.'

'He had a suntan,' said Turner.

'They all did – them lads. The Laurels has got a garden and a pool. They used to lounge about if they'd nothing to do, so they'd lounge about a lot. It was lovely. Specially last summer. I went up and there were a couple of other girlfriends. It was fun.'

Turner let the subject drop, although it was clear Basford's suntan had been burnished more recently.

Brooke thought about the latest addition to Dr Comfort's mortuary, the body found in the shelter on Parker's Piece.

'Do you know if any of the other boys left at the same time as Philip?'

She shook her head. 'They just said he was gone when I rang. Nothing more.'

'You said he had mates. Did he have any close friends?'

'Not really. He was so shy.'

'I'm thinking of a friend who may have had a health issue – poor skin. Psoriasis.'

'Oh, that's Jonathan. Jonathan Ambrose. Yes, he was at the Laurels too. In the sun he never took his shirt off – nothing at all. Terrible really. It would have done him good – the sunlight. But he wouldn't. They teased him, but nothing too bad.'

Brooke took a note of the name.

'I'm afraid we may have to ask you to identify Philip,' he added. 'I am sorry.'

Peggy drank her tea. What little colour she had in her face drained away.

The front desk rang to say her mother was downstairs, so they let her go. Turner said they'd ring in the morning to arrange for identification and that she should sleep if she could.

Which is when it hit Peggy; that this was it, and the rest of her life was about to begin.

Her face just collapsed, and so Turner helped her out and down the stairs, because the tears weren't going to stop any time soon.

Alone, Brooke wondered if she'd told the whole truth. It made some sense for Basford to pay for a funk-hole in the country – but not a lot of sense. If he'd wanted to avoid any nastiness in public, he could have worn his glasses – presumably with their giveaway thick lenses. He could have picked up a room near his girlfriend for a fiver a week. A few white lies and they could have shared a bedsit. Instead, he'd invested in a country hotel. And then, quite quickly, he'd amassed enough to buy a house in a fashionable part of Cambridge – even if it was a small house. How?

CHAPTER FOURTEEN

Ten minutes later Brooke was on the doorstep of the Spinning House when the doleful wail of the siren wound itself up, and then settled into the mournful rhythm they'd all come to loathe. He should go home, or dash for a shelter, but the first light of dawn was less than two hours away, and sleep was impossible, so he walked into the city as searchlights over the southern hills began to criss-cross the sky.

Trinity Street was a canyon of shadowy stone. Opposite the college gates and Newton's apple tree, below his old rooms, an alleyway led to some rear yards, usually home to roadsters camping out by the bins. A metal ladder led up to a flat roof, which he crossed to another ladder, which took him to a platform, made of wood, with a parapet of sandbags, and a conical metal hut set back against a chimney breast.

Jo Ashmore, her Observer Corps tin hat set at a stylish angle, was scanning the sky to the east, waiting for a sighting of incoming bombers. The city, a landscape of stone pinnacles and towers, surrounded her stone eyrie.

Ashmore didn't move, but she'd clearly heard the clatter of his ascent, as she greeted her visitor. 'Brooke. I presume that means it's time for breakfast.'

Brooke heaved himself over the railing onto the platform itself. Jo Ashmore was another one of his nighthawks. The lookout post offered a panoramic view of the medieval heart of the city east of Market Hill, but crucially gave a distant prospect of Newmarket Downs, over which the Luftwaffe might at any time emerge en route for the Midlands. Radar stations on the coast gave the city advance warning of a raid, the signal being sent to the Bomb Control Centre in the basement of the Fitzwilliam Museum, which had a direct line out to all the observation posts. Ashmore's job was to track height and speed, and if possible identify the intruder, and then log bombs dropped, ringing in locations to the 'Fitz'.

They stood in silence.

'Hear that?' she asked.

On the edge of sound there was a distant hum.

'Too high for us. They'll have come in over Lincoln and now they're going home by the shortest route. Only danger is they might jettison anything they haven't dropped already,' she said.

She gave Brooke a tired smile and disappeared into the conical aluminium hut.

Looking down, Brooke saw small groups of people –

families – making their way to the shelters. With every passing raid the exodus thinned as more and more decided to keep to their beds and trust in fate. Fatigue – physical and mental – was a national disease.

Jo's hut contained the inevitable Elsan bucket, a small desk and logbook, a phone and a camping stove. She emerged with two tin mugs of tea, laced with whisky. They leant on the sandbags and smoked, Ashmore taking the moment to reapply lipstick using a small shaving mirror she'd attached to the guardrail.

'How's Claire?' she asked.

She'd grown up in the villa next to Brooke's at Newnham Croft and shared a childhood with Luke and Joy. As a youngster she'd always been in awe of 'Mr Brooke', with his strange glasses and odd habit of appearing out of the river, the gunshot wounds on his legs still livid. Claire, who'd nursed him back to health at the sanatorium in Scarborough, had prescribed swimming as a way to heal his wounds, and his mind. Luke had told the rest of the children schoolboy stories about his father's exploits in the war, embroidering tales of Lawrence of Arabia – *El Aurens* – and the fabled tribes of Bedouin. It was rumoured that the great man had even made secret visits to the house – gossip Luke was happy to promote, even after the adventurer's death.

Brooke got her up to speed on the family: Luke, possibly now a film star thanks to the Lofoten raid; Ben speeding south for a family reunion. Claire and Joy on two days off, so hopefully asleep, luxuriating in the idea that no alarm clock would ring. Iris preparing to ruin it all.

'When was the last time a bomb actually fell?' asked Brooke.
Jo produced a calendar – a single card showing the whole

year, several dates ringed in red lipstick, a lot more dates ringed in blue ink.

'According to the official records – that is, my calendar here – that would be 23rd July – a Dornier came down if you remember, out in the hills. The bomber escaped. Some incendiaries fell on Hills Road. That was it. The blue circles are for the siren, but no action. The war's left us behind, Brooke.'

'But life and death go on. A body's turned up in a shelter,' he said.

'I saw the poster.'

'No. Another one.'

'I heard suicide for the first.'

'Yes. Unlikely. But now two, and both of them holed up in a hotel out in the sticks. Comfort's not happy and neither am I. The Yard's looking at toxicology. We need the shelters open. Not everyone's got a back yard or a cellar. For now, suicide suits us nicely. But it can't go on. The rumour mill is already whirring.'

Ashmore flicked her perfectly bobbed hair. 'You think someone killed them?'

'Odds on.'

'Evil thing for someone to do,' she said.

'Yes,' said Brooke. Perhaps that was what had unsettled him, the idea that there might be a killer at large bringing death to the one place where people should feel safe.

And then there it was – the distant 'crump' of a bomb falling.

They both looked north. A pulse of light reflected off low clouds.

'That's out on the edge of the Fens,' said Ashmore. 'As I said – they'll be heading home and dropping anything they've got left.'

There was another distant rumble, and then silence.

Ashmore circled the date on the calendar in red, then took a bearing, making notes in the log.

'How are you?' asked Brooke.

Claire would ask for news, so he tried to concentrate, knowing he'd be expected to get the family up to speed.

Ashmore's boyfriend, a pilot who'd needed surgery after a fire in the cockpit, had left for Canada to fly cargo planes. Ashmore was given the impression he'd left because she couldn't deal with the scars to his face, but she suspected he couldn't deal with them.

For the first time Brooke thought of the OC post as a form of escape from the complications of life below. She'd volunteered for the job when war broke out, ditching a life in the fast set in London – which had scandalised her father, who was a historian and master of his college. She always seemed at home above the rooftops, but Brooke suspected she was unhappy, not just bored.

In answer to his question, she listed her social engagements of the week so far: a meeting with a girlfriend at Lyon's Corner House, her mother at the café in Robert Sayle's; 'And a cycle ride out into the Gogs,' she added.

This was clearly a tease. The Gog Magog Hills were just south of the city and a favourite of courting couples.

'A date?' he asked.

'Sort of. Don't tell Claire or Joy – not yet.'

'There's a second date, is there?'

'He's a copper,' she said, enjoying watching Brooke take the bait. 'Up at Ely. He'll be called up soon, they're making their way through the reserved occupations. So, he might as well volunteer.'

'Local boy?'

'Manchester. Just transferred. Looking to get out of uniform; he's tired of traffic and the duty desk. He's a sergeant.'

'Already?'

'I think he's good at his job, Brooke. What's wrong – can't abide competition?'

The phone rang and she sat in the hut dictating the readings she'd taken on the bomb.

'What's the latest?' asked Brooke when she was finished.

'Random, as I said. But the Fitz is all excited now Pye's works at Barnwell are making stuff for radar. And there's a few other targets on that bearing . . .'

She showed Brooke a map. Various sites were marked. He spotted Pye, and the army vehicle shop at Milton, and the Cavendish on Free School Lane.

'Is that the Vulcan Works?' he asked, with fingertip precision.

'Yes. They're doing Mosquito parts and Whitehall's fidgety because there's very little air cover. They're going to put some ack-ack guns on Arbury Downs but that'll take a month.'

'I know. We've checked out security in case of sabotage. They're taking on workers by the busload. And it's twenty-four-hour production.'

'Not in a raid it isn't,' said Ashmore, lighting another cigarette.

The scales fell from Brooke's damaged eyes.

Turner had mentioned the shelter at the Vulcan – and the distinctly lax security. Which made him think of the factory, silent and dark, with the workforce huddled in the shelter half a mile away.

'Can I see that calendar again, Jo – with the raids marked?'

By the time she got back, he had his notebook out with the list of dates when faulty periscopes had been shipped to Barrow.

'Right,' said Brooke, after a double-check.

It was a perfect match. Every time there was a shipment of faulty periscopes there was a raid – or a siren – the night before. The problem was that the siren went off one day in three. Brooke was a scientist. It was a match, but hardly constituted cause and effect.

'What is it?' asked Jo.

'Best I don't say yet,' said Brooke.

'I'm a spy now, am I?'

'Could be. Göring could have offered you free lipstick.'

Which made him think of a kiss on a bicycle-ride picnic in the Gogs.

'Your new beau – what's his name?'

'He isn't my beau.'

'A beau is an admirer, Jo. I think he is an admirer.'

'Sergeant Holt – Johnnie. Why do you want to know?'

'If he really wants to be a detective, and nobody in Cambridge knows him from Adam, except you, then I've got a job for him. Get him to ring me at the Spinning House. Today.'

CHAPTER FIFTEEN

Sergeant Edison swung the Wasp through the pillared gateway to the Laurels and along the dappled driveway. The gardens were unkempt, their classical design overwhelmed by nature. A copse of laurels partially concealed a small cottage, or possibly the original gate lodge to the big house.

The house revealed itself as the drive unfurled: a two-storey Palladian villa, with a *porte cochère* for visitors who had once arrived by horse and carriage. The white-painted facade was mottled with moss, the sky-blue paintwork peeling. A clematis had been allowed to run riot on one side of the door, a vine on the other.

Brooke, in the passenger seat, thought it looked like a classic funk-hole – somewhere hidden from sight where the rich could see out the war away from the bombs, the ration books and Whitehall's nosy parkers. Great Wilbraham was eight miles from King's College; Little Wilbraham a mile further, while the Laurels was a mile beyond that along a lonely dead-end track known as Mill Lane.

'Blimey,' said Edison. 'Seen better days.'

'It's the back of beyond,' said PC Turner, from the rear seat. Turner's file had revealed that she'd been born and brought up in London's fashionable Kensington. Brooke suspected any trip out of the city constituted a safari.

A sudden burst of sunshine sent a sharp pain through Brooke's eyes, so he swapped the green tinted spectacles for the black, stepping out of the car and getting his first waft of newly-mown grass. An effort had been made to keep back the encroaching wildness, and from somewhere Brooke thought he could hear a tennis ball being struck.

'We'll tackle the owner, Turner, if you could circle the house. Anything catches your eye, investigate.'

She set off towards the sound of tennis balls.

Brooke and Edison shared a moment to smoke.

'Let's play this gently,' said Brooke. 'We're here because a former guest has been found dead in a shelter. Suicide presumed. They don't know another former guest has – probably – joined him in the morgue. This place is the link. It's actually the only link we've got. But let's stick to Basford for now – until we get a positive ID on Ambrose. Who do we want, Sergeant?'

Edison produced his notebook. 'According to the electoral roll, the owner is a Dr Charles Watt Hayle, sir. Aged sixty-eight. No other permanent residents listed.'

Brooke retrieved his hat from the seat and led the way.

The door was opened by a young woman in a pinny who asked them to wait. Inside, the house was spartan. The paintwork was dingy and the rugs musty. But there were echoes of grandeur. The furniture was all sturdy – a pew, a sideboard, a hatstand – although it could have all done with a polish. A small round table held keys on fobs in a bowl. On the wall hung a set of pigeonholes, a few holding letters.

There were footsteps, and they turned to see a woman coming down the hallway from the shadows beyond. She was perhaps thirty-five years of age, agile, brisk and fresh-faced, with frizzy ginger hair. As Brooke took off his glasses she looked directly into his eyes. Claire would have said she was 'outdoorsy'. Brooke imagined her wiping down a glistening colt, or lugging milk pails.

'Jackie Brodie,' she said, not offering her hand. 'I'm the manager here at the Laurels. Can I be of assistance?' Accents again: Brooke judged Irish, west coast, Kerry, perhaps.

They heard skittering claws and a greyhound loped into view wearily, trailing its mistress.

The dog stood beside her and she laid a hand on the head.

'This is Rochester. He's retired now, but once – back in the day – he was a champion. He fits in here just nicely.'

'Likes the country?' offered Brooke.

'No. He's been put out to pasture.'

Her eyes were transformed by a smile. Brooke thought the accent was a little false – not the accent perhaps, but the vocabulary, as if she was trying to be a cut above.

'Is Dr Hayle at home?'

'He's away on business. He has been for some time. It's all a bit hush-hush. Washington, I think. I can't tell you any more – because I don't know any more. The War Office takes messages for him if that helps – I have a number?'

'A medical doctor?' asked Brooke.

'No. A scientist, at the university. I'm sorry, I don't know the details. Something to do with geology . . . ?'

'Thank you,' said Brooke. 'But when he's at home he lives here . . .'

'And you are?' she asked, taking a step forward. The breezy good humour had vanished.

Brooke showed his warrant card.

'I see. No, no. Dr Hayle lives in the Lodge. It's back by the gate. It's just him. He owns the whole estate – it was in his wife's family. She's long dead I think.'

'I see. I have a few more questions that may take time,' added Brooke.

She led them into a drawing room. It was spotless, the plasterwork of the ceiling an extravagant field of flowers and leaves. A grand piano reflected the sunlight. But nobody would have said the room was 'lived in'.

The dog threw itself down on a rug.

Brodie didn't suggest sitting down.

'You run a guest house?' asked Brooke.

'A hotel,' she said. 'Before the war most of our guests stayed for a night, a few nights – often visiting the university. Now we tend to offer long-term rates due to the current interruption in normal business.'

She'd made a world war sound like a blown fuse.

Brooke had read that in neutral Dublin the word 'war' was avoided, replaced by 'The Emergency'.

'We've six rooms on the first floor for long-term residents, and eight box rooms in the attic. What is this about?'

She was smiling, but the lack of patience was becoming audible.

'A former guest – Philip Basford – has been found dead, in one of the city air raid shelters. His girlfriend tells us he lived here until last year when he checked out suddenly.'

She nodded. 'Yes. He did.' Her eyes were switching from Brooke to Edison, but her hands hadn't moved. 'I'm sorry to hear that,' she added.

'Why did he go?' asked Brooke.

'I can't recall. He was from Chester I think – so maybe he went home?'

'He'd been dead for about twelve hours at least when his body was found. He'd cut his wrists.'

She didn't miss a beat. 'That's terrible. A strange young man. Nearly blind – he was always knocking things over. Taught history, I think.'

'Can I see the register please?' said Brooke. 'And the ID numbers for the current residents. I'm sure you are well versed in the regulations, Mrs Brodie.'

She went and got the register and put it down on the table.

Brooke turned a few pages. The complement of residents was listed at the start of each week on a Monday. Beside each name was the ID number.

Brooke flipped back until he saw Basford's name, and then forward a few weeks until his name appeared on Saturday, 31st August. By his name it said: Checked out – paid in full. CASH.

With it were three other names – all checking out, all paying cash. He noted Jonathan Ambrose amongst them.

137

'When did he check in?' asked Brooke.

'I need to look at last year's book,' she said. 'But by memory most of the boys arrived around Christmas '39.'

'The boys?'

'Yes. That's what they liked to call themselves,' she said, the smile manufactured. 'They stuck together. Henry – Harry – Callaghan was first. He suffers from asthma. So unfit for military duties. He liked the place, and the others followed over the weeks. It's all above board – I have their papers.

'There were eight of them to start with. Richard Underhill is the odd one out – he's a conchie, and he went to the technical college. He didn't really fit in, so he moved out of the attic when he took over as the gardener. He's got a room in the basement near the shed and the greenhouse. Then Basford and the others left and so now there's just three of them up there. Callaghan, Clifford and Tudor.'

'Why did four of them leave together?' asked Brooke.

'I think they were all good friends. They had plans.'

'What kind of plans?'

'To travel. To find the sun. Portugal – that came up a lot. South Africa. And the Bahamas. They thought that might be glamorous. Very exclusive now the Duke of Windsor's governor.'

Brooke transferred his hat from hand to hand.

'What is your room rate for guests?'

'Is this necessary?' Brodie's manner was impatient, even haughty. Perhaps it was the shock, of Basford's death, but Brooke thought she was stalling, trying to work out how best to deal with the police on her doorstep.

'Depends on the answer, Mrs Brodie. That's why I asked the question. We can resume at the Spinning House . . .'

She smiled. 'Of course. Only happy to help.' It was a studied withdrawal. She took a step back and patted the greyhound on the flank.

'We have two rates. Long-term residents pay five guineas weekly, three months in advance. Attic rooms we charge two guineas a week. Full English breakfast and evening meal are included. Lunch is extra.'

'What was Basford like? Aside from knocking things over?'

She offered some bland comments about politeness and keeping himself to himself.

'I think there was some family money,' she added at last, before watching in horror as PC Turner strolled past the window and away across the grass.

'We ask residents to keep off the grass,' she said.

'Are you surprised he killed himself?' asked Brooke.

'Not really,' she said. 'It's tough I think, for young men, if they can't serve. I know there'd been incidents . . .'

Brooke waited.

'White feathers. Drunken louts shouting out.'

'There was a girlfriend,' said Brooke.

'Yes. Sweet. She didn't stay. There are rules, and we enforce them.'

They heard someone coming down the stairs two at a time and a young man sped past without a glance, carrying a tennis racket.

In profile Brooke thought he knew him, but couldn't place the face, and the moment was gone.

Mrs Brodie looked at each of them. 'I do need to get on – if that's all?'

Brooke punched his hat into shape. 'We'll leave you to it,

Mrs Brodie,' he said, handing back the register. 'Did you ever see him again?'

'Basford? No. I don't think anyone did.'

'Right. We may have to speak to the remaining young gentlemen in due course. All very routine. I'd like you to ring my office if anyone decides to check out.'

He gave her his card.

Then he had a cruel idea. He felt this woman was hiding something. And besides, he took against anyone who seemed to think a visit from the police was an imposition.

Why not turn the screw?

'One favour, Mrs Brodie. Basford's fiancée is distraught – as you can imagine. Identifying the body would be a further trauma. We could save her from that memory. We do need someone respectable, of course. Would you identify Basford? I can arrange a car.'

Brooke counted five seconds before she answered. 'Yes. Of course. Telephone here when you have a time.'

Out in the hallway there was a pile of business cards by the keys, one of which she gave Brooke.

Back in the Wasp nobody spoke until they were out on the road back into town, as if the vigilant Mrs Brodie could hear every word.

Edison had taken a second look at the register while Brooke asked questions. 'I found home addresses for Basford and Ambrose – Chester, then Marlborough,' he said. 'I'll get the locals to deliver the bad news when we're sure. The other two who left were William Mortimer and Edmund Smith-Stanley.'

Edison spelt out each surname.

'She's scared, sir,' he said.

'Yes. Something's up. Anything in the grounds, Constable?'

'A game of tennis – they didn't bat an eyelid when I watched,' said Turner. 'Mostly elderly. One resident was in a lounger reading a book. Aged about twenty-five. Not very talkative. He had a slight stutter. I asked what he was reading and he said he didn't know – he had to look at the spine. It was *Cold Comfort Farm*. I asked if it had made him laugh and he looked baffled.'

They heard Turner flicking through her notebook.

'Oh, and two more permanent residents. Both in their eighties. Widows. Sitting down under the apple trees.'

'Anything?'

'They love the "attic boys" – that's what they call them. Giggling like schoolgirls, sir. Apparently sunbathing was a daily entertainment last summer.'

'Heliophiles,' said Brooke. 'Question is – where did our sun-lovers go? But the real question is why didn't Basford tell his sweetheart he was leaving? Why did they come back? And why on earth did he have the Borough's telephone number on his hand?'

CHAPTER SIXTEEN

Security at the Vulcan Works had been stepped up to reflect, at least to the workforce, the pastoral visit of the Borough a few days earlier. Brooke was back now, officially, to check on the new procedures. The guard on the gate not only checked their ID cards and warrant cards, but insisted on looking in the boot and under the car, a liberty Edison took as an invasion of his personal space.

They were escorted to Chubb's office by the security guard.

'How can I help, Inspector?' asked the factory manager, standing, running a nervous hand back through the thinning red hair.

'Tell me what happens when there's an air raid, Sir. In fact, if you wouldn't mind, show me, if you would,' said Brooke.

Chubb told Mrs Bavidge, the company secretary, not to bother with tea and led them upstairs to the flat roof of the office block. The factory had its own siren, he explained – leading them to the machine itself, set on one corner of the roof. It was operated, Chubb said, by the night watchman in response to a call from the Fitzwilliam – unless they'd heard the Guildhall siren, which at two miles wasn't always a given, especially against a wind from the north-west. This siren was clearly audible in all the sheds, stores and workshops, and across a large swathe of the northern edge of the city.

Setting aside the image of young Hood on the high ledge, Brooke followed Chubb down a spiral staircase to ground level, then took a path along the wire perimeter fence to a single locked gate.

Chubb unlocked it.

'Watchman has a key – so does the duty manager. Whoever gets here first opens up. Early weeks of the war, we were all out in five minutes. Things are a bit more sedate these days – but we're all safely inside within ten.'

They picked their way along a rough path over the downland to the grass mound, which in fact obscured three identical air raid bunkers, sunk down deep in the turf banks.

They stood at the top of a concrete stair.

'Roll call here. I'll do it if I'm around; if not, the watchman or night-shift manager. We tick a sheet compiled by the guardhouse of everyone on the shift. Nobody gets left behind – including the guards on the gate – which is locked before they leave their post.'

The steps led down ten feet to a steel door. Inside, the

standard layout matched the Trinity Shelter; two benches ran to the toilet at the back. But a small kitchen had been added with gas, and a cable had been run out from the factory to power up a pair of electric Baby Belling fires.

'It's cosy, really. And we're two hundred yards from the factory. If a direct attack was made on the site we'd still be good – unless we caught a stray shell.'

Back outside they shared cigarettes.

'The other two bunkers are identical,' said Chubb. 'We have a workforce upwards of one hundred and eighty now, so it's a good job we have the three.'

Brooke shook his head. 'I'm confused. The guardhouse gives out a list of the night shift – which is checked against those going into the bunkers. But there's three. How does that work?'

Chubb straightened his tie.

'Well. When I'm on duty I visit each bunker – starting here.'

Chaos, thought Brooke.

The bunkers would be crowded, everyone talking, the siren wailing. It was perfectly possible for someone to miss their name when it was called out or mishear their name and call out when it wasn't them. Or shout out deliberately when it wasn't them. As PC Turner had observed, with a rapidly growing workforce a lot of people were strangers to each other. Who knew if someone answered to the correct name?

'The guardhouse list – all surnames?' asked Brooke.

'Yes. It saves time.'

So – duplicate surnames would introduce a further element of doubt, thought Brooke.

And there was the time factor. If Chubb got to the final bunker and there was someone 'missing', was he really going back out – in an air raid – to double-check?

Brooke moved on.

'The night before a shipment to Barrow the periscopes are checked, then loaded on the lorry that evening?'

'Yes. As I've said before, Inspector. Then the lorry's locked and the vehicle bay too. There's no goods in or out on the night shift. Why do you ask?'

Brooke produced his notebook. 'Because an air raid – or at least the siren – precedes every shipment tampered with. It's a perfect match. Which indicates, surely, that the saboteur may use the air raid drill to get enough time to tamper with the periscopes. They could be inside the factory while you're all outside.'

Chubb smoked, studying his shoes. 'It's an idea. But the siren's always going off. It could be a coincidence.'

'And it might not. We have no better ideas – do we? We need to work out how it might happen,' said Brooke. 'I presume you don't count everyone back in?'

Brooke took silence for assent.

'It's a pretty rickety system, sir. But for now – let's leave it like that. We want to catch our man.'

They were outside now, on the grass, and the earth beneath their feet began to shake. Looking north they saw a line of bombers rising up from an airfield on the distant Isle of Ely.

'This is what's going to happen,' said Brooke. 'I'd like to slip a detective sergeant onto your work force. If anyone asks, he will admit to suffering from asthma – and is therefore unfit for military duties.

'If the siren goes he will stay in the factory. Please make sure his name does not appear on the guardroom list. Or simply pass over it during the roll call.'

Chubb nodded. 'I'll have to give him work.'

'Good. Something mobile would be ideal – then he can move around the factory without causing suspicion. Messenger perhaps?'

'How about time and motion?' said Chubb. 'We haven't had production lines assessed for more than a year. He could time jobs, collect evidence of quality and performance. It would look like a response to accusations of shoddy manufacture.'

'Ideal,' said Brooke. 'Perfect, in fact.'

They retraced their steps to the roof of the office block. Over Cambridge, barrage balloons hung like clouds in uniform.

'When's the next consignment due to leave?'

Chubb checked the calendar on the wall. 'Two days – Wednesday morning.'

'Right. We had better move swiftly. I'll ring you when I have a name. Your job is pretty simple, Mr Chubb. Give it until midnight tomorrow and then fire up the siren. By that time the periscopes should be in the Morris Eight locked up in the vehicle bay. I'll clear it with the Fitz. We may even get a real raid, which would help. But if not, we fake one. Our man stays inside. If the saboteur is on the workforce we'll have them in a cell by morning.'

CHAPTER SEVENTEEN

Brooke spent the afternoon in his office, the blinds drawn, the phone slowly warming in his hand, engaged in a desperate attempt to entice information out of that great paper tiger: Whitehall. Secrecy had become endemic, and the Emergency Powers (Defence) Act was cited at every juncture to deflect enquiry. An endless game of pass the parcel began at Scotland Yard, who passed him to the War Office, who *suggested* the Ministry of Food. Here the first crack in the edifice appeared as a junior clerk blithely hinted he'd make more progress at Hendon Aerodrome – the capital's HQ for the Royal Air Force. But then the trail went cold again, and he was passed back to the Cabinet Office, which took a note and said they'd ring back *if* they could provide any enlightenment.

The object of his enquiry was the war again – but this time not the Vulcan Works, but the Laurels residential hotel. Mrs Brodie had said the owner, Dr Charles Hayle, was a scientist involved in secret work for the War Office, possibly in Washington. Brooke wished to know the general nature of that work, and where it took place. (The number Mrs Brodie had given him was simply a Whitehall dead letterbox where a secretary would take messages for Dr Hayle.) Brooke felt that coincidence in police work should always be accompanied by the waving of red flags. He had, potentially, a double murder inquiry – which he suspected led back in some way to the Laurels, a house owned by a scientist engaged in top-secret war-work.

Was this a coincidence?

Finally putting down the receiver, he covered his eyes. A sudden wave of fatigue drained him of all energy. The temptation to fall upon the Nile bed was overpowering, and he was on his feet when there was a cough at the open door.

'Inspector Brooke? Sergeant Johnnie Holt, sir. Jo's friend.'

'That was fast work,' said Brooke, laughing. He'd talked to Jo Ashmore just after dawn, and here was the young man in person.

'Jo's fed up with me moaning about being bored. She phoned, I'm on a day's leave. I've got a motorbike – a Bantam – so I hopped on that. Here I am.'

They shook hands. Brooke admired his fieldwork: he was wearing a set of brown overalls and had – he explained – approached the Spinning House from the rear yard, only showing his warrant card at the duty desk. His accent certainly set him apart: it was broad Mancunian, with not a trace of the lazy Fen drawl.

Brooke asked the switchboard to nudge the canteen and send up tea.

'I need a detective, Sergeant Holt. Jo says you're keen to transfer in the future?' said Brooke.

'If army doesn't come calling first, sir.'

'Jo said you were twenty-eight – you've some time yet.'

Brooke summarised the case as the tea arrived and outlined Holt's role in trying to catch the saboteur – which would begin that very day – reminding him that there was no need for Jo to know any of the details, despite the fact that it was she who'd spotted the possible link between the siren and the saboteur.

'You've squared this with Ely?' Brooke asked.

The Isle of Ely had its own police force, which must have vied with the Borough in terms of its minute resources – although it had to cover hundreds of square miles of remote fenland. But, like the Borough, it was fiercely defensive of its independence; the spirit of the Fen Tigers, who'd blazed a path for Cromwell's republic, was jealously guarded.

'Sir. Inspector Gimbert said they can spare me for a week or two, like. So, I thought I'd head for the big city. And I've spent plenty of time in factories. I'm from Oldham, we pretty much invented them.'

'You'll find Cambridge is a small Fen town, Sergeant, not much bigger than Oldham. You had a big city down the road, but there's nothing down the road here – unless you head south for fifty miles. It just happens to have a university attached. Everyone's heard of Cambridge. Run for ten minutes, it will be behind you. Manchester it isn't.'

'Sir. Looks a picture though,' he said.

Sergeant Holt fitted the bill nicely. He was sturdy,

workmanlike and at home on a shop floor. He'd need a cover story to explain the accent, but other than that he was perfect for the job. He'd been in Ely three weeks and had never been to Cambridge.

Holt had met Jo on the river towpath at Hornsea, both of them out on lonely walks. Since then their one date, in the Gogs, had been out in the sticks. The chances he'd be recognised – and recognised as a policeman – by anyone at the Vulcan Works were close to zero.

Brooke took off the ochre glasses as the dusk gathered outside. 'Any questions? What do you need from us?'

'Nowt. Jo said they'd got up to two hundred in the workforce. I'll just be a new face, me. I'll stay inside the factory. If the manager can get me copies of the keys, I'll just lie doggo in the vehicle bay at the end of the shift. The siren's fixed to go off?'

'Yes. All set.'

Holt calmly held his gaze.

'I suppose a gun might be helpful. I'll try and observe, but you never know. Apparently, Ely want me back in one piece.'

Brooke stood, considering the request. If the saboteur was in the works, they were a traitor. Under current legislation they faced the death penalty if caught. A reprieve would be out of the question in wartime. If they faced capture, they were likely to take desperate measures.

'I'll organise a firearm,' he said. 'You've had training?'

'Oh aye. Mostly shooting rabbits on Saddleworth.'

'Right. Lodgings?'

'Jo's organised all that,' he said. 'Rooms in college apparently. Who'd have thought . . .'

'Don't get too excited. It can be pretty basic. It's not the The

Ritz. Check in tomorrow at the works and with luck Chubb, the manager, will be ready to let you in for the night shift. Baptism of fire, Sergeant. First consignment leaves the next morning. You're to be a time and motion man – so I'm afraid you'll have no friends, which is just as well. Transport?'

'Bantam's ideal, sir.'

'Cover story?'

'I don't look much like an asthmatic so how about reserved occupation? Maybe lathe operator. But I've volunteered for the army and I've got two weeks to report, and I'm down to see me sister – that's Jo. Then I'm off to Aldershot.'

It would do, so Brooke let him go and locked his office.

It was just seven o'clock but dark, and the street was deserted. It was extraordinary, the extent to which the war had reduced society to medieval traditions. When the sun set everyone went home. A single tram, empty, lit up, swept past on Lensfield Road.

Edison had volunteered to fetch Mrs Brodie from the Laurels at eight, and to deliver her to the Galen to identify Philip Basford's body. As prosecuting officer – if they ever found the victim's killer – Brooke needed to be in attendance. Which was a shame, because Claire and Joy had conspired to go for a drink at the Red Bull and then pick up fish and chips. Even if he did get there in time, he suspected his appetite would be less than ravenous after a visit to the morgue.

He had an hour to kill and answers to find.

He set out north, turning down Downing Street, until he reached the lurking Gothic shadow of the Sedgwick Museum. Through the great arch and he was onto the Downing Site, and its maze of science blocks. Even in peacetime there was plenty of unused space in the university's sprawling estate, but war had robbed the city of its students, and most of its academics. The result was desolate lecture halls, laboratories and rooms. It was quite possible to wander its corridors for days without seeing another human being. Then, without warning, you could turn a corner and find yourself in a bustling laboratory: government work usually, at a frenzied pace, all part of the war effort.

Brooke was on a well-trodden path. Despite the darkness he found the door he sought down an alleyway, under a broken lamp. A short corridor led to a large lecture hall, which he crossed by his own torchlight, before finding himself at the foot of a central staircase. Up three floors he paused for breath on a landing. A light showed under a door marked simply 'H': a light always showed, because within was one of Brooke's most loyal nighthawks, his one-time room-mate and friend Peter Aldiss. He had rooms at Pembroke, but he worked here, every night of his life.

Aldiss's subject was circadian rhythms, the mysterious biological clocks which seemed to govern animal behaviour. He'd served in the Great War – on the Western Front, but this time around the government were interested enough in his research to allow, in fact order, that he continue it. Soldiers, submariners, bomber pilots – all needed to stay awake and alert beyond normal bounds. Any help from the 'boffins' was eagerly awaited. Could Peter Aldiss discover a way of keeping the Night Watch wide awake?

Brooke paused at the door. The lab within had several cells, and behind each door lurked the stuff of nightmare: cockroaches (marked with luminous paint), fireflies, fruit flies in thousands, and rats of course, scratching and nosing their paths through mazes and pipes. Behind each of these doors light came and went according to a strict schedule, temperatures fluctuated, and noise levels varied.

All of which was monitored by Dr Aldiss. Learned papers were left unpublished as there was a chronic shortage of paper, but at regular intervals he went to London to report progress to civil servants desperate for good news.

It was all about staying awake.

Brooke's problem was the opposite. He couldn't, with any certainty, predict the moment when he might sleep. It was this ironic reversal of day and night which had brought them closer together. It was Aldiss who had prescribed Brooke's new daily routines, designed to establish normal sleep patterns. So far there had been limited success, the only progress recorded in Brooke's condition for nearly a quarter of a century.

'Brooke,' said Aldiss, looking up from a lab bench strewn with papers. 'I hope you are heading home for a meal, a hot bath, a darkened room.'

'I'm to the morgue at eight. Identification of a possible murder victim. I must be there, Peter,' said Brooke.

Behind one of the doors he heard a distinctly soft, fleshy percussion. It was the moth room. (Over the months since war had been declared, he'd accompanied Aldiss into each room, an act of bravado he now regretted. The damp collision with moth wings in the dark had been especially haunting.)

'Ah,' said Aldiss, setting aside his work. 'So an evening's deduction awaits our very own Sherlock Holmes.'

This was a private joke. They both despised Holmes, mostly for the pretentious claim to powers of 'deduction'. The great detective hardly ever used this rigid intellectual tool – it was more often induction, but usually abduction, which was no more than observation and guesswork, a slapdash intellectual system at best.

'What do you know about Dr Charles Hayle?' asked Brooke.

Aldiss put down his glasses. 'I shall leave my paperwork aside,' he said. 'Gladly. Let me think,' he added. 'While I make tea.'

This was the Aldiss way – nothing flashy or showy, just a plodding intelligence, building brick upon logical brick. It was the exact opposite of Holmes's intellectual pyrotechnics. If there was a moment of logical inspiration, it was always carefully concealed.

Peter Aldiss had one other intellectual and moral gift: discretion. He was adept at keeping secrets. As a student he had concealed a very great secret.

At the moment he was still making tea.

But on moonlit nights before the Great War, he would join other enthusiasts to indulge in the city's legendary love affair with night-climbing. This sport had risked death, of course, and there was a touch of arrogance here too – one that said life was always precarious, but why not just risk losing it in a frivolous gamble. And besides, these young men were clever and had trained long – if furtively – to attain the necessary strength and skill. But did they have the nerve? That was the great question each time they set out from college windows. The fact that the university had banned the activity and threatened anyone caught red-handed with being sent down in disgrace had only added spice to the game. No one had ever been caught, which cast doubt on the university's determination, and prompted speculation that night-climbers didn't have to be young students, but might include professors, and even university dons and administrators.

For the first term of their degree Aldiss kept this secret life from his friend, with whom he shared rooms at Michaelhouse. Then, one late night, Brooke had stumbled back from the Eagle and seen a spider-like shadow traversing the ledge above the Great Court – finally slipping in through a familiar open window. Aldiss, still breathless, had to confess.

In wartime such sport was strictly forbidden – this time with some semblance of genuine disapproval. It was thought obscene that young men should risk their lives for sporting thrills while others died on the beaches at Dunkirk, or in convoys torpedoed a thousand miles from the nearest British port. And so the night-climbers had – literally – gone to ground. Brooke always felt that this aspect of Aldiss's past threw a different light on his otherwise downbeat, humdrum, academic life.

Aldiss was still considering Brooke's question: what did he know about Dr Charles Hayle?

He delivered a cup of tea, then sat down, and steepled his fingers.

'A bit shadowy, I'm afraid, Brooke. University Farm I think – out at Gravel Hill. Certainly before the last war. Then the Botanic Garden. A hydrologist – interesting stuff. I seem to recall a paper on desalination. Lot of work with the French I think on using sea water for irrigation in francophone Africa. And irrigation in the Fens of course – there might be rivers running through Cambridgeshire but the climate's dry, desert-dry to the east. I think he's done work on flood prevention, and the possibility of building a great "catchwater" – a reservoir really, to prevent the rivers bursting their banks. That's now – not sure about his student days. Trinity I think. Father was Horace Hayle – worked with Thompson at the Cavendish. Not of the first water, but a very decent laboratory physicist.'

That was it. The memory banks were empty. The verdict on poor Horace was typically brutal. That was the thing about academics: a lifetime of experimentation made them used to delivering the truth, however unpalatable. 'Feelings' either way were not considered, or at least set aside. It could make them appear cold, even heartless.

'Thank you,' said Brooke. 'Why would Hayle be in Washington on classified business for the War Office, and possibly in cahoots with the Royal Air Force?'

'Yes. Ah. Ummm. All I know is half a dozen have gone – he's among them, is he?'

Aldiss sat down, his hooded eyes just catching the overhead light. 'This is gossip, Brooke, but it's all there is these days. We might as well be Stalin's peasants when it comes to information.'

'I'll take anything,' said Brooke.

'Have you heard of Geoffrey Pyke?'

'Boffin?'

'Yes. Dreadful word. Calls to mind men with deranged hair and wild eyes. But yes, Pyke's a loose cannon, that's for sure. Brilliant mind. Totally interdisciplinary. Moved from chemistry, to mechanics, to ballistics, to biology and back again via mathematics. Like most brilliant men he does not suffer fools gladly. Which is just an excuse for impatience and a lack of manners.'

'Have you met him?'

'Yes. Enough said. Anyway, Churchill is a devotee. Pyke's specialty is madcap schemes. We need such a scheme, Brooke, because otherwise we might lose the war. So Pyke gets free rein, and financial backing.

'There's a project afoot. Very early days. Talks going on with the Canadians, and with the Yanks, but given they're still officially neutral the truth of *that* is disputed. The gossip is that they might rope in Max Perutz – an Austrian, parents fled the Nazis. He's first-rate. Works here – London mainly. Thinking is Pyke might get this going and then Perutz would take over down the line – next year, '43, something like that.'

Somewhere in the city they heard a dog barking, which, given the silence of the blackout, gave rise to a canine chorus.

'What's the project?' asked Brooke.

'No idea. But if Hayle is involved then water's involved. But he'll be well down the food chain. He's an engineer in many ways – he makes things, applies the science. But yes, no idea. What I do know is the problem the project is designed to solve, which is that we are in danger of losing the Battle of the Atlantic.

'It's Churchill's nightmare apparently – the victory of the U-boat. They're sinking thousands of tonnes of food, ripping the heart out of the convoys. We can't feed ourselves, doesn't matter how many Land Girls you call up. Apparently U-boats are susceptible to bombing – submarines spend most of their time on the surface or just below. You can see them underwater and from above in daylight. The problem is our fighters don't have the range to cover the mid-Atlantic, which is where the convoys are most vulnerable.

'Pyke's brilliant idea – whatever it is – solves that problem.'

'And Hayle's in this – but in a pretty menial role?'

Aldiss shrugged.

'Maybe. The thing with rumours is that there's always

a grain of truth. But the rest might be fantasy. So it could all largely be tripe – there's fifteen wonder weapons being concocted in Cambridge tonight, Brooke. Before dinner. It's all a bit desperate. No doubt Hitler's doing the same. Rockets, A-bombs, bacteria.'

They smoked in silence.

Aldiss had failed to ask why he wanted to know about Hayle. This was another academic trait – curiosity was largely limited to the area of expertise. Outside that, his old friend was strangely uninquisitive.

Aldiss clicked his fingers. 'One thing I do know – well, might know – is that it's called Project Habakkuk – that's the codename.'

Brooke laughed. 'How do you know *that*?'

'It's doing the rounds. There's quite a bit of jealousy here, Brooke. So there's plenty of people trying to find out the truth of it all. Thing is funding – secret stuff gets money thrown at it. The rest goes to the wall.'

Brooke was still mesmerised by the codename 'Habakkuk?'

'Yes. Book of the Old Testament, apparently. It's biblical you see – grandeur, scale, righteous anger. Apparently, we have God on our side. Which is bad news, because what we really need is the Yanks.'

CHAPTER EIGHTEEN

Brooke sat on an iron bench in the gardens which thrived in the courtyard of the Sedgwick Museum, its towers and Gothic spires a silhouette against a starry night. He was ten minutes early for the pathologist, who could not bear the unpunctual – a dislike embracing both the late and the early. Brooke, smoking, could see a torchlight flitting behind the windows on the top floor of the museum, as the night watchman made his rounds. His father had brought him here as a child as a treat, allowing him to roam the galleries searching out dinosaur bones, and drawing the tiny fossils laid out like stone butterflies in their glass cabinets.

Sir John, mysteriously, would disappear during these visits, only to emerge at the appointed time at the Tyrannosaurus – their special place. Brooke only discovered after his father's death that on such evenings he was meeting the curator on a regular basis to discuss a project hatched by Sir John, and several colleagues from other colleges, and other scientific disciplines. The idea was to found a museum of the history of science, featuring Cambridge's particular talent: the making of scientific instruments. The cellar at Newnham Croft held Sir John's private collection of medical instruments dating back to the seventeenth century. But it had been Darwin's son Horace who had started factory production of laboratory glass in the last century, and there had followed generations of enterprising scientists, and laboratory technicians, setting up small works around the city. Instruments, electronics, radar, the new-fangled television. Fortunes had been made and lost. Brooke wondered what clandestine rivalries existed unseen. If the Vulcan Works had to close down because of sabotage, who would gain, who would lose?

He ditched his cigarette as the city's clocks chimed the hour.

Turning back to the bench, he ran his fingers over the small brass plaque:

Sir John Brooke
Nobel Prize in Physiology or Medicine 1904.
Benefactor of the Sedgwick Museum

Outside the Galen Building Edison sat at the wheel of the Wasp, quietly smoking.

'I took Mrs Brodie up, sir. She looked like death. Can't help thinking she's protecting someone.'

Brooke found her sitting on a pew, alone, in the corridor

outside Comfort's laboratory. She held an empty glass, but there was a hint of whisky in the air. Comfort had clearly administered what he often referred to, unfortunately, as a 'stiffener'. The Galen's interior decor matched its facade – white tiles. Against such a backdrop Mrs Brodie's face was perfectly camouflaged.

Brooke took off his hat and knocked briskly on the door.

One of the 'servants' appeared, in an immaculate white coat, and nodded at Brooke, who invited Mrs Brodie to lead the way.

It was a tableau he'd seen many times: at the nearest dissecting table a body lay under a white sheet. The pathologist stood behind it. The servant walked briskly to the end and took the corner of the sheet in his hand. Brooke led Mrs Brodie to the table: twenty strides, the metal Blakey's on his shoes striking the quarry tiles. It was a ceremony with all the subtle horror and indecent haste of an execution.

'Shall we?' asked Comfort, not waiting for an answer.

The face was revealed.

For a heartbeat she lost her balance, rearranging her black court shoes.

'That's him,' she said, and went to turn away, but Brooke needed the formalities completed.

'You are sure this is Philip Basford?'

'Yes.'

'Perhaps a second look?'

She turned back. 'Yes,' she said. 'I'm sure.'

The face was covered. But standing back, the pathologist revealed that the dissecting table behind him also held a body, the feet protruding from the shroud.

Brooke hadn't planned this, but he felt Brodie was a

heartbeat away from a collapse, so he pressed on. He had no doubt that she was withholding some evidence from the inquiry.

'I'm sorry, Mrs Brodie,' said Brooke. 'You do not have to comply with this request. Another fatality has been recorded in a bomb shelter. We believe this may be Jonathan Ambrose. Basford's friend of course, and a former resident at the Laurels.'

'I see,' she said. Nothing more. Later Brooke would reflect that this was an extraordinary reaction. Two of her former residents had been found dead within hours of each other in separate bomb shelters. Her reaction: *I see.* And she had not asked – but may have presumed – that this was another case of suicide.

'He has an elderly mother in Wiltshire, but no other immediate family. It would be a mercy. The alternative would be visiting the Laurels and seeing if any of his former friends might help. It just means we can move on swiftly with our enquiries.'

She wouldn't look at the second table. Brooke wondered what she was more afraid of: the sight of death again, or another visit from the Borough out at the hotel.

'A minute?' she asked.

Comfort poured her another whiskey and pulled up a lab stool. They could hear rain falling on the roof, and a dog barking close by. Ordinary life unfolding outside, while they were all trapped here.

'It's a shock,' she said at last. 'The dead look different.'

She stood up suddenly, the moment passed.

'Alright,' she said.

The servant pulled back the sheet.

She studied the face. 'It's Jon Ambrose,' she said.

They all sat and drank whisky for ten minutes, against the soundtrack of a ticking clock. The servants waited out in the corridor, and there were intermittent, and inappropriate, bursts of laughter.

Finally, Brooke asked Brodie to try and remember everything she could about Jonathan Ambrose.

The summary was unemotional, given the proximity of the victim.

Ambrose had taken Room 5 (next to Basford's). The family came from Bath, or maybe Swindon – the address would be in the register. He'd presented a civilian medical board certificate confirming he was unfit for military duty at home or abroad. He'd been shy – taking food on a tray in his room. He used the library at St Radegund's College. He'd been in the third year of a degree – she thought in Classics. His conversation was limited to talking about the Grand Tour he had planned for when the war was over: Greece, Italy, North Africa, Mesopotamia. He was always being sent brochures for cruises, and the very best hotels.

Mrs Brodie was a tough customer, Brooke concluded. She had entirely recovered her composure. But he couldn't help thinking she'd just made a revealing mistake.

'What do you think these attic boys were up to, Mrs Brodie?'
She didn't blink. 'Up to?'

'Yes. Basford planned to buy a house and start a family. Ambrose the life of a gentleman scholar, by your account. Then they were off to chase the sun in the tropics.'

'As I say – I think there was family money.'

'Yes, you've said that before. But there wasn't, Mrs Brodie.

Both were scholarship boys. There wasn't a penny. So they must have gained a penny. Teaching in a crammer wouldn't come close. Or turning out for Civil Defence. Where was the money coming from?'

'I have no idea,' she said. 'Perhaps the other boys could help?' As soon as she said this she clearly regretted it.

'Yes. Good idea,' said Brooke. 'But for now, let's run you back to the Laurels.'

One of the servants took her down to the car.

They sat in silence as Comfort completed some paperwork. Brooke couldn't dislodge the idea that he'd missed something. What had Mrs Brodie said?

The dead look different.

It was a common observation. The settling of muscle and skin, the victory of gravity over flesh, the pallor. A thought occurred now, and then was lost. Should he have asked *why* Basford looked different? Specifically, why?

CHAPTER NINETEEN

Brooke walked out of the city, crossing Coe Fen towards the village of Newnham, now threatened by the suburbs which had begun creeping out along the river since the end of the Great War. Fish and chips would be long gone, so there was no urgency. And there was no siren, so a few dwindling lights showed in college windows at distant Peterhouse. But ahead everything was Stygian. The pub on the millpond was just a darker shadow against the rooftops. The scene lay under a blanket of silence, broken only by the trickling river, and a munitions train rattling through the eastern suburbs towards the coast.

He cut through the old village streets towards Newnham Croft, his shoes playing out a brisk rat-tat-tat, an owl announcing its presence, swooping over the water meadows. An ARP warden crossed his path, but said nothing, hurrying off into the shadows.

The house came into view, around a bend in the river.

Did he sense it then? What was out of place?

The light over the door was on, which it never was after blackout time. Perhaps it was too quiet. Which was odd because both Claire and Joy should have been home long ago. He strained to hear the gramophone, but the silence was perfect.

He brushed aside a feeling of foreboding and strode up the path, key in hand, and throwing open the door called out, as he always did, 'Home!'

Before his hand could find the switch they all called out '*Surprise!*' but knew better than to flood the hallway with lights. Brooke closed his eyes anyway, fumbling for the ochre pair in his breast pocket.

Then he saw them both – his wife and daughter – sat on the stairs hugging each other. Three steps up sat Ben, the Arctic submariner, his shy face just about managing a smile.

'"Home is the sailor, home from sea",' said Brooke, as he hugged the girls, while Ben preferred a brisk handshake.

'I rang the Spinning House and they said you'd be back eventually,' said Claire. 'Ben was keeping an eye out from the front step.'

Brooke thought yet again that meeting someone unexpectedly revealed a deep-seated emotional response, because there was no time to think it through. Seeing Ben had been a joyful surprise, one he could not have manufactured. His son-in-law's response was less easy to decipher, but there was no doubt his eyes shone in the light.

Claire ushered them into the front room, where a fire smouldered.

'The cellar,' announced Brooke, allowing Claire to remove his greatcoat and surreptitiously turn down the collar her husband always turned up.

'Can I help?' said Ben, following anyway, through a small blue door and down a set of steps lit by a bare lightbulb.

'The famous cellar,' said Ben. It had been Brooke's father's laboratory, but there had always been room for a rack of bottles. His mother had colonised the attic, with its claw-footed bath and Persian carpet. But this was his father's kingdom.

As Brooke turned bottles, blowing dust from labels, Ben wandered up and down the laboratory. On a previous visit, before he'd been taken prisoner off the German coast, he'd been shown the portrait in the dining room of Sir John, standing next to the King of Norway – the scroll signifying his Nobel Prize held lightly in a pale hand. Ben had been studying medicine at Durham when the war broke out, so he appreciated Sir John's achievement, in creating serums against diphtheria. Seeing the workbench, the desk, the dusty apparatus, had a profound effect: they were all symbols of lives saved, in the midst of a barbaric war.

Brooke sensed the moment.

'You'll be able to finish that degree soon,' he said, chosen bottle in hand.

'I think Hitler's bitten off more than he can chew,' said Ben. 'He'll go down in flames. But it could take years, sir. Best not thought about.'

Brooke liked the formality of the 'sir'.

He led the way back up the stairs, cradling the precious

bottle. *The boy's changed*, he thought. His own experience was that war tended to harden a man's character. Occasionally, the reverse was true.

Back upstairs Iris had been produced for general admiration. Her father sat by the fire, on the mat, with the child on his lap. Then he helped her stand, but then unaided, she subsided happily to the floor.

By the second bottle the dinner was ready – a stew of rabbit and mustard rustled up by Joy and left to simmer since sunset.

Brooke insisted on music – his beloved Beethoven, which brought cries of unpatriotic behaviour. ('Ode to Joy' was another family joke, the record played to mark Ben's first visit.)

After stewed apple, with powdered custard, Joy and Claire cleared the table and retreated to the kitchen. The only note of sadness for Brooke was Joy's obvious happiness, a reminder of how unhappy she'd been for the last three months.

'Good work on the periscope,' said Brooke, lighting a cigarette.

'Any progress?' asked Ben.

'Between us . . . I have a man in the factory on the night shift. We think the saboteur is working under the cover of air raids, or sirens, while the rest of the workforce is in a bunker.'

Ben nodded, looking into the fire.

'What kind of person am I looking for, Ben? A mechanic?'

'No. The skill is in making the washer – that could have been done in a batch anywhere. Backstreet metal-basher could do it – it's precision work, but once you set up a jig for it you could turn them out. It's just a standard washer bevelled down. Then train someone to dismantle and assemble the periscope – it's a spanner and screwdriver job. No special dexterity.'

Claire and Joy came back and they listened to *ITMA* on the radio. Claire considered Mrs Mopp a creation of Shakespearean genius. The programme was live from a hall in Devizes, and Brooke thought the audience's almost hysterical laughter reflected everyone's pent-up anxiety about the world. It was a common enough expression, but it held a great truth: they laughed until they cried.

Brooke poured drinks for Claire and Ben, while Joy went to check on Iris.

'Plans?' asked Brooke. 'How long have you got, Ben?'

'A week, then we'll go north to my folks in Ripon.'

Darkness seemed to creep out of the corners of the room. Claire was terrified they'd move away and she'd never see her granddaughter from one Christmas to the next. Brooke had assured her that Yorkshire was not beyond the Pale, and now free of dragons.

'Ben's got a plan,' said Joy, returning on tiptoes from settling Iris.

'I thought we could go greyhound racing,' he said.

'Why?' asked Brooke, before he could stop himself. He hated betting and thought making greyhounds chase a mechanical hare was cruel.

'I thought you'd like to solve a crime,' said Ben.

He got out his wallet, produced a piece of paper and read out a series of names.

Tasty Tea
Agincourt Adam
Drumdoit Ginger
Blackies Pearl
Albert's Lass

'They're all winners, are they?' said Brooke.

'No. They're all the same dog,' said Ben. 'The list is care of Able Seaman Tonks. He was ill-advised to share with me below-decks chatter about gambling scams. I warned him off – but back he bounced with this. He'd paid a fiver for it. The dog was bred in Ireland and registered as Pauline's Pet. But Pauline's Pet has never raced. Apparently, this happens. So you've got a dog with no form. She's a fast dog – well trained. They've brought her over and each time she runs she gets a new name. She's piebald apparently, distinctive. So they paint her as a disguise – just altering the distribution of black and white. Faster than light. But nobody knows it's her.'

Triumphant, Ben sat back in the armchair.

'She's a sure-fire winner. She's running tomorrow night at a place called Coldham's Lane.'

Brooke nodded. 'Evening meetings – teatime, they can't use the lights. But they get a good crowd.'

'How do you know, Dad?' asked Joy.

'Comes up on County's list, it's outside the city boundary. They put a man out just to show willing.'

'Can I place a bet before you clap the culprit in irons?' asked Ben. 'Only we've got our eye on a flat off Castle Hill. We could do with a down-payment.'

'It would be fun, Eden,' said Claire, furtively celebrating evidence that her granddaughter might yet grow up in Cambridge.

'You could cycle. I'll watch Iris,' said Joy. 'Ben can have my bike.'

The phone rang and Brooke was on his feet before anyone else. He'd used Comfort's phone to leave a message at the duty desk to contact PC Turner ASAP and get her to call Newnham Croft.

'Sir. I got a message to call.'

'You can talk? Hope you weren't asleep.'

'Sir. I'm at the studio. It's part bedsit now.'

Brooke detected a slight echo, and imagined a high ceiling, and a north-facing skylight.

Studio? Brooke had imagined her in a student flat. This hinted at a more profound interest in fine art. And not only a studio, but a studio with a telephone.

'Can you drive, Constable?'

'Yes, sir.'

'Splendid. We have two victims now. Ambrose was identified by Mrs Brodie this evening. Both suspicious deaths, both residents of the Laurels until last year. I'm proposing we go back tomorrow, rattle their cage, and see if anyone bolts. It's not just Brodie – there's something crooked about the whole set-up. Two suspicious deaths give us more than enough excuse to nose about.'

'Sir.'

'I want you to organise twenty-four-hour surveillance for three days beginning at noon tomorrow – after we've been in mob-handed at eight. We're interested in the three remaining residents in the attic – although we should keep Underhill, the gardener, in mind.

'I'll get you a full ID on each. County will help – DI Hill is your contact. This is out in the sticks – it's their jurisdiction. But the murders are ours. They've also agreed to let us have the local bobby – his name's Cartwright. Lives in Great Wilbraham. I've talked to him already by phone. Pen?'

'Sir.'

'CAM 664. Hold on,' he said, putting down the receiver and quickly locating an Ordnance Survey map from the shelf by the hatstand.

'Right,' he said, phone lodged in the crook of his shoulder. 'The Laurels is at the end of Mill Lane, as you'll recall. On that lane, set back by a stream, is Hawk Mill. Cartwright knows the miller. There's always stuff coming and going, and they're working now. Loads of bustle.

'No one can leave the Laurels without walking past the mill – or passing by car. Work out a shift pattern. As I say, County can provide manpower.

'The miller's a friend of the chief constable apparently. There's a loft in the "cap" of the mill – with louvred openings. We can keep watch from there.

'PC Cartwright has a motorbike. I'd leave him as back-up. You can have an unmarked car from the Borough's garage. Sergeant Edison might help if you ask nicely. But he'll be going in with me early doors, so maybe the night shift.

'If one of the three – or Mrs Brodie – leaves the hotel, then follow – but leave a message at the Spinning House if you can. Follow and observe, nothing else. We'll be about and ready to help. If someone slips through the net and you lose them, don't panic. Ring it in. Stay put. We'll cover the station and routes out.'

Brooke heard the sound of a map being unfolded.

'There are footpaths, too, sir. One to the next village, one across country.'

'We can't cover everything,' said Brooke. 'As long as they don't suspect they're being watched they'll use the lane – the bus stops up in the village. None of them own cars, but the hotel has a van. I'll get you the registration, but it's a Morris shooting brake. Black.'

There was another voice on the end of the line, and then Turner said something, a hand over the receiver. Then a man's voice, low, sleepy.

'I'll leave you in peace,' said Brooke. 'If you need me early tomorrow, get a message to Radio Car 2.'

'Sir.'

He put the phone down, surprised as always that police officers had private lives.

CHAPTER TWENTY

The thought of getting to grips with the residents of the Laurels put a spring in Brooke's step, so he set aside his morning swim and was at his desk by six-thirty. There was immediately a knock at the open door and Sergeant Johnnie Holt stood before him, to attention.

'We tend to dispense with the formalities, Holt. Relax. Anything at the Vulcan?'

It had been Holt's first night. There had been no air raid warning, and no shipment ready for Barrow, so he'd simply given his plan a dry run: at the end of the second shift he'd gone to Chubb's office while the two shifts swapped over at the security gate. In the brief interlude in production, he'd been taken to the overseer's office in Shed 4 – the main production line for periscopes. This office, closed during the night shift, was reached by a spiral staircase. It provided a panoramic view of the shop floor – and the entrance to the vehicle bay, which was locked. He'd settled down to watch the workers.

'Anything untoward?' asked Brooke.

'The usual give and take, sir. The breaks are half an hour, not ten minutes. There seemed to be a supply of beer bottles from somewhere. Nowt riotous. The chargehand seemed to be in on the fun – bloke called Enderby. There was even a spot of dancing: just lasses. Someone had a record player. But everyone worked – and according to Chubb all production targets were bang on. It's mindless like, the work: I'd last ten minutes. There was a game of football in the next shed I think, I couldn't see, but they made a racket. Then they filed out good as gold – butter wouldn't melt.'

Holt looked at his boots.

'But?'

'Between the shifts the place is empty – 'cept for the night watchman, and I didn't see hide nor hair of 'im. Ten minutes of silence. I just thought, sir, that there was someone else there – you know, listening. Common enough illusion, I know that. But it did make me think, if our fella is on my shift and does what I did: hides up, like, then slips out later the next mornin', he'd get away with it. 'Cos that's the loophole, sir. They count them in, they don't count them out.'

They heard the 'pip' of a car horn from the motor yard, and Brooke rolled up the blinds. The Wasp purred, its maroon paintwork bathed in soft sunshine.

'I must run,' said Brooke, selecting his black tinted glasses. 'Tonight?'

'Yes, sir. Consignment tested at six o'clock then locked in vehicle bay 'til six the next morning. I'll be in my glass box. All eyes and ears.'

'Right. There will be a siren, Sergeant. It has been arranged. Chubb's left us a message . . .'

He sorted through the paperwork on his desk.

'Here. Yes – three a.m. Any other time it's a real raid. But either works. Armed?'

Holt patted his overalls at the left chest pocket.

'Good. Let's catch our saboteur,' said Brooke, in full flight, so that he nearly collided with Dr Comfort halfway down the stairs.

Brooke checked his watch.

'Sorry, Brooke. This won't wait. File's on its way up from the Yard, but they rang through the results from toxicology on Basford and Ambrose.'

'Quick work,' said Brooke.

'I had a word. Two victims, danger to the public etcetera . . . They worked round the clock. Result is not cyanide, or barbiturates. Carbon dioxide – the blood was steeped in it.'

'No doubt?'

'None. The pillbox found with Ambrose contained a residue of an anti-inflammatory, possibly used to reduce the pain of the psoriasis.'

Brooke offered the pathologist a Black Russian, which he examined with elaborate care.

They shared a short silence, watching the cigarette smoke rise up through sunbeams which fell into the cool stone hallway of the Spinning House.

'They breathed in the carbon dioxide?' asked Brooke.

'Yes. Wouldn't take long – a minute, two. They'd need to be in an enclosed space. You can buy the cylinders. Or lock them in a garage and run a pipe in from a car exhaust. Pretty brutal, Brooke, either way.'

They walked out into St Andrew's. The air was sharp with an intimation of winter, and so Comfort buttoned up his jacket.

'Let's hope our man stops at two,' said Brooke. He watched the pathologist walk away. Four of the attic boys had left last summer on the same day: Basford, Ambrose, Mortimer and Smith-Stanley. They'd left together. Had they come back together?

CHAPTER TWENTY-ONE

They swept past the pillars at the gates of the Laurels at precisely eight o'clock, allowing Edison to complete a dramatic entrance by braking sharply on the gravel. They'd passed Hawk Mill coming down the lane, the vanes of the windmill turning briskly as they passed, a lorry loaded with flour bags in the lane.

A woman with floury hands, presumably the cook, came out of the hotel to greet them.

'I thought you were the post,' she said, adding that she'd go and fetch Mrs Brodie.

The housekeeper, when she appeared, was clearly disappointed to see them.

'I thought your enquiries would lead elsewhere, Inspector,' she said. 'I told you Basford and Ambrose left last year. They have not been back.'

'Basford and Ambrose died of poisoning,' said Brooke. 'This is the last place they were seen alive. I have a magistrate's warrant to search the house – although you are at liberty to simply allow us to conduct our enquiries.'

Mrs Brodie stood back, indicating the way forward.

'Murdered?' she asked.

'Yes,' said Brooke. 'We have to work on that presumption. The evidence of suicide was staged in an effort to fool us.'

She took them to the library, which was dusty but quiet – soaked in that three-dimensional silence which comes from the soundproofing qualities of leather-bound paper.

'I saw them go, Inspector,' said Brodie. 'They got a cab to the station. Nobody's seen them since. This is the truth.'

Brooke studied one of the books on the shelves: *The Nile and Its Tributaries.*

'We need to talk to those who knew them. Who's at home?'

Brodie sighed.

'The long-term residents, and the three attic boys – Callaghan, Clifford, they've just had breakfast. Not sure about Tudor – he has a night job and might not be back. I have no idea of their schedule today. A lot of the Civil Defence work is at weekends – so they may be taking it easy.'

Edison coughed, an eloquent commentary on the concept of taking it easy in a funk-hole in the midst of a world war.

'Underhill is out working in the garden. You're lucky to catch him – this is his last day. He's got a job at the Botanic Gardens. They've offered a room as well. Then there's Cook, me and a handyman today. He's fixing the electrics downstairs.'

'We'll talk to everyone who's here,' said Brooke. 'Let's start upstairs if we may.'

His arrival on the first floor, home to the long-term residents, caused a ripple of excitement. He was surrounded by several old ladies, who all began to talk at once. He sent Edison upstairs to find the attic boys and bring them down to the library for interview. Meanwhile he made use of two sofas on the landing to talk to the elderly guests.

One of the widows, Mrs Randolph, appearing from her room in a bathrobe, wanted to know if they were looking for German parachutists. The rest were polite, if bemused, and struggled for any memory of Basford, Ambrose, Mortimer or Smith-Stanley.

Except one: Mr Dillingham, who had been at the Laurels since 1932, said he was tired of the 'coming and goings', particularly, he said, late at night. He added that he often overheard whispered conversations below his window – again at night, although their content eluded him. He said he thought all the boys were up to no good – especially Clement Tudor and Harry Callaghan, whom he said specialised in 'backchat'.

At which point Miss Doughty appeared from her room to complain that the young men left beer bottles by the pool. Mrs Totteridge, much younger than the rest, said she'd been in Cambridge and the 'boys', as she called them, had drawn up in a taxi and offered her a lift home, which she'd accepted. She said it had cost four pounds and that the smell of alcohol had been overpowering. She added that the sunbathing fad, which had included young girls, had been 'immodest' and that she'd been forced to witness certain scenes from her bedroom window. This, she complained, had strained her eyesight. This produced silence from the other guests, who quickly slipped back to their rooms.

Brooke and Edison, having returned to the library, decided to interview Callaghan first – the original attic boy, who was seated outside in the corridor with Clifford. Tudor was expected home on the next bus.

Callaghan looked frail, with thinning red hair and sallow skin. His voice betrayed the breathy weakness of the asthmatic. Brooke thought he detected the ghost of a northern accent – Lancashire perhaps, possibly Preston or Blackburn.

'Why do you think your mates just disappeared?' Brooke asked, offering a Black Russian.

'It was Mortimer's idea. He was the only one of them with real gumption,' said Callaghan. 'Even if he did need a stick to walk. We just thought they'd hatched a plan for four and didn't need us along. They paid up – in cash. Took their stuff. Old Brodie said they'd left in high spirits.'

'They didn't say where they were planning to go?' he asked.

Callaghan laughed. 'Not really. We weren't that close.'

'Why weren't you that close?' pressed Brooke.

A shrug. 'They were a bit dull. You know – what's wrong with the odd night out, a decent meal and a trip to the races?'

'It costs money, Mr Callaghan,' said Brooke.

'They weren't church mice,' he said.

'No. But they didn't have private incomes. At least, Basford and Ambrose certainly didn't. Do you?'

Callaghan just nodded, looking at his shoes.

'Why do you think they came back to Cambridge?'

'Ran out of money?'

Which was a thought.

'Did they want their rooms back?'

'We never saw them again, Inspector. We told the sergeant.'

'They made a lot of money before they left. How did they do that?'

'No idea. I don't need to earn money, as you've pointed out.'

Brooke let him go – but repeated a warning he'd given them all not to leave Cambridge without informing the Spinning House.

Clifford, who according to his papers suffered from a heart murmur, kept to the same script. There were several occasions when he used precisely the same form of words.

Edison went to find Tudor and Underhill, while Brooke tracked Mrs Brodie down to the kitchen in the basement.

She sat at a large, plain deal table with a cup of what smelt like real coffee.

The range, the copper pans, the housekeeper's office behind glass – it all felt like a lost age. A small stencilled sign on the office door said BUTLER.

Brodie was smoking, so Brooke pulled up a chair and joined her.

He asked her to run through an outline of the daily routines at the hotel – although he wasn't really listening, because he felt much more optimistic about the inquiry. Callaghan, stupidly, had revealed a possible motive for the three murders: had the attic boys come back to reclaim their rooms, and a share in whatever scams were being run at the Laurels? Had their moral objections been set aside by greed? Brooke could only guess how unwelcome their return would have been for Callaghan, Clifford and Tudor.

Brooke stood.

'Officers from the Castle, the county force, are to undertake a thorough search of the premises, Mrs Brodie. It should take between an hour and two hours. I'm sorry for the inconvenience. They will also be taking fingerprints – perfectly routine, just to eliminate residents and staff from our enquiries.'

They heard heavy footsteps on the servants' stairs, and a thin young man appeared at the door carrying a spade and a satchel.

'This is Richard Underhill, the gardener,' said Brodie.

'I'd like a word,' said Brooke. 'Alone.'

'Your sergeant said. Can I brush up first?' he asked, showing soil-caked hands. He went to the sink and began washing his arms and hands.

Mrs Brodie said she had work upstairs and fled.

The gardener lifted the coffee pot, and delighted to find it wasn't empty, poured himself half a cup.

'Two of the attic boys have been found dead – as I'm sure you know,' said Brooke. 'We are now informed that they were poisoned.'

'Basford and Ambrose?'

'Yes.'

Underhill stood, leaning against the wall, the coffee cup perfectly poised in his scrubbed hand.

'They were up to no good,' he said. The voice was mildly wheedling. 'All of them,' he added, his eyes flitting upwards. Brooke sensed that Underhill's imminent departure had loosened his tongue. He tried hard not to look too interested in this sudden veering from the idyllic picture so far presented by everyone at the Laurels.

He offered Underhill a cigarette. 'What were they up to?'

Underhill enjoyed the first lungful of the nicotine.

'So what were they up to?' said Brooke, again.

He shrugged. 'Twice I seen them get this letter. The post's left by the front door. But one of them is *always there* when the postman delivers. They take it in turns see. Only I'm up early for work – seven. I get breakfast in the kitchen. So I see'd them. Whoever it was would check through – get their own, but often there'd be this other one, right? Typed. Addressed to Callaghan. Postmark Sleaford, 'cos I'd sort through m'self at the same time. They didn't like that.

'One day last month Callaghan was there and there was a letter, postmark and everything, and he pocketed it along with the rest of his post. Later on I was cutting the grass round the pool and they'd all been there – all three of them – and when they'd seen me coming they'd buggered off to the pub. They left their stuff – books, newspapers. One of the Sleaford-postmarked letters was in a book – *Bleak House*.'

'You read the letter?' asked Brooke, who couldn't help disliking Underhill's obvious pleasure in telling tales.

'Couldn't. No words inside. Only thing was a town map, printed like, of Lowestoft. There was a cross – hand-drawn – at a point on the front and the name "THE DOLPHIN INN", in capital letters. That was it.'

'What did you make of that?'

'Nothing good. Law's important. Keep's us civilised. They'd sell their grannies for a fiver. Law says we should fight – I know that. But law says I can stand aside – I've been up at the Tribunal. I've got the paperwork. I'm a fire warden in the village. I'll do that. It saves lives. I just don't want to take lives.'

There was a pious silence in which Brooke thought he heard

footsteps on the stairs. He went to the door and looked up, but the only living thing in sight was Rochester, asleep, his head just visible on the top step.

'That's not all,' said Underhill, dropping his voice. 'Callaghan again – Foster's Bank on Sidney Street – you know, the one with the dome. He was three ahead of me in the queue. I saw the cashier dole it out, in fivers. Nearly four hundred quid – nothing less. And he didn't keep it to himself. They called a cab that night – off to The Grosvenor for a slap-up meal. Three courses. They were full of it when they got back.'

Underhill looked bitter. The Grosvenor was on Trinity Street, one of the town's restaurants, and therefore outside the limits set by rationing, as was the Laurels. The Brookes had celebrated Joy and Ben's wedding there: fresh salmon, then rum baba. It had cost Brooke a month's wages.

'Did you ever see them again after they left – Basford, Ambrose and Mortimer, or Smith-Stanley?'

He shook his head. 'No. One day they were there, next day rooms were empty.'

'I'll need a statement,' said Brooke.

Brooke let the gardener return to his roses and went back to the library to brief Edison on Brodie, who'd effectively said nothing, and Underhill, who'd probably said too much.

'In his turn the sergeant had talked to Tudor, but he'd said nothing of note, while complaining he was dead tired. So he'd let him go off to his bed.'

'So Callaghan – why don't we take him in, sir?'

Brooke thought it through.

'What do we have? Callaghan picks up cash at a bank. A lot of cash, I know, but it could be twenty things, all innocent.

He'll think of one on the spot. A bequest, down-payment on rent, if he's rich enough it might be a private allowance. It's how the rich live. Which leaves the letters from Sleaford. Again, too easy. Any excuse would work. It's just a meeting place. Maybe Callaghan had taken the letter with him to the pub. Left the map behind. Could have been an old school friend just going into the army – a last chance to say goodbye. A couple of telephone calls and he'd have a watertight story. No. Let's stick with the plan. Let's get Underhill's statement and then slip away. The inquiry moves on.

'One of them will break cover.'

CHAPTER TWENTY-TWO

The duty desk had a message for Brooke from Kett, editor of the *Cambridge News*.

'He said – politely – that it was his third call, sir. He'll be taking his lunch in The Pickerel at one. He'd be happy to stand you a pint. He said Wednesday's paper would otherwise come as a shock.'

'Did he now,' said Brooke.

Kett had played ball by publishing Turner's sketch and sticking to suicide as the probable cause of death. Brooke suspected he might now know this to be spectacularly short of the truth. Given it was a subject of everyday gossip in the stalls at the Regal, a reporter was bound to have picked up an echo.

Lunch was unavoidable.

At his desk he made four rapid calls. One to the central post office duty man asking for all mail destined for the Laurels postmarked Sleaford to be withheld and the Spinning House alerted. (He'd cited the Emergency Powers Act – in peacetime he'd have had to apply for a warrant.)

Next, the switchboard got him through to the CID room at Lowestoft. The Dolphin Inn was a 'lowlife' fleapit, with links to prostitution, the black market and juvenile crime. He asked for a one-page résumé on the landlord to be dictated to the switchboard ASAP. And thirdly, he called Foster's Bank on Sidney Street. He knew the manager, Arthur Wilson – his wife was a nurse at Addenbrooke's – so they dispensed with formalities: he wanted Henry Callaghan's bank details, a list of deposits, withdrawals, cheques cashed. Brooke made it clear it was to aid an ongoing murder inquiry and that Callaghan was an associate of two murder victims. Wilson promised answers within twenty-four hours. He'd have to dig through the paperwork once the bank was closed.

Brooke checked his watch: his visit to the Laurels had yet again suggested that the four attic boys who left a year ago may have spent time abroad. Given the strictures of total war, was this possible? It seemed outlandish.

He called Marshall's Airfield on the edge of the city. Since the outbreak of war they'd taken on 3,000 workers patching up and modifying Spitfires, Hurricanes, Wellingtons and Oxfords. Brooke's 'oppo' was a former Spitfire pilot, shot down over Kent. Flight Officer Ray Edmunds cheerfully admitted that he was content to settle with flying a desk – as head of security at the airfield.

'Ray – Eden. A second?'

'I feel the adrenaline rush of murder. How can I help?'

Edmunds' office was in the control tower with a view of grassy runways, the hangars in the distance, barrage balloons in lines over Newmarket Downs. If not in the air, he was certainly aloft, with a wide view of open sky.

'If I had money, and time, and I was free of military duties,' said Brooke, 'and wanted to spend some time in the sun blowing a little cash on having a good time, where could I fly to?'

'Money, real money, knows no barriers, Eden. You could take a boat of course – dangerous, and slow, and not very glamorous. Most of the liners carry passengers alongside troops. You get a cabin – but do you get a lifeboat?

'Flying's a better option. Most commercial flights have moved to Bristol.

'The military uses civilian carriers – but they're still *civilian* carriers, so they can fit in paying customers. BOAC runs a scheduled flight to Stockholm – although the War Office controls permits. KLM flies a timetable to Lisbon – that's the best way out. Once you're there, the world's your oyster – Tangiers is a hop. There's an air shuttle over the Atlantic too, from Bristol – but again you'd need paperwork. But then let's be honest: if you've got that much money, you can buy the right paperwork. And if you can get to Ireland – Shannon on the west coast – you can fly out of a neutral country, although I'd avoid Axis airspace, and most of the eastern Med.

'All that's IIRC, of course.'

'Right. What does IIRC mean?'

Brooke found that most pilots talked in endless streams of abbreviation invented to make radio chat easier.

'If I Remember Correctly.'

'I owe you a pint in The Plough,' said Brooke and put down the phone. The Plough was where the pilots went, a bar steeped in peculiar emotion, a mixture of last pints and welcome back pints. Ray seemed to enjoy the vicarious thrills, and Brooke relished the atmosphere, which reminded him of Cairo once the fighting had turned bloody out in the desert.

Which brought him back to the attic boys. They certainly wanted the fun, but they might not have wanted the added spice of danger. Where had they gone?

No answers today. He grabbed his hat, checked his pockets for cigarettes, and set out for lunch.

By the Guildhall he bought a copy of the *Cambridge News:* the handwritten bill proclaimed MOSCOW BRACED FOR ALL-OUT ATTACK. As he strolled onto Peas Hill he read the lead story. The sense that a world war was being fought offstage was unsettling.

He'd almost left Market Hill when he remembered young Hood, and so he turned to look up at the great clock. He wondered if he'd ever look up at it and *not* think of young Hood. He doubted it. Perhaps it was the idea of self-destruction against the backdrop of war which made his death indelible.

The street was hot, so when he got to the Great Bridge, he stopped to enjoy the cool air rising from the green river. Then he strolled on until opposite the doors of Magdalene College, where he stepped down into The Pickerel, the sudden coolness suffused with the reek of beer and cigarette smoke. He stopped for a moment to take off his glasses.

The pub was five centuries old. It was entirely wooden, a ship at rest, just above the river. On quiet days he'd often imagined the creak of timbers as she slipped her anchor.

Frank Kett, editor of the *Cambridge News*, was at his usual table in the snug. There was a small fire here, lit each day, but even more importantly a phone behind the bar. Frank had once explained to Brooke the absolute necessity of being in contact with the news desk in case of emergencies: the king's death, the loss of a battleship, a raid on Calais, or worse – a raid on Dover.

'Brooke. Bitter? I've ordered the pie – I know you're an enthusiast.'

The snug held half a dozen customers at best, and there was an annual attempt by students to beat the record 'cram' of '63 – but that involved contortions and possibly public order offences. The other two bars were spacious, and a favourite with college fellows enjoying a light lunch before bracing themselves for Formal Hall.

Kett, tall and studious, could have passed for a professor himself. He always wore a countryman's tweed suit, with waistcoat, and he had a pocket watch in the old style on a chain. But his hands showed a different reality; two fingers on his right were nicotine yellow, and even now he had before him a pewter pint tankard.

But Brooke knew his real secret. The tankard was full of soda water. When in his office his desk was always adorned with two or three bottles of wine, all opened, and all full of tap water. He'd once told Brooke that it made him feel better, which hinted at a darker past.

Kett, in the best traditions of British journalism, could not be trusted. He'd kill for a story. Brooke spoke to him often, but never on the record. But there was also a persistent moral streak, a determination to use his newspaper to do good – on his terms. This made him much more dangerous. It was almost impossible to refuse to answer a question from anyone who occupied the moral high ground. For Frank Kett it was home territory.

'I'm told tomorrow's paper will be essential reading, Frank. Tell me more,' said Brooke.

'That was just bait. You've ignored my calls. I thought I'd introduce some jeopardy to your life, Brooke. And here you are.'

Kett drank from his tankard with a satisfying smack of his lips.

'I'm not a big fan of state censorship, as you know. But the new system is a big improvement. We're required to submit sensitive articles before publication. They come back with a lot of the detail blue-pencilled: they take out place names, times, any military detail. Which is why the paper's so dull, but there we are. There's a war on, as they keep telling us.

'"Loose talk costs lives", isn't that what the poster says? Poster art – the Russians are good at that. Not much freedom there any more. It's not fashionable to point this out I know, our Soviet allies and all that. But still, history is full of warnings. I accept the need for censorship at this time. But there needs to be checks and balances.'

It was a familiar refrain. The first weeks of hostilities had seen an almighty cock-up involving the new Ministry of Information. Details of British troop movements in France had been announced in Paris, then censored in London, but too late, and then the ban was lifted, only to be reimposed. There was a new system embracing Fleet Street editors. Churchill had decided it was best to get the papers onside. The Borough always received notice of anything sensitive in their 'manor' which had not been passed for publication. Provincial papers had to toe the line.

Kett skewered the pie, releasing a trickle of dubious gravy. 'I do have a story. The censors will rip it apart. But I'm tempted, Brooke. Sorely tempted to go ahead and put it out on the street. Stable doors and all that. I'd go to gaol. Happily. Because not publishing it is wrong.'

There was an unnatural pause, and so Brooke offered Kett a Black Russian. They set their plates to one side and smoked.

'What story?'

'One of my old lags – Jock Brewer, you'll know him. Covers magistrates' court. Well, he does if he stays awake. Mind you, he knows more about the law than many a King's Counsel. Anyway, he was on desk duty last night and took a call. We protect our sources – but this was no gossipmonger. Gist was that there are now two recorded deaths in city shelters and they aren't suicide – or natural causes. They're murder. Slit wrists for one, poison for the other. Cyanide was cited. You don't need a crystal ball to know it's a story that won't get past the censor. It will end up on the print room floor.

'Which, if you think about it, is pretty immoral. If there's a killer about, he might strike again. If he does, I am – to a degree – a guilty party because I did not share this vital information with the public.

'And you? Are you to blame? And the Borough? Quite a responsibility.'

He leant forward and stubbed out the Black Russian.

'And by the way, I'm giving you the benefit of the doubt on the artist's impression. I'm presuming you thought it *was* suicide?'

Brooke sipped his beer. One of the many facets of Kett's character he liked was its directness. It was perfectly clear where the threat to Brooke lay: let him print now, or face the consequences.

He thought it best to ignore Kett's question.

'Reminds me of the verse, Frank . . .' he said instead.

"You cannot hope to bribe or twist, thank God! the British journalist. But, seeing what the man will do unbribed, there's no occasion to."

'Unfair,' said Kett.

'I think it's an admirable description of the profession. You couldn't say it about policemen, Frank. Or politicians. Or vicars for that matter. You can't be bribed, Frank – take the compliment while you can.

'We can't have panic in the shelters,' said Brooke, tapping on the bar to reorder drinks.

'I agree. But stopping publication won't stop panic. If chummy is as keen to tell all and sundry what he thinks as he is the local rag, he'll be down his local boozer tonight broadcasting for all to hear. Half the town will know by the weekend. The other half by Sunday. I can't sell papers if it's just old news.'

Brooke leant back in his seat, suddenly tired, the snug bar claustrophobic. 'So here's the truth. These two men were murdered – *but not in the shelters*, Frank. There's no danger to the public. We've got leads, we're confident, and Scotland Yard is assisting.'

'Names, addresses?'

'No. Absolutely not.'

'Why? We're a local newspaper. People will want to know if

the victims are from their street, their pub, their church.'

'You can say they were from Cambridge.'

'And that it's murder?'

'We believe so.'

'I still can't get it past the censor unless you issue a statement – square it with the Home Office and the censor. That's the only way it'll see the light of day.'

'I'll try,' said Brooke, looking at his watch.

'I better start.'

Kett stood, and they shook hands.

'This was on me,' said the editor. 'Don't let me down, Brooke.'

Brooke made his way back through his city with a light step. He was confident he could get Home Office approval for a statement; it was in the public interest. But his real pleasure came from a double memory: on both his visits to the Laurels he'd noted that an edition of the *News* was always left by the keys in the hallway. He was confident the story would ruin that full English breakfast.

CHAPTER TWENTY-THREE

Brooke's father had always insisted that Cambridge was the nation's foremost cycling city: ahead of Oxford of course. The city streets teemed with bikes, while cycling clubs toured local villages at top speed, a blur of high spirits and college caps. The railings along King's Parade were almost entirely obscured by cycles. There were more bicycle repair shops than bakers. It was a city on two wheels.

His father had kept cycling into his eighties, commuting back and forth between college and basement laboratory. Brooke was one of life's walkers, but in a hurry he'd wheel out one of the machines from the garden shed. A coming of age had been marked for Luke and Joy by their first cycles – three-wheelers at four. Iris had already been allocated one of the old tricycles, despite having, as yet, failed to walk. This evening Brooke selected three adult bikes for himself, Claire and Ben, while Joy – gleefully – said she'd already promised to stay at home with Iris.

Brooke needed the diversion. His afternoon had been dominated by yet more red tape. He'd spent an hour convincing Chief Inspector Carnegie-Brown that they should let the *News* use at least part of the story they had. He'd then had to trudge up Castle Hill to repeat the performance for her 'oppo' on the County force – who then rang the Home Office. He'd then wasted a further hour getting their agreement on paper – signed. At six he'd phoned Kett in his office and given him the good news, for which he was touchingly grateful. Leaving aside some dubious moral faults, Brooke had always been cheered by the fact that all most journalists wanted was to print the truth, or something like the truth.

The upside of publication for Brooke was that the Laurels did not appear in the story. With PC Turner's surveillance from Hawk Mill, just up the lane from the Laurels, he hoped and prayed someone would lose their nerve and run for it – Bristol perhaps, then Ireland? Or, conceivably, Lowestoft, which might lead to a ship. Was that the final message inserted in the letter from Sleaford? With luck they could discover the path taken by Basford and Ambrose.

But first, he had to go to the dogs.

They set out from Newnham Croft, giggling like schoolchildren, transported back to more carefree days. Claire led the way, cutting across Lammas Land, where she took Iris on Sundays to paddle in the shallow pool, and then over the two bridges spanning the river at Crusoe Island. (Brooke had spent days here in school holidays pretending to be Defoe's castaway, a role he relished.) Then on past the water meadows, the station, wreathed in steam, gritty and grey with coal dust – and over Mill Road bridge into Romney Town. Railworkers' cottages ran off in a ladder of backstreets, petering out as they reached open country – low and bleak, the horizon dominated by the cement works, the old chalk pits full of black water. It was the shredded edge of town, no echoes here of the Backs and honeyed stone.

Coldham's Lane dog track had opened ten years ago, as the boom in greyhound racing swept the land. An oval track, a grandstand down one side, a terrace of railway sleepers opposite. Flags flew, and a loudspeaker system mangled announcements. But the sound of a crowd was uplifting: Claire said the paper recorded 5,000 spectators most weeks. They tied their cycles together with a lock and chain and then clanked through a turnstile, to be greeted by the sharp crack of a starting pistol, a shout from the crowd, and so Brooke ran forward to see the dogs go past: a Greek frieze of limbs, teeth and bright eyes. Then dust. As they jostled for a place the bell rang for the last lap: the crowd's voice took on a bitter edge, and when the winning dog swept past betting tickets were let fall from hands, a snow shower of disappointment.

A bookies' stall had the next five runners chalked up on a board.

Blacknose Robin	*5,3,3*	*7/2*
Vacant Trap	*2,2,1,1,3*	*11/4*

Faran's Mistress 5,4,5,3,2		6/4
Tasty Tea		10/1
Roger Unsaved 4,1,5		2/1
Luke's Luck (RES) 4,4,4,3,5		

'Eden – Luke's Luck,' said Claire, squeezing his arm.

'It's the reserve – it won't run. Probably a good thing given the last five races. Never better than third. Anyway,' he added, taking her arm and whispering in her ear, 'Tasty Tea is on Ben's list. So that's the ringer.'

He'd pretty much decided that he didn't have time to track down bent bookies. But seeing how the losers took the race result to heart made him think what low creatures they were – skinning ordinary folk for a few pennies.

They were parading the dogs for the next race. The bar – The Fenman – was packed, the windows already misty as dusk crept closer. There were only three more races, the blackout having done for floodlit sport everywhere. An illuminated greyhound track would have been a welcome surprise for the Luftwaffe.

'There's Rose,' said Claire, pointing to a mobile tea bar set up close to the bookies' stalls. Rose was Brooke's original 'nighthawk'. She ran a stall on Market Hill in the centre of Cambridge. When he'd joined the Borough his mentor – the detective inspector – had made sure he got a night beat, his eyes still sensitive after his ordeal in the desert. He'd chat to Rose every night, and drink her steeped tea, and so, gradually, grew to know the family. One of her daughters took the day shift, leaving Rose to the night-time regulars, mostly railwaymen, printers, college porters, and now a city garrisoned for war.

'I'll get three teas,' said Brooke, slipping through the crowd.

The loudspeakers announced that Vacant Trap had been withdrawn and Luke's Luck would race.

Brooke, walking past a bookie, saw him chalk up odds of 8/1. He knew with absolute certainty that Claire would place a bet, despite the fact they knew for sure the whole charade was fixed.

'Well, well. We are honoured. Her Majesty's constabulary,' said Rose, when Brooke got to the tea bar. Animated, theatrical, Rose ran a tea stall as if she were on stage at the Theatre Royal. Dark gypsy looks, with diverting jewellery, completed the ensemble.

'What's this – demotion?' asked Brooke, noting a fleeting sense of disappointment in the bright eyes.

'Marie, my eldest, just got married. New hubby's no slouch. He's had three of these built,' she said, slapping the side of the mobile tea van. 'Sport's good business now: football, horses out at Newmarket, greyhounds all over – this track's licensed but there's plenty of flappers in the sticks: Cottenham, Mildenhall. Half the crowd's in the services. Everyone's bored stiff, happy to throw good money after old dogs.'

'How's the family?'

Rose delivered a one-minute precis and Brooke strove to remember each detail.

'When are you back on Market Hill?'

'Tonight, Brooke. There's no rest . . . Marie's man's got the van to tow. He's running stuff for the military out of Madingley – for a price. He says he's "sweating the assets", whatever that means.'

Then there was a pistol shot, so Brooke turned his back on

the counter and watched the race – 400 yards, a single circuit, most of the dogs faster than the Wasp. He didn't like watching animals race; you could see their honest desperation to win, a virtue turned to a vice for the sake of a few pennies.

A white dog with black patches, won by a head. It was Tasty Tea. Luke's Luck was second.

'Bastards,' said Brooke, deciding he did have time after all. Maybe he could inveigle the Castle into a raid at the next meeting.

A fresh set of runners was already being paraded, so business was slow at the tea bar. They shared Rose's Pall Mall.

'Who do I need to keep an eye on, Rose? Any shady characters?' he said, back still against the counter, surveying the crowd: 5,000 certainly, but maybe more, the shadows filling up the gaps as the sun set behind the now redundant floodlights.

Rose made a bit of business out of swabbing up spilt tea from the counter.

'About twenty yards along the rail there's a bookie's A-frame. Bloke leaning on the counter with the dog on a bit of rope.'

'Got him,' said Brooke, using his eyes, not his neck, so his body faced the stand.

'Name of Brodie,' said Rose. 'Patrick Brodie – never Paddy, by the way. I'm told he doesn't take well to the navvy's label.'

Brooke knew it wasn't a rare name, but rare enough, and he didn't believe in coincidences. He had jet-black hair – shiny, maybe oiled – and a lean face, the bones clear-cut. The suit was sharp, slate-grey, but the tie was loose, the knot too tight, pulled down.

'What does he do?'

'Well, he says he's a bookie's runner. But he isn't. Talk is there's a gang of them. Now the big boys are behind bars, there's a gap in the market – that's what they say.'

Italy's entry into the war the year before had dealt a blow to a London-based mob who'd controlled the protection racket on racecourses. Charles Sabini – at the helm – had been promptly hauled off to the Isle of Man as an enemy alien, to be locked up in an internment camp.

'A gang? They must have a silly name then?' said Brooke.

Calling the London mob 'Sabini's' had always seemed like a stupid mistake to Brooke. Perhaps it simply radiated confidence, even arrogance.

'The Farm,' she said, which wasn't what Brooke had expected, and made him think there was something serious here, something smart.

'London?'

'East Anglia, Lincolnshire, all the way up to York apparently: including the Knavesmire. Flat racing, dogs, off-course betting, protection.'

'And he's what – in charge, or just a little cog in the machine?'

'Says he's in charge.'

'I doubt that very much,' said Brooke. In his experience you hardly ever saw the real villains.

'He's not taking your money, is he Rose?'

She laughed. 'There's a lot to be said for being small fry, Brooke. I'll let you know if I get the hard word, but so far we've been left alone.'

Brooke tipped his hat.

'If you hear anything more about The Farm, keep me in mind,' he said, moving off to find Claire and Ben, who were standing with pints of beer by the rail, where a uniformed constable was strolling by, no doubt content to simply show the County's colours to the crowd.

'Guess what?' said Claire.

'You put a pound on Luke's Luck and now you're drowning your sorrows.' said Brooke.

Claire just beamed.

'No. Ben made me put it on Tasty Tea. We're in the money.'

Ben got more chips. The bikes didn't have dynamos, so they'd have to set off home soon. They decided to see one more race. There was a dog called Hospital Pass and Claire thought that was an omen, and so she was going to give the bookies her pound back.

Brooke said he'd just have a last look round.

'I'd think twice about another bet. Given you knew the last race was fixed, I think that constitutes conspiracy to defraud. Five years is the maximum. If they send you down I'll bake a cake and pop a nail file in.'

'But you're not going to arrest anyone?' asked Ben.

'Not tonight.'

Brodie had disappeared. Brooke checked all the bookies' stands, the tea bar and The Fenman. Under the stand the gloom was gathering – a row of lightbulbs lit up the wooden terracing above. The space had been used to store beer crates, gas bottles, a rusted starting gate. A pistol shot signalled stamping above: the sound now brutal, building to a crescendo, then falling away to a hush.

Then, moving from shadow to shadow, he saw Brodie, striding away from the stand towards a group of lorries parked a hundred yards away, on the edge of one of the old chalk pits.

Brooke kept his distance, circling until he was at the water's edge. The pit was half a mile wide, the surface unruffled, a perfect deep blue studded with the first stars. Looking across, he could see Brodie and two other men using buckets of water from the pit to clean the black patches off Tasty Tea. Brooke heard laughter, skimming across the surface of the water. To one side, sitting on a small elegant folding chair, Jackie Brodie looked bored, smoking a cigarette, her hand on the collar of the faithful Rochester.

CHAPTER TWENTY-FOUR

The city was coming alive, shopkeepers opening up along Petty Cury, trams decanting office workers on King's Parade, college gates busy with porters and deliveries. Brooke bought a copy of the *Cambridge News* on the street outside Emmanuel College.

SHELTER DEATHS PROMPT MURDER HUNT
'NO THREAT TO PUBLIC' – POLICE
SCOTLAND YARD ASSISTING

At his desk, in the half-light, he realised that he felt astonishingly well; rested, in fact. It prompted a pause for thought because it simply illustrated his usual level of fatigue. The astonishing truth was that he'd yet again slept the whole night, from his nightcap with Ben to the seven o'clock alarm. The bike ride to Coldham's Lane had provided unfamiliar exercise, and the Asquith Pie (leftovers reheated) a substantial meal. He'd even run the hot water in his mother's claw-footed bath in the attic, soaking for an hour. Then he'd slept, so soundly that he hadn't heard the siren, or the all-clear, or Iris's teething cries. He'd come down late to find Ben asleep in the front room, his usual retreat if his daughter was restless. But his son-in-law hadn't been on the sofa as normal, instead curled in a ball on the rug in front of the cold fire. Not for the first time he'd wondered if his calm persona hid deeper anxieties.

By the time he got to work, after a breakfast of marmalade and toast, the sun was slanting through the blinds on to his desk, where an envelope had been tucked into the corner of the blotter.

It was marked, simply. *Brooke. Urgent.*

Inside was a handwritten note. He recognised Dr Comfort's scrawl immediately, the letters sloping forward, tumbling onwards, personifying in some way the pathologist's headlong determination to press on, whatever the ghastly realities of death.

Brooke. A confession. I should make it in person. I'm lecturing in the Anatomical School, Queens' Lane. Catch my eye. You should know as soon as possible.

A brisk walk and he was at Queens' for nine o'clock. The porter sent him across the lane, to an innocent blue-painted wooden door, which was unlocked and revealed a cold corridor, leading to a small marble anteroom in the Baroque style – sickly, to Brooke's eye. Angels and cherubs tussled with billowing clouds. He stood still for a moment, and heard Comfort's voice, beyond the double-doors marked 'Theatre'.

He cursed himself for not thinking this through, and for succumbing to inquisitiveness and haste. There was no going back now, so he pushed open one of the doors, and keeping his eyes down, slipped into the first bench on the right. The theatre was very small – no more than forty feet in diameter, perfectly round, with three rows of circular benches. Above, a circular skylight, in an ornate style, collected the daylight and directed it down onto a white marble table. The room was packed, the medical students in studied poses of concentration. Comfort wore what could only be described as a butcher's apron. On the table lay a disaggregated corpse.

'Five minutes, gentlemen,' said the doctor, holding up bloodied hands, and the room was suddenly full of light-hearted conversation. Several students smoked. It struck Brooke that medics had the university to themselves, the forces desperate for doctors at home and overseas.

Comfort, in shirtsleeves, stood before him, freshly scrubbed clean, with a loose manila file tucked under one arm.

'Fresh air, Brooke. Now.'

They sat in the garden of Old Chapel, on a carved bench embellished with stone skulls. Comfort had the stub of a cigar, which he took a moment to light.

He sunk his several chins onto his chest.

'I have to make a confession,' he said. 'You will recall the suicide at the Chesterton shelter – found 31st July. Two months ago – more. Medicine bottle of barbiturates in his pocket. We, I, assumed he was transient, possibly off-duty army, or RAF up at Marshall's. Certainly not a local because no one came forward. Thinking was that he'd be missed eventually – back in York, or Glasgow, or Bristol. But there was nothing.

'The coroner released the body for burial – death by misadventure. I think uniform from the Borough attended, as did the cheap papers.

'Clincher was the note he left. Capital letters, neatly drawn: "I WANTED TO SERVE MY COUNTRY." There was a white feather with the note. I wondered, at the time, if that was what had tipped him over. Some oafs in uniform spitting in his face. Physically fit, you see. Late twenties, possibly thirties – pale complexion, black hair, beard, sturdy.

'Never crossed my mind he might be a student. And he doesn't fit – does he? He was fit, hadn't been in the sun, and was a generation older. But given my oversight with Basford – I should have spotted the spectacle marks on the bridge of the nose, they were there, you see, if slight. Given that error, I spent some time checking all possibilities.'

He opened the file and took out an X-ray of two legs, hip joints and feet.

'Clear as crystal if I'd only looked. Flat feet – one of the worse cases I've seen. A complete collapse of the foot arch.

'You can see the deformation of the knees here, in compensation for this. I checked back and looked at the original file notes. He was found in his socks – no shoes. I did query this, but was told the Chesterton shelter asks people to leave their footwear at the door because it's by the river and muddy. The shoes were never found. I should have raised a concern about that. But there we are.'

'The shoes?'

'I suspect they had supports inserted – possibly handmade by the cobbler.'

He took a final puff on the cigar, smoke drifting across the chapel garden.

'Which means?' asked Brooke.

'Which means he'd have been shown the door at the army medical. A waste, given he could have been posted to a gun emplacement, or a job in the quartermaster's stores. The rules are rigid – every soldier has to undergo basic training. If they can't pass that, they don't get in.

'So – a match with Basford and Ambrose, given the extreme myopia, and the psoriasis. The only thing missing is a suntan. He was pretty much as white as a sheet.'

'But possibly a third victim,' said Brooke, checking his notebook. He'd listed the medical reasons for the four attic boys' failure to serve king and country. 'Yes. Mortimer had flat feet. Aged twenty-nine. A PhD student. And a bookworm, if I remember, who spent most of his time in his room. Shy of the sun. Hardly a surprise he nearly fell through the net.'

'Thank you for that – but it's my oversight,' said Comfort.

'If we add him to the list, then there is a pattern – of sorts,' said Brooke. 'This would be the first victim – unless of course our fourth missing man, Smith-Stanley, died even longer ago?'

'And why was *he* not good enough for the army?' asked the doctor.

'Hypotension.'

'Well, I'm not going to spot that, am I? But I checked the files – for the Borough and the Castle. I think we're clear back to last October. So no – this one's first, Brooke. All other suicides were identified.'

'Right. So – the pattern,' said Brooke. 'First victim there's a suicide note, the empty pillbox, the white feather. No other apparent cause of death. Then we move to Basford – evidence of suicide, but botched. Then the third victim – the subterfuge by that point is perfunctory. The pillbox found with Ambrose's body looked like an afterthought. A pretty half-hearted effort to throw us off the trail. They either don't care if we know it's murder, or they were panicking, or they think they're getting away with it.

'And – given *four* young men left the Laurels together, and we may have three of them in your morgue, we have to fear for the life of Edmund Smith-Stanley.'

Brooke thought that if this *was* the truth, then it begged other questions. Why the gaps between the murders? Were they returning to Cambridge individually, alone? Were they prisoners, together?

Comfort stood. 'I must go. The gentlemen are keen to see the large bowel, the liver. Brooke, it may seem callous, but they are incredibly grateful for the gift – the body. This is the third dissection – although the first time I've officiated. We'll stitch him back together and the students will undertake the autopsy themselves. At the end of the term the body – in one piece – will be buried. There'll be a service – here, at the theatre, and we'll all attend. In the meantime, we have to do our work. Just as you do.'

'What was his name?' asked Brooke, sensing the truth.

'Well, he is referred to – always – as Erasmus. That's a tradition. But you've just told me his real name, Brooke. It's William Mortimer. Yes – he could not stay in the morgue for ever. The coroner released him for a pauper's burial. The city council takes possession and can authorise the use of the body for medical research. There's a fee. But now at least we'll know his family. That's part of the tradition too. I'll write to his mother, father, next of kin. And every student will sign. So, some good has come of the whole sorry story.'

CHAPTER TWENTY-FIVE

Two messages awaited him back at the Spinning House – the first a (badly) typewritten paragraph from Sergeant Johnnie Holt:

> *15th Oct. 9.45 a.m.*
>
> *Sir. Morris Eight is on its way to Scotch Corner. Nothing last night despite siren. Workforce of 192 on gatehouse list. All listed as safely in the shelters by Chubb. I took precaution of counting them out at the 6 a.m. shift: all present. Morris Eight still locked, and Chubb and I checked the wax seals on cases. Untouched. Will return for night shift.*
>
> *J. H. Holt (Sgt)*

The second, expertly typed by Mrs Muir, the chief inspector's secretary, was on headed notepaper, incorporating the crest of the Borough:

15th Oct. 10.00 a.m.
Brooke, siren last night so I presume consignment already en route for Barrow. The Yard has requested update for Home Secretary. Please advise on situation at Vulcan Works. ASAP.

'Bumf,' said Brooke, screwing the note up into a ball and bouncing it off the far wall and into the wastepaper bin. What was the point of an update now? The van was on the road.

A wave of fatigue swept behind his eyes, making the lids droop, the call of the Nile bed almost audible. If the Morris Eight reached Barrow tomorrow with faulty periscopes, the case was mired. The War Office would close the Vulcan Works, or at least terminate the Barrow contract, and the saboteur would be free to strike again: who knew where? And beyond that lay Carnegie-Brown's departure for the Yard, and his own – unwanted – promotion.

He stood, steeled to make his way upstairs, when he heard instead footsteps rising. Fast, tap-dancing steps.

It was one of the switchboard girls, breathless, holding what looked like a scribbled note.

'Sir. Duty sergeant was dealing with someone in the cells, so I took the call. They said it was urgent.'

She began to read from her own note.

'It's from Borough Radio Car 2, sir, at Great Wilbraham crossroads. PC Turner has observed a young man in a herringbone overcoat, no hat, thinning red hair, walking towards the bus stop by Wilbraham Post Office.'

She paused to check her watch.

'Half an hour ago. Seen carrying a leather briefcase, and a copy of the *Cambridge News*. This morning's edition. Caught the Number 8 bus for Cambridge Station at 8.10. Turner reports suspect likely to be Harry Callaghan – resident.'

Brooke grabbed a spare hat he never wore – a flat tweed cap – and a lightweight mac.

'Get the sergeant to radio them back. Turner should stay at the mill. Tell her we're in pursuit.'

He dashed past the girl, then returned and took four packets of Black Russians from his desk, a notebook and pencil.

Running, Brooke got to the station in fifteen minutes and was in place on a crowded Platform 1 at the railway station, in time to see Callaghan show a ticket to the collector at the barrier. They stood, waiting, each studying a newspaper twenty yards apart. Callaghan had bought himself a Sporting Life and was immersed in pages of data. Brooke tried to put his mind in neutral: there was no point second-guessing Callaghan's destination or purpose. All he had to do was make sure he didn't lose him. The thinning hair and pale skin were a gift to spotting him in any crowd. Brooke wore the black tinted glasses, which he had not worn inside the hotel the day before, and kept his cap tipped forward, and his back to his quarry as best he could.

The train was late, the platform heaving. Physical discomfort had become a wartime affliction, like nits and insomnia. Nobody complained. Brooke found the mood of stoicism strangely moving. Less uplifting was the irritation he always felt at the decision – imposed by the university – that there should be only one platform at Cambridge: up-trains duelled with down-trains, and cross-country trains. All this confusion and crowding to dampen the liberating freedoms of the railway system. The result was pandemonium: trains going north had to vie with trains going south. Liverpool Lime Street one way, and London Liverpool Street the other. King's Lynn one way, King's Cross the other. Stories of the uninitiated being sent off in the wrong direction were legion. The *News* had run a story of an eight-year-old going home from the Leys School who'd ended up in Glasgow when he should have been in Gorleston.

It didn't make Brooke's job any easier either. Where was Callaghan headed? By now the throng on the platform was reminiscent of a football crowd. There was applause when the arrival of a train was announced – the details lost on the wind. According to the mechanical board of DESTINATIONS, it was set for Liverpool.

Whistles, flags waving, a cloud of steam, and the matter was decided: according to a guard with a flag shouting from the steps of the engine, this service was for Merseyside. Brooke slipped through the melee, watching Callaghan, who seemed agitated, shouldering his way roughly through the crowd, elbowing several people out of his path. Was he bolting? Did he really think he could simply walk away from the Laurels?

Callaghan had a second-class ticket, and so took a seat in the third carriage from the engine. Brooke had shown his warrant card at the barrier, and so simply chose a seat ten rows back, out of line-of-sight. He settled in, thanking fate for that good night's sleep, and Claire's insistence on breakfast: toast and homemade marmalade.

Once inside the carriage Brooke dispensed with his glasses – he enjoyed 20/20 vision – in case Callaghan glanced his way.

He'd interviewed him the day before from behind the green tinted spectacles. Without protection for his eyes he had to squint, to cut down the light. He felt half blind. But he was confident he'd avoid detection.

Given the state of the railway network, a journey to the end of the line could take days. Thrillingly, he had the four packets of cigarettes. Deciding on strict rationing, he lit one after the train left Queen Adelaide and swung west towards Peterborough, across the Fens.

The train was worn out, like the country. Brooke felt that the scratchy seats, and the odour of tobacco and dust, perfectly caught the touch and feel of a mildly gone-to-seed England. His quarry sat alone, breathing heavily, occasionally coughing into his handkerchief. The rapid departure and exertion had clearly aggravated his asthma.

As each station approached, Brooke watched for Callaghan to make sure he didn't suddenly decamp. But he looked settled, and as the train ran over the Bedford Levels – with a sea of autumn floods on either side – he saw him slip inevitably into sleep. At Peterborough an entire platoon of soldiers took the carriage, their sergeant diplomatically allocating himself a seat in the next one. The result, until sleep descended, was pandemonium. Card schools broke out; there was arm-wrestling, and general high jinks. They could have been on a school outing before the war.

For an entire hour the train stopped at a nameless junction, until a munitions train crossed their path, rattling through. Brooke, unable to curb a childhood habit, counted sixty-one carriages.

Then they were on the move again. The countryside slipped

past, occasionally enlivened by a cartload of Land Girls, or plodding shires. He counted thirty church spires, another childhood obsession, saddened by the thought that their bells were silent, in readiness still to signal an invasion – or one day, victory.

Brooke, overheated in the airless carriage, tried to think clearly: there had been eight attic boys (including Underhill – who had clearly been excluded from the group, probably on the basis of class, and eventually given his own room in the basement). So seven; with four leaving a year ago, three of whom had been murdered. They had died over a period of ten weeks. They had not been seen alive for a year. Were they hiding? Were they being held against their will? Why were they being murdered at intervals?

He felt sleep edging closer, so he fetched tea from the buffet car after Newark. England clattered by as the train cut a neat cross-section through Sheffield, Glossop, Manchester and Stockport; although all that was surmise, as the station signs had been taken down to confuse German parachutists. The sun, intermittent in the east, was soon shining through the windows facing west. The day slipped by. Callaghan, plainly groggy, staggered to the buffet in the early afternoon and came back with a pork pie and a bottle of barley wine. He took his briefcase with him – while leaving his coat and newspaper.

At Runcorn, the whole train now comatose with heat, they crossed the ship canal and opening the window Brooke heard seagulls. Dismal terrace streets heralded Liverpool; barrage balloons jibbed in a stiff sea breeze over dockside cranes. A brief vista of the estuary flashed by, the Irish Sea milky with a slight Celtic mist.

And then they arrived, the air rent by several whistles. The soldiers, hauling kitbags, blocked the doors.

Finally, Brooke stepped down from the carriage under the great glass dome of Lime Street Station, miraculously intact.

At the barrier Callaghan showed his ticket, and Brooke saw that he had a return in his hand as well, as he slipped it back into his wallet, then walked briskly out into the sunshine. Unless the return ticket was a feint, it meant Callaghan wasn't bolting.

The station might have been undamaged, but not so the city beyond. If he hadn't been on Callaghan's trail, he'd have sat down on the station steps. Cambridge had been bombed – houses flattened, the railyards pitted – but this was, perhaps, the shape of things to come. St George's plateau and the great concert hall itself were intact, as was the Walker Art Gallery – even if they looked to be coated in grime. But beyond lay ruins – street upon street, then the broken teeth of warehouses and fine buildings leading down to the waterfront. He could just see the Liver Birds atop one of the dockside buildings, ghostly in the murky coal smoke of the Mersey, seemingly on the lookout for German bombers. No wonder that news about Liverpool – and Portsmouth, the East End and Newcastle – was strictly controlled. If the country could *see* this, morale would collapse.

But Liverpool wasn't done yet.

Callaghan headed for a pub fifty yards from the facade of the great station, called The Crown.

Inside, it was glorious – a great Victorian confection of gilded mirrors, etched glass and painted plasterwork. Brooke got a whisky and a cheese sandwich and picked up a *Liverpool Echo* left on the bar. He pretended to read the latest list of convoy ships due to dock that day. If Callaghan wasn't on the run, what was the reason for this trip? Was he working, was he going home? It showed a bizarre level of confidence, or arrogance, to defy instructions and leave Cambridge without informing the police. Why did he think he was above the law?

Brooke checked his notebook for Callaghan's home address: Southport – just up the Lancashire coast.

It was nearly five o'clock and the crowd was growing louder. The men looked tired, even broken, and most were in dusty overalls. Callaghan, who'd sat by the window, was joined by a young man of his own age, balding, with a skimpy moustache. A workman certainly, with filthy hands, and what looked like white paint on his hobnailed boots. They shook hands and in one of those odd silences which can descend on a crowd, he heard Callaghan ask distinctly, 'John Boyle?'

And the reply, 'I go by Sean.' They sat and talked, but both looked ill at ease and quickly abandoned half-finished drinks, Boyle leading the way out to the great stone plateau of St George's.

Brooke made himself linger for a moment, in case he bumped into them on the step, and then followed, slipping on the ochre glasses. Ahead he saw them making for the Walker Art Gallery – now home, according to a series of hand-painted signs, to the Ministry of Labour. They stood on the steps smoking. Brooke walked past and found a spot amongst the Ionic columns, hidden by shadows. They waited; Brooke recalled an episode from his childhood. He'd have been five, and his mother had driven north from Cambridge in her role as a trustee of the Fitzwilliam Museum. It was the summer, so there was no school, and they'd spent an hour in a deserted room, where the light danced as rain flowed over the skylights, looking at the masterpieces of Degas and Monet. (Brooke suspected that the gallery had been closed, momentarily, so that his mother might enjoy the work without the interference of the public.)

That night they'd stayed at the Adelphi, and had turtle soup, the principal ingredient – it was said – scooped from the dark pool in the basement where the sluggish giants were kept fresh and alive. They'd taken a ferry across the river, and peeked into the cavernous interior of the new cathedral – half finished. His mother had died a month later.

Daydreaming, he nearly missed it. A man, shrugging himself into a suit jacket, with a white shirt and dark tie, came out of the ministry entrance and strolled away with Callaghan and Boyle. Brooke got a good look at the newcomer's face: round, run-to-fat, maybe fifty years of age. They stood close together and Brooke was sure he saw an envelope passed to the newcomer by Callaghan. Business completed, their contact fled, back inside the gallery.

Boyle and Callaghan set out towards the docks. Brooke stayed in the shadows for a few minutes. The Ministry of Labour's powers were considerable in war – encompassing all forms of everyday work. On his return to Cambridge, he would have to alert Scotland Yard. Given the city's role as the principal port of the kingdom, employing thousands of dockers, it was possible the Laurels was a tiny cog in a much larger criminal machine.

Having given them a hundred-yard start, Brooke was back on the trail. A strange tour of the city began. They walked to the Albert Dock, bristling with a convoy unloading from

Boston. Brooke noted they watched from the quayside but did not attempt to pass through the gates, which were guarded by soldiers. They went instead to yet another pub – the Manx Arms. Someone had wedged the doors open to catch the breeze off the Mersey, so Brooke was able to see Callaghan and Boyle join a group of dockers. The walls of the pub were covered in framed pictures of the docks, and the ships, from years gone by. At one point, one of Boyle's friends took down one of the pictures and showed Callaghan, who studied the image. A ship – thought Brooke – in the process of being unloaded.

Then they took a tram towards Stanley Park. It was astonishing to Brooke that the rails were clear given the devastation of the streets – rubble simply swept aside to form a canyon of bricks, shattered roofs, twisted plumbing. Across a few of the largest mounds of debris women picked their way, scavenging perhaps for food or lost treasures. The Number 7 reached the terminus, but instead of circling to return, the seatbacks were simply pushed forward, and the driver took his starting handle down to the other end of the lower deck. Brooke read his newspaper and stayed downstairs, leaving his quarry upstairs, but nonetheless it was a tricky moment: perhaps he had underestimated Callaghan. It was exactly the kind of trap Brooke would have set to see if he was being followed.

They went two stops back and then he heard them clattering down the stairs. The tram, city-bound, was crowded now, so there was little danger, but Brooke hung back until the last moment, swinging off the rear platform in the company of a six-year-old. Walking north they passed terraced streets: a ladder of them, one after the next, seemingly endless. The contrast with Cambridge was stark; it took ten minutes to walk across the Kite, but here they walked for half an hour, and the streets simply went on, a maze of brick, dusty pavements, and corner shops and pubs. A newsagent had put out a board for that evening's *Echo*: GERMAN SUB CAPTURED OFF IRELAND.

Finally, they turned into Index Street. Brooke hung back by a pub on the corner called the Dry Dock. Boyle went to a sky-blue door, Number 29, and knocked. A woman answered, wiping her hands on an apron, and had to be introduced to Callaghan. It was just after eight o'clock. Dusk was gathering, although there was plenty of light out to sea in the west. Lights came on in the house too, and briefly, as a curtain was drawn, he saw into the living room: it looked prosperous, with wallpaper, pictures, wall lights and a sideboard. He saw Boyle laughing, holding a bottle of beer.

The blue door did not open again until nine. Brooke, who'd kept watch from the Dry Dock for an hour, was by now in the doorway of a corner shop at the end of the street. Boyle and Callaghan walked past, so close he caught the scent of cigarettes, beer and possibly a chip pan.

Brooke let them get a hundred yards ahead. There was a wide bomb site, and to one side a street with lights and tram wires. A wooden shelter stood empty. The scene – Brooke had kept his distance amidst the ruins – rang with a specific tension; as if it was an empty stage, awaiting the actors.

The two men picked their way across the rubble towards the tram stop. Brooke noted that Boyle was in his shirtsleeves. It was a mild night, but turning chilly, and so it seemed he would return home once Callaghan was set on the tram for the city centre, and a hotel perhaps, or boarding house, as the mainline trains would have stopped by now, except for freight.

The wide field of rubble was unlit, but the sky above was criss-crossed by searchlights. There'd been no siren, but somewhere in the noise of the battered city there was the bee-like drone of a plane. From the edge of the bomb site Brooke watched as the few lights visible in houses around the open ground blinked out. The drone grew louder: a bomber certainly, and low in the sky.

Then the noise passed, the bomber unseen.

Boyle saw it first, the pale form of a parachute, but stood his ground, perhaps judging the threat would simply glide past and away towards the docks. Callaghan ran for cover.

But what was the threat? The parachute – about a hundred feet up – passed through one of the searchlight beams. What was slung beneath? It was easy to imagine the figure of a German stormtrooper. Fears of invasion – which had reached fever pitch a year before – were difficult to suppress.

Boyle wasn't panicking, just watching. Brooke wondered how many bombs he'd seen falling in this city, which seemed to exist on the frontline of a distant war. Callaghan was crouching in a shell hole in open ground.

Brooke subsided in the rubble remains of a corner shop, amongst burnt-out tins of soup and beans. He saw Boyle take out a cigarette and light it with a steady hand. He thought such self-possession was indicative of a calculating nature, and a degree of arrogance.

There was no wind, so the descent was smooth, silent, mesmerising. At fifty feet Brooke could see the payload: a cylinder, eight to ten feet long, held horizontal by two chains.

Callaghan stood up, 'For God's sake, run!' he shouted.

But Boyle just shook his head.

'It's for the docks,' he said, quite clearly, quite calmly. And it *was* drifting south towards the Mersey. Brooke had heard of similar raids on Lynn and the East Coast ports. It was a Luftmine – a German naval mine, designed to sink in the water and attach itself to a ship's hull like a magnet.

Perhaps this explained Boyle's calm vigil.

Brooke thought he was a fool. Ben had told him Luftmines had been used in the Atlantic and the Arctic on the convoys, but then the boffins had found a way to demagnetise ships – rendering the mines useless. As a result, the Germans had thousands of explosives they couldn't use – unless they dropped them on land and rigged them to go off *before* they hit the ground. Ben said there were already reports of this during raids on London and Portsmouth. The trigger was usually set at rooftop height – so that the blast could penetrate several hundred yards in all directions. But a lot failed to ignite. Duds were just as bad because the bomb disposal squads had to render them safe – a job that took days.

Boyle, realising the parachute wouldn't clear the bomb site, crouched down, still stoically smoking.

Thirty feet, twenty feet, fifteen feet, ten, five. It touched down. The parachute covered it like a shroud.

Boyle, thirty yards from the bomb, stood up slowly.

There was ten seconds of silence.

Boyle made a megaphone of his hands. 'Harry! It's a dud. Let's go, mate.'

But it wasn't a dud. It was a booby trap.

Brooke, half standing, heard the night sky tear itself in half. The blinding flash sent a nerve-shredding pain through his brain. He was unconscious before he hit the pile of bricks he'd been sheltering behind.

When he came round he was deaf, and bright electric lights kept flashing in his eyes. He lay flat on his back, moving both hands, both feet, his head from side to side.

He was alive, and unhurt, so he got to his feet.

Then the sound came back: glass falling, shattering, a ruined house finally collapsing, sirens everywhere, the flicker of flames.

Callaghan stood by Boyle's body, which looked like a pile of rags. Fires spluttered amongst the debris. Callaghan doubled over and threw up at his own feet. Then he straightened, hands held together, and for a moment Brooke wondered if he was saying a prayer. A dog barked, and a few lights came on, and then there was the sound of a fire engine's bell.

Callaghan knelt down and searched the body, retrieving a white envelope, which he put in his inside jacket pocket. Then he appeared to put something *back* into one of Boyle's trouser pockets. Then he stood, spun on his heels – a 360-degree scan of the bomb site. Brooke was just quick enough to drop behind a mound of bricks. When he looked again Callaghan was running away, past the tram stop, down the hill towards the city.

CHAPTER TWENTY-SIX

Brooke spent the night in a police station within sight of the Adelphi Hotel. His room was not up to Cunard's standards, but it was difficult to argue with the cost of board and lodging, which was nothing. He ate with the night shift – a concoction of stew called scouse, which looked like hotpot but contained all manner of other things, including fish. Most of the constables were Irish, as were most of the men held in the cells. The atmosphere in the station was a heady mix of the Bronx and the night ferry from Fishguard to Dun Laoghaire. There were two brawls at the duty desk, only one of them involving uniformed constables. However, the standard of the musical chorus, which punctuated the night, was far superior to that heard in the Spinning House.

He was woken, in his cell, by a Detective Inspector Jack McGuire, of the city police, who told him Callaghan – or a man matching Brooke's description of Callaghan – had caught the first train to Cambridge and Norwich at just after six from Lime Street. Boyle's body had been recovered from the bomb site and was in the city morgue, while a WPC had been dispatched the night before to Index Street at midnight to inform his widow of the circumstances of his death.

'Breakfast,' announced McGuire, leading the way to a café called the Stage Door behind the Liverpool Empire. Brooke noted black-and-white photos on the wall signed by the cast of *ITMA*. Brooke's seat was directly under Mrs Mopp. McGuire was served what he called a 'full Irish' while Brooke opted for toast. The tea – builders' – was richly tannic. The café was enveloped in what Claire would have called 'a fug'.

'So what have I got here, Brooke? What do I need to know?' said McGuire, skewering a piece of black pudding. 'Boyle was a piece of work, for sure. Violent. Used a knife. Glad to see his corpse,' he added. 'But if he was up to something, something big enough to interest the Borough, I'd like to know what it is. There's a hundred like him within half a mile of where we're sitting.'

Brooke lit a cigarette.

'It's a scam. We know that because they're earning money. There's a group of them – all medically unfit for service. They're hold up in a funk-hole in the sticks. Idle, clever – and most of them enjoy a drink, the high life. They need cash, and they've found a way to make it. There may be a link to illegal gambling, but they seemed most interested in the docks – and we know there's a link with Lowestoft. Is it theft on the quayside? Supplying the black market?'

McGuire leant back in his seat, his empty plate smeared with mustard.

'There you are. Boyle's a docker – was a docker. He got the push three weeks ago for running a book. Maybe your man Callaghan was to take his place? Maybe there's more than one scam.'

They had another two cups of strong tea, swapped telephone numbers, and set off for the police station. Brooke was braced for the all-day ordeal of the cross-country train journey, but they found a Daimler parked up under the blue lamp, with a civilian driver.

'This'll get you home. We'll do what we can,' said McGuire, shaking his hand. 'You get villains alright,' he said. 'Low life. But the Boyles of this world are feral, Brooke. Peace comes, which it will one day, God help us, they'll be running the streets if we don't stop them now.'

A constable came out of the station hauling a cardboard box and placed it on the back seat of the car.

'Some light reading, Brooke, for the journey.' Your statement said Boyle and Callaghan met a man who came out of the Walker Art Gallery. This may help. Enjoy the trip.'

He waved Brooke away to the sound of a ship's siren on the Mersey.

Inside the box were the duplicate ID cards of all those working in the Walker Art Gallery for the Ministry of Food. Due to the security level these ID cards included a small photograph. There were sixty-eight permanent staff. Could he spot the man who'd been given the first pay-off envelope by Callaghan? The second envelope, Callaghan had retrieved from Boyle's body – but had it been destined for him, to be handed over as he got on the tram? Or was it Boyle's to keep?

Brooke used an hour of the journey to study each ID photo from the ministry building. Brooke was good with faces: he could take a glimpse from one angle and rotate it, creating a 3D image in his mind's eye. He'd infuriate Claire with his constant ability to spot 'familiar faces' – Cambridge sometimes appeared to be populated only by people Brooke knew by sight.

On this occasion there was no match. If he wasn't on the staff, why had he been in the building? It was one of those irritating details which could provide the key to a case.

They pulled into the back yard of the Spinning House at just after four. A note from CID Liverpool was on Brooke's desk, taken down by the switchboard:

Suspect expected Cambridge 4.20 p.m. Mrs May Boyle – mother of three – said Callaghan was old friend of her husband's. Callaghan told her he was a travelling salesman and had booked in at Adelphi. No such booking existed. Boyle was a docker – reserved occupation. Dismissed three weeks ago after a series of warnings given for operating as a bookies' runner – dogs, crown green bowling, Aintree. They talked about football, and possibility of attending Cup Final in London. Boyle maybe involved in unlicensed football pools in the Merseyside area. Callaghan had brought sweets for children. Will re-interview if required. Boyle has previous. His file includes three prosecutions for burglary – with a total of sixty similar offences taken into consideration. He served three years for GBH 1935–38 at Strangeways. He was a member of the National Union of Dock Workers, and a convenor for the Stanley Park area. Please advise.

Brooke got Edison up to speed, outlining the events of the previous day.

'Let's keep the more lurid details to ourselves, shall we? I don't want Claire hearing hair-raising tales about her husband missing a thousand-pound bomb by half a yard.'

'Sir.'

'Can we get this on a motorbike back to Liverpool,' added Brooke, giving him the files from the Ministry of Food.

The phone rang. Edison picked it up and listened, then covered the mouthpiece.

There was a distinct pause before he spoke, which made it clear it was bad news.

'Barrow, sir. Red Caps. Checked the consignment in an hour ago. A dozen periscopes, two faulty.'

It took them both a few seconds to process this news: a consignment of high-security naval periscopes had left Cambridge in perfect condition and had yet again been the target of sabotage.

They'd reached an absolute dead end.

'Get a number, Edison. We'll ring them back in due course.'

Brooke got his hat.

'Let's take some air.'

He led the way along St Andrew's, turning away from the facade of Emmanuel College, down towards the river. The Mill Inn stood upstream of Silver Street Bridge. It was a favourite spot because the mill race – always white water – gave off a thin miasma of sparkling droplets which seemed to energise the air. Brooke found it inspiring. He often came here to think, aided by a glass of beer.

He bought two pints of Star Brewery's Best Bitter and they sat on the wall outside, the water racing past them into the millpond.

'What next?' asked Brooke.

It was time to rely on Edison's sound common sense.

'It must be Eva Mappin,' said Edison. 'We lost her twice on the way up on the Great North Road – never for more than ten minutes it's true, but she was out of sight. Part of that batch was sabotaged. Are we really sure she didn't know we were following? Unless Holt's blind, the culprit doesn't strike in the works. It's not Barrow – far too risky. It must be on the road.'

'Didn't we request her security file?'

'I'll run it down,' said Edison.

'Let's not spook her, but we can't avoid the basics. If we draw a blank we'll have to break cover – get her in for questioning. Chubb said she had an ailing aunt in the Arbury. Let's see if he knows the address – actually, he must know, because it's her current address. Get the local constable to wander past, check it out. We can't go on keeping the lid on this. I'm afraid the Vulcan Works may have to lose its contract. Which won't go down well "upstairs" – or in Whitehall. The fact is we've failed, Edison.'

'The Laurels?'

'We watch. Callaghan will be back in his room tonight. And that's what really doesn't add up. They know we're onto them. They must do. And yet he sets out, broad daylight, and it's business as usual. But for a Luftmine we'd have had them.

'If we drag Callaghan in now he'll bluster. There's no way he's an old friend of Boyle's, but the cover story will hold.

'One thing. Callaghan's hometown is Southport – just up

the coast from the Albert Dock. Given we don't believe in coincidences, why is that important?'

Brooke launched a fag end into the water. He was losing patience with questions to which he had no answers.

One of the Borough's radio cars trundled to a halt beside the mill. Brooke's habits were not a secret at the Spinning House.

A constable got out of the car.

'Sir. A Mr Hayle phoned – owner of the Laurels? Back in the country, sir. Requests a meeting.'

CHAPTER TWENTY-SEVEN

Brooke followed the instructions left with the switchboard: Dr Hayle would be on site at noon on Fleam Dyke; an Ordnance Survey reference was included in the message, as if the Borough always organised itself like a commando unit in the Brecon Beacons. The dyke, an Anglo-Saxon defensive earthwork, ran for three miles, starting at a point just south of the Laurels. Edison fetched the Wasp, and dropped Brooke off at the village of Fulbourn, before going on to relieve PC Turner at Hawk Mill.

Once the Wasp was gone the silence descended – that special kind of windswept silence peculiar to the open chalk grasslands. Brooke walked briskly east, past the church, and out across the downs towards the great dyke; visible, even from a mile away, edging up to form a long, straight embankment. It looked like one of the Earth's ancient ribs, protruding through the flesh of the rolling landscape.

Hayle was late. Brooke took in the circular horizon, encompassing the Wilbrahams to the east and the chalk hills to the west, which shielded the city beyond. It was an idyllic view of Cambridgeshire and the Suffolk borders, which hadn't changed since the reign of the Anglo-Saxon kings. A few sheep chewed their way along the embankment.

Lost in the past, he hadn't heard Hayle's footsteps.

'Inspector Brooke?'

He was short, surprisingly youthful for his age, with brown hair unsullied by grey, which he pushed back off a high brow. A worsted suit was threadbare, the trousers snagged by thorns, the leather boots weathered. His eyes flitted constantly over the landscape, rarely meeting Brooke's; but when they did, there was a hint of penetrating intelligence.

'Work's this way,' he said. 'We can talk there.'

Brooke heard something behind him on the track, skittering, and turned as a greyhound caught them up and loped by to walk beside its master. There was a collar but no lead.

After half a mile they stopped on the high dyke looking down on a set of Victorian buildings – utilities of some sort, the brickwork immaculate; a pencil chimney and a rather ornate main hall, with a low-slung addition.

'Fleam Dyke Pumping Station,' said Hayle, proudly. 'Cambridge would be a thirsty city without it.'

Brooke feared he'd been summoned for a lecture.

The dog ran ahead.

'I've been away,' said Hayle. 'Boreas has been in kennels. He needs to stretch his legs. Old greyhounds don't die, Inspector, they just become bad bets. Boreas is very old – Mrs Brodie's husband breeds them. He's got a farm somewhere. I wanted company and they said Boreas was ideal. Next for the knackers' yard otherwise. Couldn't say no.'

Boreas, thought Brooke. *God of the north wind.*

'You'll know Cambridge: the university, not the town. You're Sir John's son, I think?'

Brooke nodded.

'Thought so. Never met him. Made the world a better place. Not many of us can say that, eh? But a burden nonetheless, for sons. A weight to carry, isn't it? My father was Professor Horace Hayle . . .'

He waited, perhaps for Brooke to recall the great man's achievements. But Brooke struggled – a physicist perhaps, or mathematician. There was a dim echo from the past.

'The Cavendish?' he said at last.

'That's it. Worked with Thompson on quantum mechanics. Never got the recognition he really deserved outside the university, but inside it he was a god.'

There was something illogical, almost obsessive about that comparison: man and god. Who deserved that? Who *wanted* that?

Hayle seemed to snap out of the reverie, waving his stick at the pumping station.

'Why here?' he said. 'That's what you're asking. You're thinking – why's the old duffer brought me out here? Place runs on pluralism – thought we got rid of that at the Reformation.

Not so. Everyone has two jobs, if not five. That's allowed because people are so clever.'

He laughed at the absurdity.

'So, I'm a senior member of the hydrology department of the university – a subsection of geology and natural sciences. I'm also president of my college, St Radegund's. And – five days a week full-time, according to my retainer – I am the chief hydrologist of the Cambridge Water Company.

'Between you and I, Brooke, I'm most proud of this . . .'

He indicated the pumping station.

'It's a miracle – it's my job to make sure it keeps working as it has done since 1921. I've been away. I need to check all is well.'

He was about to set off down a track.

'And you are the owner of the Laurels?' said Brooke.

Hayle stopped, nodded. 'Indeed. I inherited it from my late wife twenty years ago. I live in the Lodge. The Brodies run it – and I get a steady income, which I need, on a personal basis, but also to further research. It's a big war, Brooke – we're a small country. We need to be smart to make up for it. Smart costs cash.'

Hayle looked confused, as if he'd said too much.

'Anyway. The Laurels, yes. They came to me with the idea. The Brodies. It was on the market – but they couldn't raise the capital. They said they'd take it on, pay the bills, and I'd get a regular income. No paperwork, no duties. I couldn't really say no.

'So there we are. And here you are – no doubt with questions about Basford, and Ambrose.'

'Basford, Ambrose *and Mortimer*,' he said. 'That's not

official. But it looks likely. Three former residents of your hotel, sir. All dead, all found in the shelters. Possibly all murdered.'

That seemed to take the wind out of Hayle's sails. He leant on his stick.

'Mortimer?' he said. 'Clever lad. I say lad – but he was a doctoral student, I think. Always in his books. Used to see him in the university library. What a shame.'

He set off before Brooke could ask any more questions, leading the way down the escarpment, to the main entrance to the pumping station.

The doors were open. Inside, there was that peculiar sound of well-oiled machinery, almost fluid, and the scent of polish and lubricating oil. Two steam engines lay in their pits, flywheels turning. Everywhere metal gleamed, or enamel shone. Brooke, breaking out a Black Russian, thought it was like being inside a fabulous clock. Or a Fabergé egg.

'The borehole is 162 feet deep,' said Hayle. 'The water . . .'

He stopped talking, perhaps sensing Brooke's innate aversion to numbers.

'But why don't I show you?'

There was something menacing in the invitation, but Brooke manufactured some enthusiasm, and Hayle led the way to an iron door which he unlocked, revealing a shaft and a spiral stairway.

Brooke started counting the steps and had reached one hundred when Hayle stopped, looking back up the shaft.

'Do not fear, Inspector, we're nearly there.'

Another iron door, another key, and they were out on a small mesh-iron viewing platform.

The scene below could have been devised by Jules Verne.

237

Journey to the Centre of the Earth had been Brooke's favourite. The sense of limitless exploration, beneath your feet, had been captivating.

They were in a large chamber, comfortably capacious enough to accommodate the audience at the Regal for the latest Humphrey Bogart. It had been carved out of the limestone bedrock and was a brilliant white. A single light over the viewing platform was enough to illuminate the whole space.

Through this chamber ran an artificial river, about twenty feet wide, not deep, but churning and flecked with white horses. The water was so pure, so colourless, that in places it seemed invisible, revealing the chalk bed below.

'Yes. A small wonder,' said Hayle. 'Borehole is upstream. Water surfaces with the aid of the pumps, then flows downhill – the gradient's a few inches – into the purifiers, and then the softeners . . .'

He pointed to the right, where the artificial river left the chamber through a mesh screen.

'I take samples from the downside pipes which go to Rustat Road – just by the station, for analysis. Water goes to Barnwell to get pumped to the good people of Cambridge. I keep a watching brief on water volume, and the duplicate shaft. If we've got a problem with the supply we need to know early – years early. Geology isn't to be trifled with.'

He threw up his hands.

'This is my world, Brooke. Mine alone. The mechanics are here to keep the engines going. Responsibility for this watery kingdom falls to me.'

Brooke filled his lungs. The air – laden with the hypnotic

tang of fresh water – was energising. Life-giving.

Hayle was checking the iron grids covering the entrance to what looked like a tunnel, disappearing into the shadows.

Then he looked at his watch. 'We should return to the land of the living,' he said, cheerfully.

The ascent left Brooke breathless.

There was a board – varnished wood – in the main engine hall, listing the Chief Hydrologist for the City of Cambridge going back into the nineteenth century – long before Fleam Dyke was built. Brooke recognised the names of several eminent scientists. The last was Dr Charles Hayle PhD, MA OXON FRGS.

Brooke nodded, determined not to be impressed. Cambridge was already bloated with self-congratulation.

A workman appeared in overalls, tipped his cap to Hayle, and disappeared behind one of the steam engines.

'Sorry for the peremptory summons,' said Hayle. 'As soon as I heard what had happened, I knew you'd have questions. I just wanted to help. And the work I'm doing – I might have to go back to the States at any time. So I thought I'd make the first move, so to speak. I'll be difficult to track down – even in Cambridge. It's a priority. All very hush-hush.'

Brooke took off his hat. 'My priority – my three priorities – lie in mortuary drawers in the Galen Building.'

'Quite so,' he said. 'Ask any question you want, Inspector.'

The dog had simply laid down on the parquet floor and fallen asleep.

'Somewhere private?' asked Brooke.

There was a glass-box office (locked again) full of pigeonholes holding record books. The deep-seated hiss and percussion of the steam engines was a constant backdrop.

Hayle perched on a high laboratory stool.

'Did you know Basford, Ambrose and Mortimer?' asked Brooke.

'In passing. I live in the Lodge, when I'm in town. On occasion I join the residents for dinner. Well – the attic boys. That's what they called themselves. The older residents tend to eat earlier. Hardly see them. But the boys were fun. A drink afterwards. Cards.'

'For money?'

'Yes. They liked to gamble – those three were hooked. It's maths of course; Ambrose was a mathematician, Mortimer a physicist. They were good scientists – could have been. They were interested in my work – what I could tell them of it, of course. Fascinated, in fact. But yes – risk, a game of cards, dice, the dogs, they loved it in theory. They just didn't have the pennies to play for big stakes.

'Oddballs I suppose. I liked Bill Mortimer, as I said. Good brain. He didn't waste time lying around the pool. Basford was shy, wouldn't say boo. Historian, so not my cup of tea. Nice girlfriend – sweet child really. They got a lot of ribbing, of course. Wedding bells and all that. Jon Ambrose was a tragic case – skin disease. Made him dreadfully shy.'

'And Smith-Stanley?'

'Yes. Blood pressure problems – I think. But he didn't let it slow him down. Used to see him out and about running.' Hayle shook his head. 'And the army turned him down – idiots. He'd have made a fine officer.'

'They don't sound like hellraisers,' said Brooke.

'No. I think that's true. The other three were a handful – but those four, you're right. They were a bit more private, I suppose. Thoughtful even.'

'My job is to find out who killed at least three of them.'

'Indeed. I wish I could help. They left a year ago. Surely that's where the real story lies – next thing they turn up dead.'

'You were in Cambridge when they left?'

'Yes. One morning they just upped sticks. Settled their bill. Off they went. I know this much, Inspector – they had plans. One night, over a drink, they had maps out, Florida, Portugal, I think. They said they were planning a trip for when it's all over. A jolly.

'Maybe they struck lucky with the horses. Got a flight somewhere sunny. Half the British upper classes are overseas. We took a break from Washington – a flight to Miami. Place was crawling with them. Bold as brass. So much for "we're all in it together".'

'You didn't see them on their return?'

A shake of the head. 'I've been abroad for four months. I'm as baffled as you are, Inspector.'

'Did any of these young men have anything to do with the project you are engaged in with the Americans?'

'No. Absolutely not. I can't talk to you about it – so I don't think half a dozen students with a war to waste would qualify for an update, do you?'

It was a sharp reply, and Brooke felt the mask had slipped.

'You said there was interest in your work?'

'Oh – they showed interest. I brought Basford and his girlfriend out here. He said he wanted to see the steam engines. And Mortimer – certainly once, if not twice. But that's one of the beauties of pluralism. You can hide what you really do behind what people see you doing. I don't think they knew anything at all about my real work.'

'Is that why I'm here?' asked Brooke, with a smile. 'To divert me from somewhere else?'

It was an off-the-cuff remark, but Brooke knew immediately he'd revealed the truth.

'It's no reflection on you, Inspector,' said Hayle, smiling. 'My laboratory holds a great secret. You would be awestruck – that's the word, awestruck – to see it. Especially you, Inspector. One day, perhaps.'

It was a sinuous and ambiguous thing to say. Sneering, even. Brooke didn't like it. It reflected privilege and ego. He made a vow then, to see it for himself.

For now, he felt he should cut to the chase.

'The Laurels is a funk-hole,' he said.

'There isn't a law against it. We ask for ID cards, medical certificates. It's a hotel. I don't choose the guests. I do need the income – my work and putting food on the table aside, it's been in the family – my wife's – for nearly two hundred years. That means something, even today. And Brodie runs a tight ship.'

Brooke noted he'd now listed three different reasons for needing the cash that flowed from the Laurels: to keep the estate in the family, to put food on his plate, and to provide income for research.

'Does she run as tight a ship as Mr Brodie?'

Hayle's face hardened. 'He's a turf accountant.'

'He's a crook. There's little doubt in my mind that these three young men lost their lives because they became entangled with him.'

The dog's jaws clacked.

'I've met Brodie once or twice. Bit of a wheeler-dealer certainly. But murder? Is that what you think?'

'Someone killed them, sir. Poisoned by carbon dioxide.'

'Good God,' said Hayle, pressing his fingers to the bridge of his nose. 'What an appalling thing to do. I wouldn't give it to a rat.'

Hayle stepped closer.

'I understand you have a job to do, Inspector. So do I. I knew these young men. Nothing more. But if you think I can help at all, leave a message up at the Laurels. I promise I'll get back to you smartly.'

Brooke walked back along the dyke alone, the countryside running out in every direction to all horizons. He'd left Hayle testing drinking water samples and checking record books against the main's pressure. His verdict on Hayle was binary: on one hand he was competent, level-headed and clearly committed to a project which might help win the war. On the other hand, there was something devious about the man. And there was an ego, only barely contained. He was a player in a top-secret project which might win the war. But that didn't mean he hadn't got something else to hide.

CHAPTER TWENTY-EIGHT

By mid-afternoon Cambridge was sweltering with an intimation of an Indian summer. The pavements were hot, the shadows short, and Brooke was sleepy. He considered walking home and trying a swim in cool water as an antidote. Then, discouraged by the walk, he thought he might sleep – briefly – on the Nile bed. The train journey north, the car back, Hayle's summons to Fleam Dyke, had depleted his reserves of energy. But the real problem was that both his cases – the Vulcan Works and the Laurels – were were at a dead end. He could see no clear way forward.

He sought inspiration. He'd reached Trinity Street, and opposite St John's stopped in the narrow shade afforded by the School of Divinity. The facade was dominated by a line of statues, elevated, standing each in a niche. As a child his favourite had been that of Bishop Lightfoot. He'd been able, from an early age, to jump up and touch the prelate's pale, slippered right foot. Others must have followed suit because it was the only limb – on all six figures – which was not dark with coal dust and grime.

As a child, and a lonely one at that, he'd used the library at Newnham Croft to look at Lightfoot's life. All was lost to memory now, except one line of his philosophy: *I will not be discouraged by failure. I will not be elated by success.* It was a timely reminder of the ups and downs of detective work. He needed to plod on for a while: the lookout in Hawk Mill would bring further rewards if they were patient, and the answer to the riddle of the Vulcan Works was within reach, in the sense that it required no more detective work on his part, no action but rather the flash of inspiration. The key to that, in his experience, was to think of something else.

On Market Hill he found Rose back at her usual station at her counter, but in daylight, not moonlight. Stalls were out, the shade cool under the coloured awnings. The drabness of war was set aside for a few hours. A horse – gleaming chestnut – drank from the old fountain, and the graveyard of Great St Mary's was bristling with hollyhocks.

'You look dead on your feet,' said Rose.

She was right. Perhaps the Nile bed was the answer, if only for a moment of oblivion.

'That'll help,' said Rose, giving him a mug of tea.

'Who's doing the night shift?' he asked.

'The new hubby. Wants to learn the ropes – it's only 'til the end of the week. That's what he says. Can't come fast enough. It's overrated, sunlight.'

She came round to sit with him in the shade of St Mary's tower, a cigarette already between her lips, leaving one of the daughters to mind the shop.

'I asked about,' she said, nudging her chair closer to the table.

'About what?' said Brooke, taking one of her Pall Malls.

'Keep up, Inspector. About Brodie, of course. A lot of it's common knowledge – above board. 'Course there's plenty they don't say – but you can fill in the gaps. The trick was there right from the start. The Farm, Brooke. The Farm. It's not here. Not the Black Fens. North – a drive anyway. Maybe the North Level.'

The Fens, as Brooke had been taught by his father, in a lecture illustrated by a map which still hung in his old bedroom at Newnham Croft, lay in three levels: North, Middle and South. The North stretched to Lincoln, across the silty fields south-west of the Wash.

'He's a farmer?'

'You got it. Well, he owns a farm, runs a farm, although there's a manager, a real farmer, on the spot. And kennels – breeds dogs. When he comes down for the racing he's got a trailer, a few hands. Kids really, but old enough for the army – but they're not in it, are they?'

Brooke dutifully shook his head.

'Now we know why. The Farm. Reserved occupation. Not just him, but the lot. Ten, twenty, who knows. All sorts of accents – Liverpool, Manchester, Sheffield, Newcastle. All reserved. So they're free to go about their business. Which is up to no good.'

Brooke was shaking his head. 'Farms are under supervision, Rose. Regulated. Every area has a committee. War Ags, they call them. God knows why. There'll be one for this farm. They tell them what to grow, where to grow it, which fields to bring in off the fen. Milk quotas, pig quotas. You name it. And then they send round inspectors to check everything's by the book.'

Rose swirled her tea leaves around, and Brooke feared another bout of amateur fortune telling, which was her great passion, but nonetheless arrant nonsense.

But she had more facts to share, 'He's got people on the committee,' she said, smiling. 'My man said he had it all sown up. These War Ags – your committees – are run by all sorts, WI, NFU, local vicar. Dogsbodies. Think he can't pull wool over their eyes?

'He had a few drinks the last time after his dog won. You'd gone home by then. He said – this isn't first-hand, I heard it from someone who heard it, but I trust them. He said the War Ag wanted him to take girls off the Land Army but he sent them back – not strong enough. That was the line. And he won't have interns – Ities. Says there's no security out there, and the locals backed him up. Plus – and I heard this twice. He's chucked money at machinery. So he doesn't need the men, not all of them. So why's he got them?

'And it's not like round 'ere. It's not sugar beet and carrots. Its *pastoral*,' she said, proud of the word. 'So cows, sheep, pigs. You set it up – feed them, milk them, then you leave them, Brooke. Then what do all those strapping young men go about?

'There's millions of them on the land, Brooke. Think you can't hide a few gangsters in that lot? Think you can't hide a gang?'

'But no name for this farm?'

She shook her head, triangular earrings dancing.

'I can't push it. But I'm sure you can find it, Brooke. As I said – it's north. But away.'

He was left with his tea. He could find it, of course. They could drag Brodie in for an interview and get his basics: name, address, ID card. But then Brodie would know they were onto him, and he'd never find out the truth about the Laurels.

Then an idea came to him: in his mind's eye he saw a moonlit swim, across a mirror-like surface.

CHAPTER TWENTY-NINE

The Crossways Café, the Red Fox Inn, Bainbridge and the sign pointing to 'AIR' came and went. The nightmare trundled on. He was looking for the Morris Eight. He couldn't find it, couldn't catch it up. The anxiety of loss was acute. Another nightmare intruded: a game of 'find the lady' in an alleyway in Cairo. Three cups, a single silver penny, the threading sinuous hands of the trickster. The nightmares merged: in Richmond, in a Pennine rain shower, a Bedouin peasant sold goat skewers at the side of the road, and giant gourds. The Morris Eight appeared at last, at Bainbridge, tyres at the right pressure. But not one Morris Eight, an infinite line, all locomotive green, which is when he tried to scream . . .

He woke; the room was dark. He was lying on the Nile bed. Sleep was so rare he felt disorientated. As he stretched, his bones creaked. *I won't sleep tonight*, he thought, and felt a familiar joy at the prospect of being a creature of the night.

Downstairs at the duty desk, there was a Delphic note in his pigeonhole.

Hayle – progress. Usual hours

Peter

The 'usual hours' were all those between dusk and dawn.

The trees along St Andrew's Street were dark, rustling, chandeliers of leaf. Turning into the Downing Site, he paused to let his eyes get used to the night. There was a moon, but just a sickle, and so his eyes still struggled to see the path.

He found the nondescript alleyway, and the door under the broken light. He'd brought a torch, but still hurried through the deserted lecture hall, which seemed to hold the ghosts of students past. Clattering up the five flights of stairs, his footfall – amplified by the Blakeys – must have alerted his old friend, who was waiting on the landing, looking down, cigarette smoke like a halo round his stolid face.

'Just in time,' said Aldiss.

Brooke detected a note of suppressed excitement.

'You asked about Hayle,' he said, pinching out the cigarette, and producing an iron ring hung with keys. 'I'm sure he won't mind if we take a look.'

'Lead the way. I presume this is all legal?' said Brooke.

'You tell me, Brooke. I'm simply helping the police with their enquiries.'

Brooke saw it then. Aldiss's left hand carried plasters around two fingers, and as he led the way along the corridor there was a slight limp. A keen observer of gait, Brooke felt sure his friend was trying to conceal an injury. He wondered if Jo had spotted him out on the rooftops. Had he returned to his old sport, despite the threat of the bulldogs?

They dropped down the back stairs and out into the night.

Dimly, they could see the Gothic outline of the Sedgwick Museum.

'Hydrology's not exactly a hive of academic activity,' said his friend, walking on. 'It's a bit of a backwater in fact.'

Brooke let this joke fall flat.

'Where are we going?'

'They've given him a broom cupboard in Geography – of all places. Not far.'

It was dawning on Brooke that this didn't make sense.

'He's supposed to be embroiled in top-secret research, Peter. In a broom cupboard?'

'Maybe he's not as important as he thinks he is,' said Aldiss. 'Won't be the first academic to have airs and graces. Maybe he's desperate to get one rung higher than his peers. You know the old saw: why are academics so mean to each other? It's because there's so little at stake.'

They found an entranceway into the geography building, and a porter smoking steadily over a copy of the *Daily Express*.

Aldiss simply nodded, smiled, and they breezed past, exhibiting that great Cambridge lesson for life – look entitled, act entitled, and all doors will be open.

Once inside the building Aldiss turned on his torch, the beam held down, inadvertently revealing that he was wearing his old, weathered pumps – the favoured footwear of the night-climber, although many went barefoot. Brooke knew this to be proof absolute, because in the years they'd shared a staircase at Michaelhouse the pumps had always been set, neatly, beneath his friend's bedroom window.

Another corridor, and a short drop to the basement, and they were at a door marked: Dr C. W. Hayle: HYDROLOGY.

The door, swiftly unlocked, released a stale breath.

Inside, they could smell the dust.

The glass beakers, Bunsen burners, burettes, flasks – all were covered in a thin white deposit. In the sink Aldiss shone a light on a dead sparrow. Most of the lab was taken up by two large mechanical pumps – disassembled, chaotic. One wall was obscured by a series of augers, and then – in glass pipes – extracted samples of soil, including rock in the form of chalk, and grit.

'Bird's flown,' said Aldiss, running down the blinds and throwing the switch on the neon lights.

The glare revealed a deserted laboratory.

'He was in America for four months,' said Brooke. 'He's been back two days. The work is top secret, urgent. Why hasn't he returned to his lab?'

Aldiss ran a finger along the bench top.

'I'm no expert, but this is more than a few months' worth of dust. He's either got another lab at home? Or they've given him something bigger, grander, more secure. Or, third option, he's a fantasist.'

He pointed at the wall. There was a calendar, with the academic year set out. It was dated 1940. Handwritten notes filled dates at random intervals from early February to March – then nothing.

'Sorry for the wasted adventure,' said Aldiss.

'Adventures are never wasted,' said Brooke.

There was a long desk, papers covered in freehand arithmetic notation. There was a radio, and several Unity Football Pools forms, two filled in with predictions for the treble chance. Above was a framed picture of a greyhound with a stylishly printed title:

Boreas
Champion 200 yards.
Doncaster Gold Cup
1936

The dog was being proudly held at the collar by Hayle. A caption described him as the owner. Standing to the other side was Patrick Brodie, listed below as trainer.

'Hayle's still got the dog,' said Brooke. 'But he lied about its provenance. One lie can tell you a lot.'

'What do you think?' asked Aldiss, leading the way out, locking the door.

'I think he might be in cahoots with a very unpleasant group of young men. The question is – is he a loser, or a winner?'

'Exciting either way,' said Aldiss.

Back at his own lab he offered tea, a shot of malt, but Brooke couldn't shake off the drowsiness of sleep, and yearned for the therapeutic jolt of cold water.

He shook his friend's hand, and swinging his own foot tapped one of the toes of Aldiss's pumps.

'I take back what I said about adventures. They can end badly,' said Brooke. 'Is it really worth the risk?'

Aldiss had the good grace to blush.

The idea that he was night-climbing, risking a fine life for a midnight thrill, seemed to Brooke perverse, even immoral. It had always challenged the basis of their friendship.

'Life's dull,' said Aldiss, and Brooke glimpsed a darker side to the dedicated scientist; lonely perhaps, unfulfilled. Was he hiding in the dark, afraid of life in the light?

'Enjoy it while you can,' said Brooke. 'And if you're really bored, have another go at finding our friend's real laboratory. It's top secret – so there's a challenge.'

Tipping his hat, he walked away.

CHAPTER THIRTY

Brooke had a spare pair of swimming shorts in his office, and he took a towel from the toilet by Cell 5. Cramming both in a knapsack, he commandeered a bicycle from the Borough's garage and set out along Mill Road, away from Parker's Piece, out into Romsey Town and over the railway. A moonlit night now, so the little terrace streets of railworkers' houses were silvery, the only light spilling from corner pubs and a Methodist church, where a congregation was emerging into the night.

Romsey Town became Brookfields, and then the city petered out into allotments, the rail line to Newmarket crossing his path, as the lane cut through an embankment. Beyond, the bike freewheeling, he burst out into open country. Three lakes now filled the chalk pits dug for the cement works. The largest was the first, about 200 yards across. The moon etched a line of brilliant white light over its surface.

On the far side, a silhouette against the sky, he could see the main stand of the dog track, and the now redundant floodlights. In the middle of the lake was an island: a spoil heap, now colonised by elder and a willow.

He leant the bike against a lamp post, secured the lock and chain, and slipped down to the water's edge where there was a thin, chalky 'beach' – the water mark indicating the high tide of last winter.

He found a bush to change behind – a charge of indecent exposure would have been a blot on his record – and slipped into the water.

It always worked: head below the surface, the icy water seemed to reset his brain. A lurking headache was gone in a heartbeat. Clarity returned, his limbs were weightless, and he felt the sensory transformation of being embedded in water, not air.

He counted ninety-one crisp breaststrokes to landfall on the island, carefully moving into the shadow of the willow on his knees, before raising his head. Children had played Swallows and Amazons here; there was an old campfire, a pin and ring for mooring a boat, and a single damp copy of *Radio Fun*. A bedraggled flag had been attached to the willow, draped now in the water.

Brooke settled down to watch the shoreline by the greyhound track. There was a fire, in a brazier, which fitfully lit up Brodie's trailer. The trailer must have a registration plate. His plan was to get close enough to see it – and then get traffic to trace the owner's address, without risking spooking Brodie. This might provide a shortcut to tracking down the elusive 'farm'.

Around the flames he could see at least three other people, and two dogs on ropes, standing perfectly still.

Had the dogs heard him?

He settled, skin pressing down into twigs and last year's fallen leaves. The dogs, statues, peered into the night. There was the sound of a smashing bottle, a chorus of laughter, and one of the dogs folded itself down, the other following suit, the spell broken.

The moon drifted behind a shredded layer of cloud; Brooke slipped into the water and, on his back, feet paddling, swam blind for three minutes. When he dropped his legs, bobbing like a fisherman's float, he pivoted and saw that he was thirty yards off the far shore.

The talk – slurred, colloquial – was impossible to follow. But he caught words: 'shaft', 'lie low' and 'Boston' – twice. The problem was they were all drunk, and each seemed to have an impenetrable accent. Each guttural slur reached him in perfect condition, skating along the flat mirror-like surface of the pit. He recognised Brodie, and a young man beside him, standing with hands held over the fire. It was Harry Callaghan. More fragments: 'Boston' again. Then 'Shannon'. Then, as clear as crystal: 'too late' and 'Fleam Dyke'.

Then a formal shaking of hands in the firelight.

Brooke wondered if Callaghan had shared the contents of the white envelope retrieved from Boyle's shattered body. Or were they celebrating future paydays? And what was he to make of 'Shannon' and 'Boston' – was there an escape route in place? And then 'Fleam Dyke'. Was Hayle involved with the gang – possibly against his will?

He edged closer, hands and feet gently propelling him forward.

The trailer was parked beside a van with a stencilled sign painted on the side. It showed a pig, a sheep and a cow. Crude, but effective. Beyond that was another smaller lorry clearly marked 'Ministry of Labour'. And finally, Brodie's trailer.

He hadn't kept an eye on the sky and so the moonlight, when it flooded across the water, was a shock. He saw both dogs skitter to their feet, growling, and the distinct click-clack of a shotgun being primed.

He dropped like a stone. Suspended by the air left in his lungs, he looked up and saw the glittering surface of the water. Then an explosion: a stone falling, dropping with its tail of bubbles, ripples in circles, drawn in light. Then a rat saved him, swimming across the surface, a perfect wake behind.

He did a jackknife dive, flattened out, and set off at right angles to the shore. His lungs were bursting, so he focused on the time: counting seconds, which equalled yards. He set himself a target of thirty, but at twenty-five headed up, forcing himself to slow at the surface, to 'sip' at the air.

The dogs were barking, but the moon had gone. He was inshore, but in the shadows, twenty yards from the trailer.

The party was breaking up, and the van with the farmyard artwork was edging out past the trailer, which was side-on, so that the registration plate was obscured.

But that didn't matter, because the farm van had a plate:

NOD 59G

He memorised it, but only as a precaution, because the back doors of the van held all the information he needed:

Cold Christmas Farm
SLE 6754

CHAPTER THIRTY-ONE

Mrs Muir, Carnegie-Brown's secretary, appeared at his office door at just after nine o'clock. The chief inspector gave orders on paper, so dispatching her assistant to deliver orders was unprecedented. An upright woman, dressed in twinsets (never pearls), Mrs Muir ran the switchboard girls, but rarely fraternised. She went home for lunch and drank tea from a flask. Brooke detected a disapproving eye, a lofty indifference.

'Inspector. Upstairs – if you have a moment. The chief inspector has a visitor from Scotland Yard. Your presence is expected, sir.'

There had been a minute hesitation before the word 'sir', and a slight emphasis on the word 'chief'.

To drive home the point she lingered on the threshold, brushing a thread from her skirt, just below the knee.

Short of putting him in handcuffs, she couldn't have made her point more brutally. Power lay on the floor above. One day, it might fall to Brooke. He wondered how enthused Mrs Muir would be about *that*.

Brooke climbed the stairs as one to an execution, passing PC Turner in the corridor, whom he asked to ring the National Farmers' Union and get them an address for Cold Christmas Farm, near Sleaford.

'Pigs, cows, hens,' he said, as if this would help.

At the chief inspector's door he didn't knock. Carnegie-Brown was standing behind her desk.

'Ah, Brooke. Assistant Commissioner Sir James Cray,' she said. A man in a suit, broad-backed, was at the window smoking. Late fifties, a round boxer's head, no neck, laughter lines from his eyes, but no smile on his lips.

'Good of you, Inspector. Know you're busy. Just touching base,' he said. His voice betrayed a familiarity to cigarettes, or alcohol, or both.

Something was going on, or had gone on, and Brooke was clearly an outsider. He could speculate only that the subject of Carnegie-Brown's successor had been discussed. The decision might fall to Sir James, in which case this was the ritual 'laying on of hands'. The mystical notion persisted that those in power could instantly appraise a job applicant's virtues; an invitation to men of a clubbable disposition.

Brooke leant back against a filing cabinet, fishing for a Black Russian, while Sir James sat, or rather perched, on the window ledge. Carnegie-Brown, outmanoeuvred, simply subsided, inch by inch, into her captain's chair.

Brooke felt an almost overwhelming urge to misbehave. The problem with deliberately sabotaging his chances of the job was that someone else would get it.

'Sabotage?' said Sir James, and for a moment Brooke thought he could read minds.

He had grey eyes, and an unsettlingly direct gaze. The single word was a question, but he helpfully added another.

'Progress?'

'Sir. I've had a man undercover inside the factory. Sabotage only becomes apparent the day after an air raid. Our theory was that while the workforce is in the shelter the saboteur strikes. It was a good theory. The siren sounded the night before last. My man was in position in the factory while everyone else was in the shelter. The van was under surveillance from the testing of the periscopes, by the factory manager, to being driven away the next morning. We've checked the road journey already – I'm pretty sure nothing can happen en route. Examined at Barrow, the consignment had two faulty periscopes.'

Carnegie-Brown went to speak but Sir James cut in, 'Theories?'

Brooke managed to stop himself shrugging his shoulders.

'The obvious answer is the driver – Eva Mappin. But we really did shadow her every inch of the way last week, and the consignment arrived with two faulty periscopes. Which leaves Barrow,' said Brooke.

He was pretty sure the answer wasn't Barrow – but he felt he had to offer something.

'I checked security there myself. It seemed watertight, fittingly. But it's worth a double-check. It has to be possible because everything else is impossible.'

The deliberate echo of Conan Doyle brought the ghost of a smile to Sir James's lips.

'Is any part of your investigation still active, Inspector?'

Brooke looked at his watch. 'I'm seeing someone from the Ministry of Labour in an hour, sir. They cleared Mappin for the job at the Vulcan. I've asked for the security file. But she got the job – so it's hardly likely to contain any great surprises. I have one detective constable looking into her background – everything that won't be on the file. And as I say, I'll run through the procedure at Barrow one last time.

'And I'd planned to talk to the Vulcan's shadow factory – up on Tyneside. The owner is happy to run me through their procedures. He may have a theory. He'll know the process back to front. But it's difficult to see any cracks big enough to allow the saboteur to operate undetected.'

Brooke placed his shoes apart and pushed his shoulders back. 'I'm not hopeful. But we'll do our best.'

'Good. Carry on. I'll get one of my lads onto Barrow. We need to tread carefully. Sensitive souls, the Red Caps. Maybe it is this driver. Get her in for questioning?'

'Last resort, sir. I think there's every chance the contract may be terminated. If it is then we have nothing to lose. But while the consignments are going north, I'd like to leave her at the wheel.'

Sir James stood. 'Very good. I'll brief Mr Morrison.'

'Thank you, sir.'

'Priority, Brooke,' said Carnegie-Brown, rising, checking her watch. 'No distractions.'

'Indeed,' said Sir James. 'But these shelter deaths are

disturbing. This was brought to my attention . . .'

He produced a copy of the *Cambridge News* from his briefcase.

'The artwork's innovative. Good idea. Well done. Any joy?'

Carnegie-Brown nodded. 'Sir. Rapid developments. We now have three victims – first back two months ago. All former residents at a funk-hole out in the sticks. Looks like poison.'

Sir James lit a cigarette. 'Charming.'

'It's a vipers' nest, sir,' added Brooke.

Carnegie-Brown was still standing. 'If you'll excuse us, Brooke. We're expected at the Castle. Home Office briefing on juvenile crime. It's a plague.'

Sir James grabbed an overcoat.

'It's what's coming that scares me,' he said. 'Fathers in the forces, not enough coppers for the beat, not enough decent detectives, chaos on the streets – bombed-out cities, the blackout, the black market. Imagine what it will be like when these thugs grow up.'

Despite Carnegie-Brown's impatience to leave he offered Brooke a cigarette, then settled back down on the window ledge seat.

'Always instructive to look at real crimes, Brooke. Not statistics. I saw the charge sheet on this one. Bunch of kids in Stockwell, just south of The Oval, terrorised an old man, holed up in the last house standing in a bombed-out street. It would have been rubble but for a shoring squad; two beams set at an angle on the end wall, propping it all up. Kids broke in at night, then in broad daylight. Took his cash, pictures off the wall, food from the kitchen.

'There were five of them – ages from ten to fifteen. Junior

hoods. So the old man goes to the station and asks for help. Not unreasonable, even in the Blitz. They send round a constable who talks to some kids in the street. Lays down the law. But, sadly, he couldn't enforce the law. No time, no manpower.

'There's a raid that night and a few fire-bombs drop harmlessly in the ruins around the old man's house. In the morning the council sends a lorry round to clear rubble off the street. By the time they're done with the shovels it's lunchtime.

'There's a pub on the other side of the wasteland. Landlord chucks them out at three. They get in the cab of the lorry and drive off.

'Man at the wheel sees it all in his rear-view: the kids had tied a rope round his tow bar at the back and then round the wooden props holding the house up.

'It took them two days to find the body. That's what's in store if we don't deal with this menace. They're feral, Brooke – a generation. Gangs of the future. Gangs of the here-and-bloody-now.

'So that's one of our jobs at the Yard,' he said, setting a cap on his head. 'Know who told me the Stockwell story? Home Secretary. Born there, you see. Father was a police constable. Poor house, one of six children. They didn't run wild. Knows London. Loves London. Which makes my life a misery.'

Carnegie-Brown looked at her watch.

'Give us a minute, Jean,' Sir James said. 'I'll see you in the car.'

The chief inspector had just been ordered to quit her own office.

'One thing, Brooke,' he said, when they were alone. 'Your initial report on the Laurels mentioned the owner – Dr Hayle.

Charles Hayle? He's a person of interest. At the Yard, Downing Street. The Yanks too. Any developments in that direction, let me know. Immediately.'

Brooke opened the door. 'It would be a great help if I knew something of this project he's caught up with – Habakkuk?'

Sir James's face briefly registered astonishment. 'How the hell do you know the codename?'

'A university is a school for gossip.'

'Nothing else?'

'He's a hydrologist, so the surmise is it involves water and trying to win the war.'

Sir James smiled.

'Good. Let's leave it at that. The prime minister is a patron of this work – if I can put it like that. Hayle is a minor cog. But a cog nonetheless.

'Anything goes wrong at this end, the buck stops with me. So – if Hayle becomes of interest to *you*, ring me.

'It's Whitehall 1212 – but you'll know the number.'

CHAPTER THIRTY-TWO

Brooke, back in his office, felt a profound distaste for the politics of policing. He had a clear-cut view of humanity: there were villains, and there were honest people, living their lives. The idea that this world view needed to be mitigated by policy, by the passing fads of the age, made him despair. If he accepted promotion his career might soon be dominated by juggling the sensibilities of the Castle, with Scotland Yard, the chief constable, the local MPs, Whitehall, even Downing Street.

The mere thought made him feel the need to get back to straightforward coppering – so he picked up the phone and asked the switchboard for a Newcastle telephone number: the Walbottle Works, five miles west of Newcastle, a village in the lee of Hadrian's Wall, and, by the look of the Ordnance Survey map, the ruins of a Roman fort.

It was time the Vulcan's shadow factory came into the light.

The phone was picked up. 'Sorry, hold the line, love,' said a man's voice, thick with a Geordie accent. He was out of breath. 'Wakenshaw, here. Factory manager.'

Brooke said who he was, that he'd been cleared by the Ministry of War to make the call, and that they should have rung him in advance.

'Oh aye. We'd heard – you know – down t' grapevine as well. Common knowledge up 'ere.'

There was a muffled conversation and then Wakenshaw, clear again. 'Thanks, love.'

Then a slurp of tea, perhaps. 'We've had notification by letter an' all, 'cos if they have to shut Arbury down we'll get extra work. Which means we have to be ready. And we are. But chap from Whitehall said you'd have an update on that. That right?'

Brooke lit a cigarette. 'Yes. Sabotage, I'm afraid. So I just want to know, briefly, your MO, your modus operandi, Mr Wakenshaw. I thought there might be something I'm missing.'

He heard another slurp of tea.

'Like the dog that didn't bark?' said Wakenshaw.

Brooke, not for the first time, reminded himself not to underestimate anyone because of their accent. What had he assumed? That the broad Geordie dialect must indicate a poor education, or a sluggish mind.

'Indeed. So we're Holmes and Watson, Mr Wakenshaw. Tell me what I should be looking for.'

Wakenshaw was meticulous, smart, brief. The periscopes

were tested, what he called the 'crux of the matter', and then loaded in the van the night before the delivery. He was always present for the test, with one other licensed official. The works had three technical experts, all outsiders on retainer, who could do the job.

He was present at the loading, directly after the test. He then locked the van. The vehicle was left in the yard. He locked the yard, which had a twelve-foot-high wire fence. It wasn't twenty-four-hour production – there were two shifts, and the factory was closed between six at night and eight in the morning. But there was a night watchman.

'What about air raids?'

'Not regular. And rare in daylight. But if the siren goes out 'ere, we use the shelter in the village. Workforce is only eighty.'

'Anyone left on-site?'

'No. There's an ARP warden who keeps watch from outside in case of fire. I have a register of those on the shift and I take a roll call once we're all tucked up, like.'

'The van leaves for Barrow when?'

'Nine.'

'Police escort?'

'Not at all. They see us off. Yorkshire pick us up at Scotch Corner for a half-hour and that's it. No point in making a fuss. It's all organised by CID here on Grey Street. If you want to chat it through, it's Inspector Joyce. Bob Joyce.'

He gave Brooke the number.

'And you trust the driver?' asked Brooke.

'I've had me doubts over the years, but yes – I trust him.'

'Why so sure now?' asked Brooke.

''Cos it's me, Inspector. It's the only delivery we make of

finished goods where the transport and fuel are provided. It gets me out of the place. I live here. No – I do. Flat above paint shop. Wife's been dead ten years so what's the point of a house? It's my life, this place. And why employ a driver for one trip a week?'

'And you drive directly to Barrow?'

'Aye. It's 130 mile odd. Roads aren't great, and you never know what with the bombing if they'll be open, but I always make it by teatime. I stop over in Vickerstown – old mate, ex-navy, runs a doss house for labourers, and he's always got a spare room. Costs nowt. I'm back for me lunch next day.'

There was a pause for more tea sipping. 'Anything different?' asked Wakenshaw. 'Silent dogs, that kind of thing.'

'Not really. It's broadly the same. It takes them two days to deliver, of course, and the driver's a woman . . .'

'Bloody 'ell.'

'Good apparently. The manager signs off the tested goods if he's about – but otherwise he leaves it to the technical expert. He's an academic. Needless to say, the workforce has no idea sabotage is underway – or that we're trying to catch the bastard.'

Wakenshaw laughed. 'You reckon? I wouldn't put money on that, Inspector. Factory life is dull, gossip is fun, and it's free. They'll know something's up. Mark my words.'

Brooke sighed. He was probably right. 'Anyway, sir. I don't need to remind you . . .'

'Understood. Mind you, we have nowt to do with Cambridge directly. But I won't breathe a word. Let me know if you crack it, Inspector. If you don't I'll know soon enough – cos we'll have to double production.'

And then a dog barked. 'That's Banna,' he said.

'Another fort on the wall – like Walbottle?'

'Aye. That's it. And there's Bottle too – for Walbottle. You need dogs, Inspector, better than a lock and key any day.'

'There's no dog at the Vulcan,' said Brooke. 'Last one bit the postman.'

'Well, there you are then. That's where they've gone wrong.'

CHAPTER THIRTY-THREE

Opposite the Spinning House was the New Theatre – currently offering *Orchids & Onions*. Brooke hated musical theatre, but Claire and Joy had gone together and ever since had hummed forgettable tunes. Next door were the offices of the *Cambridge News* – with SHELTER DEATHS 'SUSPICIOUS' – POLICE sharing the billboards with FOOTBALL POOLS COUPONS INSIDE and STALIN STAYS IN MOSCOW DESPITE GERMAN ADVANCE.

Brooke, cowering under the brilliance of the late autumnal sunshine, passed swiftly by, making a conscious effort not to dwell on the news from Russia, and headed for the shade afforded by the wrought-iron arcading which formed the front porch of the University Arms – the name in gold-painted letters artfully entangled with the fretwork and glass.

Cambridge's smartest hotel stood on the corner of Parker's Piece, its hundred windows a permanent challenge to the management to adhere to blackout regulations. It was a thankless task. The hotel was fined on a regular basis for letting light spill out into the night.

Enveloped in the soft silence of luxury, Brooke stood for a second in the cool lobby, taking off the black lenses and retrieving the ochre from his inside pocket. Lunch was on the Ministry of Labour, which had promised sight of Eva Mappin's file. Not for the first time Brooke noted the cosseted lives of Whitehall's civil servants – even if they had been relocated into the wilderness of the Fens.

'Name of Keeble,' he said to the maître d' at the doors to the restaurant.

His host had chosen a table with a view of a cricket match underway on Parker's Piece, lacrosse in the distance, and finally schoolboy football in the far corner – all of which overlaid the oval, white-lined course of a 400-yard running track. It looked like the setting for a reborn Olympics – but for the six bomb shelters, and a small nest of army bell tents.

A window was open and the smell of freshly cut grass was hypnotic. Brooke thought that it might be the last cut before winter struck, which made the aroma all the more elegiac.

Eric Keeble, according to his card, was a civil servant based on Brooklands Avenue, a leafy suburban thoroughfare just beyond the Botanic Gardens, earmarked for Whitehall ministries if invasion necessitated a full-scale evacuation from London.

Several hundred pioneers of this plan were already in the city.

Keeble ordered a bottle of white wine, and two glasses of beer.

'I used to go home for lunch before all of this . . .' he said, gesturing at the interior of the restaurant, as if it represented a descent into barbarian standards.

'We've a house at Vauxhall,' he added. 'Now the family's there and I'm here. Blazing a trail. My wife will see more active service than I will. Blitz was beastly.'

Brooke sipped the beer. 'So your job is . . .'

'To find men, and women, for the services – key positions, engineers, wireless operators, drivers, medics, anything specialised. And, at the same time, secure the right people for the key factories in armaments, instrumentation, and so on. And we run background checks on the existing workforces. The Vulcan Works is in my purview. Someone in the office – a local – said I could trust the Borough, and especially Inspector Brooke. I'm here to help.'

He lit a cigarette, took a lungful, and swung his hand away with a brisk military action.

'Questions? You wanted background on the manager, I think, and a driver?'

Brooke took a further inch off his beer. 'Yes. Do you do the interviews?'

'Some. We've got people, locals again, who do the rounds. But I select a few, just to keep an eye on supply as it were, rather than always worrying about meeting demand. The "workforce", the national "workforce", is a strange animal. Women, COs, pensioners, the idle, tearaways. It's a nightmare, Brooke, but I accept not as dire a nightmare as an Atlantic convoy.'

Brooke liked him, so felt he could ask. 'Last lot?'

'Cairo. Flying yet another desk.'

For ten minutes they swapped their military careers, inevitably finding mutual friends. Keeble, it was clear, had been in military intelligence.

Eventually, as the wine was being uncorked, Keeble picked a set of files out of a leather satchel hung on the back of his chair.

'Right. Chubb first. Degree in metallurgy from Glasgow. Did research at Birmingham. Married, three boys – all in the services. Wife runs a branch of St John Ambulance. House at Milton – cycles into work. Born in Cambridge, so came back and got work as a lab technician. Worked his way up. No red flags at all. A bit dull, but very dependable.'

'Dr Ralph Stephens,' said Brooke, realising with a shock that the pea soup actually had peas in it.

'He's the periscope test man, am I right?'

'Yes. With Chubb.'

'Born in Edinburgh. Went to Fettes, so no lack of money. Degree at Cambridge in natural sciences. Fell in with Horace Darwin, the great man's youngest son, of course. He set up Pye – precision equipment for labs. Now radios and much else. Stephens invested in several small industrial start-ups. House off Trumpington Road. Wife died twenty years ago. Like most rich people, he drives a hard bargain. They needed a good name to sign off on the periscopes. They pay a retainer of two hundred pounds per annum. Sorry – guineas. Another trope of the rich.'

'I see,' said Brooke, leaning back, thinking yet again how valuable a university degree could be, especially with the imprimatur of Cambridge. Stephens got a decent annual income for a few hours' work every two weeks.

Brooke looked at his own notebook. 'Which leaves Mappin?'

'The driver? Let's see.'

The waiter went to pour the wine but Keeble intervened, clearly out of patience with the useless affectation of tasting the first glass.

'We can pour our own,' he said, dismissing the waiter. 'If this bottle was corked we'd all know it by now,' he continued, filling Brooke's glass. 'The rank smell would empty the room.'

He read for a few seconds. 'Yes. Born Sheffield, 1901. Father ran a cab company on Fargate, which is in the town centre. IIRC.'

Brooke smiled. It was extraordinary that you could hear something for the first time in your life on a Tuesday and then hear it again on Friday.

'Fully qualified on larger vehicles too. Clean licence – reliable. And to hand. Moved down last year to look after an aunt. Current address 16 McCord Close – just by the Jenny Wren public house. Husband stayed up north – he's got a chargehand job at Stanley Tools. The aunt's eighty-six – bedridden.'

'So they've got two decent wages between them?' said Brooke.

'Yes. She works five days on, two off. That was a condition of employment because she drives home to see her husband each week. Busman's holiday.'

They smoked in silence, awaiting their main courses.

'On paper she's a clean sheet,' said Keeble, eventually. 'Sorry. I had a look through all the files,' he added. 'I can't see anything untoward at the Vulcan. Is there something untoward?'

'Possibly. We just need to be sure we've done the obvious.

When I can spill the beans, I'll buy you lunch.'

'Right.' He refilled Brooke's glass. 'I was a bit surprised you hadn't asked to see me last week, actually.'

Keeble produced a copy of the *Cambridge News*.

'I rang into your switchboard. I expected a call back. Maybe I wasn't clear enough. I interviewed this chap Basford, do you see? The fatality from the Trinity Shelter. He wanted a job at the Vulcan Works. He came to our offices on Brooklands. It counts as war-work and that's his category. Poor eyesight – but that needn't be a bar to manual labour, or indeed repetitive production line work. Most of the able-bodied complain they could do it with their eyes shut.'

'Date?'

'24th August last year.'

The week before the attic boys checked out of the Laurels, thought Brooke. They'd had so many calls they'd simply noted any sightings older than a year, leaving time to track down more recent ones.

'An odd one, certainly,' said Keeble. 'I asked for his address and he gave me a residential hotel out in the sticks. Must have cost a few bob, I said. He said, "That's the problem. Can't afford it any more. Not just me. So a few of us are off."'

Keeble kept nodding as if recalling the exact moments of the interview.

'Sorry. I can reconstruct conversations. Old trick. Bloody useful in Cairo. He said they'd got a house, cheap, rented at Landbeach. They were after a quiet life.'

'Is that what he meant by "a few of us are off", do you think?'

'That's how I understood it, yes. It stuck in my mind particularly, because it felt . . . well, slightly dicey if you know what I mean. Like a moonlight flit. He was frightened – I could see that, and he wanted help but felt he couldn't spell it out.

'I've got a son, his age. They can be young for their age, not like the girls. They're grown up before you can blink.

'I wanted to help but he clammed up. I said Landbeach was out of the way. He said, "That's the idea. We're leaving under a bit of a cloud, but we're all paid up. Last supper this Friday. The food's good."

'His words, Brooke. "Last supper". Odd thing to say. I said something about the canteen at the Vulcan being A1 and offered him the job. Signed all the forms – never turned up.'

CHAPTER THIRTY-FOUR

A taxi – from the Market Hill rank – had arrived at the Laurels at noon and Edison – from his eyrie in Hawk Mill – saw Marcus Clifford, one of the attic boys, jump in the back carrying a small briefcase. The Wasp was hidden behind the barn, and by the time he'd got it on the road the cab was out of sight, but he'd built a career on not panicking and so simply assumed it must be headed for the railway station. Parking on the forecourt, he slipped a Borough Police permit under a windscreen wiper and showed his warrant card at the ticket barrier. He was just in time to see Clifford getting on a north-bound train to King's Lynn.

He'd no time to call the Spinning House but assumed, again,

that their destination was the seaport on the Wash, just fifty miles north. He sat tight in the next carriage to Clifford. They rattled out through railyards marred by several wayward bombing raids. At Abbey, where the Newmarket line swung away east, a nest of barrage balloons protected the railway bridge over the Cam, and Edison's allotment came into sight, its little steamboat hut marked out by a chimney from his potbelly stove. He took some pride – even at a distance of 200 yards – in the neat beanpoles, the espaliered apple tree, the nest of globe artichokes pointing at the sky like ack-ack guns. He felt a familiar pang of loss, for the quiet life, and a rest with his feet up.

Then the Black Fens opened out, the eye constantly drawn to an horizon which gave few rewards: the church tower at Waterbeach, James Watt's old steam pump engine at Streatham, and finally the Ship of the Fens itself – the great cathedral at Ely looking exactly as its makers intended, the city of heaven a mass of miniature spires, towers, walls, windows and gates. It was an illusion of course, but on such bright autumn days with fine-weather clouds, the cathedral seemed to set sail, leaving those stationary clouds in its wake.

He was lost in this thought as the train pulled out of Ely, only to see, with horror, Clifford, standing in the shadows by a cafe. Edison, with thirty years' experience in the job, thought it plain that he'd been deliberately wrong-footed. A guard, flagging the departure of the up-train, announced that the next down-train was for Soham, Bury St Edmunds, Norwich and Lowestoft.

Edison deserted his seat and stood by the doors, checking his watch, cursing assumption. Six minutes later he got out at Littleport and accosted the signalman, who let him use the railway's phone to speak to Cambridge, which in turn patched him through to the city exchange (directly opposite the Spinning House) and then to Brooke's office. The inspector had just returned from lunch. Edison gave a brief summary of events.

'I lost him, sir. At Ely. I'm pretty certain he knew I was following. I think he's headed east towards the coast. Lowestoft is the end of the line. It was a slow train due in at 3.32 p.m.'

Brooke, his mood soft after the beer and wine, considered the coincidence: Underhill, the Laurels' gardener, had stumbled on a map of Lowestoft by the hotel's pool, a cross marking the Dolphin Inn. According to the local police, the landlord of the inn was heavily involved in the black market for petrol. And Lowestoft was a port, of a different magnitude to Liverpool, but a port nonetheless. Patterns were emerging, if slowly.

'We'll pick you up outside Ely Station in half an hour,' said Brooke.

In the files he found a note on Edison's preliminary interview with Marcus Clifford at the Laurels. He was twenty-four. He'd been in Room 3 for eighteen months. His disability was hidden – a distinct heart murmur, resulting in periods of extreme fatigue and breathlessness. His lungs were also poor, rated category C. He'd been in the first year of a degree in history at Pembroke when war broke out. His home address was in Norwich – just twenty miles from Lowestoft, which provided another chiming detail with Callaghan, who'd been brought up a few miles from Liverpool. Was local knowledge key to the scam?

Brooke commandeered Radio Car 2 and PC Turner. They were in Ely at two thirty to pick up Edison, and despite encountering an entire battalion of army lorries heading for training in Thetford Forest, they passed Norwich just after four thirty, a few barrage balloons marking the winding course of the Wensum past riverside factories, and a looming sugar beet mill. Brooke had time to catch sight of the cathedral's great spire, almost lost in a hollow beyond the foursquare castle, before they set out on the arrow-straight road across the Broads. He recalled happier days hiring a boat on the maze of lakes and rivers, now deserted, except for a brief glimpse of an army patrol boat checking out the backwaters.

Before leaving Cambridge Brooke had spoken to his 'oppo' at Lowestoft. He'd given him a description of Clifford, his estimated time of arrival, and asked for discreet surveillance. He was told that a detective constable would wait for him opposite the Marina Theatre, 200 yards north of the Dolphin Inn.

They had the windows down and so Brooke smelt the sea before he saw it, a decent lungful of salty fresh air. Lowestoft was on the frontline, facing what had once been called the German Ocean. Britain's most easterly town had been bombarded in the Great War, and was now part-fishing port, part-naval base, its outer harbour bristling with the masts of trawlers. The beach was wired and studded with pillboxes. Ack-ack guns graced the end of the Claremont Pier. They had to show paperwork at two checkpoints before entering the town centre, which seemed to be populated entirely by men, and women, in uniform.

They left the radio car a street away and met the CID man – a detective constable called Patten – on the pavement. The Marina Theatre, a wedding cake of white stucco, pillars and onion domes, looked down-at-heel, the windows taped.

'We followed your man to the pub, Inspector,' said Patten.

'He's met someone inside – we're keeping well out of sight, but our lot know the landlord and had a chat on the blower. The guv'nor's a villain, but a local villain. They don't take to outsiders muscling in. He was happy to help: says Clifford's met a local man off the railways, and they're on their third pints already.'

They let him go and then they spread out: Turner going beyond the pub to a bench in a set of parched gardens, Edison slipping into the bar of the theatre, which gave views to the sea and along the esplanade, while Brooke waited in the shadowy doorway of an electrical shop which had a CLOSED sign hanging, the interior obscured by dust.

He didn't have to wait long. Clifford appeared, matching steps with his contact – a man about the same age and height, but of slightly heavier build. His fists hung from his arms like wrecking balls. A similar tour to the one endured by Callaghan in Liverpool now began, but at a much faster pace: a football ground, St Mary's – the town's main church – and finally a terraced street slightly inland.

Clifford's new friend used a key to enter 51 Yare Street. Ten minutes later a woman let them out, while two small children clung to her skirt.

The men walked back to the Marina and bought two tickets for the next showing of *Love on the Dole*, with Deborah Kerr and Clifford Evans. Brooke told Edison to stay in the bar while he bought a ticket for the circle. The theatre – converted to a cinema – was cavernous, and almost entirely empty; clearly the tale of poverty in the industrial north was not a winner in down-at-heel wartime Lowestoft. The main feature had yet to begin and so the lights were up and he could see the men below, sat side by side, talking.

The lights dimmed, the curtain went up, and this seemed the cue for Clifford to abruptly leave; there was the ghost of a handshake in the gloom, and Brooke was sure he saw a white envelope change hands.

Outside Brooke simply followed Edison, who was fifty yards behind their quarry. The sea was to their left, the beach cordoned off, bathing huts boarded up. Halfway to the horizon a fleet of trawlers sat at anchor. A minesweeper headed in on the tide towards the docks.

Brooke caught Edison up as Clifford reached the dock gates, where he turned sharp right towards a nondescript red-brick office block of three floors. As he climbed the steps he took off his hat and brushed a hand back, lifting the hair from his forehead.

A stencilled stone beam over the doors read MINISTRY OF LABOUR.

Brooke's brain folded several disparate images into one as a woman walked past with an old greyhound on a lead.

Brooke took out Eric Keeble's business card, which he'd pocketed at lunch.

Eric John Keeble
District Administrator
Eastern district

Ministry of Labour and National Service
Ironside House, Brooklands Avenue
CAM 78784

And then he had it. The solution to the mystery as mundane as ration books and bomb shelters.

But he wasn't sure, so he left Edison on watch outside and, after a two-minute interval, went inside. There was an anonymous counter manned by two men in suits, in front of which twin queues had formed. A board listed various departments: Fisheries and Food, Royal Naval Patrol Service, Lowestoft Depot.

But on the wall by the stairwell there was a botched poster, the letters written in jagged capitals.

ARMED FORCES MEDICAL BOARD

An arrow pointed left down a corridor.

REPORT TO THE NURSE

Did he need to see it with his own eyes?

At the end of the corridor there was another arrow to the left. A man sat at a desk, a clipboard in front of him with a list of typed names. As Brooke came round the corner he was hastily slipping a white envelope into his inside pocket.

Ahead there was a long corridor and a line of about twenty chairs. Clifford was in the last seat. Young men sat on all the other chairs. A nurse with a clipboard was moving down the line.

A door opened and a doctor came out in a white coat, stethoscope around his neck.

He lit a cigarette. 'Right. Who's next up for king and country?'

CHAPTER THIRTY-FIVE

They left Marcus Clifford in a cell at Lowestoft police station. The man he had tried to impersonate – the tenant of 51 Yare Street – was James Roland Butcher. The police file on Butcher was an inch thick and lay on Brooke's lap as Edison nosed the car through the centre of Bury St Edmunds, en route for Cambridge.

'Previous?' asked the sergeant.

'You could say that. Theft, breach of the peace, and illegal off-course bookmaking – Newmarket, Great Yarmouth, Fakenham. It's a mirror image of Boyle's CV from Liverpool, right down to being in a reserved occupation. This time it's the railways. Ticket collector at Norwich. But again, age was catching up on him. He's twenty-four – so less than a year and he'd be in a uniform.'

'Unless he could fail his medical,' said Edison.

'Which he was about to do,' said Brooke. 'Clifford's condition would have ruled out James Butcher from all military service. Butcher didn't have a medical history, no records or documents – just a birth certificate, like millions of others. And an ID card – which he gave to Clifford, because we found it in his wallet on arrest.'

Brooke watched the countryside slip by, an image assembling in his mind of Boyle's shattered body in Liverpool, Callaghan carefully returning something to his trouser pocket – an ID card surely, which he would have used at the next day's medical and then returned, but for the Luftmine.

After skirting Norwich, he took up Clifford's story again.

'The trip round Lowestoft was designed to get him up to speed in case the doctor asked questions. There's a bit of standard patter, most doctors use it to relax the patient, while they observe. But you don't want to botch the chit-chat. Same routine in Liverpool. Church, pub, work, family. And a bit of practice getting the local accent up to speed. That's where Clifford scored – born and brought up in Norwich.

'Butcher would have spent the war as an ARP warden or limping through civil works for the council. Which would have left him free to go on running a book or trading in the black market, as per usual.'

Lowestoft had made one further arrest. The clerk at his desk, supervising the arrivals for the medical, was also in a cell. He'd bolted, but Edison had grabbed him at the doors, the white envelope still bulging with £25 in one-pound notes. He was the middleman, in pole position to make sure the doctor, a GP from Cromer, or nurse, from the general hospital in Norwich, did not know Roland Butcher by sight.

Brooke, tired, closed his eyes. He saw the track at Coldham's Lane, the greyhounds speeding, the 'ringer' coming in first. This was the opposite. The 'ringer' was supposed to fail – fail the medical before slipping back into a life of civilian crime.

Night had fallen, and with headlamps swaddled, the road ahead was treacherous. Edison, slow and steady, pushed on westwards for home.

After thirty minutes of silence, in which they left Thetford Forest behind, and the final stretch to Cambridge lay ahead, Brooke finally spoke.

'I can see how you find the impostors – young men, a dull life, and presumably a decent cut of whatever it costs to take the marginal risk of discovery. But how do you find the men who, A, want to dodge the army, and B, are happy to risk getting caught. If your doppelganger is rumbled it's your name they've got. And you *are* fit for the army – which means spending the Duration in the Glasshouse at Colchester. Or worse – Catterick or Aldershot. They'd end up wishing they were facing a German bullet.'

Brooke lit a Black Russian.

'It's got to be Brodie,' he said. 'Or Brodie's the link and it goes further, wider. So far the two customers we've seen – Boyle in Liverpool, and Butcher here – were involved in illegal gambling. I think we need to raid Cold Christmas Farm, tomorrow at dawn. By then Suffolk should have got Clifford over to us. We'll get Brodie into the Spinning House – and the wife – and see who cracks first. My money's on the wife.'

They edged their way, finally, into Cambridge, and after

parking behind the Spinning House went straight to Brooke's office to divide up urgent duties.

Edison went to the Clarendon Arms, just across Parker's Piece, and filled a gallon tin jug with Ridley's Best Bitter. Brooke went to Rose's tea hut on Market Hill and ordered a brace of bacon sandwiches.

They ate and drank in Brooke's office.

The switchboard came through with a line for Brooke to a Liverpool number. It was the night watchman in the Walker Art Gallery. He confirmed that while currently housing the Ministry of Labour, one room – that once held the Pre-Raphaelite collection – was used three days a week by the Armed Forces Medical Board to carry out examinations, the results of which were used to determine conscription, or allocation to other duties, or to release a certificate of 'unfit for duty'. Brooke rang Inspector McGuire at the city's main police station and asked for copies of all ID cards held by staff working for the medical board to be sent south as soon as possible.

They set about organising operations. Brooke rang Lincoln and the Yard, while Edison got together manpower for a dawn raid at the Laurels, assisted by constables from the Castle.

Two hours later Brooke picked up a sandwich, while his sergeant, replete, settled with his beer. There was a long, satisfied silence, spoilt by Edison.

'But we still don't know who killed Basford, Ambrose and Mortimer.'

'No, Edison. We don't. But we do know the business they were mixed up in – of their own free will, remember. A lucrative business; one that they threatened to destroy. And who knows, Edison, how many other funk-holes might be involved. Think about it: how did Boyle in Liverpool, or Butcher in Lowestoft, know they could find a doppelganger – with a suitable medical issue – in Cambridge? If Mortimer, Basford and Ambrose threatened to blow the whistle, it's no wonder they're dead.'

CHAPTER THIRTY-SIX

Dawn: the sound of ducks on the river, even the trickle of the water itself, weaving through the flooded meadows. Brooke watched the light creep across the room as the sun rose over Coe Fen. The bedside clock read five-thirty. By now Operation Cold Christmas was, with luck, drawing to a close. He'd wanted to be there, but it wasn't his 'manor', and the Borough didn't have the manpower, even with back-up from the Castle. It was Lincoln's job – with Scotland Yard in the loop. A judge in Spalding had issued warrants at just before midnight.

Claire was asleep so he slid out of bed and tiptoed to his study, where he always laid out his clothes for the next day. He had time, so he put on his bathing shorts and a minute later –

he'd timed it often – he was in the river. He emptied his mind of all concerns and focused on breathing. At the 'hanging tree', the stump where Luke had stashed his cigarettes as a teenager, he did a tumble turn and raced back with the current.

Hauling himself out of the river, he found Ben was sitting in the front garden, cradling a mug of tea. Iris, who must have woken early, was lying at his feet on a blanket blissfully unaware that she was supposed to be learning to walk.

'Bravo,' said Ben.

'Your element, not mine,' said Brooke, letting himself drip-dry in the brisk morning air.

'Sea water's not so benign,' said Ben, and a shadow crossed his face.

Brooke sensed tension, or worse. He didn't have the time to stop and talk, but the boy was so self-contained, solitary, that he felt this might be his only chance.

'Not enjoying it any more?' he ventured. 'You couldn't get me on one of those things in dry-dock.'

Ben's eyes flooded. 'Sorry,' he said, trying to look anywhere but at his father-in-law. 'I've made a bit of a mess of things,' he added.

Brooke knelt down on the grass and sat on his heels.

Ben took a deep breath. 'Since the fire on *Silverfish* I've been on tenterhooks – spooked really. I had a bad turn last time out – passed out, clean away. The skipper didn't flinch, said it happens to everyone. But I'm not sure, sir. I might not go back. It's a volunteer service, so I can just put in for a transfer. Army maybe.'

Brooke knelt on the grass. 'Spoken to Joy?'

He nodded.

'Good lad. What did she say?'

'She said she wanted me back in one piece.'

'We've all got secret fears,' said Brooke. 'In the desert the Turks used the sun to try and make me talk. That's because they were afraid of the sun. They know what it can do. But I wasn't afraid of it. It was painful, a nightmare. But one I could endure. If they'd dug a hole and put me in a box under the sand, I'd have spilt the beans in a minute – less. We've all got an Achilles heel.'

'Thing is, I love the sea,' said Ben.

'Navy then.'

'I need to decide,' said Ben.

'Don't think too much,' said Brooke, standing. 'Tell her how you really feel. That's more important than logic.'

He was dressed, making tea in the kitchen, when he heard the sound of a car on gravel, and the unmistakable skid of the Wasp coming to an abrupt halt. Which meant Sergeant Edison was at the wheel, which meant something had gone wrong, for he was supposed to be supervising a contingent of constables from the Castle, tasked to secure the Laurels until the Lincoln raid was over.

The engine was still running, so Brooke simply climbed in on the passenger side.

'Holt rang the station, sir. He's got our man by all accounts. There was a siren last night, and there's a consignment ready to go. Given the Yard's interest I thought you'd want to see for yourself. PC Turner's gone out to the Laurels in one of the radio cars.'

Brooke lit up a cigarette. 'Good. Nothing more?'

'No, sir. Holt couldn't say much apparently, he was going to bang chummy up in one of the air raid shelters 'til we get there. Chubb's on his way in too.'

They hit fifty along the Backs, King's College Chapel a blur beyond the riverside trees.

'Lincoln?' asked Brooke.

'They went in at two apparently. Decided dawn gave them a decent chance of scarpering. They dropped Brodie off for us at five. He's in Cell 4, and Norfolk delivered Clifford overnight. I put him in Cell 3 – so he'll know we've got Brodie, and vice versa. I put a constable on a chair in the corridor so they can't cook anything up. Fifteen arrests at the farm – stolen goods mainly.

'A few surprises: Brodie had a trailer, but there was an office at the farm. Cash in a safe: five thousand in used tenners.'

'Good God,' said Brooke. 'A king's ransom.'

'And not just the farm. There's a big house – lord of the manor, that kind of thing. Rebuilt. Now a residential hotel – same deal as the Laurels, a few old-timers in the main rooms, second floor crammed with another set of lads, the halt and the lame.'

They went round Mitcham's Corner, the tyres screeching, a queue at the bus stop watching blankly.

'But the office at the farm was the thing, sir. Twenty typed letters ready to go – with maps. All addressed, so that's helpful. Funk-holes in Maidenhead, Devizes, Southend, Brighton, Accrington, Whitby. You name it, sir.'

Brooke lit up a Black Russian with satisfaction.

'A network based on gambling – dogs, horses, football – taps into anyone who wants to avoid the army in order to make the most of the rich pickings on the Home Front,' said Brooke.

'Then the funk-holes supply what's needed, to order. Right height, right accent, right age, plus a disability that suits the life you're impersonating. You can't have a dock worker turning up with a wooden leg. Or a teacher with a ghastly skin disorder. As long as the doctor doesn't know you from Adam, all you have to do is roughly match birthdate, religion, address. Pay someone on the inside to make sure there's no obvious cock-ups and the plan is pretty much foolproof. The only people who can't buy in are those with photographic ID cards – and given that's largely policemen and government officers, that hardly robs them of customers.'

Edison blithely ran the lights across Mill Road.

'Yard's sending a team up,' he said. 'But we've got Brodie to ourselves – for now.'

CHAPTER THIRTY-SEVEN

It was six-thirty when they reached the security gates at the Vulcan Works, edging through the crowd of workers ready for the first shift, while the night shift was heading home. They parked facing the vehicle bay. In the shadows they could see the Morris Eight – ready for its run north.

Holt met them before Edison had cut the engine.

'Let's keep this private. Chubb's office,' said Brooke, leading the way.

Mrs Bavidge, the secretary, was already at her post.

She unlocked the manager's office door and promised tea.

'Who is it?' asked Brooke, once they were alone but before any of them had sat down.

'Name's Arthur Benet,' said Holt. 'He's on the payroll – night watchman. If he was there last night, perhaps he's always been there, sir – perhaps he slips out the back door by the Elsan in the shelter?'

Brooke checked his watch. Where was Chubb?

Holt gave them a precis of events.

After the siren went off he'd patrolled the factory and found several indications that someone else had evaded the bomb shelter and was still in the building. A hint of cigarette smoke, a mug of warm tea, footsteps heard on the overhead gangway.

He'd been loath to break cover and make a direct challenge.

'To be honest, sir, I couldn't be sure it wasn't me mind playing tricks. Then I saw him – plain as a pikestaff in the radio shed. It were Benet. And he had all the keys o' course, so that's how he flitted about. But silent. Like up to no good.'

'Where is he?'

'Shelter 2. He cut up a bit rough, sir. Kept shouting that he'd done nowt wrong. I got the cuffs on him and took him outside. I thought it were best to try and keep it all quiet, like. I waited for the night shift to leave the shelter when the all-clear sounded and then took him out. I had the gun in the holster, so he knew there was no argument. He's cuffed to one of the iron rings they use for lanterns. He says it's all a misunderstanding.'

They left Edison to brief Chubb when he arrived, and set off for the shelter using the spiral staircase down from the flat roof of the office block. Holt had the watchman's ring of keys, so they unlocked the security gate, and finally Shelter 2.

Benet was sat on one of the side benches, his left arm hanging down from the iron lantern ring. He was holding a large mug of tea in his right hand and at his feet was an ashtray overspilling with stubs. He looked angry, bored, belligerent.

'Mr Benet,' said Brooke. 'I'm Detective Inspector Brooke. Care to tell me what you were up to in the factory when you should have been in here?'

'I told this idiot,' said Benet, and Brooke knew immediately he was going to tell the truth. The righteous indignation was palpable.

'Now you can tell me,' said Brooke, sitting down opposite the night watchman.

'It's your own fault,' said Benet. 'Nobody believed all that tosh about security checks. That girl of yours snooping about and Chubb having you up in the office for an hour.

'Eva's a good girl. She wouldn't say a thing. But the de Havilland driver who brings in the parts said the gossip was shoddy workmanship – here, in the factory.

'Well, that's a nonsense. Chubb's a cold fish but he runs a tight ship. We worked it out, didn't we? If the periscopes are faulty, and it's not us, then it's sabotage. And Eva's as honest as the day is long, so that meant sabotage in the factory. You lot were getting nowhere so we decided to keep watch – it is my job after all.'

'Who else was party to this?' said Brooke.

'Martins – the shelter warden, he fiddled the roll call. Everyone else turned a blind eye.'

'So, the entire workforce?'

'Pretty much.'

Brooke lit a cigarette.

'Let him free,' he said, and Holt unlocked the cuffs.

'I thought I'd got him too,' Benet said, nodding at Holt.

'Creeping round like that. I presume he's a copper?' he asked, massaging his hand. 'And I wouldn't mind a fag. I've been looking at an ashtray full of butts for an hour.'

Holt, showing admirable charity, gave him a cigarette and lit it.

'My detective sergeant is armed, you're lucky he isn't trigger-happy. He was well within his rights to shoot you on the spot.'

With that, Brooke left Holt with his prisoner and went back to Chubb's office. The shifts had changed. The manager, red-faced and out of breath, arrived clutching a briefcase and hat.

Tagging along with him was an officious-looking man in brown overalls.

'This is Lionel Martins,' said Chubb. 'He tells me he has a confession to make. Would anyone like to tell me what the hell's going on?'

Getting the truth out of Martins required no pressure. He was proud of it. His story matched Benet's. Edison was delegated to get statements from both, but they were free to go, although they must not leave Cambridge until given permission.

Brooke and Chubb were left alone.

'Arthur's been with us from the start, Inspector. Great War. George Medal.'

Brooke held up his hands in defeat.

Then the factory manager pushed a piece of paper across his desk.

'Ministry. Contract officially terminated – all production switched north. Last delivery leaves today. We'll survive, but for how long? Not the best advert in the business is it – we've got a saboteur in the factory but we can't find them.'

Chubb looked a beaten man.

'I rang Walbottle – the shadow factory. They deliver to Barrow the same day as you?' asked Brooke.

Chubb nodded, calling for tea from the secretary's office.

'Yup. 'Course they're much closer, so there's no overnight stay at Scotch Corner. They get to Barrow a bit later than we do, I think. Why?'

The secretary had left the door open so they heard a knock in the outside office, and then a woman's voice.

'That's Eva now,' said Chubb. 'All this kerfuffle has set the schedule back a bit.'

They heard Mappin ask for cash for fuel on the trip to Barrow and back.

Mrs Bavidge asked how she was, and her ailing aunt.

What she said was 'Same old, same old.'

And then the secretary, 'There you go, Eva. Good trip.'

'Ta. Might get a bit o' sunshine, eh? One last cuppa and I'll be off.'

And then she was gone. Brooke knew from the file that she was from Sheffield. But he was pretty certain that her accent, which had been strong, clear, characteristic, was not from the great Steel City.

He saw it then, plain and simple. The mystery of the Morris Eight solved in a second. The flood of relief, and satisfaction, was like a drug.

Chubb had a clean desk, but there were three ornaments: a framed photograph of a Mosquito, a silver cigarette box engraved with the university coat of arms, and two horseshoe-shaped magnets locked together north–south, south–north. One was etched with a P, one an C.

They waited for Mappin to trip down the stairs to the canteen.

Brooke picked up the magnets.

'Can I . . . ?' he said, picking up the phone with his other hand.

He put in a call to Newcastle police on Grey Street – he had the number in his notebook thanks to Wakenshaw at the Walbottle Works.

He asked the switchboard for Inspector Bob Joyce. The van for Barrow would be leaving the Walbottle Works at nine the next morning. Could the local constable note its number plate and colour? On no account was the manager of the works, the van's driver, to be alerted to the presence of the police.

Joyce had questions, but Brooke promised answers in twenty-four hours. Then he cut the call. 'Eva'll be in the canteen, now?'

Chubb nodded.

'Can you show me the Morris Eight.'

They slipped down the outside fire escape and across the yard into the vehicle bay.

Brooke showed Chubb the coupled magnets. 'These precious?'

'Not at all. I stick stuff to the filing cabinets with them. Ferrite – we did some of the chemistry for them at the lab in Birmingham. This was a leaving present – my initials.'

The magnets were extremely powerful, and so Brooke had to use all his strength to separate the two horseshoe halves.

Then he knelt down, reached under the van, and attached

one magnet to the frame just behind the rear left tyre, and then one behind the right.

He dusted grit off his hands.

'One piece of advice, Mr Chubb,' he said, straightening up. 'Don't dismantle the periscope production line just yet.'

CHAPTER THIRTY-EIGHT

They brought Clifford up in cuffs, betraying a shuffling walk Brooke had noted in Lowestoft, which made him seem a decade older than his twenty-four years. Fair hair, thick and unruly, with a face apparently reflecting rude good health: almost rosy cheeks, and full lips. His eyes, grey, shone. But sitting down he had the slightly crouched body shape of the chronically ill, the shoulders forward, chin down.

'They let Brodie smoke,' he said, before a question was asked. 'I shouldn't breathe the fumes.'

He eyed Brooke's desk ashtray, a tin boat made by Luke at school.

'Your exemption from military service cites heart defects,

Mr Clifford.'

'I suffer from asthma too – they didn't bother with it at the medical because the heart's so weak,' he said.

Brooke opened the window but left the blinds down.

They'd discussed the order in which to interview their prisoners. Most importantly, they'd focused on *why* they wanted to interview them. The Yard would squeeze every last detail out of Clifford and Brodie about the Laurels, The Farm, the wider network. It was an inquiry which might involve every major constabulary in the country.

But the Borough's concern was the three murders in Cambridge. Who had killed Mortimer, Ambrose and Basford? And why?

The strategy was to interview Clifford about his trip to Lowestoft, then switch back to the Laurels, and the four attic boys who'd left a year earlier.

Edison went to get tea.

Brooke, annoyed he couldn't smoke, ran out of patience.

'Was it worth it?' he asked, putting on the blotter the envelope Clifford had been handed in the Marina Theare. 'Fifty quid in pound notes? Have you any idea how a judge will view this crime? There are young men dying, Marcus – right now, on ships, in submarines, on raids into Norway or France. And you'll be standing there in the dock. You can't fight. But you didn't have to help others duck their duty – did you?'

Clifford looked as if he'd planned to stonewall with 'no comment', but his resolve ebbed. 'I didn't see the harm,' he said, looking at his shoes.

When he did look up, his grey luminous eyes spilt tears.

Edison appeared with mugs of tea. Clifford, whose spirit

appeared broken, looked pathetically grateful.

In ten minutes they had the entire operation mapped out. The attic boys had been recruited after failing their own medicals. The Cambridge medical board had a spy within. No name, but they'd come back to that once they'd laid charges. The offer was made by Patrick Brodie: £20 a month, plus full board and £50 per 'satisfied customer'. Brodie, presumably, collected a fee directly from the 'client' long before the day of the medical. There had been seven of them at the start – plus the 'conchie' in Number 8. Mrs Brodie ran the Laurels, and clearly knew the set-up, but never got involved. After the initial meeting with Brodie, at the trailer on Coldham's Lane, all communication was via the postmarked letters from Sleaford. He knew nothing about the funk-hole at the farm, or any other funk-hole run by Brodie.

'The twenty pounds was doled out by Callaghan?' asked Brooke.

Clifford nodded. Brooke made a mental note to chase the bank and find out where the money came from. He'd been promised the details in twenty-four hours. Did the trail lead to Brodie, or beyond?

'Basford, Ambrose, Mortimer. What can you tell us about them?' asked Brooke.

Clifford painted a vivid picture. They were 'oddballs'; unlike the other attic boys, they actually needed the money and saved what they didn't spend, avoiding the high life in town.

'And then they just left like that, no explanation?'

Clifford laughed, shaking his head. 'They wanted out, see? They didn't give a toss about where to. Just not here. All very moral about it – but they still took the cash until they went.

Smug, the lot of them. Bleeding hearts, that's the truth of it. They'd all lost someone – Basford's uncle I think, in the RAF over the Channel. Ambrose had a brother, drowned at Dunkirk trying to get to one of the small boats. Can't remember Mortimer's little tragedy – but they all chimed in. Smith-Stanley was a communist I reckon – said we were allies now with Stalin. Every man who could fight should fight to bring down the Fascists. Made you sick to listen to it.

'But, like I say, they'd been happy to take the cash at the start. Once they'd filled their pockets they had time for a conscience.

'When they did go, it wasn't popular with the Brodies. I got the impression – we all did – that they were told to stay put and shut up, but they wanted out, so they went.'

'Where do you think they went?'

He shrugged. 'Brodie said he had contacts, Liverpool, Dublin. That they'd be on a beach somewhere and that meant they'd keep their mouths shut.'

'We know for a fact that they actually had plans to stay in Cambridge,' said Brooke.

'Not after a chat with Brodie they didn't.'

'Were they scared of the Brodies?'

'Mr Brodie. The wife runs errands. She's a housekeeper. Brodie had friends – friends you wouldn't want to upset. We all went to the dogs. Lost money of course. But we didn't care much. Basford and the rest went once or twice – then never. But you know, you could see the people Brodie was with. Low life.'

Brooke let that hang in the air for a moment.

'Did they say they were in danger?' he asked, finally.

'The last night at dinner, they'd told Mrs Brodie they were

off when she brought in the soup. Then Brodie turned up by the time the pie was on the table. We wolfed it down and tripped off to the Hole in the Wall. Left them to it. Got back late – lights out. I heard them go next day. Never saw them again.'

Brooke got up and feathered the blinds, letting sunlight fall in strips over the desk and Clifford's shoes. They could hear birdsong from Downing's lawns and trees.

'One more question for now. Why did you, and Callaghan for that matter, keep your appointments in Liverpool and Lowestoft when you knew there was a murder investigation, and that we were particularly interested in the Laurels?'

'Brodie said we had to go. He's not the boss really – there's bigger fish, Lincoln, Sheffield, Norwich. They'd already taken the money off the "clients" – they always called them that. Like it was respectable. Our fee, which we collected, was chicken feed to what they paid. Brodie said we could lie low once we'd cleared our jobs. I don't think he let on, you know, to the real bosses. It had to be business as normal. And anyway, he said they couldn't lay a hand on us for the missing attic boys. They'd walked out a year ago – and that was that.

'What do you think I'll get?' he asked, at last, looking at Edison, then Brooke.

'Magistrates, judges, they don't like conspiracy. It undermines justice, and the state. A lot will depend on you – the degree to which you can help us,' said Brooke.

In truth, Clifford would be extremely lucky to find himself in any court. The idea there'd be a public gallery, or the press, was fanciful. It was a case destined to be heard *in camera*. Making the story public would constitute a blow to public morale. And an invitation to others.

Clifford bit his lip.

'Jonny – Jonathan Ambrose, we used to play chess. He'd been a schoolboy champion. He was good. I played at Repton. It used up the hours at the Laurels. He said it wasn't right – what we were doing. The boys we were standing in for had a duty to serve. We didn't have a choice. They did. He said it was wrong. So, when they did leave, the four of them, he said they were going to tip off the police. The Spinning House. He said I should come with them.'

His head dropped.

'Did you tell the others?' said Brooke.

He shook his head. 'No. I told Brodie.'

CHAPTER THIRTY-NINE

Mrs Brodie met them under the *porte cochère* of the Laurels. Brooke, hauling himself out of the Wasp, thought that the gravel drive made a stealthy arrival impossible: footsteps, car tyres, even a bicycle's approach – all would be betrayed.

The Castle's paddy wagon was parked up in the shade, and PC Turner was standing at attention to one side of the front door, under the trailing ivy. The hotel was locked down, but the general atmosphere was still rather sleepy.

'Where is my husband?' asked Brodie. She wore cleaning gloves and an apron, a model housekeeper. 'And why are these policemen here? Why can't we leave? It's a free country.'

'It's our job to make sure it stays that way, Mrs Brodie,' said

Brooke, tipping his hat. 'My sergeant and the detective constable need to caution Callaghan and Tudor. They will accompany us back to the Spinning House.'

'And my husband?'

'We'll talk about that – inside, perhaps? The dining room would be a good place to start. Do lead the way.'

The room had been set for dinner. It looked like the captain's table on the *Marie Celeste*. Neat, spartan even, but the cutlery caught the light, and a marble centrepiece, in the shape of Britannia, gave it a hint of luxury.

'On the night before Basford, Ambrose, Mortimer, and Smith-Stanley checked out they announced their intention to go, just after the soup course, I understand. Do you serve dinner?'

She'd expected questions about the farm, the funk-hole, the scam. Brooke could see her sudden alarm.

'A girl comes in from the village. I can give you an address. Maisie Trinder. And Cook lives in the village too – she'd be in the kitchen. If I can, I serve the meal and let Maisie help cook. It's a good way to check everyone is happy. No complaints brewing.'

'That night?'

'Possibly.'

'We'll have this discussion again, Mrs Brodie. Under caution. Tomorrow. So I'd think carefully about sticking to the truth.'

'I served the meal that last night,' she said.

'One of the attic boys told us your husband turned up by the time the main course was served. Did you ring him? He was clearly concerned anyone might be leaving the Laurels. Given what we have discovered at Cold Christmas Farm, it is pretty clear why he'd be worried.'

'I rang him. I thought he should know.'

'What you may not know, Mrs Brodie, is that he'd been told, by Marcus Clifford, that the four of them – Basford, Ambrose, Mortimer and Smith-Stanley – planned to inform the police of the Laurels' part in an illegal network of personation, designed to allow perfectly able young men to dodge military service.'

Mrs Brodie opted for silence.

'I think your husband confronted them that night. They had plans to stay in Cambridge, plans to go the police. Secret plans. I think he bought them off. Or he scared them off. I think there was a deal: their silence in return for a trip to the sun.

'But they came back – didn't they? So your husband killed them, then dumped the bodies.'

They heard a dog's claws clacking on the tiles in the hallway, and the door swung open to admit Rochester.

'Where is my husband?' she said, like an incantation.

'In a cell at the Spinning House. I'll be interviewing him later. I have to tell you his liberty is in doubt. It may be in doubt for several years, if not decades.'

The greyhound placed a paw on her shoe. She pulled out a dining chair and sat down.

Brooke lit a cigarette; the window behind him – open – served as an ashtray.

Mrs Brodie was pale, and Brooke thought she'd caught sight of the future.

'He's not a bad man,' she said.

'Good men do bad things,' countered Brooke.

She nodded at that. 'I met Pat at a kennels in Limerick,' she said, a hand now on Rochester's head. 'This would be '35, '36. I was daft on dogs. It was all I wanted. He's off a farm, always had a dog at his heels. So that was the dream – I'd have a kennels to run. We'd breed them to race – greyhounds, whippets.

'His dream is to be free of other people. Free of being told what to do, what not to do, where to be. Money's the key. So – bookmaker. There's been temptations, Mr Brooke. But he's no killer. I'll tell you that – I'll tell you that under caution.'

'Limerick?' asked Brooke. 'So – Shannon airport just up the road. Was that it? What did he promise the four of them, in return for their silence? A holiday, a trip away? Shannon, then Lisbon, or Boston?

'Then they came back – not all together I think, but one at a time. What did they want, Mrs Brodie?

'Whatever it was, they didn't live long. Three dead: 31st July, 8th October, 12th October. Is that by way of mitigation, Mrs Brodie, that they were killed by a good man?'

Brodie smiled. It was the least anxious he'd seen her since their first visit. He didn't like the look of that smile.

She produced a set of keys on a chain and led Brooke to the office off the kitchen. There was a safe, which she swiftly opened, producing a pair of passports, placing them on the plain deal table in the kitchen.

'Citizen of Ireland,' she said, passing the green one to Brooke, with its golden Irish harp on the cover. 'Paperwork's in order. They're stamped for entry and exit.'

The passport was dog-eared, the stamps revealing regular trips across the water.

'Pat runs a book at Leopardstown, Limerick, Greenpark. It's his business.'

Brooke got to the last page: the entry stamp at Dun Laoghaire, the port for Dublin, was 28th July, the exit 13th October.

He couldn't be the killer.

CHAPTER FORTY

Cell Number 4 was the only one in the Spinning House to have a narrow, glazed grating into a short shaft which led up to the pavement on St Andrew's. It was the cell Brooke always chose – if vacant – when he was at work but knew that a deep sleep was about to descend, not just a nap on the Nile bed. The final trigger to a loss of consciousness in this cell was the gentle footfall from above, a distant echo of conversation, a horse plodding by, a news-seller opposite outside Kett's offices, calling out that day's headline.

Brodie lay on the bunk. Brooke took the stool and left the door open, telling the duty sergeant he'd be fine, and offering the prisoner a Black Russian.

They smoked, listening to the sergeant taking the slow stone steps back to the front desk.

Clifford had been allowed out into the station yard – still cuffed but free to walk the wheel, on the grounds, Brooke felt, that he might as well get used to prison routines. Callaghan and Tudor were giving formal statements to Sergeant Edison upstairs.

'Here's a funny story,' said Brodie, the accent west coast Irish, soft and sinuous. It was odd that a man incarcerated, and facing a lifetime in prison, could still radiate a sense of calm violence. He seemed entirely at home, as if Brooke were the prisoner.

'I volunteered. For king and country. We were here, in the Fens, trying to make a go of the kennels. But no luck. I needed a job. I needed money. You were taking the Irish for the army by then. Here, in Cambridge. Army Medical Board in the Guildhall. Turned me down – lungs are weak apparently, though I never noticed.'

Brodie gave him a cold stare. He had small, dead brown eyes.

'Was that where you got the idea to provide doubles so men could duck their duty?'

'That's it,' he said. 'If they'd let me in, we wouldn't be here. See – that's irony. And the result was a nice little business to see out the Duration.'

He laughed at the notion.

Brooke's stool grated on the limestone floor. 'You'll go down.'

'I'll serve my time,' he said. 'Maybe it'll all be over when I get out.'

'They'll look after Mrs Brodie, will they?'

Again, the cold stare.

'Lincoln will want you back. Then the Yard will be keen to know about your associates. You won't tell them. You'll go to gaol. They'll play fair when you get out. Bleak, but it could be worse.'

Brodie was nodding.

'I didn't finish my story, Inspector. So I couldn't join up. Then the government closed down the racecourses, then the football, then the dogs. Do-gooders. Churches. Bleedin' hearts. I just needed to earn a few bob. That's why we came over in the first place.

'Not sure who got hurt, you know? The boys got paid, a few scallywags got to sit out the war at home. No danger in that, 'cos there's no proper coppers about and the ones you do see are the halt and the lame. Nothing personal. What's the glasses for?'

Brooke took off the ochre set. 'You're happy with that, then? Ten years. Maybe fifteen.' He lit a fresh cigarette. 'Problem is, that's not what's going to happen. I think you killed those boys when they came back to Cambridge. Not with your own hands – I'll give you that. But your orders. And you'll hang for that.'

Brodie let a heartbeat pass.

'Wasn't in the country, Inspector. Check the passport.'

Brooke ignored him. 'When the boys, the four of them, said they wanted out, you got up to the Laurels pretty fast. Clifford told you they were coming to us. That they'd hand you in. What did you do?'

Brodie shook his head.

'I told them – you turn up pointing fingers, the first thing they'll want to know is what did *you* do? I said – you'll get promises. Soft treatment, a nod to the magistrate, or a judge. Wouldn't wash – never does.

'That made them think twice. They were going down if I went down. I told them to bugger off. Don't come back.'

'You helped them on their way?'

'Sure. I've got contacts in Liverpool, Dublin. A bit of paperwork and some tickets and they were on their own. No idea where they ended up.'

'But they came back.'

'You tell me. I never saw them. Isn't me. Can't be me, can it?'

Brooke stood. 'I think they came back here and threatened to go to the police unless someone paid up. You didn't pay up, did you? I think you killed them – or as good as. You run the gang – the gang killed them. All we need to do is get someone to tell us where the orders came from, and the cash. Conspiracy to murder. There's a rope for that too.'

Brodie lay back on his cot and closed his eyes.

Brooke knew it wasn't enough. Brodie would be 'looked after', his wife payrolled until he got out. Then a nice nest egg to start again. The killers would get a pay-off too – but only if they kept quiet.

He stood, determined to ruin Brodie's sleep.

'But you'll want to know what's going to happen next. The Yard. Probably tonight. I promised your wife I'd pass on any messages. She'll get to visit – maybe the Scrubs. Message?'

Brodie looked at the ceiling. 'Tell her to look after the dog.'

CHAPTER FORTY-ONE

The duty sergeant had an envelope ready for Brooke as he came up from the cells. It was marked in a neat copperplate:

FOSTER'S BANK.

'A Mr Wilson, sir. Dreadfully apologetic. He'd been ill and your enquiry was set aside. He hopes it isn't too late. He advised immediate action, sir, but wouldn't elaborate.'

Brooke took the steps two at a time to his office, dropped the blinds and discarded his glasses, switching on the low beam of the desk light.

There was a written note inside the envelope attached to a typed summary of transactions into, and out of, the current account of Henry Francis Callaghan.

Eden.

Apologies. As you will see, Callaghan's account was credited monthly by a series of deposits transferred from the savings account of Dr Charles Watt Hayle. Hayle has an account with us too. Anticipating your next request, and given your assurance this is information required in pursuit of criminal activity, I can add that Hayle's current account benefits from a monthly deposit by cheque at the Sidney Street branch. The cheque is in the name of Cold Christmas Farm Ltd. The amount exactly matches the withdrawal by Callaghan.

So – money goes into Hayle's account, only to be paid out to Callaghan. The hallmarks of what we would call 'cleaning' – a banking practice for 2,000 years. The problem is much worse in the US, largely thanks to Mr Capone.

Hope this helps.
Arthur.

Give our best to Claire.

Brooke pocketed the letter, found Edison distributing leeks to the switchboard girls, and set off for the garage. The Wasp had been given a clean, which seemed to add to its speed as they set out towards the chalk hills and the Laurels.

The Hawk Mill surveillance had been terminated, but replaced by two constables from the Castle barring the gates of the Laurels.

Brooke showed his warrant card and asked Edison to edge

the Wasp under one of the great cedar trees by the boundary wall.

The Lodge, Hayle's residence, was dimly visible beyond a hedge and a small orchard of pear trees. It was a miniature Georgian gatehouse: two floors, white stucco, a green door – ajar.

Brooke knocked.

'What?' The voice came from deep within.

They found Hayle up the short stairs in a study behind a desk. Books, half open, were spread out, several packing cases full of papers.

Brooke thought he looked diminished, older certainly, and his shoulders slumped at the sight of the Borough. The house was dusty, unlived-in, even ramshackle. Through a door they could see a bedroom, the mattress bare, the window without curtains.

'Home sweet home,' said Brooke.

'Inspector. I am busy. This will have to wait.'

Brooke took off his hat and studied the spines of several books: hydrology certainly, fluid mechanics, biochemistry, a study of the Amazon river basin.

'Who pays £520 into your account each month? I ask because Callaghan, one of the attic boys, drew it out promptly a few days later. Every month. I'm pretty certain it was Mr Brodie. Given the size of the deposit, a swift ID parade at Foster's Bank should settle the matter. Bank tellers have excellent memories.'

Hayle was thinking. Those dancing eyes were fixed now on Brooke. They heard the clatter of claws and Boreas appeared from the bedroom, his great head a burden, carried on a drooping neck.

'My sergeant would like to look around, sir. I can get a warrant.'

Hayle held a hand up by way of permission. Edison set off – finding a further short staircase to the attic.

'I owed Brodie money,' said Hayle. 'The dogs. A weakness nurtured. Several thousand pounds by the time the war started. I had shares in one or two animals – they didn't pay out. I needed the monthly cash from the hotel, so he agreed to keep paying despite the debt. In return I set up an account at Foster's. The money goes in. I make a cheque out to Callaghan to withdraw. He said he couldn't do it because of regulations on Irish citizenship. It's a tax issue – he said it was above board. I didn't ask questions. I have no idea where the money came from, or what Callaghan did with it subsequently.'

Brooke looked out the window and saw the distant attic dormers of the Laurels.

'That may – just – keep you out of prison,' he said, as Edison descended the stairs and carried on down to the ground floor. As he passed the door, he brushed dust from his fingers and jacket.

Hayle held his hands together, head down, and Brooke felt for the first time the focused energy of the obsessed.

'The work – my work – is of the utmost importance, Inspector. The income from the Laurels goes almost exclusively into my research. Mr Churchill has – is – taking a personal interest. So's the White House. I don't think I'm going to court, do you?'

'Project Habakkuk?'

'I'd be careful with that information, if I were you,' said Hayle. He leant forward, hands extended now as if indicating the width of an invisible object. 'I really cannot say anything, Brooke. The work is top secret.'

Brooke was increasingly aware of Hayle's powers of persuasion and narrative. He'd make a first-class con artist. He wondered how big his betting debts really were. Which made him consider how damaging to Hayle it would have been if Basford, Ambrose and Mortimer had rung the Spinning House. the Laurels would have closed, and presumably Hayle's debts would be collected by Brodie's henchmen. Hayle's reputation would have been dirt, and his place in the Habakkuk project forfeit.

'Sir?' Edison's voice floated up from below.

There was a back room with French windows, but little light thanks to heavy curtains, and a large card table – round – covered in a baize cloth. There were several packs of cards, one of which had been splayed out in the shape of a fan. Brooke ran a finger along the cloth: it was thick with dust.

There were eight chairs.

'Who do you play?' asked Brooke.

'Friends.'

'How about Basford, Ambrose and Mortimer?'

Hayle took the lid off a wooden box on the table to reveal matchsticks.

'High stakes, Brooke. Yes – they played. The rest were a bit fast, if you know what I mean. Preferred the high life. But those three, and Smith-Stanley, just wanted to be left alone. So, yes. We played. Cribbage, usually. And a drink. Why not?'

'On 31st August last year, they all checked out of the hotel. Did you play cards the night before?'

Hayle held out his hands, palms up. 'I have a decent brain,

Brooke. Memory isn't in the same class. I've no idea.'

'That night Mr Brodie was informed that these three young men – and a fourth still missing – had decided to leave, and that they were determined to inform the police of various illegal activities. Did you help Brodie try to persuade them otherwise? Did you connive with him to get them out of the country? A funk-hole in the sun in return for silence?'

'No. As I have said, I have no idea how Brodie makes his money.'

'You left for the United States shortly afterwards I think?'

'What's that got to do with anything? Someone killed them here, Brooke – in the city. I was in Washington for the entire period. I'd look closer to home.'

'And you never saw them again – not here, not in the US?'

'Certainly not.'

'We'll need a statement,' said Brooke. 'On the bank account issues. The station will be in touch. We will almost certainly need to speak again. You don't appear to live here?'

'I have a flat in town – handy for the laboratory. The work is intense. I also need a transatlantic telephone link. This is provided by the exchange on St Andrew's. I am here, packing some papers, because the work will transfer soon, probably to Halifax.'

'Nova Scotia?'

'Yes. Not Yorkshire. Well done.'

It was an ill-judged jibe.

Brooke got out his notebook. 'Your current address, sir?'

'That, I'm afraid, is most definitely classified. As I think I have had to say before. You'll need to go through the War Office, or even the Cabinet Secretary.'

It was a stand-off. But Brooke thought he could smell blood.

'I know who to ring, Dr Hayle. Habakkuk is a matter of interest at the highest levels, as you rightly say. I am not the only one with unanswered questions.'

He tipped his hat and they left.

In the car, swinging out through the gates, he checked his watch. Sir James Cray had said Hayle was a person of interest. Now he had good cause to demand to know why.

CHAPTER FORTY-TWO

PC Turner met them on the threshold of the Spinning House.

'Sir. Castle's been in touch. They have a match between Ambrose's pillbox and Clement Tudor – the last of the attic boys. He's downstairs in Cell 2.'

Brooke sat at his office desk. Slatted sunlight fell across a pile of typed statements. It was a moment to savour: the first direct link between the Laurels and the murders.

Brooke lit a cigarette and opened a box which had arrived by courier from Liverpool. Inside were the photographic ID cards for all those working with the Armed Forces Medical Board at the Walker Art Gallery.

There were thirty-five cards, and Brooke had almost given

up when he reached the penultimate.

'Got you,' he said.

The culprit was Arthur Wherry, aged 42. Employed as a casual desk clerk. With luck they'd have him in a cell by dusk.

Brooke was about to call Inspector McGuire, in Liverpool, when he heard footsteps and Tudor was brought in. Brooke vacated his desk and let Edison take the chair, while he sat on the window ledge to observe.

As soon as the boy was brought in, Brooke realised he'd seen him on that first visit to the Laurels, jogging past in the corridor with a tennis racket. He'd thought then that he'd seen him somewhere before. But when, where? The memory still eluded him.

'Is your name Clement Arthur Tudor?' asked Edison.

'Y-y-yes,' he said, a stammer seeming to tie up his tongue.

Which was all Brooke needed to make the link with the past. He was taken back in time, running up the steps of the Guildhall, hoping the young man on the roof hadn't jumped, rehearsing what he might say to save his life. At the top they'd found the night watchman, desperate not to be blamed for leaving a door open, desperate to stay in the shadows.

'I didn't k-k-kill them,' said Tudor now, looking at Edison, and then at Brooke. 'They were our friends. I never s-s-saw them again. I've told the truth.'

The stutter was debilitating, and the left side of his face juddered with a twitch. His skin was bathed in sweat – as it had been that night. Brooke recalled that the reason he'd failed his army medical was 'nervous disability'.

Edison leant back, and Brooke took up Tudor's original statement.

It was a warm day, and the prisoner was giving off a lot of heat, but Brooke felt cold, a shiver running across his shoulders. It had happened to him only once before. In the desert, after the trip from Gibraltar on the *Invernia*. The troop ship had been overcrowded, stifling, insanitary. He'd found evidence that someone was beating up the newer recruits – volunteers – and taking their rations and water. The culprit was a TA sergeant, an old lag. The violence had been vicious, lingering. His name was Ritchie. Standing in front of him, he'd felt the distinct presence of evil. He'd known a lot of men with vices: cruel, unthinking, selfish, calculating, thuggish. But this was something quite different. The violence wasn't part of Ritchie, it was Ritchie.

That's what made him shiver, because he saw it in Tudor too, despite the weak nerves, the unsteady hands.

'Of course,' said Brooke, rereading his statement. 'It says here you work for the city council. Job?'

'Night w-w-watchman.'

'At the Guildhall, I think. Where of course they conduct army medicals. You're the inside man, aren't you? The others travelled round the country when a letter from Sleaford arrived, but you just went to work at the Guildhall. If any young man in the city wanted to avoid conscription, there was a local service. Very enterprising.

'How did you snare young Hood? Not the usual type – not a bookies' runner certainly.'

And then he had it. 'He loved dogs, young Hood. So Coldham's Lane perhaps, to see them run. Did Brodie spot him then? Does the boss have a nose for fear, for anxiety?'

Tudor was silent so Brooke went on.

'All you had to do was make sure the doctor didn't know

Hood already. Simple enough – they're mostly family doctors. But there'd have been a fee. He didn't have the money, did he?'

Tudor, despite himself, looked away.

'You told him it was no deal. Then you sat there and let him walk out on that roof.'

Brooke remembered the scene as he'd entered Market Hill. Inspector Norton had said the alarm was raised by the constable on his rounds. Not by the night watchman.

'You didn't do a thing. How long was he out there? You couldn't even watch. You just left him there, in his own private hell. Until he took that final step.'

The pillbox they'd found in the shelter with Ambrose's body was in a specimen jar on the table.

Brooke picked it up. 'You'll recall this. You left, planted it, with the body of young Ambrose. I realise the Laurels is very comfortable, Mr Tudor, but I'm afraid you'll be staying with us for a while.'

'I didn't kill him,' he said again.

'You just dumped his body? Where did you fetch it from? Where was he killed?'

He clasped his hands together and looked at his shoes.

'If promises have been made, Clement, they are worthless. I think we'll let you sleep on that.'

They'd let him stew overnight with the rest, and a constable outside on a chair. There was nothing quite like the imposition of silence to invoke fear and dread in the guilty, and to loosen tongues.

CHAPTER FORTY-THREE

Brooke was asleep on the Nile bed when the telephone rang. He'd asked the switchboard to take messages for an hour, unless an incoming call was urgent, so he swung his feet to the floor, and grabbed the receiver.

'Brooke.'

'James Cray, Inspector.'

He imagined the assistant commissioner's office; but there were no sounds of Whitehall, no clanking trams, or the hoot of barges from the Thames. In fact, he was pretty certain he could hear the *thwack* of a cricket ball against the bat, and then polite applause from the boundary.

'Yes. On your patch, Brooke. I'm in the bar at the University

Arms – ten minutes?'

'Sir.'

Brooke grabbed his coat, wondering why Sir James had thought it necessary to travel north, when all Brooke had done was leave a note with his secretary outlining the evidence gathered at Foster's Bank, and during his visit to the Lodge. Clearly, Hayle was still a person of considerable interest.

The bar was next to the restaurant where he'd met Keeble. It was festooned with the usual stage-props of Cambridge life: rowing pennants, photographs of crews, oars and caps, while the bar itself was fashioned from the keels of two boats. Out on the river all of this was a joyful sight, less so nailed to the walls of the Eights Bar.

Sir James was in a lounge suit, no tie, and brown shoes. Brooke detected a rebel beneath the urbane exterior.

He ordered a fresh whisky for himself, and – pointedly – a fresh bowl of ice, and a soda water for Brooke.

'I don't take ice with my Scotch,' said Sir James. 'That's a clue, Brooke.'

The lines on his face indicated a smile, but it never got near his eyes.

They were at a table removed from the bar, by an open window, looking out over the game of cricket. The outfield was currently dotted with pigeons, which the man at square-leg was trying to chase away.

The drinks arrived. Sir James ignored the ice and sipped his whisky, his large boxer's hand enclosing the glass.

'Tomorrow morning we're going to arrest Charles Hayle,' he said.

'Why?'

Sir James leant forward, as if talking to a child. 'Brooke. I'm sorry, it's not been possible to keep you entirely in the loop on this. About a month ago Hayle was given the word, unofficially, that he was no longer required on the project. It's been decided to forge ahead, you see. The Americans found Hayle uncooperative, haughty and grasping. The Canadians thought his work so far was substandard. He was out. There was too much at stake to have a loose cannon on board.

'Now – the last twenty-four hours – there's been a security breach. Details of Project Habakkuk have surfaced in Abwehr reports in Berlin. The Yanks are furious, apparently. Hayle is a suspect.

'The man is desperate for fame. The feeling is he may well have decided that if he has no future here, he might as well court the enemy. Our intelligence suggests he may be about to bolt. Ports are on alert, aerodromes. But we'll forestall him.'

'He's been under surveillance for the last twenty-four hours. We'll scoop him up at dawn. I've a unit coming north now. It shouldn't trouble the Borough.'

Sir James had the decency to look away.

'If it's any consolation, I am to report, after his arrest, to Chartwell. The prime minister wishes to receive a personal briefing. He is not a happy man. I fear a position in the provinces may be about to open up, Brooke. I appear to be the only candidate.'

Sir James looked around the bar as if he'd found himself in some outpost of the Empire.

There was a catch, in the slips, out on Parker's Piece, and a sprinkling of applause.

'I thought it only decent to finally answer your question,'

said Sir James. 'You wanted to know about Project Habakkuk. Given the work will continue here, this may now be appropriate. I'll be brief.'

He picked an ice cube out of the bowl and set it on the table.

'Hayle's a bit of a red herring, you see. He's a hydrologist. Habakkuk is about water, certainly, but in its rather startling but frozen state. Ice, Brooke. That's the key. A man called Pyke . . .'

'Geoffrey Pyke?' asked Brooke. Aldiss had mentioned him as the inspiration behind the project. And now Brooke recalled something Luke had said about him when he'd come home on leave from commando training: he'd been pivotal in designing vehicles to travel over ice and snow.

'Indeed,' said Sir James. 'His idea is to develop a new material – pykcrete – which mixes ice and wood chippings. Hayle has done some work on this problem – using his own expertise, especially in the temperature of sea water. So far only small blocks have been developed. Incredibly strong. Apparently, you can fire a bullet at it and it won't shatter.

'The idea – which certainly doesn't lack ambition – is to build a platform out of it for use as a floating air base. A giant aircraft carrier, if you will. Just the deck. It would be created, and stationed, in the North Atlantic, somewhere east of Newfoundland. It would thrive, apparently in what they like to call "iceberg alley". Once stable we'd get a bomber squadron to it – probably by ship, or flying out of Canada, and from this base protect the convoys by picking off the U-boats.

'Sounds far-fetched, I know. Apparently, the Germans were trying out similar ideas in the thirties. On the Bavarian lakes. This is altogether on a different scale. If you wanted long-range bombers to use this thing, we're talking two thousand feet in length. To give you an idea of the problems involved, an ice structure that long would have to deal with issues involving the curvature of the Earth.

'Anyway, Churchill's gung-ho for it. Another reason for my invitation to lunch at Chartwell.

'If we lose the battle in the Atlantic, we lose the war. *Ipso facto*, it could win the war. Pyke will run the show, until he puts backs up, which he will, because he's a difficult man. But other scientists will assist. Hayle won't be one of them.'

Sir James popped the ice cube back in its bowl and ordered a fresh whisky. His eyes drifted to the cricket match.

Brooke would never forgive himself if he didn't speak up.

'I'm really interested in who killed Philip Basford, Jonathan Ambrose and William Mortimer,' he said. 'It seems to me Charles Hayle is my prime suspect, assisted by Patrick Brodie.'

Sir James threw back the whisky. 'I think we've got bigger fish to fry, Brooke. We'll give Hayle to SIS. The spooks can keep him. I'm not sure you've got the evidence to charge Hayle with three murders, or anybody else. The fact is they went missing a year ago, and you can't tell me, or a court, where they were until they turned up dead. When they did turn up, both Hayle and Brodie were out of the country. Any prosecuting barrister would advise you that you haven't a case. It's not injustice, it's life.'

Brooke understood now why Sir James had ventured north. He needed Hayle under arrest before his appointment with the prime minister. And he'd effectively removed Brooke – and the Borough – from the inquiry. The Yard would deal with Cold Christmas Farm, and Dr Charles Hayle.

Sir James checked his watch and stood, shooting the cuffs on his jacket.

'Forgive me. All that's secret of course – top secret. Not a word. But I know I don't need to tell you that.'

There was a final smile, wrinkles splaying from the corner of each eye. The handshake was muscular, and possibly Masonic.

'I'm sure our paths will cross,' he said, and was gone.

CHAPTER FORTY-FOUR

Brooke needed fresh air after the stuffy bar, so he was striding around Parker's Piece when he saw – sensational sight – Peter Aldiss, his most dedicated nighthawk, lying on the grass bank sunbathing while watching the cricket.

'There you are,' he said, rising up on one elbow. 'They said you'd be back soon but that you often circled the park. You're a man of habit, Brooke. I have news of the elusive Dr Hayle. Or more precisely, his secret laboratory,' he said. 'Beer?'

'Beer,' agreed Brooke, leading the way to the invigorating air rising from the river in front of the Mill Inn. They bought pints and sat on the grass by the sluggish green water. A few people had dared to take out punts. The social stigma of public enjoyment was perhaps, at last, fading with time.

'Hayle?' prompted Brooke. He felt humiliated by the Yard's invasion of his 'manor' – not to mention the pilfering of his case. But he felt no inclination to quietly melt away. Quite the opposite.

Aldiss took two inches off the top of his pint. 'Yes. This lab of his is in the William Hardy Building – opposite the Hopkins, just into Pembroke Leys, where the long line of trees runs into Downing.'

Some cows had wandered into the water meadow off Coe Fen and had begun chewing grass close to Brooke's hat. They picked up their drinks and scuttled upstream, towards Newnham Mill.

'But we can get *into* the lab?' pressed Brooke.

Aldiss shook his head, watching a duck and ducklings paddling past.

'The work's still top secret, Brooke. And the rest of the building's no better. It's been taken over by the Food Investigations Board – sounds dull but it might – you know - win us the war. They're trying to find out how to dry food – anything, fish, meat, cereals – dry it, then pack it tight. That way you can get three times the food on the same ship. This isn't some starry-eyed project – it's already paying dividends.

'There's no way through the front door of that building without a gold-embossed invitation from Downing Street.'

At this dramatic point Aldiss went for more beer – leaving Brooke to dwell on the telling phrase 'through the front door'.

When his old room-mate came back he sat on the grass, kicked off his pumps, and massaged his bare feet.

'How badly do you want to see this laboratory, Brooke?'

The smile on Aldiss's face was all it took to reveal the plan.

'Don't tell me. The Hardy has an accessible roof,' said Brooke.

'Yes. There's a door – a way down. No one locks a door on the roof. It's one of the golden rules of the rooftop world.'

Brooke closed his eyes in the autumnal sun, thinking of Hayle, out at Fleam Dyke at their first meeting, boasting – sneering – about the awe-inspiring secret held within his laboratory. And then there was Sir James Cray, loftily hijacking the whole inquiry. Had he even told Brooke the truth about Habakkuk? An awe-inspiring secret didn't sound like a block of ice mixed with wood chippings.

'I could let you in,' said Aldiss.

'Tonight,' said Brooke.

CHAPTER FORTY-FIVE

Footsteps on the towpath, the rhythmical tapping of the metal Blakeys, the rusty squeal of the broken hinged gate, then measured strides to the front door. It was Brooke, of course, so Claire just lay still, a sideways glance revealing the luminous dial of the alarm clock: 10.30 p.m. A good time, with a late shift off still to come, so she stretched out and donated one of her three pillows to his side of the bed.

Three knocks, loud enough to wake the house.

Claire met Joy at the top of the stairs, Ben in the half-light of the bedroom, holding Iris.

Joy threw the front door open, despite the hall light.

'Sorry. Lost my key,' said Luke, grinning widely, a

commando beret – without a badge – set at just the right angle.

Joy took his arm, while Claire enfolded her son in a hug. Ben stood back shyly, Iris now aware, dimly, of a homecoming.

'Where's Dad?' asked Luke, swinging off an army greatcoat, and giving up a knapsack.

Ben had already noted the absence of the cap badge, any insignia on the coat or his tunic, and the expertly made canvas knapsack – again without any military identification.

Claire and Joy took him to the kitchen to make sweet tea and find cold bread pudding – his favourite, even without the brown sugar. Everyone studied his face as he talked, but only Joy spotted the suppressed excitement of adventure, a hallmark of childhood.

'I've got news, but where's Dad?' he asked again.

Luke consulted a fine watch they'd never seen before; a circling second hand, the phases of the moon shown at the centre, a second smaller dial set for a stopwatch.

'I've got 'til seven – it's crazy I know. We're in transit. I got a pass-out because the train's in a siding at Ely. A signalman ran me to Coton and I've walked the rest. It's a lorry then – from Madingley, after a briefing, to London. But that's not the news. Where's Dad?'

It was clear Luke would not tell them anything of substance until Brooke was home. They had eight hours and Luke needed at least a few hours' sleep.

'I'll find him,' said Ben.

'Would you?' said Claire, desperate for this homecoming to be remembered as a moment of happiness. 'They'll know where he is at the duty desk at the station. If he's gone to see Doric then its Michaelhouse, if it's Rose he'll be on Market Hill. Tell them it's urgent. There'll be a radio car out somewhere which might spot him.'

She helped Ben on with his coat, and Joy gave him her scarf, knotting it smoothly at the throat.

'And check his office. He might have taken to the Nile bed,' she said.

CHAPTER FORTY-SIX

For Peter Aldiss, leaving his rooms at Peterhouse was a religious ceremony, encompassing life and death; for one night he might not come back. Every time was, in some sense, in the moment, the last time. First, the snuffing out of the final candle, so that his eyes could switch to night vision. Then the vestments of the mystical church of night-climbers: the black Guernsey, the canvas trousers and the grubby grey pumps, which he only ever wore to climb, so that now – in the twenty-fifth year of his obsession – they were gloves for his feet, the thinnest of coverings for prehensile toes. And no socks. A pocket torch, attached by a string to his belt. The pale bare hands were unavoidable, so he always dabbed ash from the grate on the backs, just before checking the trouser pockets for loose change.

He stood, breathing in, breathing out. Then listened. The college was asleep, the night porter at the east gate in his lodge. The night watchman's dog – Hobson – no longer patrolling the grounds with his master, but in his kennel by the King's Yard. Phipps, the Classicist, had padded to the toilet one last time down the corridor outside.

The clocks struck midnight. (Most were muffled after ten, but not so the Guildhall, or Great St Mary's.) Communication with fellow night-climbers was limited in wartime, given the draconian attempts by the authorities to stamp out what they considered an unpatriotic sport. In peacetime they met in The Radegund, or the Champion, huddled in a corner, swapping stories and pathways, routes and tracks over the rooftops. In war they went out alone. One night in three, Aldiss would see a distant silhouette and, if his hands were free, essay a brisk salute. But it was impossible to judge the scale of the activity. At this hour, how many other enthusiasts were gently lifting sash windows, and sniffing the air?

He'd already lifted *his* sash – the unavoidable squeal of warped wood obscured by the brouhaha of Formal Hall six hours earlier. He stepped out on the ledge – an extraordinary manoeuvre involving flexible joints, and the balance of a gyroscope. Glimpsed from below – and he had seen a similar exit looking up from St Andrew's Passage one night in his first year – the effect was eerie, the image an unlikely mixture of spider and sloth.

On the ledge, sat like a Brahmin, he looked down into the Great Court fifty feet below. There were 'drops' and 'lethal drops', and this was of the second variety. He'd land in the flower beds, but that would do him no good at all. One night at Jesus they'd sneaked away to The Radegund and a physicist named Joyce – an Irishman with a grim sense of humour – had worked out the depth of the crater a human body would make from eighty feet into well-tended shrubbery. Terminal velocity would break every bone. The thick peaty loam would capture an imprint of the outflung arms.

Still on the ledge, he savoured the moment. The adrenaline flowed, smoothly inevitable, lifting his spirits, a moment of joy which threw a soothing light across the rest of his methodical, lonely life.

He stood, hooked an arm around the stone lintel of the window, swung out with one foot on the sill, and found the onward ledge with the other. This stone lip provided what the night-climbers called *passage*, a sideways perch designed, in this case, during the reign of Henry VIII, to provide nothing more than horizontal decoration. It was two inches wide, and given – on at least three occasions – to sudden, brittle collapse. (The debris, he'd collected by dawn.) So he edged carefully, testing each foothold with a light, brisk tap of his toes. He faced the wall, his back to the drop, his hands limpet-like against the limestone, his heartbeat now at a steady eighty, measured by the pulse within the inner ear.

Twenty feet and he came to the first 'chimney' – shorthand for any gap between buttresses narrow enough to allow the climber to use his body as a brace, facilitating a methodical ascent to the gutters above. Crablike he inched upwards, until close enough to swing out one arm through the iron gutter ring, and bring one leg up and over the gutter itself, the body following. He was six foot one inch tall, and a fraction under ten stone. The upward roll of the body over the edge and onto the roof was balletic.

His world, which existed above the mundane world, was now revealed. Pembroke ran west along Downing Street, a single apex until it reached the corner of the Sedgwick Museum. To the north lay the town, dominated by the Guildhall, the turrets of King's College Chapel and the tower of Great St Mary's, while to the south lay what they were now calling the Downing Site – the brick maze of science blocks, dull tokens of expansion after the Great War. Flat roofs, skylights, water tanks – a nondescript skyscape compared to the Gothic splendour of the old colleges.

By touch, eyes shut, he could reach his own laboratory from this spot. He could reach *anywhere* from this spot, anywhere on this heightened plane. But tonight his target was the William Hardy Building. First the jump – a modest five foot six, hardly the sickening yawn of the Senate House Leap, but the rule applied. Stop, consider, one practice run-up, then go. Airborne for a second, he thought of the vision from below – a man, flying, his limbs set as if for flight, and then the running touchdown, the slight sound of the gritty stone. A life resumed.

The Sedgwick's roofs were a Victorian maze of chimneys and skylights, spirettes and flues. Then came Biochemistry, Natural Sciences, Physical Sciences, Geology, all with Regent's Street to his left, the long double line of lime trees to his right, running down to Downing College. He moved with familiarity along this aerial street. The Downing Site might be mundane, but it led to rare treasures: Downing's dome, or the vast expanse of the Regal, where the night-climber could pause by the air ducts, listening to Humphrey Bogart below on the silver screen.

The William Hardy was a cubical building, built in the

twenties, in a brick even duller than its neighbours'. At its centre was a yard, used for deliveries and serviced by lifts, reached through a double-doored archway. He noted that the doors were open.

The square block was four storeys high, with metal Crittall windows, and a little playful elaboration – a mathematical matrix of light brick picking out diamonds. Derricks, for lifting heavyweight laboratory equipment, studded the outside walls. Again, embellishments: iron gargoyles, playful spiral drainpipes. All these buildings boasted these indulgences in stone – Dr Comfort's Galen, for example, a Greek-style frieze of naked athletes at roof level, the biochemistry building – inexplicably – the signs of the zodiac. None of these artistic touches compensated for the forgettable buildings.

But he'd been wrong to ignore the William Hardy. When he executed the final leap – a two-foot minnow – he was delighted to find that, while the roof was flat, it was extraordinary. There was a greenhouse, full of exotic plants, although when he touched the glass he felt the bitter coldness within, despite the balmy night. It was surrounded by raised beds, rows of seedlings just visible, but – again – when he pushed a finger into the soil he felt the icy temperature within. There was a small weather station, a boxed thermometer reading 48°F. Peering into the glasshouse with the help of his torch, he saw another – reading 20°F. A rain gauge, an anemometer, a silk-like screen – perhaps designed to catch insect life – completed the rooftop laboratory.

A pitched skylight gave a view of what might be a canteen. There were several flues, all new. There was a hut, with a door leading to a staircase, which was open: a lifeline for night-climbers. The rule in the university estates department,

343

ostensibly a safety regulation, was that rooftop doors did not need keys, or even latches. A decision taken, perhaps, by a clandestine night-climber.

He opened the door, pausing only for a second to brush aside a rare intimation of danger. What was amiss? A footstep perhaps, a door closing with studied care? The stairwell dropped to the top floor, but the door into the laboratories was padlocked, and carried the warning NO ENTRY – BY ORDER OF THE WAR OFFICE, so he went down another floor and found the way forward open. Aldiss's torchlight ran along a corridor into the gloom. On one side was an open laboratory, serried benches, fume cupboards, sinks and various apparatus. On the other side of the corridor a series of six doors – each identical, cell doors by design, each locked tight shut by a heavy steel lever. There was a sliding spyhole window to each.

A sign, hanging on two chains, read:

FOOD INVESTIGATION BOARD

He heard clocks chiming the half-hour. Intense curiosity made him pause, but he was late, and turned away.

Another double flight of stairs ran down to the first floor, yet another to the ground. The heavy-duty concrete floors allowed for an almost silent passage. The ground floor was conventional offices – but again with a central corridor. He flashed his torch and thought he saw a rat, running along the skirting board, then disappearing down a vent.

He jogged the length of the corridor to a set of main doors, which were locked and bolted. Beside them was a narrow casement window, which he opened.

The distinct aroma of a Black Russian cigarette entered, followed by Brooke's pale moonlit face.

Aldiss offered a hand and pulled Brooke in from the dark.

'This might be the William Hardy Building on the outside,' said Aldiss, 'but it's not what it says on the inside. Look . . .'

The torch revealed the name etched in the lintel above:

THE LOW TEMPERATURE RESEARCH STATION

CHAPTER FORTY-SEVEN

They stood together for a moment in the silent building.

Even Aldiss's breathing was now shallow. Brooke's ears scanned the night, but only found a distant percussion of freight trucks in the marshalling yards a mile to the north.

'Is the place empty?' asked Brooke.

'Top floor's locked – that's Hayle's lab. The rest is for the boffins trying to shrink food. But yes – I think we're alone, although the doors to the vehicle yard are open. Which is odd.'

Their voices echoed in the corridor, and with theatrical timing an owl hooted somewhere in a leafy college garden.

'Scotland Yard are arresting Hayle tomorrow. They have him under surveillance tonight, so we'll get no visitors. We can consider ourselves special constables, Peter. I've still got three murders to solve. Come on . . . lead the way.'

They crept forward by torchlight to the end of the corridor, wary of the light switches. Briefly, they considered the lift, which showed a dull, flashing blue light. But a lot of university buildings cut power if the siren sounded, which was the last thing they wanted, so they took the stairs.

At the third floor they paused, and Aldiss used the torch to pick out the six chambers and the sign for the Food Investigations Board.

They went to the first chamber. The peephole revealed various glass cases – frosted, dimly discernible, within which they could see what looked like withered corn.

'Of course,' said Brooke. 'That at least should have been obvious. You said they're looking at ways of drying food so you can pack more into a convoy of ships. Well – dry it, freeze it. Pack it away. It's the Low Temperature Research Station. This is all about ice, Peter.'

Aldiss led the way up the final flight of stairs.

Brooke, revealing a touch of forward planning, had a burglar's jemmy, and so they levered the padlock off the door with ease.

Torchlight played over a laboratory within. The temperature was brisk, even chill. A lab coat hung from a hook. Two large logbooks were open on a lab bench, etched with lines of figures in various colours of ink. On the floor was a dog bowl.

All this to the right. To the left was a line of six chambers identical to the ones below.

They abandoned silence and searched the laboratory – every corner, save the six cells.

Brooke threw the switch to the overhead neon lights. The room blazed into view: whitewashed, surgical, reflective, deserted.

The six chambers were numbered. Beside each handle was a temperature dial. Above each chamber there was a box marked ALARM, etched with a handmade sketch of a penguin wearing a scarf. A sign ordered NO SMOKING IN THE CHAMBERS.

The first two doors were open. Number 3 was shut, and the temperature dial read 20°F. Brooke flipped the peephole cover and saw within various blocks of ice, flecked with wood, resting on metal stands. And two metal chests, frosted. Pools of water had formed on the floor, then frozen. Inside Number 4, the temperature set at 10°F, the blocks of ice were frosted and looked as hard as concrete. Inside Number 5, the gauge of which was set at minus 10°F, various blocks of wood stood on their plinths. Again, there were two metal chests.

Aldiss tapped one of the copper pipes which ran along the walls and through all the chambers.

'Cooling agent – probably carbonic acid, or ammonia. Clever. The control is extraordinary – that's what's new here, Brooke. These temperature gauges are set to warn of any deviation. Must have cost a fortune.'

The last chamber, Number 6, was a surprise. They opened the door but the interior wasn't cold. It comprised a bedroom, as if caught in ice itself, or the glass of a paperweight. But the temperature was ambient. A bunk bed was piled with army surplus blankets. An electric cable serviced a kettle, and a reading lamp. There was a pile of books, even an ashtray. There was a notebook under the pillow which Brooke collected.

He wondered if Sir James Cray had missed a trick. If Hayle

was selling secrets, it might be an idea to secure his diaries and logs.

'The man's obsessed,' said Aldiss, flipping the blankets back off the bed. 'Even I go back to my room in college to sleep.'

'You've got nothing to hide, Peter.'

They went back to chamber Number 4 and levered open the door. Air escaped like an icy breath. Aldiss flipped the lid on one of the metal chests to find various samples of ice, each set in its own glass tray.

There was a blackboard covered in cyphers and equations. Aldiss stood and read them as if casually appraising a destination board at the railway station.

Brooke turned, to the other horizontal cabinet, and lifted the lid.

The frosted seal gave without complaint. Again, a slight hiss, like a shallow breath.

One heartbeat was lost, and for a second Brooke's sense of balance fled, so that he took a rapid step backwards, which alerted Aldiss, who steadied him with his arm.

Locked together, they stood looking into the cabinet.

'God, Brooke. The colour.'

There was *no* colour, which was what was perhaps most shocking. The man lying in the cabinet was frosted, the iced lapels of his jacket as white as his eyelids, or his half-hearted moustache, or – horribly – the eyes, which were open but glazed with ice.

He had no shoes, or gloves. His fingers were animated – or had been, before freezing point; ice had turned them to stone. With one hand he seemed to be beckoning an unseen waiter, with the other about to pat a dog. The lips had not held their natural position, but were drawn back slightly from the teeth: enamel incisors shone like ice cubes. It was a face in agony.

But Brooke knew what wouldn't be pale once the frost had gone: the skin.

'Edmund Smith-Stanley, I suspect,' said Brooke, his voice recovering after an initial swallow – the cold air penetrating his throat.

'The fourth attic boy.'

They searched all six chambers, opened all the other chests, but young Edmund was alone, although Brooke knew now that he had not always been alone: Basford, Ambrose and Mortimer had endured this purgatory too, released only to die again and be set aside in yet another dark metallic coffin in Dr Comfort's morgue.

'They all died that night a year ago,' he said. 'With their Blitz summer suntans. Their killers? Brodie and Hayle's my guess. With Mrs Brodie in the background. And it's not difficult to guess where they died, is it? Did he offer a glimpse of the secret laboratory?

'They couldn't dump four bodies – every path would lead back to the Laurels. So they kept them here, left the country – both of them, Brodie to Ireland, Hayle to the States.

'The lab was locked up. But they left orders for the henchmen, and no doubt the keys, so they could dump the bodies at intervals in the shelters. They got away with Mortimer, and but for my telephone number on Basford's hand they'd have got away with that too. The others would have followed.

'Then Hayle gets the push in Washington, and faces losing the laboratory – and its frozen secrets. He didn't panic, but it looks like the foot-soldiers did. Basford and Ambrose just hours apart – botched. I wonder what he had planned for young Edmund here? Whatever it was, he ran out of time.'

Aldiss closed the chest, unable to look away.

'I don't think cold-hearted does it justice,' was all he said.

Brooke checked his watch: 1.55 a.m. They'd reseal the chamber and return with Dr Comfort in the morning. But overnight there should be a vigil for the dead.

He gave Aldiss instructions: he was to report to the duty desk at the Spinning House, then return with two constables from the night shift. He should leave one at the door of the research station, and the other would take up the watch outside the chamber, until dawn.

'I'll stay with him until relieved. Go.'

Brooke checked his watch. He listened to Aldiss's steps descending.

Then he was alone with young Edmund.

For five minutes he gathered up documents, searched the filing cabinets, and went through Hayle's 'bedroom' where he found an address book, and yet another notebook. He put all the paperwork on the lab table.

Then he returned to Number 4.

'And what did he have planned for you?' he asked, out loud. 'Cold-blooded,' he added, and the sound of his voice, trapped, without echo, made him realise the danger a moment too late.

He heard a single footstep.

Dr Hayle stood in the doorway, a small pistol in his hand.

'Inspector,' he said, the word inscribed in a thin mist of condensation.

Brooke thought the only weapon he had was time.

'Was it worth it?'

'Love to chat,' said Hayle. 'I was going to give Edmund a decent burial. But my transport has fled. I suspect my driver may be in one of your cells. There we are. I have what I really want . . .'

He held a briefcase, and a satchel over one shoulder.

'Good of you to tidy things up. I need to go, Brooke. I've shaken off one set of detectives. They've been watching my flat. They're not as alert as they should be to the shadows of the blackout.

'I won't see you again. And I don't want to be followed. I think I have a better chance of getting away without you on my trail. I suspect a noose is tightening.

'I'm afraid the night-climber won't be in time. Goodbye.'

Hayle took a step back and slammed the door; the lever was compressed. He saw Hayle's face at the peephole for a moment, then he was gone.

Brooke ran to the door, his breath clouding the glass of the peephole, his full weight on the lever.

The lights went out.

Outside he could see the dim outline of the laboratory in darkness, through which a shadow fluttered, like a dark flame. It moved to the door; there was a small light, perhaps a torch, and it caught Hayle's eyes: he looked through Brooke, as if he were as alive as poor Edmund in his frozen chest.

Then another noise, a rubbing, a turning, a valve giving way. And then the gentle *sssss* of gas escaping. The copper piping groaned, ticked, as the pressure changed.

A cloud of mist rose from the valves which joined the copper pipes. Brooke took a breath, and it caught in his throat, doubling him over. Kneeling on the floor, he heard the distinct pitter of falling raindrops.

What had Aldiss said: *carbonic acid, or ammonia.*

It didn't smell like ammonia. And there were raindrops. Brooke's chemistry was elementary, but he was pretty sure carbonic acid – exposed to oxygen – would break down quickly into water, and carbon dioxide.

He kicked the door, which didn't move.

The gas made him choke, so he knelt.

He looked at his watch and it read: 2.12 a.m., and then, instantly, 2.13 a.m.

His life was ticking away.

CHAPTER FORTY-EIGHT

The night was clear, sharp, lightless, until Ben crossed the river at Silver Street and saw the moon rising, full and almost flaring with light – a bomber's moon.

The duty sergeant was on the phone, but read his lips, and so pointed at two constables emerging from the mess, straightening caps; a tall man with fair hair stood to one side, leaning against the wall on one leg, the other tucked up and held by his hand.

Ben noted the sockless feet, inside flimsy gym pumps.

'I must find Inspector Brooke,' said Ben. 'It's nothing awful – his son's come home but can't stay. There's just a few hours.'

Aldiss shook Ben's hand. 'An old friend. Just in time.

Come on. It's best on foot,' he said, the constables following, abandoning a radio car parked in the street.

'What's up?' asked Ben, taking two paces to every one of Aldiss's strides.

'Brooke's managed to find a corpse. We're the relief column. You can take him home after these constables have been set on guard. Then it's all down to the pathologist. It's not always this exciting,' he added.

The Low Temperature Research Station betrayed itself with a single light on the top floor. As Aldiss prepared to hoist himself through the narrow window, one of the constables tried the door and it swung open. Someone threw a switch and lights, dozens of bare bulbs in a string, lit the way ahead. They left a guard and moved quickly into the building.

At the foot of the stairwell Aldiss called a halt.

'Look. This place was locked when I left half an hour ago. Either someone has entered, or someone has left. We need to proceed with caution.'

The constable drew his baton. By the lift doors was a fire alarm box, on top of which was a hammer to break the glass. Aldiss took the hammer. Ben, unarmed, led the way.

They climbed silently the eight flights of steps to the fourth floor, a single neon light at each landing. Ben, with his ear still tuned to the mechanical world of the submarine, picked up several noises: a generator buzz, the 'ticking' of pipes, the random creaking of metal beams.

The door to Hayle's lab was open, a white mist within, which grew denser towards the ceiling. The neon light was a dim glow within the phlegm-like cloud, the hissing of gas persistent.

Ben's eye for detail etched the picture on his brain: six

doors on the left, a porthole in each, the horizontal copper piping – which ran along the wall but rose to circumvent each door; then temperature dials at each, and the pressure handles. A mechanical world, claustrophobic, pressurised, reeking of metal, the surface of everything cool and smooth. His heartbeat rose at the visual echo of the interior of *Unbowed*. He felt the North Atlantic closing over the building, here, on a leafy backstreet in Cambridge.

Then they all caught the gas in the throat.

He heard Aldiss coughing, in retreat. The constable was on his knees, and so Ben grabbed him by the collar and towed him back out to the stairs.

'Where's Brooke?' asked Ben, his head close to Aldiss's right ear.

'The fourth chamber.'

Ben went back through the door, Joy's scarf covering his mouth. On his knees he found the gas was thinner. He tried a breath, his throat contracting, but he filled his lungs with what oxygen was left. Closing his eyes, he set his memory to basic training: *exiting the boat during a fire*, the procedure he'd failed to follow that night on board *Silverfish*, off the German coast. How long did he have? A minute, ninety seconds. So thirty seconds, forty-five, to get to Brooke, then get them both out and down the stairs.

I can do this, he thought. *As long as the lights stay on.*

He followed the copper piping to the first chamber. His eyes were streaming now, so he left the peephole shutter closed and moved on to the second, his hand dancing over the temperature gauge, the pressure cylinder, the riveted door.

Then a sound – strangely inevitable, even ordained. An air

raid siren, the Guildhall roof a cricket ball's throw to the north. The wail deepened, gathering strength, and then the lights went out.

Ben's fingers closed around a copper pipe. The darkness pressed against his eyes. It robbed him of motion. For several – precious – seconds he was below decks, the sea above, and he entered the third stage of fear in battle: *I won't die, I may die, I will die.* The building spun on a vertical axis. No one was coming. They'd find Brooke dead in the chamber, six feet from Ben's body, his own fingers locked in a rictus around a useless copper pipe.

His cause of death would be stasis. Fear froze his muscles, as effectively as ice. Forward, backward, up, down – all directions were unthinkable. A second had passed, perhaps three. Unconsciousness circled. Then an auditory hallucination filled his mind: Iris breathing, wetly, into his ear. He reached out to touch her, to feel the comforting heat of her skin, and so let go of the copper pipe.

He had motion, forward motion, and so he shuffled on his knees, his fingers running free over the metal riveted walls. The gas had thickened, even close to the floor, a milky stream he must not breathe. Then the peephole ahead lit up – blueish, a half-light, the chambers running on an emergency generator.

At the peephole glass he found Brooke's face. Eyes open but blank. He was never sure, looking back, if there were tears.

He leant down on the pressure handle and the door popped.

Brooke's body fell away, and so Ben had to struggle to get it open, down on his knees again, the final seconds now, as his lungs screamed for oxygen. They wouldn't scream for ever. His body would give up soon, a dreamy conscious half-world, would give way to darkness, a beckoning stillness.

It was the last moment of hope.

He hauled Brooke onto his feet, the detective's shoes sliding, trying to support his own weight. Then they both went down, a deadweight. Ben's vision began to blur. He knelt, took Brooke by the lapels of his coat, and got him into a sitting position, then he slung him over his back – a deckhand again. The strength came from somewhere, but where he never knew.

Counting the paces he walked out through the door, his eyes almost blind, the room a threaded chaos of half-light and gas. He wouldn't have made it, but as he fell Aldiss emerged, hands outstretched, and caught him long enough for his legs to recover, to bear the weight. Then, in memory only, there was the stairwell, a corridor and the night sky, the bomber's moon sailing through the sweet night air between canopies of autumn leaves.

CHAPTER FORTY-NINE

The suffocating effects of the gas were real enough, but the symptoms wore off rapidly. Nonetheless Ben elected to sit on the steps of the Spinning House while Brooke set in motion the hunt for Dr Charles Hayle. Half an hour later he appeared and sat down beside his son-in-law.

'I've sent orders to watch the railway station; checkpoints will stop all road traffic. But he'll make a port – or an airstrip. We may never hear of him again. I suspect, if I've read between the lines correctly, that he may well be heading for France, then on to Berlin. A small boat perhaps, then a U-boat off the Goodwin Sands. It all depends if they think he's worth it.'

Ben announced that he was feeling sick, so they spent twenty minutes in the first-aid post on Sidney Sussex Street, which had been set up to treat injured pets during air raids. The all-clear had yet to sound, and so they sat diligently in a dingy waiting room while a member of St John Ambulance tried to calm a small dog which had run wild at the sound of the Guildhall siren, while also attending to a child holding a guinea pig in a box, which had clearly died some time ago.

Ben was given a glass of liver salts which did make him sick, and therefore instantly better. Released, they strolled through the dark city. At Rose's tea stall they ordered tea with sugar, and the necessary whisky bottle was left on their table. Rose, retreating to serve an early-shift tram driver, said simply, 'I won't ask', which must have been a comment on their appearance. Brooke smoked steadily and drank a tumbler of the whisky in three gulps.

'You saved my life,' he said eventually, his throat sore and his voice a tone lower than usual, thanks to the gas. (Which was only now making *him* feel sick.) His last memory had been banging on the door of Number 4, peering out through the peephole, as the shadowy form of Dr Hayle calmly selected papers from the lab bench and slipped them into a briefcase.

'Oddly, I think in some ways you saved mine as well, sir,' said Ben, who'd never smoked a cigarette before in his life, but calmly accepted one of his father-in-law's Black Russians.

Brooke, who felt desperately tired, thought this was a remark they'd come back to one day.

'Why did someone try to kill you?' asked Ben.

'A scientist, probably a gifted scientist, felt that his life could only be justified if he achieved fame – or at least the admiration of his peers. Glittering prizes, Ben. I was going to take those glittering prizes away. He was the son of a famous father who cast a long shadow. I left the shadow cast by my father a long time ago.'

Ben smiled, thinking, *Did you?*

Dawn, beams of golden light, swung over Market Hill, like a hawk's gyres, catching the four great pinnacles of King's College Chapel.

'Thank you for saving my life,' said Brooke. 'That's twice. There won't be a third time, but I'll never forget it, Ben.'

The clocks marked three o'clock.

Ben leapt to his feet. 'I'm an idiot,' he said. 'We should go. There's a surprise for you at home. You have four hours – four precious hours.'

As they stood, limbs aching from the rictus inflicted by the gas, a radio car slipped smoothly onto Market Hill and parked close by, a constable jumping out smartly.

'Sir. PC Turner said you might be here. Telephone message from the guardroom at Barrow arrived, sir – apologies for delays, due to operational difficulties. DC thought you'd like to see it tonight.'

He handed over a slip of paper.

MAGNETS MISSING.
TWO FAULTY PERISCOPES.
REQUEST ORDERS.

It was the perfect outcome. Now Brooke knew the identity of the Vulcan Works saboteurs, their *modus operandi* and their motive.

'Tell the duty desk to get Sergeant Edison to pick me up at six. Orders then.'

CHAPTER FIFTY

There was a long, slow unfurling bend in the river just beyond the millpond, and then the house came into view. There was a bench on the towpath, donated by Brooke's father to the parish council, bearing a plaque in the honour of local men who had died in the Great War. A man was sitting, smoking, in a dark jacket and trousers. He'd clearly been waiting for Brooke to appear because even from a distance of fifty yards there was a slow smile, and then a hand raised lazily in greeting.

Brooke ran; Ben held back.

Luke rose to meet him, so it was over in a few seconds. He couldn't remember the last time he'd hugged his son. It seemed to have been a habit which died with the coming of age.

After a moment he held him at arm's length.

'The hero of the Lofoten Islands,' he said. 'No doubt there are medals.'

'Everyone got one – except for the captain who drew his pistol going ashore and shot himself in the foot.'

They were laughing when Claire and Joy came out with a tray of glasses, a bottle of wine, a teapot, teacups, milk and– the most sensational item – shortcake, a present from Scotland.

'We couldn't sleep,' said Claire. 'We thought you were going to miss him.'

'Where's Ben?' asked Joy.

'He's here,' said Brooke, looking back along the towpath. His son-in-law was standing, hands in pockets, watching the family from afar.

Joy ran to fetch him and the rest waited for them, sitting down on the wicker chairs in the pre-dawn light.

They were locked in an embrace, talking, each gently holding the other's face.

'You two. Stop canoodling,' called Claire. 'Luke won't say anything until we're all here.'

So they came back.

'He won't tell us what's up,' said Claire, turning to Brooke. 'It's infuriating. He just arrives, no warning, and there's no uniform and he announces he's not a commando any more – after all that training. And he won't tell us what he *is*.'

Then, watching Ben and Joy and Brooke, she sensed a shared secret. 'What's happened? You're not telling us something,' she added. 'This is intolerable. Everyone has a secret except me.'

'One day,' said Brooke. 'One day, soon, all will be revealed. But for now the stage is Luke's . . . You'll have to tell us something, otherwise we'll imagine worse. Have you been keelhauled for drunkenness?'

'I'm to be a Baker Street Irregular,' said Luke.

'SOE?' asked Brooke, who had feared as much.

The identity of its headquarters, not far from Madame Tussauds, was about the only reliable detail amidst all the gossip.

'I couldn't possibly say,' said Luke, enjoying himself.

'What's SOE?' demanded Joy.

'Special Operations Executive,' said Brooke. 'Being a spy, working behind enemy lines in occupied Europe.'

'Oh God,' said Claire.

'I might be good at it,' said Luke. 'They asked. I felt I couldn't say no.'

'Not now – not right away?' said Joy, putting an arm around her mother.

'No. I've to report to Station XV – otherwise known as the Thatched Barn. Elstree, just north of London.' He looked at his watch. 'Transport goes in three hours from Madingley.'

'Good God – the Thatched Barn,' said Brooke, turning to Claire. 'We used to drive past it on the way to Dover. Huge place – mock-Tudor. All the rage then. Film stars used to stay there.'

'That's it,' said Luke. 'Great North Road. The film studios are just behind it. I checked – they're filming now. It's all good stuff apparently. That one we saw last time I was home is one of theirs. Remember? *Old Mother Riley Joins Up*!'

'Instead of which it's you,' said Brooke.

'Thing is, they use the studios – make-up, disguise, tricks of the trade. After all, it *is* acting. Apparently, there's a resident magician. I thought it sounded like fun.'

'You'll have to speak French,' objected Joy. 'You can't speak French.'

'When you go in there's three of you. That's the idea. One's a local, they do the talking. This could be years away. I'm hoping for the quiet life. It might be over by Christmas.'

For an hour the Brooke family talked, aware that they were eking out their precious minutes.

There was a long silence, in which they heard something slip into the river and swim upstream, then there was the unmistakable sound of a car pulling up at the front of the house.

Brooke stood, hugging Luke again. Joy went to fetch Iris, whose waking cries could be heard from an upstairs window.

'Eden, really?' said Claire. 'You've only just got home.'

'A lot's happened,' he said. 'One more cup of tea – and one for Sergeant Edison by the sound of it. We can run Luke out to Madingley if he's ready to go.'

His sergeant was ushered into the family circle and given a large wicker chair. Cradling his tea, he listened as Brooke summarised Luke's news.

'And you, Sergeant?' asked Claire. 'Family, allotment, that polished car – is all well?'

Which is when Edison gave up the struggle.

'Well. If Mr Brooke doesn't mind, I've got some news.'

There was complete silence. Edison never had news, it was one of his accomplishments.

'It's the wife's sister, you see. In Galway – well, on the coast near Galway. A farmer's wife. But old John, that's the farmer, he didn't survive the winter. It's wet, and stormy there. And he was seventy.

'So Mrs Edison has decided, and the sister, that's Kate. We're to move there and I'm to farm. It's livestock – cattle, goats, a few pigs. But there's a vegetable patch – so that's good. And a hired man from the village.

'So that's it, sir. I am sorry.'

Brooke had imagined far worse.

'You must go with our best wishes,' he said.

'Yes,' said Claire. 'And when it's all over we'll visit – won't we, Eden?'

He nodded, knowing they wouldn't.

Standing quickly, Brooke shook Luke's hand in farewell. 'Write. If you're going over behind the lines, use *Village* in the address not *Croft*. It's half the battle – knowing where you are.'

The picnic was over. Joy began to clear up Iris's toys, which she'd brought down with the child and set out on a blanket. Brooke noticed two small Dinky toys – both vans, not Morris Eights, but battered beyond recognition by Brooke's childhood games.

He held Iris's fidgeting hand. 'Can I borrow these?' he asked.

CHAPTER FIFTY-ONE

Hayle's car, an ageing Rover, was logged through a checkpoint at Royston at 2.40 a.m., where he presented a warrant for blackout travel, and his ID pass, with photograph, issued by the Ministry of War. That put him on the Cambridge Road to London, which meant he could be anywhere in the Home Counties by dawn, including aerodromes at Lydd, Hendon and Southend. Brooke, at his desk by nine, felt sure he'd never see him alive again. His flight proved guilt; his attempt to murder Brooke had been a desperate last throw of an already loaded die.

At ten Mrs Muir rang through to tell him the detective chief inspector was free. She was smoking, reading *The Times*, and he felt immediately that something had happened: the eyes failed to meet his, and her offer of a chair was half-hearted. If Brooke did not know her character better, he would have said she was depressed. Idleness did not suit her.

She'd backed the wrong horse, demanding resources were used to track down a saboteur, instead of closing down a nationwide conspiracy. Now, things were about to get worse.

'Brooke,' she said. 'Latest?'

'Ma'am. We'll conduct formal interviews this afternoon but Hayle's flight has loosened tongues. Brodie will never talk – but Callaghan, Clifford and Tudor can't stop. Finding Smith-Stanley has changed everything.'

Carnegie-Brown indicated for him to take a seat.

'That last night – when they were coming back from the pub – Hayle passed them in his car. The four attic boys were passengers. Brodie gave them the story: they were off to find the sun, with a bonus each to keep quiet. Hayle was showing them the lab as a farewell treat. Which is where he killed them, in exactly the same way as he tried to kill me.

'There was no plan, not at the start. Then they hit upon the shelters – and Callaghan, Clifford and Tudor did the dirty work. They had little choice – but that won't save them in the long run. I'll make a full report, ma'am. Perhaps you could forward it to the Yard? It's out of our hands. There's no way any of this is getting into a public court. The bigger picture must remain a secret. I'm told they've made nearly sixty arrests already. More by the day.'

Brooke let a silence stretch.

'And you'll get a separate report from Dr Comfort. He's planning to write up a piece for *The Lancet* on the case – although publication may be long delayed. But for that telephone number on Basford's hand, Hayle might have got away with the whole thing. Comfort thinks some publicity is required – an alert to pathologists.

'The trick, I'm told, was the use of the ice chambers to increase the temperature of the frozen bodies by a few degrees each hour for several days, if not weeks. Comfort, blunt as always, says it was a bit like defrosting a turkey. You can't do it too quickly – the skin layer will appear normal, but the icy core will linger. It had to be done slowly, so that the whole body was the same temperature, below that at which decomposition would begin.

'Comfort insists that if he'd known the body had been frozen, he might have detected the signs, particularly the consistency of the blood. But at first sight, and after autopsy, he spotted nothing awry.

'I should have spotted that. Mrs Brodie, who identified the first two victims, said "the dead look different" – which they do, but not that different. I should have pursued the point.'

Carnegie-Brown nodded, closing a file on her desk. He doubted she'd listened to a word he'd said.

He was dismissed, but he hadn't finished. Brooke asked if he could clear the desktop.

'Why?' she asked.

'I've found your saboteur – in fact, two of them. I should illustrate.'

He placed the two toy vans on the desktop.

'For the sake of the demonstration, these are identical green Morris Eight vans – provided by the War Office to carry periscopes from the Vulcan Works here . . .'

He put one van at one end of the desk. 'And from the

369

Walbottle Works here outside Newcastle.'

He placed the second toy van at the other end of the desk.

'Walbottle is a shadow factory – providing a vital back-up supply of a key component. They both deliver on the same day, let's say Thursday. On Wednesday Eva Mappin leaves Cambridge and stops overnight at Scotch Corner.'

He ran the van to the centre of the desk. 'On Thursday an identical van leaves Walbottle – which is much closer to Barrow, of course. A day's journey, not two.

'On Thursday morning the Walbottle van reaches Scotch Corner, but drives on to catch up with the van from the Arbury. They meet, probably at a garage in Bainbridge, where the first to arrive parks behind the garage. There's a yard for checking tyre pressure, water and oil.'

He brought the two vans together.

'I'm Barrow for the sake of this recreation.'

He lit a cigarette.

'They swap keys. Mappin arrives first at Barrow. No record is taken of registration numbers. Her consignment, manufactured in Walbottle, contains faulty periscopes, but this is not discovered because no tests are undertaken on the dockside. The driver from Walbottle then arrives with the consignment from the Arbury, which is in *perfect condition*.

'They meet again the next day – having, I suspect, enjoyed a night out together in Vickerstown. That's what got me thinking, ma'am. It's not a big place. Both of them said they stayed within *walking* distance of the naval yard. It seemed obvious they would know each other. Next morning they rendezvous at Bainbridge and swap keys again.

'The saboteur was never in Cambridge, ma'am. Nor is

this the work of foreign agents, or agents provocateurs. It is industrial sabotage. The Walbottle Works relies heavily on the Barrow contract. They were desperate to increase production. The sabotaged periscopes were given Vulcan Works serial numbers – in case anyone checked, which they never did.

'The sabotage was designed to wreck Chubb's chances of keeping the contract in Cambridge. I've briefed Newcastle. An arrest has been made.

'Eva Mappin is in a cell downstairs. She may well live in Sheffield, but the accent is pure Geordie. The driver of the Walbottle van is her uncle. She maintains that the plan was to tamper with the periscopes only until the Vulcan Works was shut down. They did not intend to place our boats in danger – they say. However, their plan was reckless. Lethal. I feel sure any judge will take a similar view.'

He took his seat, the two vans placed in the middle of the desk.

Carnegie-Brown flipped the top of the silver cigarette case and took one, offering one to Brooke, again with a gesture. For the first time Brooke thought she looked like a broken woman.

They smoked in silence.

CHAPTER FIFTY-TWO

Brooke was at his desk two hours later when the inevitable call came through from Scotland Yard.

'Owe you an apology, Brooke,' said Sir James.

Given he was calling from Whitehall it seemed he had kept his job, if only for another day. Brooke wondered how.

'Our surveillance of Hayle was clearly abject. Questions will be asked.'

'Sir,' said Brooke, lighting a Black Russian.

'And we should have secured the lab. Hayle got away with some of his papers. However, fate has intervened on our behalf. A light aircraft attempted to take off from Lydd just after dawn. This was ill-advised due to fog. The pilot flew out to sea and then, lost, swung back north and collided with cliffs east of Hastings.

'No survivors. Pilot and passenger's bodies in the wreckage. I'm awaiting a positive ID but I have no doubt it's Hayle. Perhaps it's for the best – I doubt his new friends in Berlin would have made him comfortable.'

Brooke thought this scenario might have happened. Or had they picked Hayle up, and this was the story they were going to tell the world? It was an unsettling thought that he could even consider such Gestapo-like machinations, here in England.

Whatever the truth, Hayle's death had kept Sir James in post.

'Cold Christmas Farm?' asked Brooke.

'It'll be months, then a closed court for Brodie and his henchmen. A couple of vague sample charges under Emergency Powers and they'll be breaking rocks somewhere dreary – Portland, Dartmoor. I doubt they'll see freedom for a decade or more. Not a merry prospect. Serves them right.'

'And the murders?'

'Your killer will be on a mortuary slab by nightfall. We'd like Hoyle quietly forgotten - especially as Habakkuk is still very much a live issue. The rest will go down with Brodie for the army medical scam - and much else, God help them.'

'I see,' said Brooke. 'Have you been to Chartwell yet?'

'No. That's off. Downing Street are, quietly, delighted at the success of the Cold Christmas operation. We can all take some benefit from that, not least yourself, Inspector.'

Brooke heard a knock on a door at Sir James's end of the line.

'Better go. One other thing. This is between us, strictly.

Carnegie-Brown's appointment has been blocked. She didn't exactly cover herself in glory here: sidelining a case which effectively exposed a national network set on subverting enlistment, on two fronts; the personation of recruits, and the use of reserved occupations as a fraudulent excuse to avoid military service. On the other hand, she inflated the danger posed by a single saboteur, or two, not engaged in enemy action but run-of-the-mill industrial sabotage.'

'I got the impression she was under pressure from the Yard to that effect?' said Brooke. He hated the rewriting of history just because it suited the winners. It was extraordinary that Sir James's duplicity had actually made Brooke feel sorry for Carnegie-Brown.

'That's the problem with the Yard, Inspector,' said Sir James.

Brooke could tell by the tone of his voice that he'd stood up.

'Mixes politics and justice. She stays with you. Which means, I'm afraid, your promotion is also set aside, at least for now.'

Silence.

'Anything to say?'

'Not all the sons of great men feel the need to secure the glittering prizes, sir.'

'Indeed. However, if you get bored, ring. I am quite sure we could find you an office here. A supple mind is a rare virtue, Inspector. The rank might not change, but the capital has its attractions, when it's not being bombed.'

The line went dead.

CHAPTER FIFTY-THREE

Edison's farewell party was a matter of secret discussion and planning for several weeks. The invitation reached Newnham Croft and desired the pleasure of the Brooke family at The Rose public house on 5th November. Mrs Mullins agreed to babysit, and Claire and Joy had enough advance warning to secure leave in lieu of holiday. Luke had disappeared. There had been one card, addressed to Newnham Village. *Unbowed* was awaiting her refit at Rosyth, and so Ben had ample time to attend a party. Peter Aldiss, abandoning his lab for a rare nocturnal outing (at ground level), completed the party finally setting off on foot along the towpath.

Brooke should have known, but the penny failed to drop

until they were crossing Christ's Pieces, the night sky already a backdrop to several fireworks. The blackout's rules had been quietly set aside – there was little choice – for Bonfire Night, although all fires had to be out by eight o'clock. Cutting though the side streets of the Kite, they'd noticed one party – on a bomb site – about to light a makeshift fire under a Guy in the unmistakable shape of Adolf Hitler.

The Rose was a street away from the Cricketers and was the public house Grandcourt had admired that evening six weeks earlier, after Brooke had inspected poor Philip Basford's body in the Trinity Shelter. He recalled Grandcourt's wistful ode to a lost public house, a sad relic of happier days.

Tonight, Grandcourt was behind the bar, absurdly proud of his new position as landlord.

It transpired that his savings, of nearly £200, had been enough to secure the freehold. A small flat above was big enough, his grown-up children having flown the coup long ago. His wife, Jenny, had taken command of the kitchen. The interior of the pub had been painted, lampshades replaced, the wood polished, and in one corner, half in shadow, a photograph had been framed showing Grandcourt on a camel, the pyramid of Giza a silhouette on the horizon.

'Pint, sir?' said his former batman, beaming. Claire had a snowball, Joy a half of mild, Aldiss – sensationally – a large medium-dry sherry.

Grandcourt waved aside Brooke's money. 'All paid for, sir. Sergeant Edison is in the chair.'

Which he was – guarded by his wife, who had his arm. The widowed sister had taken up position at the bar, with a pint of stout. A whip-round had raised £18 – enough to secure a gentleman's shooting stick, and a hip flask inscribed with the coat of arms of the Borough – three ships on a river, under a great bridge. Brooke imagined it on an Irish dresser, pride of place in a kitchen of stone and tiles. Finally, there was enough left for a waxed overcoat for those Atlantic storms, of summer and winter.

The switchboard girls, who had colonised a round table, sang songs from the shows and proved to be tuneful, suggesting regular practice nights after work. Claire, Brooke noted, joined them but did what she always did when happy. She sat back, and drank it all in, each person, each moment, because this was the deal she'd struck with God: she'd look after the frail and ill, and he would look after 'her' people. Brooke dared not think what would happen (to God) if this arrangement faltered.

Joy, controversially, had stood down Mrs Mullins, and brought Iris, who was set up on a tabletop as far away from the dartboard as possible, and visited by everyone in turn. Ben, arriving late, revealed that he had just signed papers to buy a flat on Castle Hill, with a view of Chesterton Windmill and the river, widening out towards Fen Ditton. Brooke saw Claire's eyes flood, before she pulled herself together and offered them the spare double bed from Newnham Croft.

Jo Ashmore arrived on Sergeant Johnnie Holt's arm. Brooke thought they looked proud of each other, which was always a good sign. But he also thought it wouldn't last, but that the war – and the probability Holt would be called up – made that largely immaterial.

Be happy in this moment, this moment is your life, he thought.

No sooner had the door closed than it opened again, and PC Turner fell into the light. There was a brief silence, partly due to her multicoloured dress, perfectly cut, which made her look like a snapshot from *Vogue*, but mostly due to the young man who had her arm, who was short, pale, with the facial bone structure of the Slav – high broad cheekbones, dark deep-set eyes and a hero's jaw.

Brooke saved the awkward moment by asking what they'd like to drink, which allowed Turner to introduce Jan Kazinsky, a pilot at Marshall's with one of the Polish squadrons. His English was entertaining, and so he was soon surrounded by the switchboard girls who wanted to know his life story.

Edison made a speech, having been encouraged to stand on a chair for best effect, in which he promised to return one day laden down with produce from the farm. He said he'd been happy at the Spinning House, then faltered, and for a horrible moment it looked as if he might burst into tears; but he rallied, and said all good things had to come to an end.

Then his wife burst into tears and had to be consoled by her sister, who in turn needed a fresh pint of stout.

Later, privately, Brooke handed Edison a sheaf of petrol coupons he'd drawn from the Borough's garage, in case he had needed a car in an emergency while the Wasp was up at Hawk Mill.

'Don't know your plans,' he said to Edison. 'But it crossed my mind you might need these?'

For the first time that evening, his sergeant looked as if he was actually enjoying himself.

'We were taking the train to Dublin, then on to Galway. I've had a decent offer for the Wasp – but I may have just changed my mind, sir. This would get us to the car ferry with miles to spare. We've a barn at the farm, so I can keep her out of the salt winds.'

Grandcourt rigorously imposed last orders at ten, and so there was a gaggle of rushed farewells on the pavement – Edison giving them all a last salute before strolling home.

The last surprise was Aldiss.

They were about to part at the lamp post at the centre of Parker's Piece.

'Just to say, Eden. I won't be in the lab for a few months, possibly longer. Thought I'd break the pattern. A couple of graduate students – conscientious objectors – will keep up the observations, so the work will continue. You can even pop in for a chat. Decent types.'

'Where will you be?' asked Brooke.

'I was inspired,' he said. 'By Luke, Ben – others. I'm to go north to Achnacarry.'

Brooke laughed. 'At your age?'

'Ah. Yes. I'm not commando material, it's true. But Gardiner – at Pembroke, who used to run the PT classes for the cadets – said the army was short of trainers, especially for rock-climbing. I passed some kind of test, at Cambridge City's ground. Just me and a brick wall. I think they were a bit surprised. Couple of phone calls and I'm all set for Fort William. I think I can teach them a few tricks.'

As Aldiss walked away, Brooke wondered if he'd see him again. Age was no bar to commando adventures.

Back at Newnham Croft they were already on the nightcaps: whisky and water, or port.

Ben said it was a good night to see the aurora – although principally in Ireland and Scotland.

'But you never know,' he said, mildly unsteady on his feet.

Outside, the sky still held a little light, and at one point Ben said he thought he saw a green shadow to the north-east. And then Brooke – who'd judged this to be wishful thinking – saw it too: green, and just a hint of pink.

Ben fled to get refills and Joy came out carrying Iris. Brooke got the distinct impression this little meeting had been engineered.

'Mum says I should tell you now,' she said.

Pregnant again, thought Brooke.

'No. Not that,' she said, reading his mind. 'Mrs Mullins. I hate the idea that Iris is growing up out of sight. But I can't cope alone with the baby and work. There's so many women working now, and hubbies away. I'm going to quit the hospital and set up a nursery. A dozen babies, all under one. Well, maybe two and three. I'll easily keep up on wages.'

'Where?' asked Brooke, knowing the dreaded answer.

'The new flat – on Castle Hill – is pretty small. So . . .'

She kissed her father and fled, leaving him holding Iris.

Which was the cue for Ben to reappear, trailing the family radio behind him, the lead just reaching the garden table by the towpath.

'The skipper – he's been on Arctic boats all his life. He says even if you can't see the lights, this can work. He gave me the right wavelength and everything.'

For a moment he turned the knob and they swam through static, then the BBC, then a foreign station – possibly Danish – then a snatch of French, and then a silence interspersed with what did in reality sound like disparate birdsong, interspersed with an occasional clap or rattle.

'That's it, sir. You asked once – if I'd heard the sound of the aurora. That's it.'

They listened to birdsong under a clear sky for half an hour. Even Iris, wide awake, lay on her blanket and kicked her legs in the air. It came and went – and once or twice the loudest claps coincided with the faint green light to the north.

'You're going back, aren't you?' said Brooke. 'To the boat. To *Unbowed*.'

'Yes, sir,' he said, fleeing again to get refills.

Brooke was alone, and so this was the cue for Iris to stand up, take three steps, and then sit down again with a thud that made her cry. He kept the moment to himself, knowing it would be repeated, one day, for others.

ACKNOWLEDGEMENTS

Who to thank? I must start with Adam Copeland, estate manager for the Department of Geography at Cambridge University. It was entirely due to his perseverance that we were able to discover the hidden remains of the LTRS – which I will not spell out, as it gives the plot away. Also in the first rank of those to whom I am indebted is Albert Howard-Murphy, formerly Coroner's Investigation Officer for Liverpool & The Wirral. Without his expertise the central plot of the novel would have no spine. *The Night Climbers of Cambridge* – by Whipplesnaith, is yet again a key text, and still in print with the Oleander Press. I should add my thanks to Tony Gimbert for generously lending me his copy of the invaluable *Police Almanac and Diary*, for 1944.

And finally I must thank Steve and Gabrielle Bennett for letting me write the final draft of *The Cambridge Siren* at a window with a view of the Lunigiana.

JIM KELLY was born in 1957 and is the son of a Scotland Yard detective. He went to university in Sheffield, later training as a journalist and worked on the *Bedfordshire Times*, *Yorkshire Evening Press* and the *Financial Times*. His first book, *The Water Clock*, was shortlisted for the John Creasey Award and he has since won a CWA Dagger in the Library and the New Angle Prize for Literature. He lives in Ely, Cambridgeshire.

jgkelly.co.uk
@thewaterclock